CARRIER wAR

US Navy Thriller Series
Book Two

Irving A Greenfield
writing as
Roger Jewett

SAPERE
BOOKS

CARRIER WAR

Published by Sapere Books.

20 Windermere Drive, Leeds, England, LS17 7UZ,
United Kingdom

saperebooks.com

ISBN: 978-1-80055-011-7

This book is sincerely dedicated to all of the men who served during the Korean War.

It is also dedicated to the memory of United States Army Air Force Sergeant Max Strolovitz, who had 41 missions to his credit as crew chief of the Rita, *a B-24 that flew out of Guam during WWII; and to the memory of Chief Petty Officer Harry Stitch, who served aboard several different ships and participated in many battles, including the one for Okinawa.*

My last dedication is to my first grandchild, Anne-Sophie Pascale Greenfield, who I hope will never have to "also serve" by waiting for a sweetheart, husband, or son to return from a war.

CHAPTER 1

The klaxon aboard the CVL *Shiloh* screamed with an insistent, whooping cadence for 30 seconds, and the instant it stopped the ship's general announcing system blared: "General quarters, general quarters. All hands man your battle stations. All hands man your battle stations." Throughout the ship men raced to their assigned stations. The clanging sound of watertight doors being slammed shut and dogged down could be heard until, finally, an eerie silence embraced the ship and there was only the pervading throb of her main engines to be felt.

The pilots of Air Group Eight streamed into the fighter and torpedo squadrons' ready rooms and hurriedly donned their flight gear. Moments later, the squawk box in the fighter ready room came to life and an authoritative voice commanded: "Pilots, man your planes. Pilots, man your planes."

"Move it!" Lieutenant Commander Jacob Miller, Commander, Air Group Eight, and Commanding Officer, Fighting Squadron Eight, shouted to his fighter pilots. He led the way from the ready room and headed for the catwalk ladder leading to the *Shiloh*'s sun-drenched flight deck. The carrier was already turning into the wind, and the signal flags — F for fox — were flying at the dip from the *Shiloh*'s yardarms, indicating to other ships that the carrier was preparing to launch and recover aircraft.

Jacob clambered into the cockpit of his Hellcat. With the help of his brown-jerseyed plane captain, he stowed his chart board, buckled his chute and shoulder harness, and connected his oxygen hose and radio line while plane handlers spread the aircraft's wings and locked them into place.

"Stand by to start engines. Stand clear of propellers," the flight deck address system ordered. Once the air officer, surveying the scene from the open wing of the bridge, was satisfied with what he saw, he pressed his microphone button and ordered, "Start engines."

Jacob thumbed his engine-starter button. The propeller began to swing, and several seconds passed before the engine coughed and bursts of blue-white smoke erupted from the exhaust stacks on either side of the cowling. The propeller began to spin rapidly and the engine roared into life.

He followed the hand signals of yellow-jerseyed taxi directors and moved into his take-off position. The launch officer raised his right arm and with a circular motion of his hand indicated full take-off power. Jacob pushed the throttle as far forward as it would go with his left hand, held it there, checked his instruments and saluted, indicating he was ready to go. The launch officer dropped to one knee, extended his arm toward the bow, and touched the deck with his forefinger: take-off.

Jacob released the brake pedals, and the aircraft lurched forward. As it accelerated toward the carrier's bow, Jacob lowered his feet to the rudder pedals and felt the rudder begin to take effect. His plane lifted off the deck, cleared the carrier's bow, dipped slightly toward the sea and as he eased back on the stick, it started to climb in a gentle right turn. He raised his flaps and retracted his wheels with a fleeting, grateful thought that he didn't have to crank them up by hand, as he had done earlier in the war. A quick scan of his instrument panel showed all readings normal.

"Red Leader, this is Red Rover," the *Shiloh*'s fighter director called. "Do you read me?"

"Five by five," Jacob answered. He looked back over his right shoulder and saw his 12 fighters leave the *Shiloh*'s deck at 20-second intervals.

"We have six bogies bearing zero-nine-zero-true, 25 miles out, angels ten… Stand by."

"Roger," Jacob answered. "My guys are joining and I'm climbing to angels 15." Below him, the island of Okinawa appeared to be a large green patch in the expanse of the blue sea crowned by towering cumulus clouds. From this height, the multitude of American ships off its southern coast looked like floating toys.

For Jacob and the other pilots of Fighting Eight, this was their third foray since dawn, when the first of the kamikaze attacks had begun. It was now 1600, and fatigue was Jacob's cockpit partner.

"Red Leader, vector zero-nine-zero. Six bogies, angels eight. Ten miles out."

Jacob acknowledged the order and, turning to the heading, advanced his throttle to bring his Hellcat to near top speed. His wingman was tucked in on his right wing and he could see the others close astern in his rear-view mirror. As he passed through 14,500 feet, he eased forward on the stick to level off.

Suddenly he spotted in the glare of the sun three black specks below and ahead of him. "Tallyho! 12 o'clock low," he radioed to the other pilots. His adrenaline began to pump. He pushed the stick forward and dived. There was no doubt about it: Japanese aircraft. Within moments, he saw three more enemy planes above and to the left of the first group.

"Red Leader," the *Shiloh* called, "four more bogies following the others about ten miles back, angels ten. Keep a sharp lookout."

"Roger," Jacob answered. Wetting his lips, he said, "Gus, Frank, the four new ones are yours. Break your sections off and go get 'em."

"Hot damn, Skipper," Gus responded.

"Yeah man!" Frank exclaimed.

Jacob watched the four Hellcats at his rear break away and begin to climb. Then he concentrated on the six enemy aircraft directly ahead and below him. Moment by moment, they were becoming more sharply defined. Three were VALs, the others were Zeros. Were they all on kamikaze missions? Were the Zeros escorting kamikaze VALs to dog fight? He flicked his master armament switch on and charging his six 50-caliber machine guns, he felt the thud as rounds were chambered. Barreling down at the lead VAL, he saw the red rising-sun insignia growing larger.

The air screamed past the Hellcat's canopy. Jacob's right forefinger rested lightly on the trigger. So far he and his men, coming out of the sun, seemed to be undetected. He flicked his eyes to the altimeter; he was rushing toward 10,000 feet. "Open out and pick your targets," he radioed to his pilots. Glancing over his right shoulder, he saw his eight planes string out behind him.

Suddenly, the last VAL in the lead group peeled off to the right and began to dive.

"They've spotted us," Vinny called as the VAL formation broke up and scattered.

"It's a free-for-all now," Jacob radioed back, following the VAL in front of him as it twisted and turned. For a few seconds, the meatball on the Japanese aircraft hung in his gun sight. Jacob fired a long burst. Smoke spurted from the engine of the enemy plane, and it rolled and plunged toward the sea. Jacob followed in hot pursuit.

"Skipper, you got a Nip Zero on your tail," Carl warned. "He's coming up under you."

Jacob kicked the plane over into a right turn. Without warning, he heard the thwacking sounds of machine-gun bullets chewing into the metal skin of his Hellcat. Forgetting the VAL, he pushed the stick forward and dived more steeply toward the sea. The altimeter needles rapidly unwound.

At 7,000 feet, he pulled back hard on the stick. The force of six Gs drove him down into the seat. His vision blurred; for what seemed an eternity he floated in a hazy, semiconscious state. Slowly his vision cleared, and he realized he was over the top of a loop. He rolled into an Immelmann turn and found himself within range of the attacking Zero's tail. He instinctively squeezed the stick trigger, and as his tracers smothered the Zero it exploded into a thousand fragments.

"Jesus, Skipper!" Steve called.

"I got another one," Bill shouted. "I got the bastard!"

Jacob saw a burning VAL plummet toward the sea. "You sure as hell did," he answered, scanning the sky for another target.

"Skipper, it's Frank. I'm hit," Jacob heard in his earphones as the melee developed. "I'm hurt bad... Can't move my arms... Can't control this mother... Christ, help me!"

"I don't see you, Frank. Can you get back to the ship? Is your wingman with you?" Jacob radioed.

"Negative, we got separated," Frank responded with panic in his voice. "I'm going to try to get out now."

"Red Rover, Red Rover, this is Red Leader. Red 10 is wounded. He's trying to bail out. Alert one of the destroyers."

"Can he come close to Red Rover?" the fighter director asked.

"Negative. He —"

"Frank's in a spin, Skipper. I'm closing on him!" Gus shouted.

Jacob still did not have Red 10 in sight.

"He's not getting out… Holy mother of God! He's gone," Gus exclaimed with an infuriated sob. "I'm going after the bastard Zero that got him."

"Red Rover, this is Red Leader," Jacob said, swallowing hard before he spoke. "Red 10 went down, Red 8 saw him go in." Jacob suddenly spotted a VAL at three o'clock low and kicked his Hellcat over to the right. White streamers of tracers floated up toward him: the Japanese rear gunner was firing long bursts.

Jacob bored in on the enemy plane with renewed vengeance. Once he had him in his gun sight, his six machine guns hammered. The white lines of his tracers seemed to wrap themselves around the fuselage of the VAL. Jacob stopped firing and pulled back on the stick. His Hellcat angled up and over the plane.

"You got him, Skipper," Vinny called. "Black smoke is pouring out of his engine."

Jacob banked slightly to the left and looked back over his shoulder. The VAL exploded into a ball of fire.

"Skipper," Gus called, "two VALS going in on the deck, I can't catch 'em!"

"Red Rover, two kamikazes from the second group incoming on the deck," Jacob radioed. "The first are no longer a problem."

"That's bad news and good news. We're ready. Stand clear."

Within moments, Jacob saw puffs of smoke erupting from the guns of the American ships steaming off the coast, and the sky around them turned black with deadly antiaircraft fire.

"Vinny, guard your ass. There's a Zero behind you!" someone frantically called.

Jacob swiveled his head and spotted the Zero closing on a Hellcat. He threw his Hellcat into a tight left turn, and the Zero came broadside into his sights. He pressed the trigger, and tracers enveloped the enemy plane. He saw the pilot attempt to turn toward him. He fired another short burst.

The pilot slumped in the cockpit. The plane suddenly swung off to the right and Jacob watched the Zero go into a long, smoking glide. It smashed into a hill just behind the beach. Jacob then knew the Zero pilots were escorts for the kamikaze VALs and had been ready to fight them through. But it had not been a good day for the Japanese pilots.

"Skipper," Vinny radioed, "looks like one of our ships has been hit."

Jacob looked toward the amphibious force. A thick column of black smoke was climbing into the sky. At least one of the VALs had managed to complete an attack.

"Red Rover," Jacob called, "this is Red Leader. My sky seems to be clear of bogies. I know five have been splashed, maybe six." His shirt was soaked with sweat as he looked at his watch. He'd been in the air less than an hour.

"Good show, Red Leader," the fighter director responded. "Return to Red Rover and take up combat air-patrol station until Charlie time — about one hour."

"Wilco," Jacob answered. Hearing the weariness in his voice, he said to his men, "Join up, let's go home." He made a wide turn and headed toward the *Shiloh*.

On the way back, Jacob had time to reflect. This was his second combat tour in the Western Pacific. He'd served aboard the carrier *Endeavor* and had taken part in the strikes against the Japanese bases in the Gilbert and Marshall islands and fought in the Battle of Midway. He'd been shot down once and had been awarded the Distinguished Flying Cross with several Gold Stars.

Now, at twenty-six, he felt like an old man. The war was grinding away at him. He, along with his pilots, was dog-tired and weary. These past two weeks off Okinawa had sapped his vigor as nothing else had, and once the island was taken and secured, he knew the invasion of Japan itself would begin. If the toll in taking Okinawa was any indication, the cost in terms of men and equipment would be staggering.

Jacob spotted the *Shiloh* and its escorts ahead of him. He assumed his CAP station at 10,000 feet and circled at slow speed to conserve fuel. As the sun sank toward the horizon, the *Shiloh* radioed, "Red Leader, this is Red Rover. Your signal Charlie." With a wave of relief, Jacob led his flight down into the holding circle at 1,000 feet. At 200 feet, he peeled off and entered the landing pattern. He lowered his landing gear and flaps, locked his shoulder harness, and as he entered the cross-wind leg of his approach to the fantail he picked up the landing signal officer's orange paddles signaling a slight correction to the right. Jacob made the necessary adjustment so that the orange paddles were straight out on either side of the LSO's body.

At the cut point over the ship's fantail, the LSO made a precise slashing movement across his chest with the right paddle. Jacob cut the throttle and flared for a landing. The plane touched down and rolled forward. An instant later, its hook grabbed an arresting wire and the Hellcat jerked to a stop. His shoulder harness held him from being thrown forward into the instrument panel. Jacob slid the wing-unlocking lever forward, allowing the plane handlers to push the plane's wings back into a folded position, and the yellow-jerseyed taxi directors led him toward the other parked planes on the forward part of the flight deck.

For several moments Jacob remained in the plane, too tired to move. The plane captain clambered up to the cockpit. "You okay, Skipper?" he asked, peering closely at Jacob's face.

"Beat to shit," Jacob answered, unbuckling his harness and then his chute.

"Yeah, the Japs keep coming and we keep shooting them down. But they still keep coming."

Jacob lifted himself out of the cockpit, found the toeholds in the side of the aircraft, and dropped to the deck.

"Looks like you caught a few rounds," the plane captain said, pointing to the rough-edged tears in the right wing.

Jacob eyed the holes. He'd forgotten that he'd been hit. "Nothing serious," he said.

"Just holes," the man said. "I'll make sure they're patched up tonight."

"Thanks," Jacob said and started to walk to the ready room, where he'd be debriefed, when the Klaxon screamed. "All hands topside. Take cover. Inbound enemy aircraft," the all-too-familiar voice ordered over the flight-deck address system.

One of Jacob's pilots was on his final approach and three others were still in the air. He looked at the yardarms: the fox flags were being hauled down.

"He's being waved off," the plane captain shouted as he ran for cover.

At full throttle, the Hellcat roared over the *Shiloh*'s flight deck and pulled up.

Jacob looked up at the unrecovered planes. They didn't have much fuel remaining, 30 minutes at the most. Not enough for further combat and they would be ordered, no doubt, to clear the area.

"Incoming bogies. Incoming bogies. Bearing zero-five-four relative. Range eight miles. Angels two," the 1MC blared.

The four Fighting Eight planes turned to the left and headed away from the *Shiloh* to a carrier in another task group where they could be recovered. The ship's guns were now the only defense.

Rather than go to the ready room, Jacob remained topside to see the show. In a jaundiced way he had concluded that if he weren't in the air, it really didn't matter whether he died on the flight deck or the ready room in an attack. For the past two weeks at sunset, after fighter cover was no longer in the air, Japanese Bettys — Louie the Lamp Lighters, as they were known — had bored in at low level for suicidal torpedo attacks.

Suddenly, the ships on the outer perimeter of the *Shiloh*'s screen erupted with a barrage of antiaircraft fire.

"Incoming bogie, zero-five-zero degrees. Low on the water, one mile."

The escort ships on the *Shiloh*'s starboard side were firing with furious intensity as a twin-engine Betty skimmed the surface and headed for the *Shiloh*. The carrier was heeled over to starboard, responding to hard left rudder; then her guns opened up. The noise was deafening. Black smoke poured out of the Betty's port engine, but it kept coming. Its right wing began to shred and break away from the fuselage, making it pitch violently to the right.

For an instant, Jacob was sure the plane would fall short of the ship. But the very next moment its remains slammed into the *Shiloh*'s starboard side, within a few yards of the fantail, below the level of the flight deck and into a 40mm mount, where it exploded into a ball of fire. Within seconds the unreleased torpedo it carried in its open bay exploded underwater, showering debris in all directions.

Jacob ran toward the stricken gun mount. Damage control firefighters were already battling the inferno.

One of the men in the gun crew was screaming in agony as he staggered out of the smoke and flames. His clothing was charred and seared flesh peeled from his arms. "I'm blind," he yelled. "I —" Blood gushed from his mouth. His knees gave way and he dropped to the deck.

"Incoming bogie," the 1MC blared. "Bearing zero-four-five relative. Range four miles, low on the water."

The ships screening the *Shiloh* once again opened fire on the inbound enemy plane, but it, like the first one, kept boring in despite the intensity of fire. Just as it passed over an outlying destroyer, Jacob saw it. It too was headed straight for the *Shiloh*'s starboard side when, in a hail of gunfire, it lost altitude and plowed into the water. Its wings broke off as it tumbled across the water and disappeared below the waves.

The *Shiloh* remained at General Quarters until 2000, when the fire in the after starboard section of the ship was finally extinguished. Damage control parties started making temporary repairs. The physical damage caused by the Betty attack was relatively minor, and at 0800 the following morning Jacob's pilots returned to the *Shiloh*. Throughout the day, he and his men were once again flying combat air patrol for the ship.

On the morning of April 16, 1945, Commander Warren Troost sat before the desk of Captain George Munson, aboard the attack transport *Iroquois*, the flagship of Amphibious Task Group 56.6, where tactical planning for the invasion of Okinawa by Marine assault forces was being completed.

"Ordinarily," Captain Munson said, "a job like this might be given to a sub. But all of ours are now otherwise engaged and Admiral Harly, in Special Operations back at Pearl, suggested you and your PT boats for the task."

Troost, a solidly built young man with blue eyes, brown hair and sensuous lips, studied the captain. Less than an hour before, he had radioed Warren to report to the flagship. "Sir, you haven't told me what the mission is."

Munson took out a silver cigarette case, opened it, offered a cigarette to Warren.

"No, thank you, sir. I'm a pipe man myself."

Munson nodded. Taking a cigarette from the case, he tapped the end of it against the cover of the case before he lit it. "We know there's a Japanese prison ship hiding in a cove in one of the Amami Islands in the central Ryukyus." He opened a manila folder, removed three glossy eight-by-ten aerial photographs, and showed them to Warren. "These were taken just seventy-two hours ago. As part of the Okinawa campaign we're planning to capture the ship, take it to sea, and rescue the prisoners."

Somewhat startled, Warren examined the photographs. On each a white circle and a red one had been overlaid. A small boxlike ship was clearly visible inside the white circle. Several buildings, which Warren guessed were some sort of prison camp or a defense headquarters, possibly both, were included in the red one.

"You'd have to get in and out fast," Munson said.

Warren shifted his gaze from the photographs to the captain. "Getting in fast wouldn't be a problem, but getting out — well, that will be a different matter if I'm to take that ship to sea."

"Getting the ship out is the essence of the operation," Munson responded blandly, blowing smoke toward the ceiling.

"Obviously, unless you do, we won't be able to rescue the prisoners."

Warren smiled wryly. "Sir, I see what you mean… But getting out fast, is that realistic? If that barge makes ten knots, we'll be lucky… But first there's the matter of capturing her. What's going to be involved in that?"

"We estimate a thirty to forty member crew."

"That's three to four times the size of one of mine, and there'll be at least that many troops in that base."

Munson nodded. "Could be," he said. "But you'll have two dozen really mean Marines with you."

"How many of my boats go?"

"Two. Yours and one other. Once you take the ship, you'll move her out to sea and rendezvous with the destroyer *Ferris* that will tow your boats to within fifty miles of the island to begin with."

"And our boats?"

"Totally expendable," Munson answered. "Once you take possession of the Jap ship, you'll destroy them."

Warren tried not to show his surprise. He'd been in PTs since '42 and loved them. The idea of destroying his own boats didn't sit well.

"After this mission," Munson said matter-of-factly, "you're going to be reassigned."

"You mean my squadron will —"

Munson shook his head. "PTs will be phased out. You're headed for a more important slot." He smiled. "I probably wasn't supposed to tell you anything about that plan, but I'm sure I can rely on your discretion."

"Of course, you can, sir," Warren answered simply, though he wasn't sure he liked what he'd been told. He liked the freewheeling independence that he had in the PTs.

"Captain James Connely will be the Marine platoon commander. First Lieutenant Clifford W. Dawson will be his second. There will be two experienced gunnery sergeants and the rest combat veteran EMs," Munson explained. "Their job will be to neutralize enemy opposition. After you leave the *Ferris*, you will be in overall command."

"Have you any charts of the cove?" Warren asked.

"None that are modern," Munson answered, stubbing out his cigarette in a metal ashtray.

"The PTs have a shallow enough draft to bring them close inshore without any difficulty," Warren said. "But maneuvering a ship —"

"She's about the same size as AKO-96, and as I recall, you did well with her."

Warren flushed. In the early days of the war he had become skipper of the 96, a one-of-a-kind combination oiler and supply ship, after its captain and executive officer had been killed.

"Well enough with her," Munson repeated, "to bring her safely to Pearl and get yourself a Navy Cross for doing it."

Warren felt his cheeks burning. Despite the fact he was young to be a full commander, he was a quiet, self-effacing man. The horrors of war had developed a degree of humility in his approach to life.

"The *Ferris* will take you, and whatever other boat you choose to go with you, in tow at 0330 on April 18. Should the previous day's aerial reconnaissance indicate that the ship was moved, the mission will be scrubbed. The same will hold true up until the morning of the attack. You will be advised whether or not to proceed with the mission, which has been codenamed Operation Cut Out."

"How many prisoners are aboard the ship?" Warren asked.

"We don't know."

"Will any of the prisoners be ashore?"

"Again, we don't know."

"Assuming we are successful in seizing and getting the ship to sea, where —?"

"The *Ferris* will escort you back here, where the prisoners will be transferred to one of our ships and be sent to either Perth or Pearl. A decision where to send them won't be made until we know how many are involved and where they are from. That really is not your problem."

Warren nodded. That was clear, but as far as he was concerned, it was the only aspect of the scheme that was clear.

"Have you any questions?" Munson asked.

"When do I get to meet Captain Connely and Lieutenant Dawson?" Warren asked.

Munson looked at his watch. "They should be coming aboard just about now. It's up to you to plan the details with them."

"Reporting, as ordered, sir," Lieutenant Commander Glen Lascomb said, looking down at Commander Harold Ross, the *Ferris*'s skipper, who was seated behind a small desk in his sea cabin.

Ross leaned back in his chair and, without inviting Glen to sit down, said, "I found something for you to do while you're waiting for your new orders. I don't like to see an officer sitting around doing nothing, even if he is a hero."

Glen stiffened. A few days before a kamikaze had sunk his ship, and after being rescued by a PT boat skippered by his old friend Warren Troost, he had been temporarily assigned to the *Ferris*. Commander Ross, learning of Glen's combat background and heroism, had taken an instant, jealous dislike to him.

"We're being detached from the task group to rendezvous with two PT boats and take part in a highly classified rescue mission. You will be my liaison officer with the PT attack unit. You will accompany them to their objective and radio me when, and if, the job is completed. Otherwise, for the protection of this ship, strict radio silence will be maintained, regardless of the situation ashore. Is that understood?"

"Yes, sir!" Glen answered. He was a tall, blond, handsome man with blue-grey eyes and an easy smile, who had been decorated several times for conspicuous gallantry and bravery in action.

"Have you any questions?" Ross asked perfunctorily.

"Three, sir."

Ross scowled. "Ask," he answered. He was a short man with a round face and small green eyes.

"Where are the people we're going to rescue? Who are they? And when will this mission take place?"

Ross leaned forward and placed his elbows on the desk. "We're scheduled to depart at 0300 the day after tomorrow. For now, that's as much as you need to know."

"Yes, sir," Glen answered. "Is there anything else, sir?" he asked, purposely assuming the demeanor of a young, inexperienced officer in the presence of a god.

Ross's full cheeks colored. Glen looked straight at him. "Nothing," Ross finally answered.

Glen saluted, did a smart about-face, and left the captain's cabin. But as soon as he was outside, he slammed his fist into the palm of his other hand, and muttered, "What a turd bird!"

CHAPTER 2

After an uneventful air patrol, Jacob taxied smartly out of the *Shiloh*'s arresting gear into his parking spot. Over the noise of the wind and the clatter and roar of other aircraft in his flight being recovered and taxied, Jacob heard the powerful flight-deck bullhorns come to life: "Forward on the deck. Air Group Commander Miller to the bridge, please." As Jacob climbed out of the cockpit, he glanced up at the ship's primary fly location, just aft of the bridge, and saw the air officer, Commander Ed Fredericks, leaning on the handrail and smiling down at him. Shying from the rain beginning to fall, Jacob gave the thumbs-up signal indicating he had heard the request and was on his way.

"Any problems?" the plane captain asked, handing him the customary form to record any maintenance discrepancies.

Jacob answered by scribbling *None* on the yellow sheet and signing it. He patted the plane's wing. "She ain't broke, so don't let anybody fix her."

The plane captain grinned.

As Jacob ducked low and made his way through the maze of parked aircraft to the island, the cold rain became heavier. He noticed that the destroyer, *Currie*, operating on the *Shiloh*'s starboard quarter in plane guard position, was no longer visible. He entered the island, passed through a short passageway and up the ladders to the bridge.

The *Shiloh*'s skipper, Captain Paul Schooner, a burly, red-faced man with beefy hands and gray hair, was seated in his high, swivel-back chair overlooking the flight deck below and the building sea ahead. "Afternoon, Miller," he said. "The stinking weather is closing in fast."

"From fifteen thousand we could see the front coming in from the southwest, Captain," Jacob said, feeling slightly uncomfortable, as he always did, in the presence of the older, imposing man.

"Sometime tomorrow, we're going to have news media people on board for a short — I hope — period. They're interested in air operations and have been cleared to discuss them with you and Fredericks. Newspaper reporters and two liaisons: one from Admiral Nimitz's staff and one from Washington. Get together with Ed and plan what you can and cannot tell them."

Jacob saluted, left the bridge, and made his way back to a small compartment where Fredericks had taken refuge from the rain. The air officer was puffing on a stubby cigar and offered Jacob a fresh one. Jacob declined, saying, "The old man tells me we have some planning to do and that you have all the dope."

Ed motioned for his friend to sit down and said, "With all the emphasis in the past on censorship and security, this deal beats the hell out of me. Somebody must figure we're winning and can afford to let up a little." With a snort he blew a cloud of smoke at the overhead and observed, "Seems that the people back home are fascinated by the kamikaze business, and the powers that be believe it's good politics to keep them that way."

"So how long will they be on board?" Jacob asked.

"It depends on how long it takes to get what they want. Captain Horace Dean —"

"Dean? If it's the same Horace Dean I remember, he's a stupid son of a bitch. He and I had a run-in after Midway when he was a lieutenant commander."

"It's probably the same guy," Ed said. "He wants the people with him to interview you, and the captain wants you to be as cooperative as common sense allows."

"I will even if it hurts."

"It shouldn't hurt all that much," Ed said, his eyes suddenly twinkling.

Jacob caught the change and cocked his head to one side. "Why? Is he bringing Lana Turner or Betty Grable with him?"

Grinning, Ed said, "Better, as far as you're concerned."

Jacob sat upright and his heart began to race. "Are you about to tell me what I think you are?"

"Your fiancée, Miss Connie Burke, that female paragon of the fourth estate, is part of the party," Ed said. "This is the first time a woman reporter is being allowed on a warship at sea."

Jacob took one of Ed's cigars and stuck it in his mouth. He hadn't seen Connie for almost four months. In her last letter, she had not mentioned a word about coming anywhere near the Western Pacific.

"How does that grab you, amigo?" Ed asked, still smiling.

"I'm going to be worried shitless all the time she's here," he answered. "What if we take a hit and —"

Ed held up his hands and, with mock seriousness, intoned, "The captain says we've been hit once and that's it. No other hits will be permitted. He doesn't give a damn who's flying the fucking kamikaze. Another hit will make him very angry."

"I'm sure the Japs are terrified of that," Jacob joked. "I'm sure they speak in dread, over their sake, of Captain Paul's wrath!"

The two of them looked at each other for several seconds and then burst into laughter.

"The captain says he'll put his in-port cabin at Connie's disposal while she's on board," Ed said.

"She'll love that," Jacob commented; then he asked, "Who else will be in the party?"

"Four others, including two cameramen. If this weather continues to build," Ed continued, "they might have to remain on board longer than a day."

"With all due respect to Washington and Pearl," Jacob said worriedly, "this visit will put civilians at great risk and —"

"The way I see it," Ed broke in, "it's one way of readying the American public for what's coming when the invasion of Japan begins. Everyone out here knows that the cost of taking Okinawa will be small compared to what it will be to take Japan. Maybe the brass are trying to get the people to understand that the Japs aren't finished yet. Once the war is over in Europe — and that, if what we hear is correct, might be only a matter of days — the effort out here will have to be redoubled to finally end the whole bloody mess. I don't know if I'm right, but it seems logical."

With a nod Jacob said, "Yes, it does." Then he asked, "Did you ever get the feeling that we're fighting one war and the men in Europe are fighting a different war?"

"Very often," Ed responded. "And in many ways, I think we are. Someday it will become clear … but only after it's all over!"

Jacob tapped the ashes off the end of his cigar into an ashtray made from the end of a five-inch shell casing. "I should thank the captain for letting you tell me about Connie."

"No doubt he would have told us if his wife were coming aboard," Ed said.

"Yes, but would we have had the same restraint? We might have said something like, 'Your wife's coming, and you and I both know she has no damn business being here.'"

Ed smiled. "I doubt it, but —"

The phone rang.

"Fredericks here," he announced. He listened for a few moments before he snapped, "The captain's going to general quarters." He put the phone down. "The destroyer *Byrd* reports a sonar contact." The *Byrd* was one of the destroyers on the perimeter of the *Shiloh*'s antisubmarine screen. Her station was five thousand yards ahead.

The Klaxon began to scream.

The 1MC came on. "All hands man your battle stations. All hands man your battle stations."

On the run, Jacob headed to the fighter ready room. The rain was so heavy he couldn't see the end of the flight deck. Men were racing to their stations throughout the ship.

Suddenly the awesome sounds of two exploding depth charges, amplified by the heavy atmosphere, rolled over the ship. After a pause, two more deep booms came out of the driving rain.

The muffled explosions of eight more depth charges, dropped in pairs, sounded, and Jacob and his pilots could feel the concussion of the relentless destroyer depth charging in the ready room. For the next fifteen minutes, quiet pervaded the *Shiloh*.

Despite the tension, Jacob found himself thinking about his on-again, off-again relationship with Connie. The last time he'd been with her in Honolulu, they'd agreed to wait until he was rotated again before they married.

"I don't want to make you a pretty young widow," he had told her after they'd made love for the last time. "I want you and I to have children and raise them together. I want to know that we'll have time to quarrel and make up, that we'll be able to share a secure future."

Jacob's thoughts were interrupted by the squawk box from the primary fly. Ed's voice said, "Jake, the captain says that the *Byrd* reports she has lost contact. Could be she got the sub. Anyhow, Captain Paul intends to remain at GQ for at least another forty-five minutes."

Jacob said to his pilots, "Let's hope they got the bastard."

Within the hour, secure from general quarters was sounded and Jacob headed back to the bridge to see if the captain had any more instructions for him. He found the CO talking with his executive officer, Commander Henry Blake. "I had Fredericks brief Miller about our guests," he said as Jacob entered. "Seems he knows at least two people in the party. One rather well!" The two of them laughed as Jacob blushed.

Blake grinned. "Really... I bet I know which one."

He and Blake were friends from the time they'd served together earlier in the war. Blake knew about his rollercoaster relationship with Connie.

"Some men have all the luck," Schooner commented wryly.

"You can say that again," Blake said.

The two of them laughed.

"Bridge, target bearing zero-seven-five," the combat information center reported. "Range two thousand yards, speed ten knots. Could be a surfaced sub, Skipper."

"The son of a bitch got through the screen. I have the conn," Captain Schooner exclaimed. "Alert the screen commander," he ordered. Then to the helmsman, he commanded, "Right full rudder."

"Right full rudder," the helmsman answered.

"All ahead flank," the CO ordered the engine-room signalman.

"All ahead flank," the man answered.

Heeling sharply, the *Shiloh* began to answer the full right rudder.

The CIC continued to report the bearing, range, and speed of the contact, and said, "The destroyer *Currie* is placing herself between us and the contact."

"I have the sub on my scope," the deck officer said. "She's nine hundred yards off our starboard bow and closing."

Jacob looked toward the bridge's windows and could just make out the silhouette of the *Currie* close aboard on the starboard quarter.

"Torpedoes broad on the starboard bow, one thousand yards, closing fast," the voice of a lookout screamed from the bridge squawk box.

"The *Currie* is coming up fast," the OOD reported.

Jacob began to sweat… It was a race between the torpedoes and the *Currie*. All at once, there was a tremendous explosion. The gray outline of the *Currie* flamed red and yellow. The destroyer heaved up, and when it fell back into the sea there was a second thunderous roar.

"God help her, she took one of them for us," Schooner said.

"Where in hell is the other torpedo?" Blake questioned in a tight voice.

Anticipating a third explosion, Jacob sucked in his breath.

"It passed ahead of us," the OOD exclaimed excitedly. "It passed ahead of us."

Jacob wiped the sweat from his brow with his shirt-sleeve. There hadn't even been time for Captain Schooner to order "general quarters."

The *Currie*, on fire and racked by secondary explosions, was falling rapidly behind the *Shiloh*. The captain came up to Jacob and, looking out at the burning ship, he said, "That gallant ship deliberately went 'in harm's way.' Blake, tell the screen commander to render all possible assistance."

"Yes," Jacob whispered to himself, "certainly 'in harm's way.'"

"Bring us in about five yards off her starboard side," Warren told the man at the helm. "Use just enough throttle and rudder to keep us alongside." He picked up the radio microphone and, glancing over his shoulder at the second PT, said, "Sean, lie off my stern."

"Aye, aye, Skipper," Lieutenant Sean Devlin answered.

Warren raised the loud hailer to his mouth and called, "Ahoy, *Ferris*. Ahoy, *Ferris*. PT 501 here. Commander Troost requests permission to come aboard."

A few moments passed before the *Ferris* answered, "Permission granted."

The *Ferris* was moving ahead slowly and holding a steady course. "Ease her in alongside," Warren said. Warren's helmsman pushed the throttles slightly forward and at the same time turned the wheel over to the right to bring the boat through a full three hundred and sixty degrees turn and alongside the *Ferris*, amidships where a cargo net had been put over the side.

Warren left the cockpit and grabbed hold of the rope webbing. "Take off," he ordered as soon as he began to climb. "Commander Warren Troost," he said, as he stepped on to the deck.

The petty officer in charge of the deck detail saluted and said, "Please follow me, sir. Captain Ross is expecting you." The man led him to the wardroom. "Commander Troost, sir," he announced, stepping aside to allow Warren to enter. There were three men in the room: the captain, a Marine captain and a Marine first lieutenant.

Warren and Ross exchanged salutes.

"Commander Troost, Captain Connely and Lieutenant Dawson," Ross said. "Please, gentlemen, sit down."

Summoning a steward, Ross ordered coffee and cake brought to the table. "The ship's baker happens to have been a baker for Sutters in Brooklyn before he was drafted," he said proudly. "I've been told by a few of my men who come from Brooklyn that Sutters Bakery is considered one of the best French bakeries in the city." He spoke with a decided nasal tone. "My liaison officer is on his way here," he continued, "but we needn't wait to lay down the ground rules. He already knows what they are. From the outset it must be understood —"

Another officer stepped into the wardroom.

Warren instantly recognized his old friend Glen Lascomb, but Glen pretended not to know him.

"Gentlemen," Ross said, facing Glen, "Lieutenant Commander Glen Lascomb." Glen shook hands with the three men. "All right, Mr. Lascomb, sit down and I'll get on with what I was telling these gentlemen."

"Before you go on, Captain," Warren said, sensing his command responsibilities were in jeopardy, "I think I'd better lay out for all of you what my sailing orders are as I understand them."

"Please," Ross responded, making an open gesture with his right hand.

"I'm sure all of you know this," Warren said, "but I'll say it anyway. For this mission, particularly after my boats part company with this ship, I am in command. Is that understood by everyone here?"

The other three nodded before Warren turned to Ross. "Captain?"

Ross stiffened and said tersely, "While you are in my company and in matters where the operation and safety of my ship are concerned, I, as the senior officer present, must retain final say."

The steward came in unobtrusively and placed pots of steaming coffee, cups, and a large plate of several slices of cake on the table.

"My orders give me overall responsibility for the operation," Warren continued, speaking in a matter-of-fact manner. "But if you perceive 'overall' to exclude your ship — and I certainly appreciate your position — then I suggest you clarify the matter with Captain Munson. I have been told the *Ferris*'s job is to tow my boats where I want them, to retire, wait for us to return with the prison ship, and then escort us back."

The skin around Ross's jaw tightened. "I see, Commander," he answered. "I will be compelled to ask for a reconsideration of your role, as you understand it."

Warren didn't bother responding. Instead he said, "I'd like the *Ferris* to take my boats in tow at the ends of one-hundred-yard lines. I will have three men aboard each of the boats to ensure that they hold their positions with respect to each other and the *Ferris* during the tow. Regular watches will be maintained, and that means at the end of each watch the *Ferris* must slow down and haul the boats in to allow watch personnel to be changed."

"That will cost us some time," Ross observed.

Warren agreed, but added, "It will also ensure the safety of the boats and lessen fatigue of my crews." He turned his attention to Connely. "Your men will board when we cast off from the ship and make the final run to the island. You already know your objectives."

"Yes, sir," Connely answered. He was a short, wiry man with a thin, pugnacious jaw and a small moustache.

Warren added, "You and twelve of your men will be in my boat. Lieutenant Dawson and his twelve men will be aboard the other boat."

"That's the way I figured it," Connely said.

"Good," Warren responded and looked at Glen. "Since you're liaison between my strike force and this ship, you'll be aboard my boat. Once the attack begins, you will keep in contact with the *Ferris*."

"Yes, sir," Glen answered.

Warren shifted his gaze back to Ross. "I don't anticipate having to do it, sir, but should I call for gunfire support, I expect it to be provided."

"But that means coming close inshore," Ross protested. "My orders say that I'm to tow you within fifty miles of the island and —"

"I agree, but they also say you are to support me," Warren told him. "Therefore, as soon as we begin the assault, I suggest you close within range of your five-inch guns should we need that kind of help." He paused for a moment to lift a cup of coffee to his lips. "As soon as we get the prison ship underway, Lieutenant Commander Lascomb will signal you to stand by to cover us as we make for the open sea. We'll be lucky if we can make ten knots with it. Are there any questions so far?" he asked, helping himself to a piece of cake.

"Commander, have you received any new information about the kind of opposition we might have?" Dawson asked.

"None, Lieutenant," Warren answered. Dawson looked as if he were fresh out of officer-candidate school. "But given the importance of the installation, the number of garrison troops is probably close to what you have been told." Then he said, "I have several charts of the island that date from some years ago and, of course, we have the aerial recon photos. But that's it. Any questions...? None... Okay! Captain Ross, with your concurrence, I'll have my boats come alongside, pick up the tow lines and transfer the men." Then, in a much lighter vein he said to Ross, "Sir, my compliments to your baker. This cake is delicious."

"OK, gentlemen," Warren said, "unless someone has something else, I move we adjourn." He looked at his watch. "Captain Connely, Lieutenant Dawson, we'll meet at 2000 to go over details of our assault plans."

Everyone rose and began to file out of the wardroom with Captain Ross in the lead. Warren turned to Glen and said, "Mr. Lascomb, could I have a few words with you before you leave?"

"I had no idea you were aboard," Warren said warmly, as soon as he and Glen were alone. "What the hell is going on with you? Why didn't you let on that you know me?"

"Am I glad to see you," Glen said, reaching for Warren's hand. "You sure took the wind out of Ross's sails."

"Just before you came in, he began to tell me what he wanted understood. At that point, I figured it would be best to straighten him out."

"He and I rub each other the wrong way, to put it mildly. That's why I acted as I did. I didn't want to make your job more difficult," Glen said. "I'm temporary here and surplus — like tits on a bull. That's why he's sending me with you."

"Listen, if you'd rather not go, I'll ask for someone else," Warren offered. He dug into his pocket and pulled out a pipe.

"I'd far rather be with you than stay here," Glen answered. "My orders to a new ship probably won't come through for a while."

"Probably," Warren agreed with a nod. "How's Lucy and the baby?"

"Doing fine, at least they were according to Lucy's last letter," Glen answered. "But I haven't had any mail for the better part of two weeks… I guess," he laughed, "the guys who sort the mail don't know where I am."

Lighting his pipe, Warren commented, "Tell me about Ross."

Glen shrugged. "He has a good enough reputation. Runs a tight ship."

"What's his beef with you?"

"My medals, I think. I think he might be jealous."

"You can bet on it," Warren said. "Well, as long as he doesn't interfere with my job, he and I will get along."

"You can bet you're on his list, too."

"Don't doubt it," Warren said. "But I've been places like that before and probably will be again!"

Glen laughed. "I like your attitude, and you, too, Commander!"

"The feeling is mutual," Warren answered with a grin, throwing his arm around his friend's shoulder.

At first light the next morning, the rain had passed. From the *Shiloh*'s primary fly, Jacob and Ed watched the first CAP of the day take off. Six aircraft left the flight deck. Sam Thorpe the Fighting Eight XO was Red Leader for the flight.

"Well," Ed said, turning to Jacob, "all we have to do now is relax and wait until Connie and the others arrive."

"I'm going to take a few turns around the flight deck," Jacob said with a note of tenseness in his voice.

"A cold shower might be better," Ed observed with a straight face. "It would help to cool that hot Hebrew blood."

"A point well taken," Jacob responded and, changing his mind about the walk, suggested to Ed that they go to the wardroom for breakfast. "Some food might be as relaxing as some exercise. What do you think, Ed?"

"Good idea," Ed said. "For some reason, my appetite is really running high this morning," and leered knowingly at Jacob.

"Enough!" Jacob exclaimed, as the two of them left Pry-Fly and headed for the wardroom. "If I get ten minutes alone with Connie, it will be a lot."

"Warren!" Ed said with a smirk. "Five to seven minutes is all that it takes to do it! If you were a rabbit, you could do it again in ten more seconds ... then do it again ... and again ... and..."

Jacob pretended not to hear as they entered the wardroom and sat down at a table. A steward in a white jacket immediately came to the table to take their orders.

Ed asked for a full breakfast, but Jacob ordered only a cup of black coffee and slice of toast.

"You're going to need more than that to keep your energy up," Ed commented. "Promises to be a big day!"

The phone near their table rang.

"I'll get it," Ed said and got up to answer and, returning to the table, he reported, "Bridge says the Destroyer Escort *Cyrus* will be alongside in half an hour. Our high-line detail is manning its station now. We're going to have to hurry here."

Jacob nodded. "I got more butterflies now than you'd believe…"

Jacob and Ed made their way up to the bridge to be on hand when the press party arrived. Captain Schooner again was seated in his elevated chair. A gyro compass repeater and array of instruments before him indicated the ship's course and speed as well as wind velocity over the flight deck. The executive officer, Commander Blake, was standing beside the captain outlining his plans for below-deck operations that day. Jacob and Ed entered, saluted, and said, "Good morning, sir." Both the captain and XO said, "Good morning," and resumed their conversation. Jacob could overhear the captain saying, "To change the subject, Henry, I think we should have some kind of mild celebration when victory finally comes in Europe."

"I'll see what we can do. What does it look like to you?" Blake asked.

"I make it a matter of a few days," the CO said. "The Allies have massed for the final assault to retake Berlin."

"Too bad Roosevelt didn't live to see it," the XO commented. "What a job he and his generals have done. He's another Nimitz!"

"I wonder how this man Harry Truman is working out in the hot seat in Washington?" Blake continued. "I mean, while he was vice-president we didn't hear much about him other than he once sold haberdashery someplace in Missouri."

"Don't forget he was an army captain in World War I and that should qualify him to be commander-in-chief," Paul responded with a note of uncharacteristic sarcasm.

Jacob thought to himself, *Sometimes the office makes the man, and, then, the man can make a difference in the office.* The squawk box in front of the CO came to life, and a voice said, "Captain, CIC here, we have *Cyrus* on radar. Ten thousand yards, bearing one-one-zero."

Schooner instructed the deck officer to complete preparations for receiving *Cyrus* alongside.

Jacob said with a spurt of temerity, "Captain, I'd like to be down there when they come aboard."

"Sure, go ahead," the CO told him, getting to his feet. "I sure as hell would like to see your face when your ladylove rides across on that high line, but I'll forego that pleasure."

"Thanks, sir," Jacob said.

"Henry, bring them to the bridge when they're all on board," Schooner said.

"Aye, aye, sir. Let's go, gents!" Blake answered.

Following him, Jacob and Ed went down to the hangar deck, where a large door to starboard was already open. The chief boatswain mate in charge of the high-line detail had his men setting up the various supports that would hold the line once it was passed between the ships.

Jacob stood off to one side and hoped that the ship wouldn't suddenly be called to general quarters while Connie was being transferred from the *Cyrus*. The vision of her dangling between the two ships made his stomach churn.

Jacob sensed that the *Shiloh* had slowed to ten knots, and he could see the *Cyrus* closing on a parallel course. Within moments, the *Cyrus* was alongside. She slowed and held a position about a hundred feet away from the *Shiloh*.

Connie and the other members of the party were at the *Cyrus*'s high-line station, outfitted in kapok life preservers. Suddenly, she saw Jacob and waved.

Slightly embarrassed, Jacob waved back.

The chief ordered his man with the line-throwing gun to fire the first small line across to his counterpart on the *Cyrus*. It took another few minutes for the heavier lines to be threaded through various pulleys, slack taken up, and the breeches buoy attached before it was ready to be used.

From the *Cyrus* a voice boomed, "Ladies first!" and Connie was placed in the buoy seat. She was wearing khaki slacks and a khaki shirt. Her blonde hair was held in place by a red headband. Within moments, she was off the *Cyrus*'s deck and on her way to the *Shiloh*.

The closer she came, the more anxious Jacob became.

"I have my eyes shut," Connie shouted.

Some of the men in the detail laughed and Jacob smiled.

Finally, she was close enough to the *Shiloh* for the chief and another man to grab hold of the breeches buoy and ease it into the hangar.

The chief assisted her out of it, and Jacob went to her side. "You can open your eyes now," he said.

"Oh, my God," she exclaimed, throwing her arms around him and kissing him smack on the lips.

The rose scent of her perfume filled his nostrils, and he shivered at the delicious press of her body against his. He held her closer and longer than he meant to. Suddenly aware that they were far from alone, Jacob gently separated from her. The men in the detail would certainly have something to talk about with their shipmates. How come the air group commander gets so lucky? How about us?

"I was never so scared in my life," Connie blurted. "I had visions of becoming a shark's breakfast." Not realizing the need for military formality, she linked her arm with his. "That's Horace Dean coming across now," she said. "You remember him, don't you? He was at the table the night we met."

"I remember," Jacob said, acutely aware that the two of them were the center of attention.

"He arranged this whole thing. He's very close to Admiral King."

Dean was hauled into the hangar and managed to extricate himself from the breeches buoy.

Jacob disentangled his arm from Connie's and saluted him.

Dean returned the salute and said, "Good to see you, Miller. I keep hearing about the remarkable things you've done."

"Thank you, Captain," Jacob answered stiffly.

Dean, a tall man with movie-star good looks and presence, gave him a big smile, but didn't say anything else.

Lieutenant Charles Preston came across next. He was very young and nervously saluted when Commander Blake greeted him. He was followed by the first cameraman, a short, rotund man named Eric Stempler. The second, whose name was Peter Boon, had the tell-tale, spidery-red veins of a heavy drinker tracing around his nose and cheeks.

Captain Dean took charge of the introductions, and when he was finished, the XO said to all of them, "Captain Schooner requested I escort you to the bridge. Please follow me." As he led the group away, he turned to the chief. "Miss Burke's bag goes to the captain's in-port cabin, and all of the other luggage can be brought to the wardroom."

"Aye, aye, sir," the chief answered.

"Thanks, guys," Connie called out to the men in the detail. "That's one ride I'll never forget." Then, linking her arm with Jacob's again, she said, "Which plane do you fly, Admiral?"

Embarrassed, Jacob cleared his throat. "She's over there on the other side of the hangar."

"Can I see it?" Connie asked.

"The captain is waiting for us —" he started to say.

"Oh, please, it'll only take a minute."

"Let her see it," Blake interjected. "The captain will understand, Miller. A few minutes more won't really matter."

Jacob guided the press party to the parked plane.

"There are thirteen Jap flags painted on it," Dean exclaimed. "Thirteen kills?"

Jacob nodded. "Yes, sir."

"I had no idea you had that many to your credit."

Jacob flushed.

"Can I look inside, Jacob?" Connie asked.

Jacob guided her up the steps of the maintenance stand alongside the plane's cockpit.

"I love you," she whispered as she bent over to look into the cockpit. Then aloud she said, "I'd never be able to think in a place that small, let alone do what you do."

"Why are there little metal patches on the wings and the fuselage?" Lieutenant Preston asked.

"To repair bullet holes," Jacob answered, preceding Connie off the platform and catching her when she stumbled on the last step. "I took a couple of Jap rounds the other day." He put his hand on one of the patches. "But she's as good as new now."

"This is going to make great stuff for us," Dean said, pointing to the Japanese flags painted on the fuselage below the cockpit. "Does anyone else on the *Shiloh* have as many kills?"

"No," Jacob answered.

"We can feature him and —"

The Klaxon began to sound the general alarm.

The 1MC came on. "All hands man your battle stations. All hands man your battle stations."

As men began to run in various directions, Connie grabbed hold of Jacob's hand.

"You have to get the hell out of here!" Jacob exclaimed.

"Get the cameras," Dean ordered. The two cameramen ran to their piled equipment and pulled out two cases. "I want them to film this," Dean shouted to Jacob, following him.

"You and the rest of your crew are going to the wardroom," Jacob shouted.

"No way," Dean answered. "Connie —"

"I'll go with the camera crew," she said. "Go do what you have to do, Jacob."

The voice on the 1MC announced, "Two bandits have broken through the combat air patrol. Incoming at bearing two-five-zero. Range twenty miles. Angels three."

"Just point us in the direction of the flight deck," Dean said.

"No —"

"That's an order, Commander," Dean said.

"Take the order —" Jacob stopped and forced himself to growl, "Aye, aye, sir." He reluctantly turned to go to his battle station in his ready room.

Even before the news people reached the flight deck, they could hear the sound of antiaircraft fire coming from the screen and, when they were finally outside they could see black puffs of smoke filling the sky on the western horizon.

The 1MC came on again. "Incoming bandits. Bearing two-four-zero. Range ten miles. Angels one and closing fast."

The *Shiloh* heeled sharply to port, answering the full right rudder. Captain Schooner was turning the ship away from the contacts.

Dean assigned one cameraman to the forward part of the flight deck. "Connie, I'll cover the bow. You and Preston and Stempler go aft. Preston, make sure you get everything she wants."

Wide-eyed with fear, Preston managed to answer, "Yes, sir," before leading Connie and the cameraman toward the stern of the ship.

The sounds of gunfire became more intense.

"Incoming bandits from the stern. Low on the water," the 1MC blared. "Incoming bandits!"

The ship's after five-inch mounts began to fire.

Suddenly, one of the enemy planes became flying fire and curved toward the *Shiloh*'s fantail. The 40mm guns kept barking as the burning plane bored in on the ship's stern. The flaming mass faltered, slowed, and plunged into the carrier's foaming wake.

The guns were blasting away at the second plane as it roared over and crashed into the *Cyrus*, which had broken away from the *Shiloh* and was steaming toward a defensive position ahead of the carrier. A huge explosion sent flames high above the ship, and its hull broke in two.

"Oh, my God," Connie cried out to Preston. "Oh, my God!" She desperately wished she could be safely in Jacob's arms. "Did you get that? Did you get that, Stempler?"

Explosions rocked the *Cyrus*'s two halves. The bow turned on its side and began to sink. The after portion of the ship remained afloat and continued to burn. The cameraman, seemingly oblivious to the danger surrounding them, continued to shoot. "Jesus, what pictures!"

At that point Jacob appeared on the flight deck, having learned flight operations were not possible until the attack was over. He spotted Connie's group aft and raced to her side.

"Thank God you're here," she cried. "We're scared out of our wits."

"I am too. Out here if you're not scared, you're a fool." Then he said, "You shouldn't be here, Connie. Christ knows, none of you should be here."

She shook her head. "But I am here, and that's what matters." She took hold of his hand and squeezed it as Jacob led them toward the island.

"Terrific stuff," Dean exclaimed as he and Boon joined them. "I mean first-rate. It's going to knock the socks off the people back home."

"Captain, Miss Burke, as I started to say before, please follow me to the wardroom," Jacob said, leading them inside the island. "When we collect our wits, we'll go to the bridge and meet Captain Schooner."

There were no other kamikaze attacks that day, and after dinner in the wardroom Jacob and Connie took a walk on the flight deck. The blacked-out ships around the *Shiloh* loomed as dark forms. The night was moonless, but the sky was brilliantly starlit.

"This is the strangest place for two people in love to be," Connie said.

"I was thinking the same thing."

They stopped several feet from the end of the deck.

"Except for the sounds of the wind and the ship slicing through the water, everything is so quiet," Connie said. Then, turning to Jacob, she added, "For a couple of moments there this morning, I didn't think I'd —"

He put his finger across her lips. "Try not to think about it."

"Or talk about it?"

Jacob nodded.

"Is that the way you manage to live?" she asked.

"Yes," Jacob answered. "The more you think, or talk about it, the more difficult it becomes to do the things you must do to survive."

She hugged herself. "It's cooler than I thought it would be out here."

"Here, take my jacket," Jacob said, unzipping it and helping her into it. "The wind makes it feel cooler than it actually is." They started to walk back to the island. "Are you going back to the mainland after you've finished here?"

"By way of China," Connie replied flippantly.

"Come on, be serious."

"I am. I'll be in China for a week, India for another week, then Egypt and Paris for a few days before going back to the States, or, as you call it, the mainland."

"When you get back to New York, I want you to visit my mother," Jacob said.

"Are you sure —"

"I wrote her all about you. I told her that we plan to be married."

Kissing the back of his hand, she said, "The very next time we're on the same piece of dry land together, unless Captain Schooner can marry us now — can he?"

Deciding she was teasing, Jacob played it straight. "He doesn't have the authority to do that," he said.

"What about the chaplain? I'm sure he does."

"He probably does," Jacob said after a moment's thought.

45

"Well?"

They went below again to the wardroom. "Would you like something hot? Coffee or chocolate?"

"You haven't answered me," Connie said.

"You're not just teasing, are you?"

"No, I'm not… I love you, Jacob."

Jacob uttered a deep sigh before he said, "This isn't the time or the place."

"For the question or the marriage?"

"Both," Jacob answered.

Connie stopped.

"This is a warship in a hostile zone," Jacob said. "What you saw this morning is what all of us out here have experienced for weeks. When we marry, I want to be able to be with you for a while. I don't want to marry knowing that the next morning I might be blown to smithereens." He paused. "And there's another reason. There are men on board this ship who haven't been home in months. Even if the captain allowed the padre to marry us, and I guarantee he won't, it would blow hell out of their morale."

"Are you trying to tell me that you want to wait until the end of the war?" she asked.

"Yeah, I guess I am," Jacob answered. "The Japs still have a lot of fight in them."

"I'm going to my cabin," Connie said, turning away from him in a fit of pique.

"Connie, wait. I'll go with you."

"I can find my way on my own," she answered.

"For Christ sakes, you can't roam around this ship by yourself!" Jacob stopped. He went after her.

"I said I could find my way on my own," she said stubbornly.

"Connie, will you stop and listen?"

Suddenly, the Klaxon rang out its raucous alarm. "All hands man your battle stations. All hands man your battle stations. All visitors proceed to the wardroom. All visitors proceed to the wardroom."

"What is going on?" Connie asked in a low, frightened voice.

"Go back to the wardroom… Go!" Jacob said.

"But —"

"Go!" he commanded.

She hurried down the passageway. Jacob waited until he saw her enter the wardroom. Then he turned and ran to his ready room.

"What's going on?" Gus, his wingman, asked.

"I sure as hell don't know," Jacob said. "But I'm going —"

The *Shiloh* started to heel to the port side.

"That's a goddamn tight —" Gus started to say when an explosion aft threw him and Jacob against the bulkhead. Instantly the 1MC announced, "Fire. Fire in the after ammunition handling room."

Three more secondary explosions followed.

"Okay, guys, just sit tight," Jacob said. "The skipper knows what he's doing." Concerned for Connie's safety, he stepped out of the ready room and went to the flight deck. Looking aft, he saw flames spewing from two holes in the deck. Firefighters were already hosing water into the infernos below. With dread racing through his mind, he returned to the ready room.

Two more explosions deep in the hull shook the *Shiloh* from stem to stern, and she suddenly listed heavily to port.

Jacob contacted the bridge. "Smoke is about to drive us out of this ready room!" he said excitedly to the OOD.

"Stand by," the OOD answered.

Jacob held the phone slightly away from his ear. He fought down a powerful impulse to run to the wardroom. No, his place was with his pilots.

"The skipper is coming on the 1MC," the OOD said. "He's worried the torpedoes stored in the hangar will cook off. Damage control reports many fires aft out of control." Jacob put the phone down and waited.

The 1MC came on. "This is the captain speaking. We have sustained two damaging torpedo hits. We must abandon ship. All hands abandon ship. All hands below come topside and abandon ship from the port side. Destroyers are closing to pick you up there. Keep calm. All hands abandon —"

Another huge explosion in the bowels of the ship plunged the ready room into darkness. Suddenly the smoke was unbearable.

"Everyone out! Head for the port side. Every man for himself. Help your shipmates if you can," Jacob ordered between coughs.

Jacob waited until every man was out of the ready room before he left it. He glanced into the passageway leading to the wardroom, and with a broken heart saw nothing but crumpled bulkheads and roaring flames. As he and throngs of others reached the flight deck, the holocaust in the after section of the ship cast an eerie red glow through several gaping holes blown through the flight deck. Heavy black smoke poured into the starlit night. Three or four miles away, destroyers were laying down full patterns of depth charges. Maybe the bastard sub would not get away.

"All hands abandon ship. All hands abandon ship," again came over the 1MC.

Two destroyers were standing off about thirty yards from the *Shiloh*. Their powerful searchlights illuminated the water between the stricken carrier and themselves. Hundreds of men in bulky kapok life jackets were already in the water and more were jumping in.

"All right, let's go over," Jacob shouted to the pilots around him. "Try to stay together and swim for the nearest destroyer. Remember, inflate your life vests as soon as you hit the water."

His wingman, Gus, was at his side as the men began to jump.

Jacob looked up at the island cocked crazily in the air.

"There's no way you could have gotten to her," Gus said, "even if she was still in the wardroom."

"God Almighty, I knew she shouldn't be here," he sobbed. "Why couldn't I have saved her from this?"

Gus put his hand on Jacob's shoulder. "Come on, Skipper, the men need you."

"I'll follow you."

Gus leaped into the water.

Jacob was about to jump when he heard someone shouting, "Commander Miller, Commander Miller. Wait. Wait!" He turned and saw two figures stumbling toward him. Behind them, the after section of the ship was an inferno.

"Jacob," a woman's voice cried. "Jacob!"

"Connie," he yelled and ran to her. The other person was Preston. "Get over the side, Preston, right now! There's no time left!" he ordered and scooped Connie up in his arms. The scent of her perfume that had so thrilled him earlier in the day was gone. In its place was the smell of scorched clothing and flesh. Her tattered shirt seemed to be smoldering in several places. She clung to him and whimpered, "Oh, Jacob!"

"Below," he shouted to the men in the water. "Stand by below!" and, holding her over the side, let her drop. An instant later, he jumped into the sea.

Within moments, Jacob was on the surface. "Connie?" he shouted. "Connie?" Searching for her in the darkness, he swam in frantic circles.

"She couldn't swim." Preston appeared at his side and gasped, "She couldn't swim. I couldn't hold onto her!"

Suddenly one of the destroyer's 1MC came on. "Men in the water. Men in the water. Swim well clear of the *Shiloh*. Swim clear of the *Shiloh*. She's going to go over any minute."

"Head for the *Emerson*," Jacob yelled to the men around him.

Within moments, an enormous explosion tore through the *Shiloh*'s hull amidship; the torpedoes had cooked off. Amid hellish steam the ship plunged nose down, stern high in the air, and disappeared with a great roar.

Those men unable to get clear were sucked down in her deadly whirlpool.

Jacob grabbed hold of one of the cargo nets over the *Emerson*'s side, pulled himself out of the water, and climbed slowly up on the deck. Two pairs of strong hands reached down and, catching him under his shoulders, lifted him up. A blanket was thrown over him as he was handed a mug of hot black coffee.

"Skipper, you all right?" Gus asked.

"Yeah, I'm okay," Jacob answered, sitting down on the deck alongside his wingman. "All the men —"

"Everyone made it," Gus said. "We just got lucky."

"That young kid… Preston, is he here?"

"I'm here," Preston said.

Jacob nodded. "The skipper and XO? Dean and Ed?"

"I haven't seen them, sir. Let's hope another ship picked them up," Preston answered.

"God, I hope so," Jacob said. He looked down at the steaming coffee and as he lifted it to his lips, tears welled up in his eyes and coursed down his cheeks. It hadn't occurred to him to ask Connie if she could swim. "She didn't tell me and there wasn't time to put my life vest on her!" he whispered aloud.

"What?" Sam asked.

Jacob shook his head. By dropping Connie into the water, without a life jacket, he surely had caused her death... What terrible irony! Suddenly, he could no longer hold back. He put the cup down on the deck, pulled his legs up and, burying his face in his hands, he wept and wept.

CHAPTER 3

The "GO" signal had come earlier in the day and the *Ferris* had taken two of Warren's PT Boats in tow at the end of 100-yard lines. Sean Devlin and a two-man crew manned the helm in one of them and Harry Fox, with two men, was controlling the rudder of the other to keep the boats apart. The boats were riding easily behind the *Ferris*, gently rolling in an easy sea; while on board the *Ferris*, Warren, Glen, Connely, and Dawson were relaxing after dinner when Captain Ross entered the small wardroom.

One of the *Ferris*'s junior officers saw him and called out, "Attention!"

"As you were, gentlemen," Ross said and went directly to Warren's table. "May I join you?" he asked.

"Please," Warren responded.

Ross seated himself and, smiling at the group, said, "About ten minutes ago, I received an answer to my query about my role in this operation."

Warren glanced at Connely, but remained silent. Ross produced a piece of paper from his shirt pocket. "Captain Munson said, and I quote, 'Use your best judgment in any matter concerning the safety of your ship.' I think that clearly defines my authority, don't you?" he asked, looking straight at Warren.

Warren rested his elbows on the table and laced his fingers together. "Absolutely," he answered. "You are, of course, assuming that any gunfire support from the *Ferris* will be met by counterfire." Ross looked as if he was about to speak, but Warren continued, "If you please, Captain, hear me out.

Nothing in the recon photos suggests that there are shore batteries on the island, or for that matter, any kind of artillery. If there is, my plan is that it will be neutralized by Connely's bazooka men. I asked you to be available to give fire support in the event that the garrison is larger than we have been led to believe and need suppression fire to take the prison ship. In such a situation, the *Ferris* would be a couple of thousand yards offshore and in no peril from troops ashore. Obviously, if for any reason your ship is in danger, you would be remiss not to defend it."

Stung, Ross stood up. As everyone at the table started to stand, Ross commanded, "As you were." Fixing his small eyes on Warren, he said stiffly, "I can read recon photos as well as anyone. We'll see what develops."

Warren nodded.

"Goodnight, gentlemen," Ross said and, leaving the table, he walked out of the mess area.

"Well done!" Connely exclaimed.

"You put the screws to him," Glen said gleefully. "You didn't give him any way to go, except the way you want him to."

Warren smiled. "We might need him, and I want him to be there if we do."

"How about a few hands of poker before we turn in?" Dawson asked.

Glen threw up his hands. "Not with me… You already took me for a sawbuck."

"I'm going to check on my men," Connely said. "I want to make sure everything we need is ready to go."

"What about you, Skipper?" Dawson asked.

"You're too good for me," Warren said.

"I'm just a Marine trying to make an honest dollar," Dawson responded.

"He's just a Marine with a second income," Connely said. "When he leaves the Corps, it will be a blessing to all of us who have lost to him."

Dawson took a deck of cards out of his back pocket, removed them from the box, and executing a professional shuffle, he made the cards fly in a continuous stream from his right hand to his left and back again. "Maybe I can find a couple of players —"

"The wind has picked up," Warren commented, as the *Ferris* began to roll more than she had been.

Glen nodded.

"Better check the tow lines and see how the boats are riding," Warren glanced at the wardroom clock. "Sean and Harry still have another hour to go before their watch changes."

The phone rang. One of the ship's officers answered it and called, "Commander Troost, the captain requests your presence on the bridge."

"I'm on my way," Warren said, getting to his feet.

"Make sure you get some sleep," he told the men at his table. "We head for the beach at 0500."

Glen stood up. "I'll go out with you."

They walked down a passageway without speaking, but as they started up the ladder Glen said, "There's something I've wanted to tell you ever since you came aboard. It's about your sister, Lillian."

Warren stopped at the top of the ladder. "Go ahead."

"You know about us — I mean that she and I were … uh, intimate," Glen said, locking his gaze to Warren's.

"I'd heard something about it."

"I would have married her," Glen said, "but —"

"You don't have to explain anything to me," Warren said, feeling embarrassed and trying not to show it. His sister, a gorgeous twenty-four-year-old blonde, still had, according to his mother's last letter to him, illusions about becoming an actress. Warren had little doubt that she had been around as far as men were concerned.

"I know I don't. But even before you fished me out of the drink, we were friends. And now that we're going on this mission together, I just want you to know that I really loved her and still do."

Warren nodded. He felt even more uncomfortable than he had a few moments before. Lillian was engaged to a Marine lieutenant colonel, and he realized Glen didn't know.

"I just wanted to tell you that I still have deep feelings for her," Glen said. "But I have a wife and a son to think about. Lucy is a good woman, and I'm having trouble deciding how to handle the problem."

"Sometimes things just don't work out the way we want them to, especially when it involves a relationship with a woman," Warren responded, remembering his own torrid love affair with Irene Hacker, an army nurse.

"I'll check our tows now," Glen said abruptly.

"And I better get to the bridge," Warren told him, "or Captain Ross will begin to think I'm purposely avoiding him."

As Warren entered the bridge, Ross said, "Radar shows some heavy weather. Squalls ahead and the barometer is falling."

Warren went to the chart table and picked up a pair of dividers. He walked them from the *Ferris*'s last position, fixed just before sundown, to the target island. Then he checked the ship's pit log: she was making fifteen knots. "We're about a hundred and twenty-five miles away from the objective," he said. "Less the fifty —"

"That puts us approximately five hours away from your departure point," Ross said. "That's with good sea conditions but from the looks of it, we may not be able to maintain this speed."

Warren nodded. Ross had obviously gone back to his original stance.

"We're rolling ten degrees to a side on this course," Ross observed, "and that could increase as we get into the weather ahead."

The phone rang.

The OOD answered and said, "For you, Commander Troost. It's Mr. Lascomb."

Warren went to the phone. "Troost here."

"We're going to have a problem with our tows if the seas become any rougher. Lieutenant Devlin is sure the lines are not going to take the kind of stress that's on them much longer. They're about to part now," Glen reported.

"Can we get heavier lines to the boats?"

"I doubt it. The boats are plunging like corks already."

"Where are you?" Warren asked, knowing that Devlin and Fox and the other men aboard the boats would soon be in real danger if the seas continued to build. He feared the boats themselves couldn't sustain much more pounding and still be ready for action in a few hours.

"I'm on the fantail," Glen said.

"Stay there," Warren ordered.

"Aye, aye, sir," Glen responded.

Warren put the phone down and returned to where Ross was standing. "We've got a problem," he said, "and it will be very serious if, as you think, the weather worsens."

Ross said nothing, but Warren knew drastic measures had to be taken at once, or the success of the mission would be jeopardized. He took a deep breath and said, "Before the problem becomes unsolvable, I'd like for us to avoid it altogether."

"'Us'?" Ross questioned.

Warren pursed his lips. He'd purposely used that inclusive term, hoping that it would make it easier for him to handle Ross.

"It's not an 'us' kind of problem," Ross said. "It's an *I* kind of problem, and you're the *I* who has it. They're your boats, and you're in charge of them."

Connely appeared at the door of the bridge. "Request permission to come onto the bridge, Captain," he said.

"Permission granted," Ross answered.

"How are your crews doing?" he asked, addressing Warren.

"They probably feel as if they're on a rollercoaster," Warren answered, "and wondering why they volunteered for PT boats." He looked at Ross. "The captain and I were just discussing the situation. It could turn real ugly."

"With all due respect, I'd bring those men back aboard the *Ferris* until the weather moderates," Connely said.

"I was just about to recommend that."

"If I come dead in the water —" Ross began.

"OK," Warren cut in. "Do that, sir, but first turn into the wind and then use just enough power to hold steerageway until we can get my men safely on board."

"We can't keep those boats in tow with nobody at the helms. They'll crash into each other."

"We're not going to continue to tow them, Captain," Warren said, suddenly realizing that the time had come for him to take the bull by its horns. "As soon as my men are aboard, I'm going to destroy the boats."

"What?" Ross practically shouted.

"You and your ship will have to get us to our target," Warren answered, feigning nonchalance though his heart was racing. It was coming to the showdown between him and Ross, and he was certain Ross was as much aware of it as he.

Ross's small eyes went from Warren to Connely and back again.

"Let's get my men aboard as soon as possible, Captain," Warren said.

Ross glared at him.

"Now, Captain," Warren said, knowing what he was about to say might well cost him his career. "I do not intend to abort this mission. To put it directly to you, the *Ferris* will now have to take us to our target. Later on you can complain to Captain Munson, or Admiral Nimitz, or anyone else if you want to. I hope we understand each other."

Ross's eyes went to slits.

Warren faced him down. It was a test of wills.

"Very well," Ross snapped at last.

"Connely," Warren said, "I'm going to need your men aft to lend a hand in getting those boats close enough to get my men on board. And bring a half dozen grenades ready to use on the boats."

"Aye, aye, sir," Connely answered.

Using a megaphone, Warren ordered Devlin and Fox to bring the boats, one at a time, close into the *Ferris*'s stern. "She's going to turn into the wind," he shouted, "and will hold a heading."

"Roger," Devlin answered over his loud hailer.

"Stand by. The ship is turning to starboard," Warren informed him.

"Coming to zero-three-five-true," the talker on *Ferris*'s fantail reported. "Reducing speed to dead slow ahead."

Warren relayed the information, but as the *Ferris* began to slow down and turn, she was struck by a fierce rain squall.

"Skipper," Devlin called over the loud hailer, "I can't see where the hell you are."

For his part, Warren couldn't see the boats. "Put your running lights on," he shouted.

"Lights on," Devlin answered.

"Can you see them?" he asked, turning to Glen.

"No."

"Connely?"

"I can't either. The goddamn rain is too heavy."

"Ask the bridge to turn our stern light on full bright," Warren said to the talker.

Within moments, the stern light blazed brightly.

"Have you in sight," Devlin reported.

The *Ferris* was rolling heavily and Warren could see she had lost all headway. "Bring those boats in. You first, Devlin," Warren said, holding onto the flimsy lifeline around the fantail to keep from falling.

The throbbing sound of the PT's powerful diesels increased.

Warren wiped the rain from his eyes. "I see you. Come ahead easy," he shouted.

The sounds made by the diesels diminished.

"Keep taking in the slack on the lines," Warren ordered the deckhands around him.

Ross came on the *Ferris*'s 1MC. "Bear a hand on the fantail. We're sitting ducks out here, all lit up like a Christmas tree."

"Commander, the port line has gone slack," the chief boatswain mate in charge of the line handlers reported excitedly.

"Harry?" Warren shouted. "Harry, answer. Sean, can you see Harry?"

"Negative," came the response.

"Christ, he's gone over!" Warren exclaimed. "God help 'em in this sea!"

"Line snapped," the chief reported, holding the end of it up.

"Sean, what's your condition?" Warren asked.

"Shipping a lot of water. Pumps can't handle it."

"Can you make it to us?"

"I'll sure as hell try," Devlin answered.

"Keep on taking up the slack," Warren ordered. He could clearly see the boat about fifty feet away from the fantail. It was pitching and rolling violently.

"She comes anywhere near us, she's going to crash against us," Glen said.

"And if we don't get those men off, we're going to lose them too," Warren answered. He shouted to Devlin, "Come in on the starboard quarter. Run parallel to us. You and the others are going to have to leap across to the *Ferris*. There'll be men here to catch you. Come as close as you can. Sean, hold her steady until everyone else is off."

"Aye, aye, Skipper," Devlin answered.

"Connely, get your men over to the starboard quarter," Warren ordered.

"Aye, aye, sir," Connely said.

The PT boat crested a wave, dropped into a trough, and as it struggled to climb out, it was smashed down by another wave.

"Line's gone slack!" the chief exclaimed.

"Sean?" Warren shouted through the megaphone.

Suddenly the boat reappeared.

"That was a bad one, Skipper," Devlin cried over the loud hailer. "Took a lot of water."

"Do you still have power?"

"Affirmative."

"Bring her alongside," Warren said. He could see Devlin and the other men now. Sean was at the helm, while the two crewmen were clinging to the gunwale amidships on the boat's port side. "Connely, as soon as Devlin is clear, destroy the boat. Use two grenades."

"Aye, aye, sir."

Warren watched the pitching of the PT boat. Under the terrible circumstances, Devlin was doing a masterful job of handling her.

As the boat drew alongside the *Ferris*, Warren shouted, "Sean, make your move."

"Easing over," Devlin answered.

The gap between the boat and the *Ferris* narrowed. Suddenly the throb of the diesels died. "Go!" Devlin shouted to his men.

The first man flung himself toward the *Ferris* and was caught by two of Connely's men. The second man struck the side of the hull and dropped into the water.

"Grab the line," Glen yelled, throwing a length of line to the bobbing man.

In a matter of moments, the man had tied the line around his waist and was hauled up on deck.

The *Ferris* continued to plunge and roll.

Devlin leaped across the everchanging gap toward the *Ferris*, but as he jumped, he lost his footing and dropped into the water. He started to swim, but a wave smashed him back against the boat's hull.

"He's not going to make it!" Glen yelled.

Warren grabbed a line, quickly tied it around himself, and without a second thought dived into the tumultuous sea. He had no alternative. Devlin had earlier saved his life after their boat had been shot to pieces by a Japanese destroyer during the crucial battle for the Solomon Islands.

"Sean went under," Glen shouted. "No, he's drifting facedown off the stern."

With powerful strokes, Warren battled the waves toward Devlin. "Got him," he yelled as he grabbed hold of Devlin. He secured the line around his lieutenant and, holding onto it, shouted above the howl of the wind, "Bring us in!"

It took more than ten minutes for the deck detail to pull the two of them back to the *Ferris*.

"Get the bloody water out of him," Warren managed to gasp as soon as he was on deck.

Glen had already begun to give Devlin artificial respiration.

Suddenly, two grenade explosions turned Devlin's boat into flames as it drifted away.

"Tell the bridge they can go ahead now and darken ship," Warren said, looking at the talker. Turning to Connely, he said, "Good work, my friend."

Within moments the ship's propellers began to turn, and the ship went dark.

Devlin began to cough. An oxygen-charged breather was put over his face.

"Take him down to the sick bay," Warren ordered.

Devlin pushed the breather away and tried to sit up. "I'm okay," he protested.

"Sick bay," Warren ordered.

For a few moments, Devlin looked questioningly at Warren. Then in a quiet voice, he answered, "If you say so, Skipper."

After Warren had changed into dry clothing, he returned to the bridge. The *Ferris* was emerging from the squall area, and the wind and sea were beginning to abate. He thanked Ross for his cooperation during the rescue.

"We were working together," Ross answered.

Warren nodded. "Just the same, thanks."

"My suggestion, Commander, not that I expect you to take it," Ross said, "is to cancel this mission. You have lost three men and two boats before you start."

Warren felt that another confrontation was in the offing and that the bridge was not the place to have it. "I suggest we go to your sea cabin, sir, to discuss the matter."

Ross turned the conn over to his OOD and led the way to the cabin, where he said, "Well, Commander, now what?"

Warren rubbed the balls of his fingers up and down the sides of his face. "Let's sit down, sir, and keep calm," he answered, pointing to the chair at the captain's desk. "I'll sit here."

The two of them sat down. "I greatly lament the loss of those three fine men and the boats, sir," Warren said quietly. Harry Fox had been a brand-new officer in the squadron, and because he was inexperienced, Warren had planned to use him as his second aboard his own boat during the attack.

Ross shrugged. "I'll let others be the judge of what has happened so far as a result of your decisions. But your numbers have now been significantly reduced, and I question whether you can, or should, continue."

"That's a risk I must take. I still have all of my fighting Marines," Warren answered. "If that prison ship holds any of our people —"

"That's only one *if*," Ross interjected. "There are several more, and any one of them could spell disaster. Has it occurred to you that you yourself and all hands in your group might wind up as enemy prisoners, or dead, as a result of your persistence?"

"Why didn't you voice your disapproval, sir, at the time that you were assigned to this task?" Warren asked.

"For one very good reason," Ross said, looking squarely at Warren. "At the time, I had no idea that I wouldn't be in complete charge of the operation. You see, Commander, I find it hard to live in the shadow of my heroic — and I use that word advisedly — juniors. I mean you and your friend Lascomb. I have eyes. I see what's happening aboard my ship."

Warren lit his pipe. *So, I was right,* he thought.

Ross lit a cigarette, but said nothing more.

"As I see it, Captain, you'll just have to come to terms with the situation in the best way you can," Warren said. "Now, more than before, the *Ferris* is vital to the success of the mission, and I am determined to carry it out."

"Hell or high water, eh?"

"As I said, I plan to continue, and I trust you will do everything in your power to see that we do not fail," Warren said. "The *Ferris* will have to put my landing party ashore as close to the enemy base as possible and be ready to provide gunfire support on call. That's the way it looks to me."

"I see," Ross said without emotion.

Warren nodded and said, "Now, if you will have the word passed for Lascomb, Connely, and Dawson to report to the wardroom, I'd appreciate it." He stood up. "I think, sir, it would be good if you joined us with your charts of the island."

"Very well," Ross said resignedly, and picked up a phone to the bridge.

Warren left the sea cabin. But before going to the wardroom, he went down to the sick bay to see Devlin, who he found trying to convince the doctor that he was in good condition.

"What about it, Doc?" Warren asked, standing at the foot of Devlin's bed.

"Some rest would be best," the doctor answered. "But I won't keep him."

"That's a prescription all of us could use," Devlin said flippantly.

"Get your clothes on," Warren said, "and come with me to the wardroom."

"Aye, aye, Skipper," Devlin answered, already out of bed.

Warren looked around. The sick bay was a small area with half a dozen beds. "How many corpsmen do you have, Doc?"

"Three."

"Can you let me take one or two with me tomorrow when we land?" Warren asked. "One would go with Captain Connely's assault team and one will be with my team. If yes, they should report to me in the wardroom at 0430."

"All right," the doctor answered. "What can I expect to get down here later on?"

"Let's hope not too many casualties," Warren answered. "But there's no telling what we'll find aboard the prison ship."

"Ready," Devlin announced. Turning to the doctor, he said, "Thanks for your hospitality. *Su casa es mi casa*, to re-coin a phrase."

"That's what all of you say, one way or another," the doctor responded, "but if someday in the far, peaceful future we should meet in a bar someplace, you'd probably say, 'Doc who?'"

"Didn't anyone ever tell you that it was an ungrateful world out there?"

"Tell me about it."

Devlin looked at Warren. "He's the one that needs a rest, Skipper, or he'll want to start sending bills to his patients for services rendered."

"Not a bad idea," the doctor said, walking to the door with them.

"I owe you a drink, Doc," Devlin said, offering his hand.

"You're a witness, Commander," the doctor said, shaking Devlin's hand.

"Absolutely," Warren responded.

"Good luck tomorrow," the doctor said to Warren.

He nodded and started down the passageway. Devlin fell in alongside of him. "I owe you a drink, too," he said softly.

"We owe each other a drink," Warren answered. "But rank hath its privileges! Therefore, I claim the right to buy the first round."

"Nothing doing."

"This is something we can settle later," Warren said. "Right now, we have a very real problem to solve."

"Ross still making waves?" he asked.

"In a way. I'm sure he'll try to create a storm as soon as we return to Okinawa, especially if the mission fails."

"Sometimes I wonder if guys like him realize we're on the same side?"

"Sure they do," Warren answered. "Ross is a good skipper, but he thinks he should have been given overall command of the operation. Maybe he should have, but that's not the way it is. He sees me as unfair competition: a guy whose father was an admiral and who happens to have a few medals. He even sees Glen that way, especially since he realized we knew each other before I fished Glen out of the drink and he was brought to the *Ferris*."

Just before they entered the wardroom, Devlin said, "I'm having trouble dealing with that kind of shit. If I weren't in the Navy and ran into a guy like that, I'd tell him to fuck off, and if that didn't work I'd consider beating him to a pulp."

Warren opened the door to the wardroom. Captain Ross was already at a table with the others, but did not seem to have overheard. Everyone welcomed Devlin after his harrowing experience, and even Ross shook his hand.

Warren sat down and, spreading out the charts, said, "Without the PT boats, Captain Ross and I have agreed that if we are to continue — and I am determined to do so — the *Ferris* itself is our only means of putting our assault force ashore in the target area." He filled his pipe and lit it. "The enemy garrison is on relatively flat ground except for these low cliffs, here on the east side —" he pointed to the area with the tip of his pipe stem. "The vessel we must take is located at the end of this small cove just in front of the garrison." He began to puff on the pipe, causing a column of blue-white smoke to curl upward from the bowl, before he asked, "Does anyone have any suggestions?"

"How about bringing the *Ferris* directly into the cove," Devlin asked, "and hitting the beach right over the bow?"

Ross paled and said, "Jesus, young man, are you crazy? There's not enough water or maneuvering room for that."

"You're no doubt right, Captain," Warren responded. "What's more, we'd be spotted long before getting ashore, and the Jap commander would guess that our real objective was the prison ship."

"I wouldn't give a plugged nickel for the lives of the prisoners once that happened," Connely said. Even Ross nodded agreement to that observation. "How about this?"

Connely went on, speaking slowly. "Captain Ross, do you have inflatable rafts on board?"

Ross responded, "Yes, we have a number of ten-man inflatable life rafts."

"I'm listening," Warren said. "Go on."

Connely continued excitedly, "We divide my men: half to me and half to Dawson. Under cover of darkness, we go over the side just outside the cove and make for two landing spots on either side of the garrison. The *Ferris* closes to about three thousand yards at the mouth of the cove, and when we're ashore lays down a five-minute bombardment on the garrison buildings. That will cause all kinds of panic for the Japs. And then Dawson and I close the pincers and take care of them."

"Sounds good to me. How do I and my men get aboard the prison ship?" Warren asked.

"While the *Ferris* is bombarding, you and your men, in two other rafts, will head for the side of the prison ship and board her. After we mop up, we'll come down the pier, board from the other side, and help take the ship."

Ross's jaw tightened and he said, "I can do my part without too much of a problem."

"Very good!" Warren said.

"It can be done!" the Marine captain affirmed.

"Skipper," Devlin said, "I don't see that we have any other option. The Japs will certainly be surprised by being hit in three different places at once."

"They'll certainly radio for help," Ross said. "We'll have to be on the lookout for counter air attack when daylight comes. But they're so busy back at Okinawa the chances of that are slight. I like it better than anything else I've heard."

Warren nodded and said, "Captain Ross, I think we can rule out meeting up with any enemy surface force. But I agree there's a chance that we might come under some kind of air attack."

"That chance was there even if we went in as we'd originally planned," Dawson said.

"That's true, Warren," Glen added.

Warren looked at Ross. "I think Connely's plan might work."

"If you say so, Commander," Ross responded formally.

Warren rubbed the warm pipe bowl between his hands and said, "All right, that's it. We'll do it just the way Connely laid it out. Connely, work out the details for your part with Dawson. Devlin, you'll remain aboard the *Ferris* and be our chief communicator. Get enough field radio equipment for each of our parties so we can keep in touch with each other and the *Ferris* throughout the entire operation."

"Skipper, I'd much rather be with you," Devlin said.

"I need you aboard the *Ferris*," Warren countered. "Besides, you've had enough sport for one day." Then looking at Ross, he said, "Captain, let's set D hour for 0500. I'd like to be in and out of that harbor before dawn."

"Very well," Ross answered.

Warren looked at his watch. "I have 2100. The landing parties depart at 0500. I will go at 0530. Are there any questions?"

"Just a statement," Ross said.

"Sir?" Warren snapped, coming to the end of his patience.

"These proceedings will be noted in the ship's log for whatever future use they may serve."

"Are there any more statements?" Warren asked.

"Officially or unofficially?" Dawson questioned.

"Either way."

"Unofficially, sir, for your ears only!" Dawson responded.

"Go ahead."

Leaning close to Warren's ear, Dawson said in a stage whisper, "Sir, I think Captain Ross is a horse's ass!"

Ross leaped to his feet, eyes blazing, but before he could say anything, Warren said, "Lieutenant, none of us was able to hear you. Speak, if you have something important to say... Do you have something important to say?"

"No, sir."

"Gentlemen," Warren said, "let's get about our business."

Ross left immediately.

"You owe that man an apology," Warren said, his eyes fixed on Dawson. "He is not any of the things you obviously think he is. And, besides, he's about twenty years older and more experienced than you are."

Dawson flushed. "He —"

"I'll leave it to you how and where you want to apologize, Lieutenant, but make no mistake, I want it done," Warren said.

"Yes, sir," Dawson answered, and he too left the table.

Connely waited until Dawson was out of the wardroom before he said, "He's a good officer... Just young and hot-headed!"

"I understand," Warren replied. "But he has to learn to hold his tongue."

Connely stood up. "If you hadn't ordered Dawson to apologize, I would have."

"Yes, I know you would have."

Connely nodded and said, "I better set things up for tomorrow with my guys."

"See you in the morning," Warren answered.

"I think I'll hit the sack," Glen said. "I'm beat."

"Me too," Devlin announced.

Warren stood up and went out on deck. He was too tired to sleep. Except for some ragged clouds, the sky was clear and the stars shone with diamondlike brightness. For no good reason Warren found himself thinking about his father and Kate, a remarkable woman who had loved his father deeply before the admiral was lost during the naval battle off Savo Island in the Solomons. They had provided each other with a wonderful amalgam of understanding and physical love that brought happiness to each of them… Warren pursed his lips and wondered if he would ever find a woman with whom he could be happy? That question fluttered in his mind for a few moments; then as night and sounds of the ship underway penetrated his consciousness, he was overtaken by a feeling of great weariness… 0500 would come all too soon.

CHAPTER 4

Connely's commando force was designated Able, Dawson's Baker, and Warren's Charley. Able and Baker manned their rafts at 0500 and immediately headed, with muffled oars, toward their landing points bracketing the enemy garrison. On the beach, they would be two thousand yards from each other. The *Ferris*, completely darkened, stood dead in the water at the mouth of the cove. Her five-inch guns were trained out to starboard; the muzzles were responding to range data from the director. At 0530, Warren and his boarding party were in their rafts. His radio talker said, "Sir, Able and Baker are ashore. They have requested *Ferris* to commence bombardment."

Warren accepted the report without comment. He was concentrating on the cove, which was covered by a light predawn mist.

Almost at once, the guns forward and aft on the *Ferris* barked with round after round. The hot paths of the projectiles traced arcs across the dark sky. Seconds later, two star shells burst over the enemy buildings ashore, completely illuminating them. The guns continued to fire furiously.

At 0535 Warren said, "All on schedule. Let's head for that ship. Tell the bridge, 'Good shooting and we're on our way.'"

As suddenly as they had roared, the ship's guns fell silent after the five-minute barrage. Glen, seated next to Warren in the slowly moving raft, wet his lips and said, "Jesus, listen to the small-arms fire. Able and Baker must be having a time of it."

Warren could now see the prison ship clearly, tied up with her port side to a jutting pier. Her bridge was lighted, and there were dim lights at her bow and stern. No other lights were visible. Suddenly, all of the lights on the prison ship went out.

"Able and Baker report reaching the base perimeter," the talker said. "They are encountering moderate resistance." A few minutes later, as the raft closed in on the ship, he reported, "Captain Connely reports he and the other team have joined together at the end of the pier. Says the bombardment really leveled things and there are a lot of dead Japs. He and Baker team are going to fight onto the ship to help when we get there."

"Tell him to keep up the good work. We'll need his help getting on board."

Warren's Charlie team raft was closing the prison vessel, and so far they had not been spotted. "Make sure you have rounds in your chambers," Warren ordered his well-armed men, "and all safeties off."

"God, that's an ugly ship," Glen whispered. "The *Kiuki Maru*," he said, reading the name on the bow of the vessel.

Warren watched the distance between his raft and the ship narrow. He tensed, then hissed, "Now." Two of his men threw grappling hooks to the *Kiuki*'s deck and pulled the raft alongside. From above, there was a burst of automatic-weapon fire and two of Connely's helmeted men appeared at the rail. They immediately lowered a large cargo net over the side, and Warren's men clambered up to the deck. From the other side of the ship came the sound of intermittent small-arms fire.

"To the bridge," Warren exclaimed and, leading the way, he, Glen, and two other men raced up a ladder. Warren flung open the door to the bridge, and, leveling his pistol, fired two quick rounds at a figure crouching in the gloom. The man clutched his stomach and dropped to the deck.

A staccato burst of machine-gun fire came from the deck below, followed by a brief silence. Then a grenade exploded.

"Get our radioman up here," Warren shouted to Glen.

Glen had started for the door when a Japanese sailor blindly firing a submachine gun from his hip came charging through it. Glen staggered and fell against the bulkhead.

Warren and the other two men hit the deck and, with pistols blazing, dropped the man in his tracks.

"I have to get that radioman up here!" Warren ordered, scooping up the dead Jap's automatic weapon.

One of his men leaped to his feet and headed toward the bridge door. Just as he did, the door cracked open and just as quickly was pulled shut.

"Grenade!" Warren shouted, dropping to the deck and flattening himself against it.

The explosion lifted his man at the door into the air and hurled his body to the front of the bridge.

Warren opened fire. His bullets tore through the wooden door. There were screams, then the door opened and a Japanese sailor with one eyeball hanging down his bloody face staggered out and fell lifeless to the deck. A second Jap crawled out and, managing to sit, put his hands behind his head in surrender.

A sweating Marine appeared at the bridge door and said, "Sir, your engine men have control of the engine-room. Two standard diesel engines. They know how to start them."

"You take the helm," Warren said to his remaining sailor on the bridge. "Marine, get down on deck and tell Connely to have men cast off all lines. Move it!"

"Yes, sir," the Marine answered and raced below.

Warren found the voice tube to the engine-room, blew into it, and said, "Chief, can you give me power?"

"Yes, sir, but this is an old ship. We'll get eight knots if we're lucky."

"OK, stand by."

"Wilco," the answer came.

Warren went to the port wing of the bridge and called down to Connely, who had reported resistance on board had ceased. "I need a medic up here on the double and my radioman."

"Commander, we've found about a hundred prisoners on board," the Marine captain shouted up, "and fifty or so still ashore in that building at the end of the pier."

"Keep the people below where they are for the time being."

"Will do," Connely answered.

Warren's radio talker appeared on the bridge with his field radio, followed by a corpsman and another man.

"You," Warren said, pointing to the radio man, "raise the *Ferris*."

"Yes, sir."

Warren looked at the other man. "Get on the engine-room voice tube," he said.

"Aye, aye, sir," the sailor answered.

"Skipper, I'm sorry to say Commander Lascomb is dead," the corpsman said, bending over the crumpled body.

"And so is this man," the medic announced as he examined the grenade victim.

To ease the knot in his throat, Warren swallowed hard. Glen had been his close friend and in many ways the fun-loving man he had always wanted to be. As he looked at Glen's body, he felt sick to his stomach. Only after deep breaths could he turn back to his task.

"Skipper," the radioman said, "the *Ferris* is lying off at the head of the cove. Wants to know what's next."

"Get Captain Connely," Warren snapped, acutely aware of a sudden increase of small-arms fire coming from the base area.

"Commander, some of the people down below need medical attention," a man said, coming up to the bridge's open doorway. "There are a few women down there, too."

Warren turned to the corpsman. "Go with him," he ordered.

Connely entered the bridge. "What's your situation?" Warren asked.

"Four walking wounded, two dead. Except for those poor bastards, the rest of us are on board."

"Listen, you say there are more prisoners in that shack at the end of the pier?" Warren asked. Connely nodded. Looking at the building in the gray light of the coming dawn, Warren asked, "Can you get them?"

"We can try. How much time do I have?"

"Not much." Turning to the man at the voice tube, Warren said, "Go below and ask the prisoners down there if any will volunteer to help our Marines check that building ashore for other prisoners."

"Aye, aye, sir."

"Give those who volunteer captured Jap weapons," Warren said. Turning to Connely, he said, "Good luck, you've got ten minutes."

"Yes, sir," Connely said and left on the run.

"Get the *Ferris* for me," Warren ordered his radioman.

A moment later, the man said, "*Ferris*, Skipper. Captain Ross wants to know why we haven't moved yet."

"We have a situation to handle before we can move," Warren commented. "Tell him to stand by. We should be underway in ten to fifteen minutes."

Warren went out again to the port side of the bridge.

"I found an American guy down there; he got ten others to volunteer," Warren's man called up. "They're all armed now. But, Commander, most of those people are in real bad shape."

"Tell him to take his orders from Captain Connely," Warren answered, "and when they come back, I want to see the man you talked to. Now come back to the bridge."

"Aye, aye, sir," the man answered.

"Radio, tell Connely he's got ten more men coming and to move out when he's ready. The sooner the better."

Warren took a deep breath and slowly exhaled. Then he went to Glen and squatted down beside the body. Glen had two holes in him: one in the forehead, and the other in the neck. Warren took one of Glen's dog tags, but left the other around his neck. With a shudder, he gently closed Glen's eyes.

Suddenly the sound of small-arms fire ashore increased, and Warren stood up. Several grenades exploded. He could see a lot of movement at the end of the pier, but couldn't make out whether it was Connely's people or Japanese troops who were scurrying around the objective shack.

"They're coming!" a man on the bridge shouted.

At the same moment, Warren saw many emaciated figures hobbling onto the pier. Connely's men fired furiously, covering them as they fled toward the ship. "Get the *Ferris*," he said. "Ask them to put a few more rounds into the garrison area."

"Aye, aye, sir," the radioman answered.

Looking down on the pier, Warren saw the newly released prisoners were only yards from the ship.

The *Ferris*'s guns roared and explosions erupted in the area beyond the pier. Men were streaming aboard the ship. Warren could see Connely, but not Dawson. Jap soldiers at the end of the pier were frantically taking cover from Connely's deadly fire.

"All hands on board!" a man on deck finally yelled up to the bridge.

"Cast off all lines," Warren called. Then into the voice tube he bellowed, "Engine-room, give me everything you got. Full ahead!"

"All lines clear," a voice from the deck called out. At the same time, Warren felt the ship shudder and begin to move slowly ahead.

"Steady as she goes," Warren ordered as the ship's bow lined up with the entrance to the cove.

"Steady as she goes," the helmsman repeated.

"Signal the *Ferris* that we're underway," Warren said.

The Jap soldiers rushed onto the pier and began firing their automatic weapons at the ship, but she was already presenting her stern to them.

Connely came to the bridge.

"Good work, my friend," Warren said.

"Dawson was killed," Connely countered with a tight voice.

"Glen too," Warren answered, looking toward the body. He quietly added, "Get a detail up here to take care of the bodies. I also need help on the bridge. Some of your men will have to take over from mine, except in the engine-room."

"There were forty-five prisoners in that shack," Connely said. "Some in bad shape."

Warren nodded. "There are some women among the people below. As soon as we clear the cove, we'll bring them all topside for screening … and fresh air."

"We also have ten Jap prisoners. Two officers and eight sailors," the Marine added.

"Where are they?"

"In a small compartment below, under guard."

"Skipper, Captain Ross wants to speak to you," the radioman reported.

Warren picked up the mic and bulky headphones. "Troost here," he said.

"What is the situation aboard your ship?" Ross asked.

"I have a hundred and fifty men and a few women, and most need medical attention. I also have ten Japanese prisoners, two are officers. I have lost Lascomb, Dawson, and three others."

"My medic is ready for you, and I will take the Japanese prisoners aboard the *Ferris*. I'm glad to see you underway," Ross radioed.

"Roger," Warren answered. "Let's make the exchange as soon as the island is out of sight."

"Do you need additional food and water?" Ross asked.

"Probably. I'll know whether we do or not in a little while." Then he added, "I'm running this bucket at max speed until I clear the cove."

"You seem to be clearing now," Ross said.

"Right. Will reduce speed to eight knots to preserve the plant."

"Roger, will stay with you," Ross answered. "Out."

"You can cut back a little now," Warren bellowed into the engine-room voice tube, knowing that Ross had come as close as he ever would to congratulating him for successfully completing the operation.

Two groups of men appeared on the bridge. One detail, under Connely's direction, removed the dead, and the other stood by to take up watch duties.

Warren turned the bridge watch over to a boatswain's mate, who had been helmsman and throttle man on his boat. "Boats, hold her on this course. I'm going below. Anything unusual happens, send for me immediately."

"Aye, aye, Skipper," the man answered.

Warren left the bridge and went to the large, airless compartment amidships where the prisoners had been held. Even before he reached it, the air stank of sweat and a reek that almost made him retch. The prison area was, literally, a large cage with only one door.

A Marine guard at the door came to attention as Warren approached.

"Carry on!" Warren said and asked if there were any problems.

"None, sir," the guard answered. "Except for the men who volunteered to help, these people have had the starch taken out of them."

"Guess we would have too, if we were in their shoes."

"Yes, sir," the Marine answered.

Most of the people sat cross-legged on the deck, or with their backs against the bulkhead. Those men who had some strength left stood in groups of three and four. There was not even a blanket or mat for the starving wretches to rest on. The smell was overpowering. Men and women had been held in the same cage. All wore tattered, soiled clothing.

Dull, lifeless eyes stared at him, and for a moment he felt guilty for being healthy and clean. Clearing his throat and squaring his shoulders, he said in a booming voice, "I'm Commander Warren Troost, United States Navy. I have taken command of this vessel and you will be repatriated. If you will please follow me now, we will go topside. Shortly, a doctor will be brought on board and those of you in need of medical attention will receive it."

No one moved or spoke immediately, as though this news was too much to bear. Finally a tall, cadaverous man detached himself from the nearest group of four men, approached

Warren and stood at attention. Saluting, he announced in a clipped accent, "Colonel Robert Marsdin, Royal Australian Army, Twenty Fourth Infantry, Fourteenth Regiment."

Warren returned the salute.

"The women must be moved immediately, sir," Marsdin said, pointing to a separate huddled group in a corner.

"As soon as it is practical, Colonel," Warren said, looking at the group. There were ten women there, and three seemed hardly more than children. All of them were filthy, and the dresses they wore barely covered their bodies.

The colonel leaned slightly forward.

The man's breath stank, and Warren almost stepped back.

"They've been used by the Japanese," he said in a low voice. "All of them, including the young ones, have been raped many times."

Warren clenched his teeth. A vision of Irene's mutilated body, as he had found it, flashed into his mind along with the dreadful, now certain knowledge that she'd been raped before her ordeal had ended.

"Commander," a man shouted from the companionway. "Commander, you're wanted on the bridge."

"I'll be back," Warren told the colonel and headed back up to the bridge.

"Skipper, the *Ferris* signaled she has a sonar contact," the boatswain's mate said. "Bearing two-nine-zero. Range ten thousand yards."

Warren went directly to the radio, picked up the mic and headphones, and called his liaison on the *Ferris*. "Devlin, what do we have?" The *Ferris* was already beginning to turn toward the contact.

"Captain Ross will attempt to locate, identify, and destroy, if enemy," Devlin responded.

"We're sitting ducks in this ship," Warren radioed.

"Bridge suggests you maintain your present course and go back to max speed."

"That will give at best two to three more knots," Warren said bitterly, knowing that to do so would put an enormous strain on the *Kiuki*'s engines. "Wish Ross good luck for me. Out," he said, putting the mic and headphones down. He turned to the man who had been sent to get him. "Go below to the prison cage and ask to speak to Colonel Marsdin. Tell him there's a submarine in our area and to lead all of his people topside to the afterdeck. We'll have to pray we aren't forced to abandon ship."

"Aye, aye, sir," the sailor answered.

"Give me everything again!" Warren said into the engine-room voice tube. Going to the starboard side of the bridge, he could see ahead the *Ferris* maneuvering at high speed in pursuit of her sonar contact. If the *Ferris* couldn't find and destroy the submarine, if the submarine should manage to sink the *Ferris* instead, everyone aboard the *Kiuki* was doomed.

"Skipper," the boatswain's mate called, "there's someone who requests permission to speak to you."

Warren turned and found himself looking at a bearded, emaciated young man with bright, glistening eyes. Neither spoke as Warren stared at the man. There was something familiar about him.

Then a smile spread across the man's lips and he said, "Welcome aboard, old friend."

Recognition lighted Warren's face. "Tony Trapasso?" he said unbelievingly.

"Yes."

Warren grabbed the skeletal hand and shook it warmly. Embracing him, he exclaimed, "Glad to be aboard. My God, Tony! I'm glad to see you alive!"

Memories of the past came flooding back as he looked at his old buddy. In the early days of the war, Warren had met Tony and Jacob Miller, his brother-in-law, quite by accident in New York City as they were all preparing to leave for duty stations in the Pacific. Warren was an Annapolis graduate and Tony and Jacob, answering the country's wartime call, were newly commissioned officers in the Reserve. Despite their very different backgrounds, the three had become close friends almost at once. Glen Lascomb, also a new Reservist, was befriended by Tony and Jacob en route to San Diego where, in a short time, the four men forged lasting bonds of friendship. During the next few years, they had been able to rendezvous again from time to time on leave from the turmoil of battle. Warren had learned some months before that Tony had been taken prisoner. He said, "Jacob will be so glad to hear you're OK and free…" He had difficulty going on. How could he tell Tony that Glen had died that morning?

"And Glen? How's he doing?" Tony asked, sensing from Warren's manner that the answer would not be what he wanted to hear.

"I'm sorry to have to tell you, Tony, he was killed this morning helping me take this ship and free all of you," Warren said softly.

Tony's thin shoulder slumped as he blurted in anguish, "Jesus Christ, saving me cost him his life? I wish to God it could have been me!"

"Skipper, *Ferris* closing fast. Range five thousand yards," the man with the radio suddenly said.

"I doubt the submarine captain will go for the destroyer," Tony offered. "In these shallow waters it's just too dangerous. And unless he has learned what happened on the island — and I doubt it — he won't go after us either, because we look like a lot of other Jap ships."

Warren picked up the radio microphone. "Devlin, I want to speak to Captain Ross."

"Ross here," the *Ferris*'s captain announced.

"Captain, one of the prisoners is Lieutenant Commander Tony Trapasso, former skipper of our submarine *Tarpon*. I'd like you to hear what he has to say."

"I'm listening," Ross said.

Warren beckoned to Tony, put his hand over the mic, and said, "Tell Captain Ross what you just told me."

Tony took the mic, identified himself, and repeated what he'd said to Warren. Then he added, "I'd play this one close to the vest."

"Meaning, I take it, cover the *Kiuki*?"

"Yes, sir. That will confuse him."

"Stand by. Stand by. Sonar reports he's surfacing!" Ross exclaimed.

"He's surfacing?" Trapasso asked, looking at Warren in bewilderment.

The black hull of a submarine broke the surface and began exchanging recognition signals with the *Ferris* by flashing its light.

"God damn! It's one of ours!" Tony shouted. "It is one of ours. It looks like the *Sailfish* to me."

Warren cupped his hands and shouted the news down to the men below. "What luck!" he said, re-entering the bridge.

"Jesus, I can't believe it," Tony exclaimed.

"Slow down, engine-room," Warren called into the voice tube.

As relief swept over them, their thoughts returned to Glen. Warren put his arm around Tony's shoulder.

Tony bit his lower lip and his eyes misted over.

No more was said.

CHAPTER 5

"Lieutenant Commander Miller, reporting as ordered, sir," Jacob said as he stood at attention in front of Admiral William Gower's desk.

"Please, sit down," Gower responded, gesturing to the chair at the left side of the desk.

Jacob nodded and sat down. Though his service on light aircraft carriers during the past several years had been under Gower's overall command, this was the first time he had met the now legendary man. He had no idea why he'd been ordered to report to the admiral aboard his flagship, the large attack carrier *Vicksburg*.

Gower opened a humidor and pushed it toward Jacob. "Help yourself," he said. "They're the best."

"Thank you, sir," Jacob responded, taking a cigar.

Gower, an elfin man with twinkling gray eyes and a clean-shaven, deeply tanned face, didn't speak until he lit his own cigar. "Ernie Pyle was killed ashore yesterday by a sniper's bullet. He was a good friend of mine."

"I heard that yesterday, sir, in a news report. He'll certainly be missed," Jacob responded. Pyle, a famous war correspondent, had written about American men at war the way no one ever had before. He'd covered the war in Europe, going wherever the famous Texas Division was fighting. Recently, he'd come to the Pacific to cover the war there.

"You know," Gower said, blowing smoke to his left side, "that little man was as brave as any man I have known."

"He certainly had that reputation, sir," Jacob responded.

"You've proved yourself to be a brave man too," Gower said, squinting at him.

Jacob flushed.

Gower tapped a manila folder. "It's all recorded here, Commander."

"There are many just as deserving as I, sir, who haven't had the same recognition."

Leaning back in his swivel chair, Gower silently puffed on his cigar.

Jacob tried not to show his uneasiness, but he felt Gower's eyes bore into him.

Suddenly, Gower leaned forward and planted his elbows on the desk. "You really meant that, didn't you?"

"Yes, sir, I did."

"Humility in a fighting man is a rare trait, Commander, a rare trait indeed. But I've been told by your seniors that you are a special young man."

Again Jacob felt the color rise to his cheeks.

"My air operations officer is going to be rotated to another job in two weeks," Gower said, "and I want you to take his place."

Jacob almost stood up, but forced himself to remain seated.

"How does that strike you?" Gower asked, settling back into the chair.

"I'm honored, sir," Jacob answered firmly, knowing that the admiral's air operations officer would have heavy responsibilities as the fighting with Japan accelerated.

"Before you give me your answer — and that means I want you to accept or reject the offer of your own free will — I want you to know that you won't be doing as much flying as you have been ... and that I'm a son of a bitch to work for."

Jacob smiled.

"I demand excellence," Gower growled. "Anything less earns my unabiding displeasure."

"Yes, sir," Jacob answered. Gower's temper was a well-known part of the man's legendary personality. He was a perfectionist and demanded the same level of perfection in those around him.

"Do you want to think about it before you give me your answer?" Gower questioned.

"No, sir, I don't have to. Working for you will be an honor."

Gower nodded. "Good, your orders will be cut today and by tomorrow you'll be a member of my staff."

"Thank you, sir, I look forward to it."

"I hope you don't mind if I interject a personal note," Gower said. "I was sorry to hear about Miss Burke's death."

Jacob was too surprised to respond.

"She and the rest of her party were aboard the *Vicksburg* before they went to the *Shiloh*," Gower explained, "and I asked her why she chose the *Shiloh* instead of one of the big carriers out here. She told me that you were the *Shiloh*'s air group commander, and that the two of you were engaged."

"We were," Jacob answered softly.

"Hard to take," Gower commented in a low voice. "Hard for a man to take that."

"Yes, sir," Jacob answered. "I believe she saved my life."

"How?" Gower asked, placing his elbows on the desk again.

"She had never told me she couldn't swim … and even when I was dropping her into the sea, she didn't scream," Jacob told him. "Had I known that, I would never have left her that day. I would have gone over the side with her in my arms and neither of us would have survived."

Gower nodded understanding. "That was one hell of a woman."

"Yes, sir, she certainly was," Jacob said.

Gower tapped the ashes off the tip of his cigar and placed it on an ashtray. Extending his right hand, he said, "Welcome aboard, Commander Miller."

Jacob shook Gower's hand. "Glad to be aboard sir," he answered.

Tony's train was scheduled to arrive at Grand Central Station at 11:55. With an hour still to go, the train raced down the eastern bank of the Hudson River. Just fifteen days before, Tony had been rescued by Warren and now he was ten thousand miles away from that hellish place. He looked at his reflection in the window. His face was gaunt, and his eyes were deep in his skull. The doctors in the Naval hospital at Pearl Harbor said he was suffering from malnutrition and severe anxiety. They had wanted him to remain in the hospital for at least a month, but he'd managed to talk them into granting him recovery leave at home.

Al Flyn, an Army corporal sitting opposite, asked, "Say, Admiral, what day is it today?" The left sleeve of his Ike jacket was pinned up. He'd lost his arm during the battle of Manila.

"May 6," Tony answered. The previous night, the two of them had boarded the train together in Chicago and Tony had helped the soldier with his duffle bag. During the night, Flyn had told him that before the war he had been an ironworker.

"I mean, what day," Flyn said, gesturing with his right hand. He was a short, wiry man with a small black moustache.

"Sunday."

"Sunday," Flyn repeated. "Well, this is my special day."

"Not only for you, Corporal, special for all of the guys on this train," Tony said. Smiling, he added, "It looks like a beautiful spring day out there."

"You know," Flyn commented, "I'm not so sure I want to go home. I mean, who the hell needs a man with one wing?"

"Hey, you have people who love you," Tony said, totally unprepared for the sudden shift in Flyn's mood. Up until a few minutes ago, he had seemed to want to go home as much as all the other military people on the train.

"Love me!" Flyn exclaimed with a forced laugh. "They would have loved me much better if I had gotten myself knocked off and they'd been able to collect the insurance."

"Everyone gets the jitters about going home."

Flyn didn't answer.

"Cigarette?" Tony asked, taking the pack out of his pocket.

"Naw, but thanks anyway," Flyn answered.

Tony lit a cigarette for himself and faced the window again. He wasn't saying everyone got the jitters about going home just to make Flyn feel good. He certainly had them. Even now his stomach was churning. He had a two-year-old son he'd never seen and a wife he barely knew. Theirs had been a quick, wartime marriage.

"I'm going to the latrine — head to you, Admiral — before we reach Grand Central," Flyn said flippantly, digging into his duffle bag. "I still can taste the hamburger I had in Chicago last night."

"I know what you mean," Tony responded, turning away from the window.

Flyn smiled forlornly at him and left the seat.

Tony stubbed out the cigarette and found himself wondering whether he and Miriam would even like one another after such a long separation. He knew he'd changed greatly, and no doubt she had too —

A single shot exploded from the washroom and echoed throughout the car. Tony was on his feet the next instant.

"Came from the head!" a sailor shouted.

Tony ran to the end of the car where Flyn had gone.

"Fucking door is locked," a Marine growled, trying to smash the door open with his shoulder.

"The conductor is coming," a third man said.

Within moments the conductor had pushed his way through the crowd of soldiers, sailors, and Marines.

"I'm Lieutenant Commander Tony Trapasso. I was just talking to the guy. He needed a friend," Tony said, standing in front of the door.

The conductor nodded, took a ring full of keys out of his pocket. Finding the right key immediately, he inserted it into the lock and turned it. "You want to go in first, Commander?" he asked, looking at Tony.

For a fraction of a second Tony hesitated. Then he put his hand on the door knob, turned it, and opened the door. "Holy mother of God!" he exclaimed. Flyn had put the muzzle of a .45 in his mouth and pulled the trigger. The back of his head was gone and bloody bits and pieces of his brain were splashed all over the wall, mirror, and sink.

Tony turned to the toilet bowl and vomited.

"Listen," Tony said, looking up at Detective Spitz of the New York City Police Department, "my wife and my folks are waiting for me."

"They've been told that you have been detained for a while," Spitz answered.

"I have already told you everything I know," Tony said, lighting another cigarette.

"We're just trying to make sure we have the facts straight."

Tony blew smoke toward the ceiling. "Listen, what more can I tell you, for Chrissakes?"

Spitz, a man with beetle brows and very thin lips, studied him for a long moment. "Just seems strange that a man who manages to survive for three years comes home and blows his brains out just before —"

"The man had lost his arm," Tony said, exasperated by Spitz's insensibility.

"It doesn't seem reasonable —"

"Christ," Tony exclaimed, leaping to his feet, "you're fucking stupid. You don't know the first goddamn thing about what that man had gone through … or how he hurt!"

"What I don't understand," Spitz said, "is how he happened to have had your gun?"

"My gun?" Tony exclaimed.

Spitz nodded.

"I don't carry a gun."

"Lots of you guys bring them home for souvenirs. Something to show the wife or folks. That was a .45 and the man was just a corporal. I've never been in service, but I know that only officers carry a .45… You're an officer."

Tony shook his head. "God rest his soul," Tony said, "but the man probably stole it."

"Why didn't he kill himself before?"

"Before what?"

"Before he was almost home?" Spitz challenged.

"How should I know?" Tony snapped back. "I already told you, I didn't suspect anything was wrong in his head until a few minutes before he left his seat to go to the can!"

"Though you claim you didn't really know him, you did tell the conductor you were his friend?"

"I didn't say that exactly. I said I saw he *needed* a friend! We got on the train together in Chicago and sat opposite each other all night and talked."

"Doesn't that make you friends?" Spitz rejoined.

Tony glanced at his watch. He'd already spent more than a half hour with Spitz. He looked at the man and, making his decision, walked toward the door.

"Where the hell do you think you're going?" Spitz asked.

"Out that door," Tony answered, "and to stop me, you'll have to shoot me ... or arrest me! I've had enough of this bullshit!"

"You think you're a fuckin' tough guy?"

Tony smiled. "Tougher than you ever dreamed of being!" he said and started across the room.

"Stop," Spitz ordered.

Tony ignored him; this was almost a replay of his teens when he worked for his father as a runner for the mob. He had hated cops almost as much as he later on hated the Japanese ... and he hated them with a fury.

"That .45 has to be yours," Spitz shouted.

Tony stopped and faced him.

Spitz held a snub-nosed .38 in his right hand.

"I told you before," Tony said quietly, "I don't carry a gun." Then he turned around, opened the door and walked out of the room.

Tony entered the large waiting room on the station's Forty-Second Street side. Across the expanse, he immediately spotted his father and mother. With them was Miriam and his mother-in-law, Mrs. Miller, as well as his Uncle Mike. For several seconds he rejoiced in the sight of them. His father wore a wide-brimmed gray hat cocked slightly over the left side of his face and had a cigar stuck in his mouth. His mother was dressed in black but looked regal all the same. Miriam, no longer the girl of eighteen whom he had met by chance on

Broadway on December 7, 1941, was now a dark, exotic-looking woman. Even from a distance she seemed as nervous as he felt. Mrs. Miller was dressed in a simple floral print, with a small, cupcake-shaped hat, but looked much older than he remembered her. Uncle Mike, with his tie pulled down and the top button of his shirt open, had a brown bag in his hand and was busy cracking the shell of a roasted peanut.

Suddenly Mrs. Miller shouted, "There he is. There's Tony!"

In moments Tony was surrounded by them. He embraced his mother, who said in Italian, "I had the father say special prayers for you. I knew you were alive, I knew God wouldn't take you from me."

He was in his father's arms next. Neither one spoke, but Tony saw tears in his eyes.

"Miriam," Tony said, embracing her. "Miriam." He passionately kissed her on the mouth. "I love you," he whispered.

"I love you," she answered, clutching him fiercely to her.

"How's our son?" Tony asked.

"Sam is just fine. Your cousin Maria is looking after him."

Tony sensed a raggedness in Miriam's voice, but he figured it was there because she was nervous. He turned to Mike, and the two embraced. Then Mike, still holding his arms, took a step back and looked at him. "Hard time?" he asked.

Tony nodded. "Hard time," he answered in a tight whisper.

Mike again took him in his arms. "I love you, kid," he said in Italian. "I love you like you were my own."

Tony kissed him on both cheeks. "You're my Uncle Mike, my special Uncle Mike," he answered in Italian.

Finally he took Mrs. Miller in his arms.

"God bless you," she said and kissed him on the cheek.

"Last I heard," he said, "Jacob was doing fine. He's been assigned to an admiral's staff."

"Did you see him?" she asked.

"No, but he's okay," Tony assured her. He didn't know whether or not he should mention the death of his father-in-law and decided, because it had happened two years before, not to.

"Well, let's go home," Tony's father said. "Your mama has made a Sunday dinner fit for a king, and the rest of the family is there waiting for you."

Tony suddenly realized that a middle-aged blonde woman was staring at him and that next to her was a round-faced, bald-headed man.

"Do you know those people?" his father asked.

"I'm not sure, but I think they want to talk to me. They probably think I knew their son," Tony said. "Wait here. I'll be back." And he went to where the woman and man were standing.

"I knew it was you the moment I saw you standing in the doorway," the woman said. "I'm Al Flyn's mother and this is my friend, Mr. Loomis."

Tony shook hands with each of them. Mrs. Flyn, it seemed to him, was remarkably composed for a woman who had just been informed that her son had blown his brains out.

"Have the police given you any information?" he asked.

"Yes, we know what he did and how he did it and we were told that he became friendly with you on the way here from Chicago," Mrs. Flyn said, "and the police think the gun he used belonged to you."

"I assure you, Mrs. Flyn, the gun doesn't belong to me," Tony said. "I don't carry a gun." Then he added, "Did you know that Al had lost an arm?"

Astonished, she exclaimed, "No! How?" Tony looked at his family. "I must go," he said, "my family is waiting for me. I wish I could tell you more."

"I never knew he was wounded," she whispered. "He never wrote that he was even in the hospital."

"I wish there was something more I could say or do," Tony said.

"God bless you for coming over to speak to us," Mrs. Flyn responded.

"Thank you," Tony said and returned to his family.

"What was that all about?" his father asked, throwing his arm around Tony's shoulder as they left the waiting room.

"I'll tell you about it later," Tony answered and took Miriam's hand in his.

"I have a limousine waiting outside for us," his father added with a big smile. "One of those big Hollywood jobs with a chauffeur. Remember the guy you beat the shit out of the first time you came home on leave after submarine school?"

Tony shook his head.

"He's the driver. He's 4F. Somethin' about his back or ears, I forget which. But he did some jobs for me and I owed him, so now he's my chauffeur. You'll recognize him when you see him."

"You look very handsome in your uniform," his mother said in Italian.

And his father added, "You won't be able to keep the women off you."

Tony laughed. He knew they were trying to make him feel good, and translated what they'd said for Miriam, who blushed and tightly squeezed his hand.

The driver got out of the car and opened the rear door as soon as he saw them coming. "Remember him now?" his father asked as they approached the car.

Tony didn't, but knowing that his father expected him to, he said, "Sure, I remember." And he shook hands with the man.

"I'll sit next to my wife," Tony said. "Miriam, do you want the window?"

"You take it," she said.

Tony glanced at his mother and realized that she wanted to be near him too. "You sit next to the window," he said to Miriam, "and Mama, come sit next to me."

"Some boat, eh?" his father asked as soon as they were moving.

"I thought there are all kinds of shortages. Gas, meat —"

"Sure there are," his father laughed. "But not for me and not for mine. Miriam and her mama don't have any shortages, either, right?"

"Every Friday, Mike brings us a chicken and meat for the week," Miriam said.

Tony suddenly felt uncomfortable. He had conflicting emotions about this bit of news. Part of him was glad that his wife and mother-in-law didn't lack for things that others found rationed, but he also knew that the way they were getting such things was not right. Finally he said, "That's good, Pop."

"Damn right, it's good," his father responded. "My family gets the top of the cream, and this war has made a lot of cream. I mean a lot of cream!"

Changing the subject, Tony started to ask about various members of the family.

"Mario's boy, Victor, is in the Marines and is somewhere in the Pacific," his father said. "And Stella, Bruno's daughter, is a schoolteacher ... but you'll have all the news as soon as we get home."

"How long will you be home, Tony?" Miriam asked.

"I have sixty days' leave time coming," Tony said, putting his arm around her shoulders and drawing her to him. "Then maybe I'll be assigned to the submarine school in New London."

"You won't be going back to the war?"

"Not for a while," he answered.

"I hope never," his mother said in Italian.

Tony smiled and, in English, said, "Mama, never is a long time!"

The dining room was hot, noisy, and redolent of garlic, oregano, and cigar smoke. Tony loved everything and everyone in the room. Even if the war continued and he had to go back to the Pacific, he'd have this memory to sustain him through the hard times.

"You're not eating, Tony," a cousin on his mother's side called out.

"*Manga*, Tony, *manga*," his older sister, Iris, said.

He touched his stomach. "I'm bursting now," he responded.

"We got to fatten you up," his Uncle Bruno said. "You're too skinny."

"Let me tell you," Tony answered, turning suddenly serious, "I managed to stay alive on a plate of rice a day. Many others weren't so lucky."

The talking and laughing at the table suddenly dwindled into silence.

"I only meant—" Bruno started to say.

"It's all right," Tony said, holding up his hand. "I apologize. Come on now, everyone have some wine."

"I want to make a toast," his father announced from the head of the table. He stood up, holding the glass of wine in front of him. "To my son, Tony, health, wealth, and happiness."

Everyone drank.

The custom of his father's house demanded that Tony make the next toast. He slowly got to his feet. "Papa, Mama —" he paused and looked down at Miriam, whose face was turned up toward him, "my beloved wife —" A sound of approval rippled around the table. Tony next looked at Mike, who was seated on the other side of the table. "And to my Uncle Mike," Tony said. "I would ordinarily make this first toast to all of you, but this time the first toast I make must be to the memory of the crew of the Tarpon —" his voice faltered and he had to swallow hard before he could continue — "and to the memory of Lieutenant Commander Glen Lascomb, who was killed while rescuing me and other prisoners of war, and, finally, to Corporal Al Flyn: may all of them rest in peace." Though his hand shook, he managed to raise the glass to his lips. With tears clouding his vision, he sighed heavily and said, "That had to be done." And he sat down.

Miriam entwined her arm with his. "Are you all right?" she whispered.

He nodded and used a napkin to wipe his eyes.

"I got something to say," Mike said. "I got a toast to make, too."

"Hey, Mike, you never say nothing," Bruno called.

"I got something to say now," Mike responded.

"Let him say it," Tony's father ordered.

Mike stood up, glass in hand, and said, "Tony, I'm proud of you. We're all proud of you. You're the best of all of us. That's right, the best of us. *Salute!*" He raised his glass and drank.

Leaning close to Miriam, Tony whispered, "I've got to get out of here. I feel as if I can't breathe. I've got to have some fresh air."

"Say that you have to go to the bathroom. Then go out to the back porch," she said, smiling at him.

He nodded, and a few moments later was outside. It was the best part of the day. A late afternoon sun bathed the back of the house, and his mother's flowers were in bloom and her tomato plants were thriving. He took several deep breaths.

Miriam came out and stood alongside him. "I took a look at Sam," she said. "He's awake now, if you want to hold him."

"Sure," Tony answered. He'd seen his son as soon as he arrived home, but the child had been asleep and he had not wanted to wake him. "It's a miracle that he can sleep through all the noise."

"He's a deep sleeper," Miriam responded nervously.

The two of them left the porch and climbed the steep flight of steps that led to the second storey. Sam was in Tony's old room, which, except for the crib where Sam was sleeping, was exactly as Tony had left it almost four years ago. Tony looked down at his son and saw two beautiful but unseeing black eyes staring back at him. Suddenly, Tony began to perspire. Something was wrong. He turned to Miriam.

"I couldn't write to you about it," she said, reaching down and gently caressing the child's head.

Tony wet his lips. "There isn't any light in his eyes," he whispered. "Nothing."

"He's brain-damaged, Tony," she sobbed. "There will never be any light in his eyes."

Tony shook his head and gripped the sides of the crib until his knuckles turned white. "You sure?" he finally asked.

"I'm sure," Miriam answered.

"Who knows?"

"Your parents. My mother. Mike. Mike said God gave us one of his favorites to watch over and love."

Tony started to move his hand toward the child, then suddenly withdrew it.

"It's not his fault that he's this way," Miriam said, picking the child up and holding him in her arms. "It's not his fault."

Tony went to the window and looked down at the backyard. "He'll be a vegetable all of his life?" he whispered.

"The doctors say he won't live to be more than ten, maybe twelve years old," Miriam whimpered.

"You know," Tony told her, still looking out of the window, "when I was in that Japanese prison camp, and then aboard the prison ship, I spent hundreds of hours thinking about the things I would do with my son when I got home. Sometimes I even pretended we were at a ball game together." He turned to her. "Thinking about him made me want to live, especially after the beatings."

"Oh, my God, Tony, I'm sorry!" she cried.

Suddenly the door opened, and Mike stepped into the room. "I figured this is where you'd be."

"I told him," Miriam said.

"I thought so the minute I opened the door."

"This isn't what I expected," Tony said, still dazed.

"It's what you got," Mike answered. "He's your son, Tony, and you should love him, because God gave him to you."

Tony sighed deeply. "I'll try, Mike," he said. "I'll try."

Mike nodded. "I'll see you downstairs," he told them as he closed the door after him.

"Here, let me hold him," Tony offered, reaching for his son. When the boy was in his arms, he said, "We'll make it, won't we, Sam?" Then he looked at Miriam. "We will make it, won't we?"

"We will," she answered with a tearful smile. "We will make it together!"

The sky was filled with low gray clouds and a light rain was falling. Jacob was in the air operations office going over the previously planned strikes for the following day with his boss, the staff operations officer, Commander Russell Skirous. Because of the weather, all of the day's strikes had been canceled and Skirous was on the phone with Aerology.

"The best we can hope for, Miller, is partial clearing late tomorrow afternoon," Skirous said.

"How late in the afternoon?" Jacob asked, concerned whether the next day's strike groups would have sufficient daylight to get back on board their carriers after completing their missions.

Skirous relayed the question and then he said, "Anytime between 1500 and 1700."

"If they get a better fix on that time," Jacob said, "ask them to let us know."

Skirous relayed Jacob's request and, putting the phone down, returned to the table where Jacob was studying the charts of Okinawa. Skirous was a long-limbed man whose family owned several sponge-fishing boats in Florida. A seasoned dive bomber pilot, he had delivered many tons of bombs against enemy targets before becoming Admiral Gower's operations officer.

"You wouldn't think there'd be anything left to strike at," Jacob commented. Pointing to a spot on the chart, he added, "Today's strikes would have hit the Japanese positions here in the hills."

"We'll check with Aerology again tonight," Skirous said. "Maybe they'll have an update. The admiral wants those targets hit as soon as possible."

"Yes, sir, I know," Jacob answered. "If the weather clears by fifteen hundred tomorrow, we could launch and have the strike groups back before sundown."

Skirous scanned the air schedule. "Twelve SBDs from each of our four carriers escorted by six fighters each would have gone on the last strike today, right?" Jacob nodded. "Put them on standby for tomorrow afternoon."

Jacob indicated he understood, and Skirous suggested they go to the flag mess for coffee.

"That's an offer I can't refuse," Jacob answered.

They left the office and a few minutes later were seated at a table in the flag mess, where a steward brought them coffee.

"Well, how do you like life aboard the *Vicksburg*?" Skirous asked.

"So far so good," Jacob responded. "But I've got to get used to staff duty."

"In the early days of the campaign, it was a lot more hectic than it is now."

"I can believe that," Jacob responded, filling his pipe with tobacco and lighting it.

Skirous' tone became lighter. "You know, Miller, as we get to know each other, you'll find that, being of Greek extraction, I have a real interest in philosophy."

"Jake, call me Jake," Jacob interrupted, puffing on his pipe.

"If you're Jake, then I must be Russ. Glad to have you on board, Jake," Skirous said, extending a friendly hand across the table.

"The pleasure is mine, I assure you," Jacob answered, shaking his hand.

"As I was saying, my heritage gives me a historic interest in things philosophical —"

"Don't let him snow you," another commander, who was sipping coffee at a nearby table, interjected. "His interests are the same as all of ours, and they're mostly physical, not philosophical."

Skirous ignored the remark but said, "Jacob, I'm not pleased to say this is Commander Arnold Kelton, the senior flight surgeon aboard the *Vicksburg* doing additional duty on the admiral's staff. Not long ago, he was practicing his voodoo brand of medicine on Park Avenue. And this, Arnold," he said, looking at the doctor, "is my new air ops, Jacob Miller."

Kelton came over to the table, shook Jacob's hand and said, "Welcome aboard the *Vicksburg*!"

"Why don't you join us, Doctor?" Jacob asked.

"He's not shy," Skirous said. "He would have without the invitation."

"Russ was just telling me about his philosophical heritage," Jacob said.

"I may grow old trying to tell you," Russ responded, "if you don't let me finish!"

"Sorry, boss… Go ahead," Jacob responded.

Skirous nodded and said, "I have given a great deal of thought to what I would consider the three essentials for a man's life, and I have reached the only conclusion possible that the three essentials are: women, women and women… Do you agree or disagree, Jake?"

"Can you imagine what his dreams are like?" Kelton asked.

"I dream in full color, with a full symphonic background… But I have put a significant philosophical question to my air ops man, and I'm waiting for his answer!"

Jacob puffed hard on his pipe, squinted at Skirous, and rubbed the bridge of his nose.

"He's obviously thinking hard," Skirous commented. "I like that! The admiral will like that! So will the chief of staff!"

"I can almost agree with you," Jacob finally said with mock pomposity. "But I'd have to say that once we say women are essential, we don't have to say it again … and again! You can have too much of a very good thing!"

"An answer worthy of a gourmet rather than a gourmand!" Skirous responded with a big grin. "I respect a man with sensitivity."

Suddenly the 1MC came on. "All hands, stand by for word from the admiral."

"This is Admiral Gower speaking. Word has just been flashed to us that Germany has surrendered."

"We beat them," Jacob shouted. "We beat the Nazis. We beat them!"

Skirous put his finger under his nose to imitate Hitler's mustache and, in a bad imitation of a German accent said, "Ah, now all vee good Germans vill make like puppy dogs… Ja Wohl!"

And Kelton yelled, "My God, I'm proud of those guys in Europe!"

"The German High Command surrendered unconditionally," Gower continued. "General Jodl signed the instrument of surrender at SHAFE headquarters. The fighting in Europe will cease at 1101 on May 19 local time." Gower paused again, before saying, "I ask all of us to silently thank God for this splendid victory, and ask that He grant us prompt victory over our enemy here in the Pacific."

Skirous bowed his head, but Jacob, who had long since lost his faith, thought about his dead father. In the silence of his thoughts, he said, "It's over, Papa. Hitler has been destroyed."

Gower came back on the 1MC. "Now let's get this job over with so we can all go home. Carry on."

"If the Japanese think they've been facing military might up to now," Skirous commented, "wait until men and equipment in Europe start arriving out here."

Kelton sighed. "It's still going to cost us a lot of men. Look what has been happening on Okinawa."

"The admiral thinks it will cost us a million men to take control of Japan. We will have to land on each of their home islands," Skirous said.

"Maybe they'll just throw in the towel," Jacob suggested.

"Didn't anyone ever tell you that miracles don't ever happen in real life?" Kelton asked.

"War has nothing to do with real life," Skirous cut in.

Kelton threw up his hands. "This is where the conversation is bound to become philosophical, and that means it's time for me to go... Good to meet you, Jake."

"Always good to know a doctor!" Jacob answered.

Kelton smiled and left the table.

"It's time for us to go, too," Skirous said, stamping out his cigarette.

"A million?" Jacob asked, following Skirous to the flag mess.

As soon as he came ashore at Honolulu, Warren was ordered to report to Admiral Harly's headquarters at Pearl Harbor. Harly had arranged for Warren to command a PT boat squadron two years before and had sent him to the Philippines to support operations in that area against the Japanese. After Warren had settled into a chair, the admiral asked, "How was the trip back?"

"Almost a pleasure cruise, sir," Warren answered. "I was able to relax a bit." As he spoke, he noticed Harly had gotten grayer and heavier since he had last seen him.

"Good. You did one hell of a job out there," Harly said. "You know you've been recommended for another Navy Cross?"

"Thank you, sir," Warren responded. "But Captain Ross and Captain Connely ... and Lieutenant Commander Tony Trapasso were also instrumental in the success of the mission."

"Each will be similarly rewarded," Harly said. "But I want to discuss your future with you. I appreciate and admire a man as capable as yourself."

"Thank you, sir."

"I'm assuming that you intend to make the Navy your career."

"Of course, sir. That's what I intended when I entered the Academy."

Harly nodded. "I've spoken to Admiral Nimitz about you and I have his approval to have you assigned again to my command, but as much as I would like to have you, I will not do so unless you agree."

"Sir, other than the kind of assignment you arranged for me in PTs, I really don't know what your command does," Warren admitted.

Harly leaned back in his chair. "Taking the *Kiuki Maru* was one of our operations," he said. "I chose you to carry it out because I felt that if anyone could do it, you could."

"Captain Ross?"

"He did his job too," Harly said with a smile. "Special Operations — spook work — is my main reason for being."

He paused and smiled almost impishly before he added, "I can get anyone I need, anytime for the mission at hand."

"Then you must be in some way connected to Naval Intelligence," Warren responded.

"In some ways yes, and in other ways — well, for the moment let's just say I have a great deal of latitude."

"What would I be doing?" Warren asked.

"Most of the time you'd be involved in work that any officer of your rank would normally be doing, but that would only be for the sake of appearances. Undercover work is what I really have in mind for you."

Though Warren thought of a dozen more questions he wanted to ask, he chose only one. "Are there any other officers assigned to you under the conditions you just described?"

Harly nodded. "And several men who are not officers."

"For appearances' sake, where would I be assigned?"

"After you finish some special training I want you to have, we'll come up with a suitable billet."

Warren rubbed the side of his head. "What kind of special training, sir? Where?"

"For openers, you'll go to the Marine jump school, then for some special flight training and finally to the FBI school."

"I washed out of flight training," Warren said, looking squarely at Harly.

Harly nodded. "You're not going to be sent back to Pensacola, or, for that matter, any other Navy flight training center."

"But —"

"Wherever you are, there will be no record of your ever having been there, or any record of your having received any of the training I mentioned."

Warren nodded. Suddenly he'd remembered having read about a highly classified government organization called the OSS, the Office of Strategic Services.

"There will be, Warren — I hope you don't mind if I use your given name?"

"Not at all, sir," Warren answered, still somewhat mystified.

"There will be two Warren Troosts, so to speak, or three if two are not sufficient," Harly explained. "One will be the person you are now, and your alter egos will be highly skilled specialists capable of carrying out a variety of unusual tasks, some of which will be completely foreign to the most experienced naval officers."

"I hardly know what to say, sir."

Harly nodded. "I totally understand. Take a few days to think about it."

"If I agree, how long would I have before I have to report for training?"

"One month's rest enough?"

"Yes, sir... I've been hoping to get back to the mainland on my leave."

"No matter what you decide," Harly told him, "let me know when you want to go and I'll arrange priority transportation."

"Thank you, sir," Warren responded, sensing the meeting was over.

Harly extended his hand over the desk. "Enjoy your stay here, Warren. You've certainly earned it."

Warren stood and started for the door. Then he stopped, faced Harly, and said, "I'll come aboard, sir."

"Are you certain?"

"Yes sir. The offer is too good to refuse," Warren answered.

CHAPTER 6

"My God, Warren, you should have at least called!" his mother exclaimed, standing in the open doorway of her apartment in Waikiki with her arms around his neck. "Lill," she shouted. "Lill, Warren is back."

"Warren!" Lillian whooped and came running to the door, closing her pink terry-cloth bathrobe. "I just got out of the shower."

Warren released his mother, embraced his sister, and lifted her in the air.

"It's so good to see you back," Lillian said, throwing her arms around him and kissing him on the lips. "My God, you look as if you've spent all your time on the beach," she added as soon as they were inside.

"Don't let the tan fool you."

Lillian went to the phone. "I'm going to call Gene and tell him you're here. The four of us can go out for dinner tonight."

"The Marine colonel?" Warren asked, looking at his mother. Her hair was beginning to gray, and she seemed more serene than he remembered.

"The colonel is past history," she said lightly. "Gene is an Army Air Corps major."

Warren shook his head, but didn't make any comment.

"How long will you be here?" his mother asked.

"A whole month," he answered. "But I'm going to make a trip to the mainland… Glen Lascomb was killed and I want to see —"

"Glen killed?" Lillian asked in a shocked tone, putting down the phone in the midst of dialing.

"I was with him when it happened. He never knew what hit him," Warren told them.

Lillian rejoined them and sat on the edge of a club chair. She clutched the top of her robe and, fighting back tears, she asked, "Did he say anything about me?"

Warren glanced at his mother and caught the slight shake of her head. Ignoring it, he said, "A few days before he died, he told me he loved you."

Lillian lowered her head and said in a strangled voice, "He was such an innocent."

The phone rang, breaking the awkward silence. "It's probably Gene," Lillian said. "I better answer it, or he'll ring the phone off the hook."

"Are you going to see Glen's family?" his mother asked.

"Yes."

She nodded approvingly. "Your father would have done the same thing," she said. "The very same thing."

"Dinner at eight?" Lillian called.

"Fine with me," her mother answered. "Warren?"

He nodded.

"Does Kate know you're back?" his mother asked.

Warren flushed. His mother knew that Kate Hasse and his father had been lovers, and because he thought the subject was taboo, he hadn't expected the question.

"Don't look so surprised, Warren," she said. "Kate and I have become good friends. After all we shared — no, the truth is that we loved the same man."

He'd never before heard his mother say that she'd loved his father. For years, he had felt theirs had been anything but a loving relationship.

"Why don't you call Kate when Lillian is finished with the phone?" she suggested.

"No, I want to surprise her too," he said.

There was a momentary lull in the conversation, and they could hear Lillian chattering. Then his mother said, "I was sorry to hear that Irene had been killed. Her picture was in the newspaper."

"Her brother is an officer in the Navy," he said for lack of anything better to say.

"Yes, that was mentioned in the article, too," she explained. As a way of changing the tender subject, she said, "There's room for you here if you want to stay."

"No," he answered. "But thanks… I've become something of a restless sleeper. More insomniac than sleeper."

She nodded understandingly and said abruptly, "Warren, I don't drink anymore. I haven't had a drink in almost two years."

He smiled at her. "I knew that. It makes me happy to hear it from you."

"How did you know?"

He went to her and, lifting her into his arms, he said, "Because you look so at peace and beautiful."

"Oh, Warren," she cried, flinging her arms around his neck.

He held her very close and for the first time since he was a small boy, Warren realized how much he loved his mother.

That same afternoon, Warren left his mother's apartment and stopped at the florist, where he bought a dozen long-stemmed roses for Kate. It was his way of thanking her for the letters and books she'd sent him over the past two years. After a short cab ride, he found himself standing in front of an open door looking at a young woman wearing white shorts and a white blouse tied in a bow, exposing her tanned midriff. She had the same russet hair as Kate and some of her other good features as well.

"You must be Warren Troost," the young woman said, glancing at the sleeves of his jacket. "Or should I have said Commander Troost?"

"Warren will be just fine," he said, realizing he was facing one of Kate's twin daughters, either Tara or Riva.

"My mother and my sister will be back any minute," the young woman said and gestured him inside.

Warren removed his cap, entered the small foyer, and waited for her to lead the way into the living room. He sat down in a high-backed chair, feeling more than uncomfortable under the scrutiny of her piercing blue eyes. The silence between them, he realized, was turning into an endurance contest. He became determined to win it.

Finally she said, "I'm Tara."

"How did you know me?" he asked.

"Mother showed us one of the photographs you sent to her."

Warren nodded. There was an unmistakable note of antagonism in her voice.

"Besides, who else would be carrying roses?" she asked.

"One of your, or your sister's, male friends?" Warren offered jokingly.

She made a moue. "Neither I nor my sister is involved in that kind of relationship," she said.

Warren looked down at the flowers. "These are my way of thanking your mother —"

Suddenly the door opened, and Kate and Riva stepped into the foyer.

"Mother, you have a visitor," Tara called.

Warren stood up, and an instant later Kate entered the living room. Seeing Warren and running to him, she cried, "I knew it.

113

I knew it was you, Warren, as soon as Tara told me I had a visitor." She hugged him. "Riva, this is Warren."

"Hello, Riva," Warren responded, looking over Kate's shoulder. She was a mirror image of Tara, down to a small, delightful mole on her left cheek. "These are for you," Warren told Kate, handing her the roses.

She gently cradled them in her arms. "That was very thoughtful of you," Kate said. "When did you arrive?"

"This morning around eight," he answered. "I had something to take care of at CinPacFlt Headquarters; afterward, I went to see my mother and Lill and then I came here."

Kate took several steps back and looked at him. "Are you all right?"

He nodded.

"Really all right?" she questioned again.

"Tired," he answered.

"Tara," Kate said, "will you place these in the green vase and put them on the coffee table here? Remember to dissolve an aspirin in the water. Keeps the flowers alive longer," she explained, looking at Warren. Taking him by the hands, she led him to the couch. "I was sorry to hear about Irene. I know that must have been very hard for you to take."

"It was and sometimes still is," Warren admitted. Tara came back with the vase and placed it on the coffee table.

"They look absolutely stunning!" Riva exclaimed.

Warren smiled at her.

"I have something to show you," Kate said, standing up. "I'll be back in a few moments."

Alone with the twins, Warren could sense the hostility emanating from Tara, and at the same time a distinct feeling of sensual interest came from Riva.

"Will you be going back to the combat zone?" Tara asked.

"Not for a while."

"Were you in the typhoon that hit Admiral Gower's fleet in the beginning of June?" Riva questioned.

Warren shook his head. "I was in Ulithi at the time, waiting for a ship that would bring me to Pearl."

Kate returned. "This is an advance copy," she said, handing Warren a book with a yellow and black dust jacket on it.

"*The Hill Country* by Kate Hasse," he said, reading the title aloud and the small print below it. "A novel about a Kentucky family... Kate, I'm proud of you, real proud."

She beamed. "Open it."

On the inside cover, she'd written: *To Warren: I love you as if you were my own son, Kate.*

"Thank you," he said quietly.

"Well, what would you like to drink?" she asked.

"Something cold would do fine," Warren answered, looking at Tara, who seemed to be smoldering.

"Gin? Rum?"

"Nothing like that," Warren said.

"I'll bring some juice," Riva volunteered.

"Thank you," Kate responded.

"Mother tells me you and she see quite a bit of each other now," he said.

"Yes, you know she's really a very talented woman. She's been acting very successfully in various amateur theater groups."

"After all these years, she is finally doing what she wanted to do," Warren observed.

Riva returned carrying a wooden tray with four glasses of pineapple juice on it.

"I don't want any," Tara declared.

Kate waited until Warren and Riva took their glasses. Raising hers, she said, "To Warren Troost, welcome home."

The three of them touched glasses and drank. Then Warren lifted his glass and said, "To the memory of my father, Admiral Troost, and to the memory of your husband, Captain —"

"Don't you mention his name!" Tara suddenly screamed, her face suffused with color. "Don't you dare mention his name!"

"Tara!" Kate exclaimed.

"No," she yelled, glaring at her mother. "I know about you and his father. And I know Riva doesn't care. But I do!" And she ran from the room.

Warren lowered his glass. "I wasn't thinking," he said, looking first at Kate and then at Riva.

Kate put her hand over his and gently squeezed it.

"All air strikes against the Japanese home islands have been canceled for Monday, August 6," Skirous said, reading the information off a special order from CinPacFlt Headquarters. "In addition, all reconnaissance flights over said islands to assess damage from previous strikes are to be canceled for that day."

Jacob uttered a low whistle. "Any reason given?"

"None."

"The admiral is not going to like that one bit," Skirous commented. "During last week's OPS meeting he said how pleased he was that since mid-June, our strikes have reduced Japan's industrial capacity by a full twenty percent. He pointed out that we've succeeded in almost totally destroying their rail and shipping capability. That's not bad for six weeks of work."

"Damn good, if you ask me," Jacob responded, sitting down at his desk.

"Jake, get a message to the other carriers about the strike cancellation ready for the admiral's release."

"Yes, sir, but it seems to me we'll have to resume our strikes right away to keep them on their heels, especially when our amphibious forces hit the beach."

"Absolutely right," Skirous answered. "We must retain control of the air."

"I was hoping, after a few more weeks of our strikes on the homeland, those bastards would realize they can't win," Jacob observed.

"Possible, but not likely. They'll probably continue to fight the way the Germans did. It wasn't over there until Berlin fell. It probably won't be over here until our troops capture Tokyo."

Jacob didn't answer and busied himself with preparing the message for the admiral to release. The war had become considerably more complicated for him than it had been when he first was at sea. Then he had viewed it from the cockpit of his fighter plane. It had been a personal contest of skill between him and his opponent and their aircraft. But now, he felt the man-to-man aspect had ended. Now all of them were called upon to pulverize anything of military value and completely destroy the will of the Japanese government to continue to fight, regardless of innocent civilian victims. It was a very different kind of war men in the air were fighting now, very different. But there was no doubt in his mind he had to give to it the same zeal and dedication that he gave when he was in the cockpit of his fighter... He handed the message he had prepared to Skirous and said, "Is this OK, Russ?"

Along with the other members of Gower's staff, Jacob had been summoned to the flag mess. Gower waited until everyone was seated before he said, "Gentlemen, the following message came from Admiral King's headquarters and I quote, 'At 0815 this morning, Japanese time, an atomic bomb, a weapon of horrendous strength and the first of its kind, was dropped and detonated over the Japanese city of Hiroshima. The city has been destroyed.'" The rest of what Gower was saying became lost in a rising murmur of excited voices. Everyone in the room realized that war was about to come to an even more dramatic end than the way it began. "…and that statement, gentlemen," Gower concluded, "heralds the end of this war and the dawn of the nuclear age!"

As Gower paused, there was absolute silence in the room, but then there was an explosion of cheers, whistles; even Gower smiled.

"An atomic bomb!" Skirous exclaimed. "I can't believe it. Now we know why all of our strikes today were cancelled!"

"It's the miracle we all wanted," Jacob answered.

"Gentlemen," Gower called above the noise. "Gentlemen, may I remind you that until the Japanese actually surrender, we are still at war."

CHAPTER 7

"You can't imagine how crazy everyone is," Lillian said excitedly. "It's V-J Day and no one is ever going to forget it...! Warren, are you listening to me?"

"With both ears."

"My God, you helped make this wonderful day possible, but you don't seem the slightest bit interested," Lillian complained, pacing back and forth across the living room. "I don't understand you."

"Don't worry, little sister, I fully intend to celebrate. I might even get drunk," he said through a haze of smoke from his pipe. Lillian obviously found Warren's calm very irritating, and as he tried to understand it himself, he realized that the war's end was something of a let-down. For himself, and perhaps for tens of thousands of men like him, the bloodcurdling memories of the war would never really fade. The horror would always be there inside of him. At best, that thought made him nervous; at worst, it frightened him.

"You get drunk?" Lillian said unbelievingly.

He nodded.

"I hope so. Just once, I'd like to see you really let go. You're wound up tighter than Dad ever was." The moment after she spoke, Lillian ran to him and, bending down, kissed the top of his head. "I didn't mean that the way it sounded," she apologized. "It's just that I want you to have a good time." She settled on the arm of the chair. "I really worry about you, Warren. I know you think I'm a scatterbrain and too wild for my own good. But —"

"I never criticized you," he said, holding the pipe by its bowl. "I may not agree with what you do, but you are a woman and your decisions are your own."

"So, for that matter, are yours," Lillian responded archly. "But I'd like to see you happy, at least happier than you appear to be now."

"I'm not unhappy. I'm just not happy."

"Blah is what you are!" she said.

"Blah?" Warren questioned.

"I think you're in an emotional state of limbo," Lillian said, standing up. "You need to be with people more than you are. You spend most of your afternoons and evenings here, and when you're not here, you're out walking by yourself. Warren, you need a girlfriend."

"Thanks for the advice, Dr. Lill. I'll consider trying to follow it."

"I'm not joking."

Warren nodded. "I know you're not, and I appreciate your concern. I really do."

"Come out with me," she said.

"Not right now … but I promise I'll go out soon and go as crazy as everyone else," Warren told her. "Now, go and have a good time. Maybe we'll run into each other later."

"Are you sure you don't want to come?"

"Go," he ordered, pointing to the door.

She smiled at him, picked up her bag, and, adjusting a pert hat on her head, went to the door. "See you," she exclaimed as she blew him a kiss and left the apartment.

Warren relit his pipe and, settling back to smoke in peace, glanced at the phone on the nearby end table. Ever since the unpleasant incident in Kate's house with Tara, he'd been uneasy. Although he understood Tara's flare-up, and, indeed, sympathized with it to some extent, he also resented it. He'd offered a toast to the memory of two brave men. That's all that he had had in mind, and that was what he wanted her to understand. "Goddamn it, that's what she *will* understand, whether she wants to or not," he muttered aloud.

Picking up the phone, he dialed Kate's number. It rang four times before a woman answered. Warren couldn't tell whether the voice was that of Tara or Riva, and in his uncertainty he quickly pressed the disconnect button. He could hear the pounding of his pulse in his ears. He was strangely excited. Even though Tara had been far less responsive to him than Riva, it was Tara who stirred his imagination.

"Christ," he growled, "why the hell am I acting like this?"

Releasing the disconnect, he dialed again.

This time, the phone was picked up on the second ring and a pleasant feminine voice said, "The Hasse residence."

Warren cleared his throat. "May I speak to Tara?" he asked, hoping that it was she on the other end.

A brief silence followed before the voice said, "This is Tara. Who is this?"

"Commander Troost," Warren answered formally, but, instantly recognizing his stilted tone, said, "It's Warren, Tara." He could hear her soft breathing, and before she could respond, he continued, "There's a victory celebration at the Royal Hawaiian tonight. I would very much like to take you."

"Are you asking me for a date?" Tara's voice became defensive.

He cleared his throat and, feeling a trifle foolish, he answered, "It seems that way, doesn't it?"

She said nothing.

"I realize this is very short notice," Warren heard himself say, "and if you have other plans, I understand." He wondered why he was acting like a high school kid with her. After all, he was twenty-eight; he guessed she had to be twenty-one, perhaps twenty-two.

"I'll be ready by eight," Tara announced without further comment.

"Eight will be fine."

Tara clicked off without saying another word.

Warren put the phone back in its cradle and walked to the window. He felt mysteriously disturbed and, putting the pipe back in his mouth, he became aware of its suddenly bitter taste.

Warren and Tara left the Royal Hawaiian at one in the morning, and the revelry was still going strong. He had met several of his classmates there and introduced Tara to them. He also introduced her to Admiral Harly, who in turn had them meet his wife, Gwen. Tara had been a hit with everyone.

"Where to?" the cabdriver asked as soon as they were seated.

Warren was about to give Tara's address, but he stopped himself. Looking at her, he said, "Take us out to the Overlook on Diamond Head." The Overlook was a popular place for sightseers in the daytime and lovers at night. Warren settled back and commented, "I can't remember when I've danced so much. I had a great time."

Tara's silence disappointed and irritated him.

Warren fished out his pipe. "If you'd rather go home, I'll tell the driver."

She looked at him coolly. "If I wanted to go home, I would have said so."

Warren filled and lit his pipe. Throughout the evening, Tara had been pleasant but remote. Their conversation had been limited to inconsequential topics, and when they danced, she had made sure that there was always space between their bodies. He, on the other hand, had been extremely aware of her. She wore a sleeveless, strapless dark blue gown that seemed to be molded to her body. Her long russet hair flowed around her bare shoulders. From Kate's letters, Warren already knew quite a lot about her and Riva. Both were graduates of the University of California at Berkeley, where they had majored in art history. Both had returned to Honolulu only three months earlier from the mainland. Riva worked as a secretary at CinPacFlt Headquarters. Tara had been offered a job in the fall teaching art in a local high school, but her ambition was to be a professional artist.

"Do you intend to stay in the Navy?" Tara asked, breaking the silence between them.

"Yes, I do," Warren answered.

"And make flag rank?"

"That's certainly the goal of many career officers," Warren responded. "But it's really too early now for me to worry about that. Maybe I'll think about it in a few years."

She turned her face toward him. "Yes," she said, suddenly wistful. "It was my father's dream too, after he became a captain."

Warren was about to answer when the cab turned into the parking area adjacent to the Overlook. There were several cars already there.

"Do you want me to wait?" the driver asked as he brought the vehicle to a stop.

"Yes," Warren answered, and as he opened the door and got out, he offered his hand to Tara.

Walking together, they went to the wooden deck that provided a panoramic view of the Pacific. The softly breaking surf caressed the sands of Waikiki Beach with an ever renewed flow of irregular white necklaces. The scent of the sea was sharp and clean.

"I hope you don't blame my father for your father's death," Warren said abruptly as they looked out on the open ocean. Captain Hasse's cruiser had been Admiral Troost's flagship in the early years of the war. Hasse had lost his life on his bridge during a savage exchange of gunfire with Japanese shore batteries.

"I don't blame him for that," she responded. "Your father and my mother —!"

He turned her toward him. "My father fell in love with your mother, and she fell in love with him. They didn't plan to do that."

She turned her face away from him.

Gently, he touched her chin and brought her face back to his. "Try to understand it from their point of view."

Tara shook her head. "I hate my mother for sleeping —" She stopped and tears welled up in her eyes.

"Tara," he said, taking her in his arms, "don't hurt her any more than she has already been hurt. She lost the only two men she ever loved."

"She never loved my father!"

"She did," he answered softly. "She loved him in a very special way, but she also loved my father. That kind of thing has happened before."

"How can you accept the fact that your father betrayed your mother?" she questioned fiercely.

Warren shook his head. "Your mother made him happy," he said lamely, "and he obviously made her happy."

"That's almost obscene," she exclaimed, drawing away from him.

"It's the way things were between them," Warren said. "Neither of their mates was capable of giving them all of what they needed. My mother was an alcoholic, and living with her was no picnic for my father. And my guess is that your father was so dedicated to his career that your mother's needs were overlooked."

"I didn't know that about your mother," Tara said softly.

Warren shrugged. "There was no way you could have known."

Tara turned toward the ocean and for several moments remained silent. Then she asked, "You asked me out in order to tell me these things, didn't you?"

"Yes, I thought it was important that you see the past as it really was."

"And do you think I do now?" she asked, facing him.

"No, but maybe you will someday," Warren said, intensely aware of her loveliness. Under other circumstances, he'd have taken her in his arms and kissed her. But somehow this was not the right time.

"I'd like to go home now," Tara told him.

They left the deck, and though Warren scrupulously avoided walking too close to any of the parked cars, it was impossible to avoid hearing the sounds of passion that came from them. A particularly loud squeal of pleasure made Warren smile self-consciously, but Tara seemed not to have heard it.

"It was thoughtful of you to ask me out," Tara said as the cab began to move. "I heard you were engaged. Was your fiancée very beautiful?"

"Irene?" he asked, puffing on his pipe.

"Sorry, that was a dumb question," Tara said, suddenly remembering Irene's fate.

He ignored her words of self-reproach and said, "Not really gorgeous in a physical way, but certainly attractive … and that to me is beauty."

"Yes, I know some women who are like that," she responded. "Sometimes, I should think, a woman like that is more interesting to a man. A ravishingly beautiful woman you look at; she's there for other eyes to behold. But an attractive woman has an elusive quality, a kind of aura that gives her an air of mystery as well as beauty."

"I'd never thought about it that way," Warren admitted, becoming interested. Whether Tara knew it or not, she'd described herself. And then he realized that what she'd said held true for Kate as well. Whereas his mother could still be considered a physically beautiful woman, Kate had a certain indefinable air of elegance that his mother lacked. He could understand how fascinating his father must have found this.

They were pulling up in front of the house almost before Warren realized it. "Wait," he told the driver, assisting Tara out of the cab.

"Warren," Tara said as they walked up the path to the door, "once again, thank you for asking me out tonight."

"It was my pleasure."

They stopped in front of the door and faced each other. He desperately wanted to kiss her, but still felt the time was not right. She opened her purse and, taking out her key, said, "Goodnight, Warren."

"Goodnight, Tara," he responded and took a hasty step away. Facing her once more, he said, "I'd like very much to see you again."

She hadn't moved. "Yes, I'd like that, too," she answered. "Call me."

Warren grinned happily and started to walk jauntily back to the cab as a shore patrol jeep careened around the corner and came to an abrupt stop in front of the house.

"Commander Warren Troost?" a lieutenant asked, swinging himself out of the seat next to the driver's and saluting Warren.

Warren returned the salute. "Yes," he answered, wondering how they'd tracked him down.

"We have orders to escort you to Admiral Harly's office."

Tara came running down to the curb. "Is anything wrong?" she asked breathlessly.

Warren shook his head. "Some papers I didn't sign and should have," he fibbed. "Nothing to worry about."

"They want them signed now, at three o'clock in the morning?"

Grinning, Warren shrugged.

"You know the Navy."

There were two other officers in Admiral Harly's office when Warren arrived, a Navy captain and a Marine major, and there was a large map of Manchuria on the wall directly behind Harly's desk.

Harly, pointing to the empty chair between the two men, said, "Sit there, Commander." Then he said, "Commander Troost, this is Captain Josiah Finch, and on your left is Major Paul Boxer."

Warren shook hands with both of them. Boxer was a tall, lean man with a hatchet-shaped face and black eyes. Finch was slightly shorter than Boxer and heavier, softer-looking. Warren then remembered having seen Harly and Finch together sometime earlier in the evening.

Harly told them, "About 2330 I received word from Washington that Japanese forces are still holding twenty Navy,

Marine and Army Air Corps pilots in a special prison facility on the Manchurian coast. Those Japs have not yet surrendered." Using a wooden pointer, he located the place on the wall map behind him. "This facility is one of a kind. Intelligence has learned the Japanese have been conducting unusual medical experiments there like those carried out by the Germans on Jews and Russian prisoners at Buchenwald and other concentration camps in Europe. CinPacFlt has directed that our men at this place be rescued immediately and that the Japanese doctors and other scientists involved in these experiments be arrested and held in maximum security until Washington determines what to do with them. Gentlemen, in addition to that, Washington wants to have all records of experimental data that have been compiled by the Japanese at this facility. Some of those experiments, we understand, have been grisly beyond the imagination of anyone in this room."

Warren puffed hard on his pipe while the other two men took long drags on their cigarettes.

"It's up to us, gentlemen, to carry out this mission which the president himself has endorsed. Our sources have indicated that because of the nature of the work done at the facility, it has been, and still is, guarded by at least one detachment of Japanese Marines. What we don't know is whether they will lay down their arms, or continue to fight in an effort to gain guarantees for the facility's medical and technical butchers. Therefore, our commando team must be ready for battle when it goes in, which will be as soon as possible. We have excellent recon photos of the area, but charts are grossly out of date. Any questions, gentlemen?"

"Sir, how soon are you talking about?" Major Boxer asked.

"It will take a day to fly the three of you out to Okinawa, another day to assemble your strike team… Two to three days to reach your target. That makes five days. Add another one for contingencies and that would mean six days, seven at the outside."

"How will we get in and out?" Boxer asked.

"Commander Troost, since you've had more experience than anyone here in both hit-and-run raids and in personnel-rescue operations, let's hear your ideas on that."

Warren took the pipe out of his mouth and said in measured tones, "I would not suggest doing again the kind of operation that we used in putting our commando unit into the target area when we took the prison ship. This time, I believe we would be better off using two submarines to transport the strike team and infiltrate the area."

"Any comments on Commander Troost's suggestion?" Harly asked.

"That wouldn't give us fire support, should we need it," Boxer said.

"No, sir, it wouldn't," Warren responded. "But it would give us the invaluable advantage of total surprise."

Harly looked at Captain Finch. "How do you see this?"

"I'm inclined to agree with Major Boxer," Finch said. "Just having a destroyer stand offshore would make that Japanese commander think twice before he took any action."

Harly shifted his gaze back to Warren. "That's certainly a consideration."

"Yes, sir, it is," Warren responded. "But as you have indicated, our objective will be to get our people and theirs, as well as the records you mentioned, out without a major confrontation. Besides, the submarines could give us fire support from their deck guns as a last resort."

"Sir," Finch said, "do you know how many of our men, and how many Japanese doctors and other personnel must be evacuated?"

"A total of thirty. As I said, twenty of our people and ten of theirs."

"I believe a minimum of twenty Marines will be needed in our commando team to ensure success," Boxer said.

"That will mean there will be twenty-five additional individuals on board each of the submarines on our way out … twenty-six including Commander Troost and myself," Finch said. "Even for a few hours, it's going to be mighty cramped aboard those boats."

"Sir," Warren offered, "if you agree to use two submarines to get in and out, once we're safely out of sight of the coast, I recommend the subs rendezvous with a surface ship and transfer all hands to it."

"Major?" Harly questioned.

"Reasonable," Boxer answered.

"Captain Finch, do you have any objections to Commander Troost's proposal?"

"Sir, I would much prefer the landing and the withdrawal to be made from a destroyer," Finch answered.

"That way we'd not only have the space, but we'd also have the necessary fire support should we need it."

"Commander Troost, do you still recommend that we use submarines?" Harly asked.

"Yes, sir," Warren answered.

Harly took the cigar out of his mouth. "Captain Finch, thank you for your views. I have decided to go with Troost's idea. You may leave."

Finch stood up, saluted stiffly, and then left the office.

As soon as the door closed, Harly said, "Commander Troost, you will be in overall command of this mission."

"Yes, sir," Warren responded.

Harly said, "We'll use two of our new Gato-class submarines. Gentlemen, my watch says it is 0430. You have three hours before reporting back here at 0730."

"Yes, sir," Warren and Boxer answered simultaneously. The two of them stood up and saluted. Turning toward the door, they left Harly's office.

"You didn't exactly score points with Captain Finch," Boxer said as they walked down the hallway together.

"Don't I know it. But I had to call it as I saw it," he said as they reached the doorway.

"I have the feeling that he's not the kind of man who forgets things."

Remembering his troubles with Captain Ross, Warren said darkly, "Probably not — but what could I do?"

Warren pushed Kate's doorbell several times before one of the windows on the side of the house glowed yellow. It was another moment before Kate called out from the other side of the door, "Who's there?"

"Warren," he answered. The porch light came on.

Kate opened the door and said lightly, "Warren, what a strange hour to be calling. Come in."

Warren followed her into the living room and asked, "Kate, would you please wake Tara?"

She looked quizzically at him. "Is something wrong?"

Warren closed the door behind him. "No," he answered. "Please forgive the hour, but I just must speak to her."

"She's sound asleep, Warren."

"Please."

"All right. Sit down and I'll get her."

Warren nodded. He went to the window and nervously looked out at the garden, now awash in predawn grayness. As he had been walking down the corridor with Boxer, he had felt a compelling need to tell Tara he would be leaving Honolulu very soon. He bit his lower lip. Why did he want so badly to see her again before he left?

He heard the padding of feet behind him. He turned as Tara entered the room. Speaking very fast, he said, "Listen, Tara, I know this is crazy, but I just learned I will be going away today for a while and I wanted to tell you in person."

"What?" she asked, moving closer to him.

"I didn't want you to think —"

"Where are you going?" she asked.

"I can't tell you that," he said, dodging the question. "What is important is that —"

"You came here just to tell me you're leaving?" she asked incredulously.

"Yes." He was beginning to feel foolish.

"When are you leaving?"

"Shortly," he answered and started to walk past her toward the door.

"Must you go now?"

"I have a jeep waiting for me," he said, halfway between her and the door. He'd made a stupid mistake and wanted to leave as quickly as possible.

"Warren?" Tara called.

He stopped and turned.

"There's something you didn't do earlier this evening when you left," she said, coming close and placing her fingertips on his chest. "And I'm not going to let you leave this time without doing it."

He gulped loudly despite himself.

"Yes," she said, "kiss me."

He took her in his arms and brushed her lips. "I don't know why, but I had to see you before I left," he whispered.

"I'm glad you came," she murmured.

He kissed her again, but this time the kiss was full of passion. Tara responded with open lips hungrily seeking his.

"I must go," Warren told her as he reluctantly separated from her. "I'll be back to see you as soon as I can."

CHAPTER 8

Even with circulating air whooshing through ventilators, the interior of the *Sockeye* was hot, humid, and smelly. But Lieutenant Commander John Brisby, the *Sockeye*'s skipper, a chunky man with a ready smile, and his XO, Lieutenant Charles Samuel, had made every effort to make Warren and the ten commando Marines on board comfortable. At dinner the first evening, Warren learned that Brisby had known Tony Trapasso at submarine school and that he also knew all about the rescue of Tony and the others who had been held on board the *Kiuki Maru*.

"What you might not know," Warren said at the end of the dinner, "is that prior to that, Tony was in a submarine that saved my ship, the *Dee*, from being chewed up by a Japanese gunboat in the Philippines."

"Any friend of Trapasso's is a friend of mine. As the expression goes, 'My house is your house.' Or should I say, 'My submarine is your submarine'?" Brisby said jokingly.

This was Warren's first time aboard a submarine for more than just a visit, and he made the best of the opportunity to learn more about it. He spent a great deal of time on the bridge as well as with Samuel observing the complicated procedures needed to keep the boat in good trim and on course. Another aspect of his education, as the *Sockeye* and its companion boat, the *Bluefin*, slowly made the long voyage on the surface to the China coast, was playing cribbage with First Lieutenant Victor Borodine, a Marine officer assigned to the mission. Borodine was the son of a Russian emigre who had arrived in the States shortly after Joseph Stalin rose to power. Borodine claimed that Alexander Borodine, a famous Russian composer, was his great uncle. Warren tended to doubt that, but after consistently losing to the young Marine at cribbage, one thing he didn't doubt was that Borodine had superior card sense.

Despite Warren's effort to keep occupied, there were hours when he had little to do except think about Tara. Late in the afternoon of the third day, she crept into his thoughts as he was in the wardroom alone drinking coffee. He wasn't at all certain why he had gone back to see her that last night, or why he needed for her to understand her mother's and his father's relationship. What had he wanted? And what did she want? Love? Marriage? Didn't all young women want that? Was he ready for such a commitment? He was twenty-eight, and the only woman he'd ever loved was Irene Hacker. Would he be able to forget her if a new love came along? He realized abruptly that he was getting ahead of himself with the kind of thoughts that were racing through his mind. When he saw her again, then he'd see.

"Commander Troost, the captain requests you join him in the conning tower," a young sailor said as he entered the small wardroom.

As the *Sockeye* and *Bluefin* neared the objective area, both boats were running submerged. Warren climbed into the conning tower and found Brisby with his arms draped over the periscope handles. "Want to take a look-see at the Manchurian coast?" Brisby asked. "I sure do."

Brisby moved away from the scope. "The coast is about ten miles away. You're looking at the hills just behind the shoreline."

Through the periscope, the outcroppings stood out clearly in silhouette against the late afternoon sun, but little else was defined. Nevertheless, since Warren had monitored the plot of the *Sockeye*'s progress toward the Manchurian Coast, he knew they were close to where his commando team would go ashore.

"The *Bluefin* is a thousand yards off our starboard," Brisby said. "We have them on sonar and they know where we are. We'll remain submerged until 0100 — six hours from now. At that time we'll both surface, and you and the others will hit the beach. We'll be about two thousand yards from the shore, so it should be an easy paddle for you in your rafts. The *Bluefin* and I will go to periscope depth and wait for your return. Approximately three hours after you are back on board, we expect to rendezvous with the destroyer *Harrison* forty miles off the coast."

Warren stepped away from the periscope and Brisby ordered, "Down periscope."

"Sounds good to me. Let's hope it works," Warren said.

Brisby nodded. "All ahead one third," he ordered to the engine-room talker.

"All ahead one third, sir."

"Take her down to one hundred and fifty feet," Brisby called down to the control room below the conning tower. Turning to Warren, he said, "That is where I gauge the bottom is."

"One hundred and fifty feet, aye, aye," came the response.

The swishing sound of escaping air filled the *Sockeye* as control valves for the ballast tanks were opened and the tanks began to flood. Warren watched the needle on the depth gauge move slowly clockwise. They had started at periscope depth and were already passing through seventy-five feet.

"All engines stop," Brisby ordered.

"All engines stop," the engine-room talker answered.

"We'll settle down nice and easy and rest on the bottom," Brisby said, watching the depth gauge closely. It indicated they were at one hundred and ten feet. Brisby switched on the 1MC. "All hands brace yourselves. All hands brace yourselves. Bottom coming up. Bottom coming up."

Warren moved close to the bulkhead and steadied himself against it. The *Sockeye* touched bottom, sending a minor shock through the boat, and came to rest with a slight heel to the starboard side.

"A good landing," Brisby exclaimed with satisfaction. Looking toward the sonar officer, he asked, "Is the *Bluefin* down yet?"

"Looks like it to me, sir," the SO replied, "but I can't say for sure."

"The *Bluefin* is going to do the same as us, Commander. Nothing to do now but wait," Brisby said.

"Couple of rounds of cribbage might help to pass the time," Warren suggested. "But only with you! I can't afford that Marine!"

Brisby agreed and they headed for the wardroom.

Under a sliver of yellow moon, the large inflatable rubber raft carrying Warren and ten marines touched lightly on a narrow sandy beach, a half mile north of his objective. Coordination between the *Sockeye* and *Bluefin* had been perfect, and almost simultaneously Major Boxer and his team were ashore.

"Secure the rafts," Warren ordered in a low voice.

"Aye, aye, sir," a sergeant answered, and quickly the two rafts were pulled up onto the beach well beyond the waterline. The two groups quickly formed into their pre-planned teams and separated. Warren led his men directly up the dark beach to a line of trees while Boxer swung off to the right.

The plan called for Boxer and his ten-man assault team to take up strategic positions around the military barracks and headquarters before making his presence known to the Japanese commander and demanding surrender. If surrender was not immediately forthcoming, he was to neutralize them.

At the same time Warren, with Borodine and his marines, would free the prisoners, place the medical and technical personnel under guard, and gather up records of experiments that had been conducted at the facility.

"Radio check," Warren said, looking at his field radioman, a young corporal in camouflage gear.

A few moments passed before the marine whispered, "A-OK, sir. The *Sockeye* is coming in loud and clear."

"Move out," Warren ordered, taking the lead ahead of Borodine.

Soon they reached a narrow stand of trees that ended abruptly at a low stone wall. Warren vaulted over it, and at a stealthy trot made his way across the small, open field. Breathing hard, he stopped behind a one-storey structure that photo reconnaissance had indicated was a combination medical facility and living quarters for the doctors.

"Borodine, get five men and take the doctors and anyone else in this building prisoner. Move them down to the beach. Shoot anyone who resists. Have two men stay on the beach to guard them, and then you and the others join me back here."

"Aye, aye, sir," Borodine answered.

"Go!" Warren ordered. He pointed to a Marine gunnery sergeant. "You, take a man and get our people out of that shack on the other side. Take them to the beach and come back here to me. I'll be inside this part of the building."

"Aye, aye, sir," the sergeant answered, and in a low crouch the men ran toward the confinement barracks.

"We're going in here," Warren told his radioman and the other man remaining.

138

Suddenly, lights came on in the building Boxer's team had surrounded. The building Warren was about to enter remained dark. "Let's go!" Warren ordered, and they raced to the front of the structure.

"Door's locked," he said, trying it. "Shoot it open!"

The Marine squeezed off three rounds, shattering the metal lock.

"Guard the door," Warren shouted. He and the radioman followed by two men ran down the hall, opening doors and turning on lights. No one was in sight. Several rooms appeared to be primitive laboratories. Two were obviously offices, and Warren hurriedly piled sheaves of papers and notebooks lying on the desk tops. In a third room, he found a small safe.

The radio began to buzz.

"Go ahead," the communicator said into his microphone. "Commander, Major Boxer reports a green light — the Jap commander has surrendered. The major is collecting weapons now."

"Acknowledge," Warren said, "and tell him to send a half a dozen of his men here when he can."

The communicator relayed the message. Then to Warren, he said, "That's a wilco, Commander."

"Let's check out the other spaces," Warren responded, already starting out of the room.

"Aye, aye Skipper," the communicator answered. Suddenly two shots rang out.

"Keep checking the rooms," Warren said and ran back to the entrance. "Where the hell did that come from?" he asked the guard.

"Over that way," the man answered, pointing toward Borodine's team.

"Skipper," Borodine shouted, "one of the doctors tried to run."

"Dead?" Warren called.

"Not yet, just winged," the Marine called back. "But he will be dead if he tries to get away again."

"Get all of them to the beach."

"Yes, sir."

"Skipper, we got company coming," the Marine guarding the door said. The butt of his carbine was already braced against his hip. "It's Lieutenant Borodine and some of Major Boxer's men," the guard said in a relieved voice as he lowered his weapon.

"Tell the lieutenant that in the third room on the right there's a small safe that I want carried down to the beach. The papers we must take are piled on the desks in the various rooms."

"Aye, aye, sir," the Marine answered.

Warren hurriedly went back into the building. "Corporal?" he called, quickening his stride and flicking the safety off his pistol. "Corporal?"

"Here, sir," the man answered in a strange voice.

Warren started to run.

"Oh, God, Commander!"

Warren entered the room. The corporal was leaning against the wall, vomiting. "Look," he cried. "Look!"

But Warren had already seen the human heads in glass jars. Arms, hands, and parts of legs were in other large glass containers. A wave of nausea made his knees buckle.

"Jesus, those dirty bastards!"

"Dirty bastards," Warren echoed in a whisper. His mind suddenly flooded with the image of Irene lying in a mass grave with her breasts hacked off and her mouth open in a silent, but eternal scream of agony.

"How could they do this?" the corporal screamed.

Warren blinked the memory away and forced himself to shake his head. "I don't know. I just don't know!" he answered.

"Skipper —" Borodine entered the room, stopped short, and began to gag.

"Take it easy," Warren said. "Take it easy."

Borodine nodded. "I'll be all right… Give me a couple of minutes."

"Take your time," Warren told him.

"There's a basement to this place," Borodine finally managed to say. "One of my men found the door, but I thought I should let you know before I went down there."

Warren nodded. "Let's get out of here and check the basement out. This room is off-limits," he said, closing the door. "Get one of your men to keep anyone else out."

"Yes, sir," Borodine answered and called down the hall for a man to stand guard at the door.

"No one goes in," Warren said, "unless they're with me."

"Yes, sir," the Marine answered.

"Corporal, you come with us," Warren said, and he walked down the hallway.

"Aye, aye, sir," the communicator answered.

The basement consisted of two levels. The upper level was divided into four chambers, each with a stainless-steel nozzle in the ceiling and ventilation ducts. The interior of each chamber could be seen from a single observation area separated by heavy glass windows.

"What the hell do you think all of this was used for?" Borodine asked.

"Right now I don't want to think about it," Warren answered, but he suspected it had to do with testing the effects of poison gas on human subjects. "Let's see what's down below," he said, moving down to the lower level and switching on the light.

"Holy Christ!" he exclaimed. Three men were in trough-like structures. Each had some portion of his skin removed and replaced by clear plastic. One had the top of his brain exposed. Another's chest area was open to view and the third, his stomach and intestines.

"My God, they're alive," Borodine whispered. "They're still alive!"

Warren turned away and for a few seconds squeezed his eyes shut. During four years of war he'd seen bodies torn apart by explosions, but never had he seen the kind of horror that had confronted him in the last ten minutes. Opening his eyes, he looked at the men again.

One of them tried feebly to speak, but could make only wordless sounds.

"We can't move you," Warren said, the words coming hard.

Suddenly, the radio screeched with static.

"Somebody is trying to reach us, Commander, and we're too low to receive."

"Go topside," Warren said abruptly. He had decided to end this misery, and wanted no witnesses. "You go, too, Borodine."

Waiting until he was alone, Warren said, "It has to be this way, God forgive me."

He put the muzzle of his pistol against the head of the man who had tried to speak.

A piteous look of relief crossed the man's tortured face. He nodded slightly and closed his eyes.

Warren squeezed the trigger. The explosion filled the small room. With a silent prayer on his lips, Warren put the two remaining men out of their agony with two quick shots and went up the steps.

"Skipper," Borodine shouted, "there's a red message from the *Sockeye*."

Warren raced up to the main floor and took the headset and mic from the radioman. "Troost here," he said, trying hard to sound composed.

"We have four bogies on radar closing over your area," Brisby said.

"Could they be ours?"

"Negative. We don't have any planes around here."

"Where are they?"

"Bearing three-two-five. Range twenty miles. Angels ten. Speed one-six-zero. We've also picked up a hell of a lot of Russian radio traffic."

"Have you alerted the *Harrison*?"

"Yes, they are also aware of heavy Russian radio traffic... Stand by, I have an incoming flash message from headquarters."

"Standing by," Warren answered. "Borodine, start moving our men back to the beach."

"Aye, aye, Skipper."

Brisby came back on the air. "PACFLT says it looks like Russians invading Manchuria have reached this sector. We've been ordered to retire immediately."

"Wilco," Warren answered and, turning to his communicator, said, "Get Major Boxer on the horn."

Seconds later, the corporal said, "Major Boxer, sir."

"Pull back to the beach now," Warren ordered. "*Sockeye* has four bogies on their screen. We don't know what's up."

"Aye, aye, sir," Boxer responded.

"Let's get the hell out of here. Follow me!" Warren exclaimed, starting to run.

"Holy shit, paratroopers!" the corporal exclaimed.

Many white chutes were floating down, some landing between Warren and the beach, others in the center of the facility.

"Run," Warren yelled. "Run!" He and the corporal and the other men with them raced across the open field.

Two Russian paratroopers appeared behind them and without warning began firing at them with automatic weapons.

"The wall!" Warren shouted, vaulting over it.

His radioman started to follow. "Christ, I'm hit!" he shouted and fell across the wall. Warren grabbed him and, slipping the radio from his back, slung him over his shoulder in a fireman's carry and crashed through the stand of trees. "Cover us!" he shouted, coming out on the beach. "Cover fire!"

Boxer and Borodine, followed by ten Marines, rushed forward and fired savage bursts into the stand of trees.

"Wounded man!" Warren called out. "Give me some help!" Three men took the corporal off his shoulders and stretched him out on the beach.

"Caught one in the right leg," one of the Marines said. "He's losing a lot of blood."

"Get one of those Jap doctors to stop the bleeding," Warren snapped. "Do any of them speak English?"

"A couple, Skipper," Boxer answered.

"Have one of those bastards take care of him," Warren growled. "Make sure he understands that if anything happens to the corporal, I'll blow the son of a bitch's brains out."

"Aye, aye, sir."

"We've got company," a Marine called out, pointing to the trees. Still breathing hard and soaked with sweat, Warren turned as a small group of Russian paratroopers came toward them.

"Stand easy," Warren ordered his men. "Get your radio working," he said to one of them.

The Russians stopped. The two lead men spoke rapidly to each other.

"We are Americans," Warren said, pointing to the two submarines on the surface offshore.

"Skipper," Borodine said, "I don't think they understand. I speak Russian."

Warren nodded. "Tell them one of their men shot one of my men. Tell them that my government will lodge an official complaint. I want the name, rank, and serial number of their commanding officer and the identity of the unit he commands."

"Skipper, these are officers."

"Tell them!" Warren snapped.

Borodine nodded and, taking several steps toward the men at the head of the group, began speaking to them. The Russians listened without any change of expression and when Borodine stopped, one of them responded.

"He is the commanding officer," Borodine translated. "He is Colonel Gregor Alexander Kursk, and he considers us his prisoners. He asks that you order your men to lay down their arms to avoid unnecessary spilling of blood."

"Sergeant, is that radio working yet?" Warren asked.

"Yes, sir."

"Call the *Sockeye*," Warren said. "Tell the captain we have a Mexican standoff here with a bunch of hard-headed Russians. I want him to contact the *Harrison* and have it move in at flank speed as soon as possible. Then I want a couple of HE rounds from *Sockeye* and *Bluefin* deck guns dropped in the field behind the trees."

"Aye, aye, Commander," the sergeant responded and immediately began transmitting.

Warren smiled and said, "Tell Colonel Kursk that, given the circumstances, I must consider him and his men *my* prisoners." He looked at Boxer and said quietly, "If any one of them so much as moves, shoot him."

As Boxer and his men quickly fanned out in front of the Russians, Borodine removed his helmet and pulled his right arm across his sweaty brow. Then he translated what Warren had said.

The Russians seemed startled and uncertain.

Suddenly, the five-inch deck guns on the *Sockeye* and *Bluefin* opened fire. The echo of the heavy gunfire rolled over the water as the screaming shells passed overhead and exploded with thunderous roars in the field behind the trees. As quickly as the barrage had started, it fell silent.

The Russians were visibly shaken.

"Tell them that a surface ship has also been summoned to deliver more firepower should it be needed. Tell him, that I, Commander Warren Troost, United States Navy, will permit him and his troops to withdraw under the following conditions: one, they retire from this beach area; and two, they do nothing to interfere with our peaceful retirement."

"With all due respect, Skipper, this colonel guy seems like a real bull-head —"

"Tell him my conditions," Warren snapped. Then in a much softer voice, he added, "Lieutenant, I've won many a poker game playing with a not much better hand than I have now. I just wish I were as good at cribbage with you, but you don't have to tell him that."

Borodine grinned, translated, and listened to the Colonel's response. "He says he will agree to your terms if you leave the Japanese doctors and everything of theirs that you intend to take with you. He says that his government wants those doctors."

"Tell him that my government wants them too, and we got here first," Warren said. "Since these bastards are now our prisoners, they cannot have them. Tell him that unless he agrees instantly, I will order the two submarines to commence firing again — this time on his men. He has ten seconds to make up his mind."

Borodine began to speak.

"Sergeant, have the *Sockeye* standing by," Warren ordered the radioman.

"Standing by, sir," the sergeant answered.

Borodine stopped talking.

"I'm counting," Warren exclaimed, looking at his watch. "Ten seconds to go ... five ... two —"

Kursk exploded with a single Russian word that didn't need translation.

"I understood that," Warren said, lowering his hand. "Borodine, tell the colonel to retire behind the treeline."

"Aye, aye, sir." As Borodine stopped speaking, Kursk gestured to his men, turned, and walked toward the trees.

"Boxer, start moving our people into the rafts. It's going to take several trips," Warren ordered. "Sergeant, alert the *Sockeye* that we are now returning aboard." He kneeled down beside the corporal and said, "You'll be aboard the *Sockeye* soon, son."

"Thanks for saving —" the man started to say.

"I know you would have done the same for me," Warren interrupted.

The man grinned. "Sir, I'd walk through hell for you!"

CHAPTER 9

"Today is the twenty-fourth of August," Admiral Gower said, almost to himself, as he looked across his desk and smiled absently at Jacob. "On the twenty-seventh, our forces will steam into Tokyo Bay with the battleship *Missouri* leading the victory parade. It will be a sight to remember! All of Japan will realize what a terrible mistake Pearl Harbor was."

"Yes, sir, I'm sure they will," Jacob answered, wondering just what the admiral had in mind. He'd been ordered to report to Gower's sea cabin only minutes before.

Gower continued, "On the second of September, the Japs will sign a formal surrender on board the *Missouri* in the presence of General MacArthur. By God, I'll be there too!"

Jacob nodded. He'd known of the broad plans for several days. As Gower's air operations officer, he had been deeply involved in planning a massive victory flyover of Tokyo Bay by naval aircraft from the ten U.S. aircraft carriers stationed just outside.

Gower stood up, walked behind his chair, and, leaning over, he rested his arms wearily on it.

Acutely aware that this was a departure from the admiral's usual formal behavior, Jacob sensed the enormous weariness in the man.

"Jacob," Gower said, seemingly aware of his presence for the first time, "I've been asked to name a member of my staff to be part of a special team that will go into Hiroshima and evaluate conditions in that city for the Joint Chiefs of Staff. The group will be made up of several Army Air Corps pilots, medical personnel, and some civilian specialists. I expect there will also be newspaper people and film crews. And, because I've come to value your judgment, I've chosen you to be my representative. There will be other Navy members senior to yourself from CinPacFlt Headquarters and from Washington. Captain Kingston from the Bureau of Ordnance will be the ranking naval officer. I understand that he holds a doctorate in experimental physics from Cornell University. Because of his specialty, he was brought into the Navy as a captain for temporary wartime service. He's an expert on the effects of explosion overpressures and shock waves. You should find him interesting."

Stunned, Jacob finally managed to answer, "I'm honored, sir."

Gower nodded. "Now comes the kicker. The team will assemble ashore starting tomorrow and remain ashore until the fourth of September. Then it will be flown to Honolulu, where it will be given ten days to complete its report."

Jacob felt more than a tinge of disappointment. Though he didn't expect to be aboard the *Missouri* to witness the signing of surrender, he had secretly planned to fly one of the aircraft in the flyover. He'd wanted to be part of the event, if only as an observer from above.

"After the report is completed," Gower went on, "you might want to use some leave time to go anywhere you want to. Technically, you'll still be attached to my staff, and if you want to go stateside for a visit, I'll certainly approve your request."

"Thank you, sir. That's very kind of you."

Gower came around to the front of the chair and sat down. "You've seen the recon photos of Hiroshima, haven't you?"

"Yes, sir."

"Not much has been left standing," Gower said, opening his cigar humidor and sliding it toward Jacob. "You know the story about Lincoln and Grant?" he asked, a lighter tone entering his voice.

"Which story, sir?" Jacob responded, looking at the humidor uncertainly.

"Immediately after Grant's victory at *Vicksburg*, Secretary of War Stanton seemed critical of Grant for his drinking habits. Lincoln is said to have answered, 'Sir, find out the brand of whiskey Grant drinks, and I'll send a case to all of my other generals. Maybe it will help them win more battles.' Well, these cigars are something like that case of whiskey. President Roosevelt kindly kept me supplied with them, and President Truman has continued that much appreciated custom." He lit up and drew on the cigar with deep satisfaction. "My time in the Navy is almost over and yours, Jacob, has just begun. It's been my good fortune to have men like yourself under my command. No, let me rephrase that. It has been my good fortune to have courageous men like yourself for shipmates at a time when our country needed all they could give ... and they gave without reservation." He took a deep drag on the cigar and held the smoke a long time before releasing it. "Well!" he said with a slightly embarrassed smile, "that proves even the old admiral can get a little sentimental. Now, let's get on with it."

"Yes, sir," Jacob answered, realizing the depth of Gower's feelings.

"Those recon photos make the awesome power of atomic weapons very clear," Gower said, his voice taking on a characteristic tone of authority once again. "And if a single bomb can destroy a city, can you imagine what one might do to a Navy task group?"

"It certainly would have a disastrous effect," Jacob responded.

"It's terrifying to think of what would have happened if either the Japanese or the Germans had developed that kind of bomb first."

"Yes, sir. One kamikaze delivering one of those bombs could have destroyed a whole battle group," Jacob offered.

"You know, don't you, the Germans were well on their way to developing such a bomb. And not only that, but a new type of aircraft, one that is jet propelled — no propellers! They were seen over Europe before VE Day."

"Yes, sir, I read about it. And their rocket missiles too."

Gower nodded and pointed his cigar at Jacob. "Remember you heard it from me first. In the future, the jet engine will power all military and commercial aircraft... But getting back to your Hiroshima assignment," he said, standing, "I'm sure you will carry it out with the same level of excellence and enthusiasm that has been the hallmark of your work up to now."

Jacob stood up. "I will certainly do my best. You can count on me, Admiral."

"Good luck, Jacob," Gower said, offering his hand.

"Thank you, sir," Jacob answered, shaking Gower's hand; then, donning his cap, he saluted smartly and left the cabin.

"Tony Trapasso, Lieutenant Commander, U.S. Navy, number oh-five-three-two-nine!" He watched the black truncheon swing in a vicious arc toward him. Pain exploded in his head and he dropped to the floor. A boot pushed into his stomach. His eyes moved up the boot to the knee, then to the torso and finally to the expressionless face of Captain Yoshida. Tony cried out in agony...

He bolted upright in a cold sweat. For several moments, he couldn't remember where he was. The illusion that he was once again in that room with Yoshida was terrifying for him. But as his eyes began to pick out the pieces of furniture in the darkened room and he became aware of Miriam sleeping peacefully beside him, he relaxed with a deep sigh of relief and reached for a pack of cigarettes on the night table.

Tony slipped quietly out of bed and pulled on an old pair of pants, a T-shirt, and a pair of sneakers. He tiptoed over to the crib and, looking down at Sam, stroked the child's head tenderly for several moments before he left the room. Once downstairs, he went into the kitchen, opened the refrigerator, and took out a bottle of beer.

"Today is going to be a scorcher."

Mike was standing in the doorway. "I got two box-seat tickets for the Dodgers-Giants game at Ebbets Field for Sunday. We could take the train down on Saturday, stay over at your old man's house, go to the game, and be back here in New London Sunday night. The franks and beer will be my treat."

"I have the duty that weekend, sorry, Mike."

Mike grinned. "I don't know what the hell you're talking about, but it sounds important."

"Why don't you go?" Tony suggested, knowing how much Mike loved baseball. When he was younger, Mike had been a pitcher for a minor-league club, and might have gone up to the big leagues if he hadn't become involved with the mob.

"Nah, one game is like anudder these days. Ya see one, ya seen 'em all," Mike answered. "Up here, I get clean sea air and I get to play with Sam."

Tony finished the beer, put the bottle on top of the sink, and said, "I'm going out for a walk."

"Yeah, I was thinking of doing the same thing," Mike agreed.

Tony nodded. This exchange had become a ritual between them ever since he'd come home on rehabilitation leave. It had started that first night in his father's house, and continued through the next two months when he, Miriam, and the baby lived in a three-room apartment in Flatbush. When he had taken up his new assignment in New London as an instructor at the submarine school, Mike continued to be a frequent visitor, often spending several days at a time with them.

Outside, it was somewhat cooler. They walked toward the river, where a light mist lay over the water. "So how come you didn't say nothing to me about Miriam being pregnant again?" Mike asked as they reached the walkway along the bank.

Tony shrugged.

"Listen," Mike said, putting his hand on Tony's shoulder, "everything is going to be all right this time. You going to tell your papa and mama?"

"Sure," Tony said. "But she's only two months gone."

"Tell 'em, Tony, it'll make 'em happy. Call 'em up and tell 'em."

"Okay, Mike, if you say I should tell them now," Tony answered, "I'll do it."

For a while they walked without speaking. Then Mike said, "You been back almost four months. The war is over and you ain't said a word about it to me or Miriam. I know you ain't said nothing to her, because I asked her."

"You got a cigarette?" Tony asked. "I left mine on the night table."

Mike took a pack out of his shirt pocket and, handing it to Tony, he said, "Like when I came out of stir, I didn't talk about what it was like. Then one day, as God is my judge, Tony, I'm sitting in a greasy spoon having coffee and this beautiful black woman sits down next to me and orders coffee too. I give her a sideways glance and she just starts talking to me and flat-out tells me she's a workin' gal, but she doesn't have a pimp. She's tellin' me about her two sons. One is finishing high school and one is just beginnin'… Anyway, she says to me, she ain't looking to score, but if I want to go back to her place, it was all right. I went with her, Tony, and after we finished screwin', she says to me, 'Now, sad man, why don't you talk to me; tell me why you're so sad?' And I did, Tony, I told her. I spilled my guts out to that broad, and she took me in her arms and held me like a baby. I ain't ever had a woman do that before. But I had to tell somebody what those years in stir was like."

Tony blew smoke in the air and handed the pack of cigarettes back to his uncle. "I dream about it every night," he said. "Sometimes one part, sometimes all of it."

"There's a bench over there," Mike said. "Let's sit down."

Tony sat down. Leaning forward, he planted his elbows on his knees. Covering his face with his hands, he said, "And in all of the dreams, Captain Yoshida is there. Sometimes I even see him when I'm awake." He dropped his hands and rubbed them together.

"Say it, Tony, say it, whatever it is," Mike urged.

Tony took a deep breath. Slowly exhaling, he began to sob softly. "He beat me. Every day he beat me. He tried to make me eat my own shit, and if I didn't, he ordered the guards to rub my face in it. But I never told more than my name, rank, and serial number." Tony shook his head. "I never told him more."

Mike put his arm around Tony's shoulders.

"One day," Tony continued, "a whole bunch of us were put on board a prison ship and locked in a cage like animals. We got a few buckets of fresh water a day for over fifty men and women, and each of us got a handful of rice. There were two other buckets: one for shit and the other for piss. We were in that cage for thirty-five days before we were rescued. I saw a woman go crazy and beat her head against the bulkhead until the guards came and beat her to death with their rifle butts. The women were raped in front of us while the guards held us at bayonet point."

"Tony, Tony," Mike said. "It will go away, you'll see. It will go away!"

Tony asked for another cigarette and when it was lit, he said, "I don't know if I'm any good anymore." He faced Mike. "Do you know what I mean?"

"You tell me."

Tony shrugged. "I'm not sure I have it anymore."

He pinched off the glowing cigarette head and ground the butt into the dirt.

"What's 'it'?"

Tony made an open gesture with his hands. "I'm a commander in the Navy, but I'm not sure I'll ever again be able to skipper a submarine. Yoshida took something from me, Mike. The bastard took something from me!" Tony buried his face in his hands again. "He took it, and there's no way I'll ever get it back. One day, I might freeze when I shouldn't and then... I wouldn't want to have to live with that on my back, too. If I had any real guts, I'd call it quits, resign my commission, and go work for Papa."

"You ever do that," Mike said fiercely, "and I'll kill you myself. You ain't going to wind up a hood, not you!" Then, in a much gentler voice, he said, "That Jap didn't take anythin' from you, Tony, just like the screws in stir didn't take anythin' from me. Yeah, like you, I thought they did. But I learned they didn't. They gave me somethin', though."

"Gave you something?" Tony asked.

155

"They couldn't break me, just like that Jap couldn't break you," Mike said. "Until that woman told me that, I didn't see it either. But she said, 'Ya must have given those guards a fit when they saw they couldn't get to ya... Ya be a strong man, a real strong man.' You're strong, Tony, stronger than you know. It'll all come right for ya, you'll see."

Without saying anything more to each other, they stood up and began walking back to the house.

"You ever see her?" Tony asked.

"Who?"

"That woman you just told me about."

"Yeah, I see her," Mike said. "But never in New York. I don't want your papa or mama to go crazy. Her oldest boy is a doctor now and her youngest a lawyer."

"You helped that happen?" Tony asked.

"I didn't like the idea of her bein' on the street, so we come to an arrangement. It was good for her and for me."

"An arrangement and that's all?"

"Come on, Tony," Mike said. "You know the score. She's a good woman."

"She must be, or you wouldn't have fallen in love with her," Tony said.

Mike grinned. "You're somethin' else, Tony... Somethin' else."

A cold, wind-driven rain was falling by the time Jacob arrived outside of Hiroshima the following afternoon. He had flown from the *Vicksburg* to what was left of the airport outside Tokyo and made the rest of the journey by jeep. A Marine guard directed him toward several large tents, one of which had a wooden sign outside proclaiming it to be administration headquarters. At the field desk, an Army first lieutenant with the chemical-warfare insignia of two crossed retorts on his collar saluted him.

Jacob returned the salute and identified himself.

"Your orders, sir?" the young officer asked.

Jacob handed the single sheet of paper to him.

The lieutenant read it and wrote on a log sheet before he returned the paper to Jacob. "Sir, if you would please step to the rear of the tent, you will be photographed for your ID badge and be given a dosimeter that must be visible on your person at all times. After you have been photographed and have your dosimeter, you will be escorted to the area occupied by the Navy and will meet your team leader, Captain William Kingston."

Within the hour, Jacob had his ID badge and dosimeter and presented himself to Lieutenant Frances Martin in a temporary Navy office in another tent about fifty yards away. "The captain said he wanted to see you as soon as you reported in," Martin told him. "Please follow me."

Martin led him to the other side of the tent. "Sir," he said to the man seated at a wooden desk, "Commander Jacob Miller has arrived."

Kingston was a tall, good-looking, freckled-faced man. After he read Jacob's orders, he said, without asking Jacob to be seated, "Since you are the junior full member on our team, you will be its recorder. You will keep an accurate record of each day's events to serve as a reference when we draft our report."

"Aye, aye, sir," Jacob answered, standing at attention.

"Lieutenant Martin, my aide, will fill you in on the details about the format I want you to use."

"Yes, sir," Jacob responded, beginning to feel that he was in an unfriendly place, facing a hostile man.

"You've made quite a record for yourself, haven't you?" Kingston asked. Before Jacob could answer, he said, "Well, the war is over now and hotshot pilots like yourself will find that their days of glory are over."

"Yes, sir," Jacob answered, realizing that for whatever reason, combat pilots were not high on Kingston's list of favorite people.

"For obvious reasons, this is a very tight security area," Kingston said. "The city itself has been sealed off. None of my group will be permitted to enter unless I say so. We'll tour the area under Marine guard to make sure that nobody wanders off on his own. As a member of my team, you are not to make any statements to the press, even if the statement is an expression of your personal view of what you see. Have you any questions so far?"

"No, sir," Jacob answered with a sinking heart.

"There are various civilians in the overall group, including several women. I expect my team to stay away from those women, whether they are doctors or reporters. I don't want any trouble in that regard. I think you understand what I mean, don't you?"

"Yes, sir," Jacob replied. The tone Kingston was using gave Jacob the distinct feeling that the captain was purposely being pompous to impress him. He felt a surge of dislike for the ersatz naval officer.

"There is one more point that I want to stress, Commander, and that has to do with the treatment of the indigenous people. It is important for all of us to keep in mind that they are still our enemy and that they must be treated with firmness at all times, regardless of age or sex."

"Yes, sir."

"Lieutenant Martin will direct you to your quarters. That is all."

Jacob saluted smartly, did a precise about face, left Kingston's presence and went back to the Lieutenant, who directed him to a large tent that served as sleeping quarters for all male team members, with the exception of Kingston and two Army colonels, who both had their own small tents.

Food for the entire group was provided by an Army mess detachment in a separate tent. A Marine detachment was also present, assigned the task of keeping Hiroshima cordoned off and providing security for the group. All team members ate in the same tent at mealtimes, but officers and civilians were initially seated at different tables, and enlisted personnel ate in a separate messing facility. Kingston had gone as far as designating where each Navy team member sat at his table. Jacob, being the junior man, found himself during his first meal at the far end of Kingston's table, which pleased him considerably.

There were fifteen civilians in the group, three of whom were women, and they seemed to be enjoying themselves, especially after several Army officers, who were not answerable to Kingston, joined them. Sound of animated talk came from that table. In comparison, the conversation at the table presided over by Kingston was stilted and sparse.

Jacob, hearing the sound of rainfall on the tent, spoke to the man on his right and, leaning close to him, he facetiously asked, "Is the weather — I mean the atmosphere, expected to clear? I find it a little stuffy, especially in *here.*"

"God only knows!" the man whispered.

Suddenly Kingston cleared his throat, and the heads of every man at his table turned toward him. "Gentlemen," he said, "the newest officer to join our staff is Commander Jacob Miller. Commander Miller is air operations officer for Admiral Gower. For those of you who are not familiar with Commander Miller's combat record, let me assure you it is an impressive one. How many kills, Commander, fifteen was it and five probables?"

"Thirteen, sir, and three probables," Jacob answered, aware that all eyes were now on him.

"If my information is correct," Kingston said, "you were audacious enough to capture a Japanese officer even after you yourself had been shot down. Isn't that so, Commander Miller?"

Jacob was slow to answer. The man he'd rescued, and indeed captured, was a Lieutenant Yashi Kurokachi, a fighter pilot off the Japanese aircraft *Hiryu*. Kurokachi had been shot down just before he himself had been during the Battle of Midway. He had thought more about Kurokachi in the last few days since he'd learned about the devastation of Hiroshima than he had in the past three years. He remembered Kurokachi's family lived in Hiroshima.

"Commander, did or did you not capture a Japanese officer?" Kingston demanded to know.

"Sir, not in the sense of what it really means to capture an enemy. We were both down. I was in my raft. Lieutenant Kurokachi was in the water and —"

"Did you take him prisoner, Commander, or were all the newspaper accounts of the incident strictly propaganda?" Kingston questioned, his face becoming slightly flushed. "You see, Commander, my recall of news reports tells me you were credited with *capturing* him. Now tell us, please, did you or did you not take a Japanese flyer prisoner?"

"Yes, sir. But there was no other alternative," Jacob answered, stumbling for the right words.

"Alternative?" Kingston roared. "Why didn't you shoot him?"

A silence fell heavily throughout the tent.

Jacob looked straight at Kingston. "Sir, I could not have done that."

The color on Kingston's face deepened. "And why not?" he asked, bringing his voice down to its normal volume. "After all, you obviously killed other Japanese."

"Sir," Jacob said, staring at him, "we were out of the battle. We were just two men who wanted desperately to survive."

Kingston considered that for a brief moment before he said, "I find that a strange remark coming from one of our fighting heroes."

Jacob was about to say, "I'm sorry about that, sir," but a commander seated directly across from him made a slight slicing gesture with his hand across his throat. Nodding, Jacob remained silent.

After dinner, he sought the man out to thank him.

"Name is George Rampell," the commander said. He was a chunky man with a square, balding head and frank brown eyes. "I hate to see a man in a lion's cage," Rampell said as they shook hands and began to walk from the mess tent to their quarters. The area was splotched with yellow circles coming from Coleman lamps attached to poles, and there were Marine guards on its perimeter. A heavy rain had stopped, and now the area was misted over.

Rampell told Jacob that he was one of the men from CinPacFlt Headquarters. Before that, he'd been the XO on various DEs and, at the end, the skipper of the *Roger Williams*. He'd taken part in the invasion of North Africa, Sicily, and then, on June 6, 1944, his ship was one of many that provided support fire for the infantry landings at Normandy. "I guess I was sent out here to this team because things have eased off a bit back in Honolulu," he said with a smile.

The two of them discussed the differences between the types of naval operations carried out in the Pacific and in the Mediterranean and concluded, as others had before them, that there had been two very different kinds of naval campaigns going on at the same time.

"Speaking about differences," Rampell said, "I'd say you have some with the captain."

"So it would seem."

"I tread very softly around him," Rampell cautioned. "I was warned about him before I left Pearl. He has a great deal of influence in Washington. Knows a great many very important people."

Jacob nodded. "And it looks like he has a strong dislike for anybody who has a good combat record."

"The better the record, the stronger the dislike."

Despite his weariness, Jacob was unable to sleep. He missed the familiar shipboard sounds. With his hands behind his head, he stared at the sag of the tent's roof directly above him. His encounter with Kingston was a temporary setback, and he did not dwell on it. He had decided sometime back that he would pursue a career in the Navy. He now had leadership and combat experience, and his college education would provide a good foundation for the future. There was no reason why he should not make captain or maybe even flag rank. "Not a bad goal at all," he told himself. Lowering his hands, he was just about to turn on his side when a warning siren began to scream.

Jacob was up even before the siren stopped. He pulled on his pants and called over to Rampell, "What's that all about?"

"Marauding Jap kids."

A Marine officer stuck his head into the tent. "You guys are needed," he said. "We got them coming from three sides."

Within minutes all Navy and Army personnel were outside, and a gunnery sergeant was handing out .45-caliber pistols. A Marine colonel, head of the security forces, said, "We figure there's a dozen of them inside our perimeter. We don't want to kill any of them. We just want to scare the bejesus out of them — most of them are probably kids. Divide yourselves into service groups of four. One Army and one Navy team guard the civilian tent, just in case some of these little bastards dare to enter it; the others spread out and comb the area. Generally, firing in the air will send them running."

Kingston took charge of the Navy men and, quickly calling out individual names, he formed three groups, leaving Jacob, Lieutenant Martin, and Rampell unassigned. "You men will accompany me." Then almost as an afterthought, he added, "I hope, Commander Miller, you won't have compunction about shooting one of these bastards if necessary."

"The colonel said —"

"My order, Commander, is to shoot first and ask questions later," Kingston growled, chambering a round in the .45 and flicking the safety off.

"Yes, sir," Jacob snapped.

"We'll take a look at the far-side perimeter," Kingston said, striding off. Suddenly a flare exploded over to the right, and white light poured over a ravine, silhouetting three crouching figures.

"There!" Kingston yelled. Turning, he steadied his .45 with both hands and fired twice. One of the figures staggered and dropped to the ground.

Aiming high into the air, Jacob squeezed off two rounds. The two other figures fled madly from the scene.

Kingston headed toward the fallen body. Martin was just behind him. Jacob and Rampell followed.

"What the hell was he trying to prove?" Rampell gasped.

"I don't know. Maybe that he's a man," Jacob answered, breathing hard.

"That's a hell of a way to prove you've got balls."

Several more flares were fired, and their harsh white light illuminated the area. Two Marines raced toward the downed figure and reached it before Kingston. "Corpsman," one of them shouted. "Corpsman, here on the double."

"That's the colonel shouting," Rampell gasped.

"Get one of those civilian doctors out here," the Marine ordered.

Kingston reached the colonel's side and stopped.

"Who the fuck shot this boy?" the colonel roared.

"Boy?" Kingston questioned.

"Goddamn it, Captain, I told you, most of them are boys!" the colonel swore in rage. "They're starving, and they come inside to raid our garbage can. I want to know who was stupid enough to —"

Two corpsmen appeared and right behind them a woman arrived at a run. "I'm Dr. Ellen Lane," she announced, already kneeling beside the moaning boy. "I need some light."

The two corpsmen turned on their flashlights. The boy had taken a .45 slug in his left shoulder, and was bleeding profusely.

"I can stop the bleeding," she commented, examining the wound, "but he's going to need a blood transfusion and surgery, and I'm not really qualified to do that. The bullet did a lot of damage and it has to come out. Christ, he's not even twelve years old!" she exclaimed in disgust. Looking at the Marine colonel, she said, "I thought no one was to shoot at them."

"No one was!" the Marine answered, glaring at Kingston.

All of the teams had gathered in a large, silent circle around the boy.

Kingston took a step forward. "I shot him," he said. "I saw the three of them and —"

"We must move this boy to a warm, dry place," Dr. Lane said.

Before anyone could move, Jacob bent down, scooped the wounded boy into his arms, and said, "Tell me where you want him, Doctor."

"He's going to need surgery," the woman said, "and very soon."

"How soon?"

"A few hours at the most," she answered, "and blood immediately."

"As you know, we don't have facilities to do surgery," the colonel interjected, "but we do have plasma. Take him into the administration tent. There's an empty bed there. I'll radio for help and if we're lucky, a light plane will be able to land close by and he can be flown to a Marine field hospital. That's the best I can do," he explained, looking at the doctor.

She nodded.

Before Jacob or the doctor could move, Kingston said to no one in particular, "I'm terribly sorry about this."

"Yes, sir; I'm sure you are!" the Marine Officer responded. In a louder voice he said, "All right, the excitement is over. Let's call it a night. All hands, other than my men, return your weapons and ammo to the gunnery sergeant… Captain, give me your weapon."

Kingston cleared the chamber and, removing the clip, he handed the weapon and ammunition to the Marine officer, who said bitterly, "Thank you, sir. I, of course, must make a full report of this incident."

Kingston turned without a word and walked swiftly away.

The following morning at 0830, the members of the evaluation team gathered inside one of the larger tents for their first official briefing. Chairs in front of the podium were arranged in neat rows. The Army occupied the right three rows, the Navy the left, and the civilians were seated between them.

Opening remarks by Captain Kingston were followed by Robert Archer, a scientist from the University of California and the head of the civilian delegation, regarding the nature of the task entrusted to the team. Then the floor was turned over to Army Air Corps Colonel Bart Scovil.

"The photographs that all of you have in your orientation kits were taken by the recon plane that accompanied the *Enola Gay* to the target. Estimated temperature at ground zero was thirty million degrees centigrade, or to put it more simply, the temperature at ground zero was approximately equal to the temperature on the surface of the sun."

Jacob glanced down at his packet of a dozen color photographs, taken at specific time intervals over Hiroshima.

"Ladies and gentlemen," Scovil continued, "at that temperature, matter as we know it can no longer exist. These fantastic temperatures atomize all manmade material and structures within a radius of approximately one-and-a-half miles from ground zero. Beyond that ring, heat and overpressures are so intense that another three miles become a vast fire storm with a massive shockwave toppling any structure in its path. As the photos show, for another four to five miles, devastation from heat and shock is significant. Fire from, for example, ruptured gas lines, engulfs the area.

"As you can see from photos number two through twelve, after the initial conflagration, a huge dust cloud builds to an altitude of thirty to thirty-five thousand feet. The mushroom-shaped cloud that you see in this sequence of photographs is characteristic of an atomic detonation. The material in the cloud is radioactive, and as the cloud disintegrates over a period of hours, the radioactive dust falls back to earth. The most intensely radioactive dust comes down in and around the target area, and though less intense, areas miles beyond the shockwave ring are exposed to deadly radiation. The people who were not killed by the initial blast or the fire storm, or by destruction stemming from the shockwaves, undoubtedly are going to experience various degrees of radiation sickness. Symptomatically, there will be a range of ailments from mild nausea to prolonged illnesses and ultimate death. In that regard, it is very important as we tour the area the next few days that each of us has his dosimeter checked every evening to ensure we haven't absorbed unacceptable levels of radiation." The colonel paused to take a sip of water before he said, "I'm sure all of you have questions, but before I attempt to answer them, I want to give you some additional information that has come to me today. The Japanese authorities estimate that two hundred and forty thousand people were killed in Hiroshima, roughly about half that city's population —"

There was a sudden nervous movement in the tent, and one of the women uttered, "Oh, my God!"

"It would be heartless of me, or anyone else, to minimize what that number means in terms of human suffering," Scovil said. "But it would also be heartless to minimize the number of casualties the United States and its allies would have had to sustain to invade and conquer the islands that compose Japan. Our best estimate at this time is a million casualties."

Again there was an uneasy movement in the tent.

"Now, ladies and gentlemen, I'll do my best to answer any questions you might have," Colonel Scovil said.

All of the civilians had questions and so did some of the Army people, but Kingston said in a low voice to his group, "If any of you gentlemen have any questions, you come to me. If I don't know the answers, I'll find out what they are."

After a half hour of fielding questions, Scovil held up his hands and said, "There are buses waiting outside to take us to Hiroshima. Because the area, for a distance of two miles from ground zero, still shows considerable radiation, we will observe it only from afar. Please remember to stay together and, cameramen, please remember that radioactivity does affect film. Ladies and gentlemen, will you please go to your assigned bus."

On each bus there was a Marine linked by radio to Colonel Scovil, who rode in a jeep in front of the lead bus. "The colonel says we're now entering the zone of least damage," the Marine said in a Southern drawl. "This area is approximately ten miles from ground zero. As you can see, the surface of the ground is covered with a fine gray dust."

Thousands of homeless people were wandering over the open areas or aimlessly along the road. Many of them bore agonizing burns and ugly red blotches on their faces or bare arms. Some looked as if fistfuls of their hair had been pulled out. All of them had eyes filled with pain, anguish, and fear. One woman held her baby up for them to see. It was red from head to toe.

"We are now entering the zone where the shockwave resulting from the blast caused most of the damage," the Marine at the radio intoned. The walls of some buildings were still standing, and here and there people were picking through the ruins. Several fires were smoldering.

"Look at the pigeons," Jacob said to Rampell, "they can't fly. They're just fluttering around." Then he saw thousands of dead birds on the ground, and suddenly Jacob remembered having gone with his father a long time ago to visit his father's friend in the Canarsie section of Brooklyn to see his racing pigeons.

"Now and then, an explosion will occur and a new fire will start," the Marine said. "These are the result of combustible gas collecting under the debris. Notice that there aren't any trees standing. The shockwave either broke them apart, leaving only a stump, or completely uprooted them."

For as far as Jacob could see, on either side of the bus, the devastation was complete. A light pall of smoke hung over the area, which not only had the pungent smell of fire but frequently the stink of a decaying body still buried under the rubble.

"This is the outer limit of the fire storm that resulted from the bomb's explosive force," the Marine announced. "Here, for a split second, the temperature was millions of degrees." Everything was demolished and fused into a kind of vitreous material, like black, lustrous basalt.

The bus slowed down and rolled to a stop. "If you look over to your right, you will see what was once a small wall. If you look closely, there is the unmistakable shape of a child and a dog imprinted into the rock."

"Christ, it's really there!" Rampell exclaimed.

Jacob's stomach twisted.

"In the next few days," the Marine said, echoing Scovil's words, "you will see many different imprints like the one you are looking at."

The buses started to roll again.

"Can you believe this is the result of one bomb?" Rampell asked.

"It's unreal," Jacob answered. "Unreal."

"Ladies and gentlemen," the Marine said, "we are now entering the area of maximum destruction. In a few minutes, we will be close enough to the area around ground zero for you to see a huge crater that measures several thousand feet across and several hundred feet deep. This crater was created the instant the bomb exploded."

Once again the buses stopped, allowing the members of the group to look at the crater.

"Thirty million degrees!" exclaimed an officer behind Jacob.

"Does anyone know how much that bomb weighed?" another man asked.

"Enough to require a B-29 to deliver it," someone answered.

"Awesome power!" a third officer exclaimed.

"Can you imagine what would have happened if the Japanese or the Germans had made the bomb first?" Rampell asked. Answering his own question, he said, "It would have been all over for us. Imagine New York or San Francisco being hit with the same kind of bomb!"

"Ladies and gentlemen," the marine said, "during the next five days, all of you will have detailed opportunity to consider the total effects of the detonation of the first atomic bomb to be used against an enemy at ground level."

The bus started to move again.

That afternoon, Kingston assigned Jacob the job of developing a precise map of the areas affected by overpressures and shockwaves associated with the explosion. In addition, he was to gather a demographic representation of casualties in those areas. The Marine detachment would provide him the necessary technical assistance.

On the first day at the task, Jacob came into contact with Japanese civilians still searching among the mounds of rubble for family members. All of them bowed in subservient defeat and silently watched him and the Marines assigned to him. He often thought about Kurokachi's family, especially if a young boy or girl was among those staring in silence at his group.

After the first day, rain fell incessantly for the next two days. Typhus broke out among the weary Japanese survivors, and deaths from radiation burns increased.

Jacob and the other members of the Navy team were appalled by the extent of human suffering they saw, but at the same time, each of them realized the alternative to ending the war victoriously in this way would have resulted in hundreds of thousands of American casualties through amphibious assault on the Japanese homeland.

By the late afternoon of the third day, truckloads of food and medical supplies arrived, and the Marine colonel began the enormous task of feeding and caring for the survivors. A huge tent city was in the process of being erected, and several large tents became hospitals. Army doctors and nurses were brought in.

That evening as he was on his way to the mess tent, Jacob met Dr. Lane. Jacob greeted her warmly. She nodded and said, "I never did thank you for helping me with the boy the other evening."

"No thanks were or are necessary," he answered, aware that they were sizing one another up. She was a petite woman with a shapely body, short brown hair, and light brown eyes.

She glanced at a convoy of Army trucks that had just arrived with additional food supplies for the Japanese survivors. "First we bomb the hell out of them. Then we feed them and care for their wounded," she commented.

"Comes under the heading of 'compassion,'" Jacob said.

She faced him. "It would have been infinitely more compassionate not to have used the bomb at all, or, to go even further, to have found some way of avoiding the war altogether."

Jacob shrugged. "I can't disagree with that."

Then she said, "I heard you're some kind of a hero. Is that true?"

Jacob's cheeks burned. "I don't know what you mean by 'some kind of a hero.'"

"Medals ... that kind of a hero."

"A few," he said.

"Interesting," she commented. "Interesting."

They walked into the mess tent together, and just as they were about to separate to go to their respective tables, she said, flicking her tongue over her lips, "Sometime I'd like to hear how you got your medals."

"It would bore you."

"I doubt it," she replied and, smiling, she added, "Maybe in Honolulu, or if you ever get to New York. I live in New York."

"So do I. I was born and raised in Brooklyn."

She laughed. "Good, we have something in common," she said and went to her table.

As Jacob sat down, Kingston glared at him and later, when coffee was being served, Kingston said, "Commander Miller, please come to my office immediately after you have finished your coffee."

"Yes, sir," Jacob answered.

Kingston nodded, stood up and left the table.

"What the hell is that all about?" Rampell asked.

"He must have seen me speaking to Dr. Lane just before dinner," Jacob answered.

"What a naughty thing to do, Commander!" Rampell laughed. "For that you will be keel-hauled and maybe, because you're a hotshot pilot, plane-hauled!"

Jacob stood up. "I better go see what Captain Mastermind wants," he said.

"Mastermind? I like that. I really like that. The name fits," Rampell responded.

Jacob left the mess tent and reported to Kingston.

"Commander, did I or did I not tell you and the other officers in my team that I did not want any fraternizing with civilian women?"

"I believe you did imply that, sir."

"It was an order, Commander," Kingston said, looking up at him from behind the desk. "I am sure you know what an order is, don't you?"

"Yes, sir," Jacob snapped, controlling his anger.

"Then how do you explain your behavior with Dr. Lane earlier this evening?" Kingston challenged.

"I feel no explanation is necessary, sir," Jacob answered. "I was just being civil."

"I demand one!"

"I am sorry, sir, but I feel you have overstepped your authority. I will not say any more. If you wish, I will take it up again with you in Admiral Gower's presence," Jacob said, looking straight ahead.

Kingston stood up. "By God! You Jews are something. Do you really believe you're one of God's *chosen* people?"

Jacob's heart began to race. He swallowed before he said, "If I did believe that, I would also believe that every human being is one of God's chosen people."

Kingston perched himself on the edge of the desk. "Slippery," he said, "slippery, that's what you are, Commander Miller. It's a characteristic you share with the rest of your people!"

Jacob clamped his jaws together.

"I promise you, Commander Miller, I won't forget this," Kingston said, returning to the chair behind the desk.

Jacob remained silent.

"Dismissed!" Kingston said.

Jacob did a quick about-face and left the tent. "Dork," he growled, as soon as he was outside, "fucking dork!" And he kicked savagely at a stone, sending it hurling into the olive drab canvas front of a tent across the area.

CHAPTER 10

"That was splendid work," Admiral Harly said, leaning back in his chair. "Of course, we didn't expect the Russians to move so fast in Manchuria." Smiling, Harly put a finger against his left nostril. Then he briskly went on, "For the next month you will be on leave, Commander. Make the most of it, because after that you'll be a very busy young man for a least eighteen to twenty-four months. Very busy."

Warren cleared his throat.

"Is anything wrong?" Harly asked.

"No, sir. It's just that I have a question," Warren answered, shifting uneasily in his chair.

Harly leaned forward. "I think I know what it is, but ask it anyway."

"Sir, what will be done with the Japanese doctors and medical technicians we brought out?"

Harly frowned.

"Sir, I realize the question goes beyond my need to know, but —"

Harly made a slight waving motion with his right hand. "Sometimes," he said in a low voice, "answers to questions must be guided by more than a strict interpretation of an individual's need to know. In this case, if I knew, I would tell you. But I don't know. That's for others to judge."

Warren took a deep breath and slowly exhaled. "There's something else, sir, something you should know before I head back for my training."

"I'm listening."

"The report you read is not totally complete. I did not include one particular episode." He paused and cleared his throat. "Just before the Russian paratroopers landed, I went into the facility's basement. Sir, there were three of our men down there. All of them were restrained in trough-like beds... All of them were being used for medical experiments. Sir —" Suddenly Warren couldn't continue. He shook his head and turned away.

"Take your time, Warren," Harly said gently. "Take your time."

Warren swallowed hard. "Sir, they were still alive but really dead — can you understand, sir? Only one seemed to know that I was there!"

"You don't have to say anything more," Harly told him. He stood up and, going around to where Warren sat, put his hand on Warren's shoulder.

"They couldn't be moved, sir... I shot them."

"You were there alone," Harly answered after a long pause. "You were the only one who could make a decision. I see no good reason for you to include any reference to the matter in your official report. In all truth, I probably would have done the same humane thing under the circumstances." He returned to his chair and sank heavily into it.

"And what are you going to do now?" Jacob asked, looking at Dr. Lane across a candlelit table in the Sing Bo, a posh Chinese restaurant in the Chinatown section of Honolulu. She wore an off-the-shoulder black dress that left the tops of her firm breasts bare. The previous afternoon, the report on the effects of the atomic bomb on Hiroshima had been completed, and as the team members were preparing to go their separate ways, he had asked her to have dinner with him.

"Oh, probably spend a week or ten days here before I return home. This is my first trip to Hawaii. What about you?"

"Well, I have some leave time coming," Jacob said, "and I'm going to use part of it to go to New York. I haven't been home for a long while."

"To your going home," she toasted, raising her martini.

Jacob touched her glass with his and then sipped his bourbon on the rocks.

"You never did tell me how you got all those medals," she said.

"I'd rather hear about you," he responded.

"In other words, you don't want to talk about your exploits, is that right?"

"Not especially. As I said, I'd rather talk about you."

"I'll let you off the hook if you answer one question," Ellen said.

"To the best of my ability, Doctor!" Jacob responded.

"What happened between you and Kingston after we talked? And don't tell me 'nothing.' Everyone knew something was going on between you."

Jacob drank more of his bourbon, before he said, "We had a less than friendly exchange."

"Because of me?"

"He saw us talking and he'd previously said that he didn't want any of us to fraternize with the women —"

"That hypocritical bastard!" she exclaimed. "He tried several times to get me into a corner."

"You're joking?"

She shook her head. "He even invited me to his tent," she said.

"You're not joking!"

"What, no outrage?" Ellen questioned.

"Who am I to be outraged?" Jacob responded quietly.

Ellen fell silent.

"I feel as if you're studying me."

She nodded. "You're right, I am."

"Find anything interesting?" he asked, sipping his drink again.

"I'll let you determine that for yourself."

"And how will I do that?" he asked with mock naivety. The promise in her voice set his pulse racing.

She smiled and, ignoring the question, said, "Let's order, I'm starved."

"Come to think of it," Jacob quipped, "so am I. But for more than just food."

"You know what I'd like to do at this moment?" Ellen asked as the restaurant doorman opened the door for her and Jacob to leave.

"Ride a rollercoaster? Go skinny-dipping?" he asked flippantly.

She linked her arm with his. "Walk. I can't remember when I ate that much. For the moment, just walk."

"I wouldn't have been much for a rollercoaster ride myself. Now, the skinny —"

"It's a lovely night," she exclaimed, looking up at the sky. Then she said abruptly, "I'm forty-two years old and divorced. I have two children: a son, Keith, who just last month turned sixteen, and a daughter, Laura, twenty. How old are you, Jacob?"

"Twenty-eight."

"Then you've been in the Navy for the entire war?"

"Before the war," he answered.

They began to cross the street.

"Are you going to stay in?" she asked.

"Yes… I love to fly and the Navy is a good place to —"

Ellen suddenly stopped. "Jacob, I'm not your average woman. Had I been, I would never have made it through medical school. To do that in those days, I had to have drive and brains. I had to compete in a man's world, and that meant I had to be bold and sometimes a bit aggressive. And that brings —"

He put his finger across her lips. "Let's go back to my hotel."

"Even if I'm forty-two?"

Jacob put his arms around her. "You don't look a day over twenty-eight," he said, kissing her hard.

"I think we'd better find a taxi," she told him, "before either of us changes our minds."

He took her hand and started searching for a cab. "Don't worry about me. I won't."

Jacob was in bed, propped up by two pillows. He looked across the darkened room to the window, where Ellen's beautiful naked body was silhouetted by the light of the moon over Waikiki Beach. He hadn't made love to a woman in months, and Connie's death a while back had dulled the need until recently. Ellen had thrilled him deeply. He reached for the pack of cigarettes on the night table, took one, and lit it.

Ellen returned to the bed and sat down. "Would you consider me foolish if I asked you to spend ten days with me here in the islands?" She put her hand on his knee.

Jacob lazily blew smoke up toward the ceiling. "No."

"No, meaning you won't stay with me, or no, meaning you won't consider me foolish?"

"No, I don't consider you foolish. How could I?" Jacob told her.

"But you won't stay?"

He took hold of her hand and kissed it. "I may not be the kind of guy you'd want around for a full ten days," he said gently.

"It's a hell of a time to ask," she suddenly questioned, "but do you have a wife —"

"Only a mother and a sister," he chuckled. "I promised them I'd come home to see them."

Settling down alongside of him, Ellen said, "When do you plan to leave?"

"As soon as I can get a flight out," he answered. "Probably in a day or two."

"Will you stay with me until you go?"

He stubbed out the cigarette and said, "I was going to ask if you'd stay with me."

"You were wrong, Jacob, in what you said before," she murmured. "You're exactly the kind of man I'd want around. And for a lot longer than ten days."

"Let's make the most of what we have," he said, taking her in his arms, caressing and kissing her with abandon.

"Tony," Miriam called, "a black limo just pulled up in front of the house."

"Be there in a minute," Tony answered. It was Sunday afternoon, and he was out in the backyard resting in a hammock he'd slung between two trees. Sam was asleep in a carriage next to him. "No rest for the weary," he commented aloud to himself.

"It's your dad and a couple of other men," Miriam called.

"Coming," Tony called, entering the house through the screen door. Though it was late September, the weather was still unusually summery in Connecticut. By the time Tony reached the foyer, his father and the other two men were already inside the house. One of the men was Carlo Spilachi, the capo of the New Jersey Mafia. Tony didn't know the other one.

"You look more like a Madonna every time I see you," his father said to Miriam, kissing her on the cheek and gently patting her stomach.

"How's Mama, Mike, and the rest of the family?" Miriam asked.

"Well, very well," her father-in-law answered in Italian and asked how her mother was.

"Well," Miriam answered in Italian, "she will be coming here for a few days after the Jewish holidays." During the time that Tony had been away, she'd learned to speak fairly fluent Italian by attending classes at the Berlitz language school on Flatbush Avenue in Brooklyn.

Trapasso nodded. "I will have her driven up here by one of my men. I don't want a woman of her age traveling alone on the trains."

"Isn't he the best?" Miriam exclaimed, looking at Tony and hugging her father-in-law.

"Sure he is," Tony answered, shaking his father's hand.

"You know Don Spilachi?" his father asked, looking at his son.

Tony nodded. "Welcome, Mr. Spilachi," he said, reluctantly taking the man's hand. Spilachi hadn't changed much in the years since he had last seen him. Grayer and perhaps more sallow. But he still had the eyes of a predator.

"You made all of us very proud of you," Spilachi said.

"And this is Giorgio Ferrara," Tony's father said. "Giorgio is a lawyer in Newark and Don Spilachi's nephew."

Tony shook his hand. "My wife, Miriam," he said. Ferrara looked like a successful businessman. He wore a white linen sports jacket, a light blue shirt with a matching tie of gray with thin red stripes, and blue slacks.

"A great pleasure to meet you," Ferrara responded, kissing the back of Miriam's hand. "Your father-in-law never stops talking about you," he said in English.

Miriam blushed. "Papa, you shouldn't —"

Mr. Trapasso put his arm around her shoulder. "And why shouldn't I tell everyone that I got the best daughter-in-law in the world?"

"You keep that up, Papa," Tony said, "and she'll get the idea I'm not good enough for her."

They all laughed as Tony led his guests into the living room. "You'll stay for dinner?"

"We don't want to be any trouble to you and your charming wife," Spilachi said in a Sicilian dialect.

"It won't be any trouble," Tony answered in English. "Miriam, Papa and his friends are staying for dinner."

"That much I could make out on my own," she answered. "There's more than enough — I hope you like roast leg of lamb."

"One of my favorites," Ferrara said.

"If you'll excuse me," Miriam said, "I'll take care of things in the kitchen." And she left the living room.

Tony offered his guest drinks.

Spilachi asked for mineral water, commenting that his digestion had been acting up of late.

"Seltzer is the best I can do," Tony answered.

"That will be all right,"

"Johnny Walker Black, if you have it," Ferrara said.

"Neat?"

"On the rocks."

"Grappa for you, Papa?" Tony questioned.

Mr. Trapasso nodded.

When Tony went into the kitchen for ice, Miriam asked, "Did you know Papa was coming?"

"No, I would have told you if I had," Tony said, putting ice cubes in a glass for Ferrara and wishing he didn't have to entertain these friends of his father.

"Who are those other men?" Miriam asked, opening the oven and looking at the roast.

"I'll tell you later, Miriam," he said, avoiding the question. But he suspected Spilachi hadn't come for a social visit. He and Spilachi had exchanged more than a few harsh words some years back at his father's house. "How much longer until everything is ready?" Tony asked in a gentler tone.

"A half hour at the most," Miriam answered. "I want to feed Sam before we sit down."

"Take care of Sam first," Tony told her. "If it takes longer than a half hour, don't worry. We can wait. First things first!" And he went back to his guests with a feeling of vague foreboding.

"This is the first time I've been around a Navy base," Spilachi said.

Tony offered to show them around. "You could see some submarines. They're not far from here, and I probably could get you aboard one of the ones we use for training students."

Spilachi smiled broadly, revealing his tobacco-stained teeth. "I'd feel too closed in," he said in Sicilian. Then he added, "I don't know how you stand it."

"It's something you get used to."

Ferrara asked, "Do you still make dives?"

Tony nodded. "I'm an instructor at the school for new submariners," he explained. "I teach them what I'm supposed to have learned during the war."

"He knows," his father said proudly. "He knows everything there is to know about submarines."

"Remarkable!" Ferrara exclaimed, adding in a somewhat apologetic tone, "I couldn't serve during the war because I have a punctured eardrum."

Tony nodded. He did not say aloud that he knew many draft dodgers had had one deliberately punctured to be medically deferred.

"I certainly envy your experiences," Ferrara said.

Tony stood up. He didn't want to listen to this kind of drivel, even from someone who was a friend of his father's. "You can't envy something you don't know anything about."

Ferrara flushed. "Naturally, I meant —"

"With all due respect, Mr. Ferrara," Tony cut in, "I really don't care what you meant. The war is over. Let's leave it that way."

"I told you, Giorgio," Spilachi said with a hard smile, "that Don's boy doesn't fuck around with words the way you lawyers do. He's straight from the shoulder." Then, with the smile still frozen on his lips, he shifted his muddy-gray eyes to Tony. "Giorgio works for me. He's my sister's nephew."

Tony nodded. That was Spilachi's way of telling him that he'd reacted more strongly than he should have.

"Dinner!" Miriam announced from the entrance to the dining room.

"Dinner," Tony repeated, thankful that unwittingly Miriam had interrupted at a crucial time.

"Your father tells me that you were in a Jap prison," Giorgio said after they sat down at the table and Miriam served the baked ziti.

"On a prison ship too," Tony's father said.

"It must have been terrible," Giorgio commented, digging his fork into the ziti.

Tony remained silent.

"Ah," Spilachi exclaimed, changing the subject, "we should drink to the coming of the new child."

"Miriam," Tony's father called, "come into the dining room. Don Spilachi is going to make a toast to your next son."

She came into the room and stood at Tony's side.

"May it be a beautiful and healthy son," Spilachi said, raising his glass in Miriam's direction. "May he then grow stronger and wiser each day."

Everyone raised their glasses and drank.

Throughout the rest of the dinner, the conversation at the table rocked along uncertainly. Some of it was about Tony's old neighborhood and the people he had known, and some of it was about Lucky Luciano and Buggsy Seigel, two of the top Cosa Nostra men who were turning Las Vegas, Nevada, into the gambling capital of the world.

Spilachi said, "We're in for a few hundred thousand Gs. But in a few years' time we'll see ten, maybe fifteen million. Giorgio has set up the deal with Luciano."

"Papa, you already got more money than you know what to do with," Tony laughed. "What are you going to do with more?"

"In this country, it's always more."

"You see something you like, you buy it," Spilachi added. "A car, a house — anything you want."

Tony smiled. He'd heard words similar to those ever since he could remember.

"You don't believe that, do you?" Giorgio asked.

Tony shook his head. "It makes no difference whether I do or not. It's a question of whether a guy is foolish enough to believe that stuff. But then, that's what makes a horse race right? A difference of opinion."

By the time Miriam served the cannoli from a local Italian bakery, Tony sensed that the real reason for Spilachi's visit was in the offing, and offered to help Miriam clear the table.

"It'll only take a few minutes," she said. "Tony, why don't you show Mr. Spilachi and Giorgio around? It's still light enough to take them down to the river."

"Good idea," Spilachi exclaimed, "I could use a good walk and a good cigar." And taking out a leather cigar case, he said, "These are Havana's finest. Try one, Tony, and if you like it, the next time your papa comes to visit, I'll give him a couple of boxes for you."

Tony took the cigar, thanked Spilachi and waited until they were out of the house to light up.

"You know," Spilachi said, letting smoke rush out of his nostrils, "of all the boys I knew from the neighborhood, I always figured you to be the smartest. Giorgio here is book smart. But you were book smart and street smart. That's a hard combination to find in any man."

"Stop the bullshit," Tony said nonchalantly. "Tell me what you want."

Spilachi said, "Giorgio, you tell him."

"No," Tony snapped. "You can use your Charley McCarthy with someone else. I want to hear what you have to say from you."

They'd reached the path along the river and stopped. Spilachi took the cigar out of his mouth. "You're in the right place at the right time," he said. "There's a man in Washington who we own. He buys for the Navy and we got warehouses full of stuff we want to sell and he wants to buy."

"If you have that kind of a hook-up, why do you need me?" Tony asked, disgusted by what Spilachi was telling him.

Spilachi gave him one of his thin smiles. "I need a man to watch him. He's not like us. I need a real close man to sign off on him."

Tony shook his head.

"You work for me and your papa and I'll give you ten percent of every deal we cut."

Tony almost smiled. It was time to play games. "Giorgio, how much is your uncle giving you?" he asked in Italian.

Giorgio looked questioningly at Spilachi.

"Tell him."

"Twelve percent and twenty-five percent of those deals I initiate."

Tony took a long drag on his cigar and slowly let the smoke flow out of his mouth. "Not bad for a guy without any street smarts. But I have street smarts. You see, Mr. Spilachi," he said, starting to walk again, "I can get you guns. A man like you always needs guns. Maybe a submarine. I mean, now and then a surplus submarine comes up for sale. How would you like your own submarine?"

"Guns?" Spilachi questioned with a greedy tone.

"Sure," Tony answered. "M-ls, burp guns, .45s — a whole fucking arsenal."

Spilachi wet his lips.

"Fifty-five percent," Tony said. "No, I want sixty-five percent of every deal I cut, and fifty percent of every deal you cut."

Spilachi stopped walking. "You pulling my dick?"

Tony smiled. "No, Mr. Spilachi, that's something you probably do," he said in Italian.

"Tony!" his father exclaimed.

"No, Don," Spilachi said, also speaking in Italian, "let me deal with him. Suppose, Tony, I agree to your terms, then what?"

"Then you're a bigger fool than I thought you were," Tony said in English and, turning, he started to walk away.

Suddenly, Giorgio was in front of him. "You can't talk to my uncle that way!" he challenged.

"Spilachi," Tony said, in a low, flat voice, "tell this son of a bitch to step aside, or I'll take him apart."

"Maybe you need a lesson," Spilachi growled.

With one quick movement Tony shoved his cigar into Giorgio's mouth, kneed him in the groin, and, locking his hands together, smashed them against the side of his head. The man went sprawling to the ground. "Don't ever tell me," he said, speaking Italian and gulping air, "that I need a lesson, Mr. Spilachi." He bent over Giorgio and pulled him to his feet. Still speaking in Italian, he said, "You ever step in front of me again, motherfucker, I'll tear your heart out. Understand?"

Giorgio was mute.

Tony backhanded him across the face. "I asked you if you understood."

"I understand," Giorgio whimpered.

"Good," Tony said. "That's good." Looking at his father, he added, "I don't ever want to see this garbage around here again." Spilachi took his nephew by the arm and wiped his bleeding face.

"Tony —" the elder Trapasso began.

"You still don't understand, Papa," Tony said coldly. "You still don't understand who and what I am, do you?" Shaking his head, he walked slowly back to the house alone.

CHAPTER 11

Warren waited three days before he phoned Tara to tell her he was back in Honolulu. Most of that time he had spent alone, trying to come to terms with his unrest. He could not explain the depression that nagged him. His last two missions had affected him profoundly. He wondered if he was experiencing a cumulative response to all the missions, from the first time he'd come under enemy fire aboard the *Dee* until he faced down the Russian colonel. He wasn't sure.

Warren walked for hours on end, aimlessly exploring areas of the city he had never been in before. Honolulu was returning to normal, but not he. On several occasions he had found a lonely strip of Waikiki Beach, and, sitting on the sand, stared endlessly out at the ocean. The memory of shooting those three men in Manchuria bothered him more than anything else he'd done or seen, with the terrible exception of looking at Irene's mutilated body.

His mother had made several attempts to get him to talk it out. "I know something is wrong," she'd said. "You just don't act yourself."

Lillian had implied the same thing. Late one afternoon, when he stopped by his mother's apartment, his sister said, "You look like death warmed over, brother."

"That's the kind of remark," he answered, managing a smile, "that certainly makes a person feel better."

"Come on, Warren," Lillian said. "Like I've said to you before, and you know exactly what I mean, you should get together with people. See someone, have a good time."

"And just who do you think that someone should be?" he asked, dropping down on the sofa and stretching out on it. He knew his sister meant Tara without saying her name.

"Warren, dear, if you were the least bit religious," she answered, "as a last resort, I'd say a chaplain. But since I know you're not, I'd suggest a psychoanalyst."

Warren sat up. He hadn't thought about seeking help either from a chaplain or from a doctor, but it was an idea. If he couldn't shake this depression, he might stay in Honolulu for a while and see a civilian analyst before going to visit Glen's family on the mainland.

"I also think you should be going out with girls," Lillian said, again avoiding Tara's name.

"And I bet you just happen to have a few in mind who'd just love to solve my problem," he laughed.

"Now that you mention it —"

"Thanks, a lot!" Warren answered, holding up his hand. "I really do appreciate the offer. But I'm sure they'd find me terribly dull and I might find them terribly anxious to lead me to the altar!"

"Worse could happen to you!" Lillian observed quietly.

"I know," Warren said sarcastically. After Lillian left the apartment, though, he decided he would phone Tara after all. The hell with a shrink.

"You always ask me out on such short notice," Tara said petulantly. "I have been wondering when I'd hear from you. Don't you ever write letters?"

"If you'd prefer another time —"

"No, tonight will be fine. I'll be glad to see you," she answered.

"I'll pick you up at eight," Warren said. He left his mother's apartment and walked to the Royal Hawaiian, where he was staying. He lay down and drifted off into a restless sleep until an hour before his date.

Warren arrived by cab and told the driver to wait.

Tara opened the door a few moments after he rang the bell. She wore a simple black cocktail dress that emphasized her lovely figure. She greeted him with a kiss on the cheek and said, "Welcome back, Warren. My mother is in the den. She wants to see you too."

Warren nodded and followed Tara.

"My God," Kate exclaimed, greeting him with a loving hug, "you've lost weight!"

"I know," Warren countered with bravado, "but I'm eating a lot of bananas and ice cream to put it back on!"

"Make sure he eats," Kate told Tara, as she walked them to the door.

Tara didn't answer, but Warren said, "I promise to have two portions of everything."

Kate laughed. "Whatever you say!"

"I'll see that he eats," Tara called as she entered the cab.

Warren sat down next to her.

"There's a new Italian restaurant on Franklin Street called the Terra Verde. Riva has eaten there and she says it's very good."

"I'm game," Warren answered lamely.

At dinner, Warren tried to settle down and think of something exciting to say, but there seemed to be a strain between them. Conversation lapsed, and each seemed to be struggling to say something important. The magic of their last moments together before he had left for Manchuria seemed to escape them. Then suddenly Warren said, "Jesus, I think I see an old friend."

"Where?" Tara asked.

"Three tables behind you."

Tara turned around. "The tall officer?"

"Yes… It *is* him."

"He's seen you," she said as Jacob rushed to their table.

Warren stood up. "My God, Jake, it's good to see you!" he said, grasping Jacob's outstretched hand and shaking it. "Commander Miller, this is Miss Tara Hasse."

"Commander, how nice to meet you."

"It's a pleasure," Jacob responded, taking her hand.

"Why don't you and your friend join us?" Warren suggested.

"I'd like that," Jacob answered. "I'll ask Dr. Lane if she'd mind our joining you."

"He's one of our top fighter pilots," Warren told Tara as soon as Jacob was out of earshot.

"That's funny, he doesn't look the type," Tara commented. "Looks more like a college professor."

"Good, the two of them are coming over," Warren said, oblivious to what she had said.

With Jacob and Ellen at the table, the conversation brightened and Tara became an animated part of it. Learning they had recently returned from Japan, she wanted to know all about their experiences in Hiroshima.

After they had told of the harrowing things they had seen, Ellen said to Warren, "Jacob won't tell me anything about what he was doing before I met him."

"Just a fighter pilot," Jacob said with exaggerated humility.

"One of the best," Warren commented.

"What have you been doing?" Jacob asked, looking at Warren. "The last I heard, you were picking guys out of the drink off Okinawa."

"Had a real good time for a few days in China. Now I'm waiting for reassignment," Warren answered evasively.

"Did you see any of the other guys we know? Tony? Glen?"

"Glen didn't make it," Warren said in a low voice.

"Damn," Jacob said, shaking his head. "Damn, he was so full of life!"

"Jake, I was sorry to learn about Connie," Warren commented. Then, watching Ellen's eyebrows rise, he realized he may have made a faux pas.

Jacob also looked at Ellen. "I was going to marry her. She came aboard the *Shiloh* to do a story about kamikaze attacks, and while she was on board, we took a torpedo. The *Shiloh* went down and she was drowned."

"I'm sorry, Jacob," Ellen said, lowering her eyes.

"Thank you." Feeling the awkwardness at the table and not wanting to be its cause, he quickly asked Warren, "Do you know if Tony Trapasso made it back?"

Warren smiled. "Yes, he made it back. I saw him."

Jacob nodded approvingly. "He's not only my friend," he announced to the women, "he also happens to be my brother-in-law."

"And he also happens to be one hell of a fine submarine skipper," Warren added.

The four of them chatted for a while at the table after dinner.

"How long are you going to be in Honolulu?" Warren asked Jacob.

"I leave for the mainland tomorrow."

"I'm going back in a few days, too," Warren said. "I'm going to visit Glen's family, then go to Washington. Maybe I'll see you in New York."

"That would be great," Jacob said. "If Tony is up in New London, maybe the three of us could get together."

"I'd really like that, Jake."

The four left the restaurant together and, after Jacob and Ellen had said goodbye and entered a cab, Warren suggested to Tara that they walk for a while.

"Fine," she agreed, then said, "Warren, do you think they're lovers?"

Warren knew she was asking about Jacob and Ellen. "I don't know whether they love one another, but I'd guess they're sleeping together! You know just about as much as I do about them."

"I gathered the same impression. That's what I meant by lovers!"

Warren didn't think an answer was necessary.

"She does love him, though!" Tara said. "I could tell... She couldn't take her eyes off of him and she touched him whenever she could. Warren, who was the woman he knew who was killed?"

"Connie Burke, a reporter for the *New York Post*... I met her the same time he did," Warren explained, remembering the evening. "It was after the Battle of Midway, and Jacob had come out of it a hero." He pursed his lips. "Connie was a very beautiful, exciting woman."

They stopped for a red light and when the light had changed and they started to cross the street, Tara blurted out suddenly, as though she could no longer hold it in, "All the time you were away, Warren, I thought about us!"

He began to be very uneasy. Although she was beautiful and lovely to look at, he had found, for some strange reason, he had no desire to make love to her. And he didn't want to hear now what she seemed about to tell him. He floundered in awkward silence.

"I shouldn't have responded the way I did the last time I saw you," she continued.

"What?" Warren exclaimed, startled by her impersonal tone, feeling relieved as well.

"We — I let things get a little out of hand," she told him. "I guess I was prepared to be angry at you and when I realized I couldn't — well, I'm not in love with you, either! I know that now. I don't want anything more from you except just to be good friends!"

Though Warren had no idea how she expected him to react, he said with great relief, "Tara, dear, I've come to the same conclusion! Having you as a friend would be wonderful!"

"Ditto," Tara laughed. "Ditto!"

Jacob raised his head from Ellen's bare breasts and kissed her closed eyelids. Moments before they'd found, in each other's deep embrace, simultaneous ecstasy.

She ran her hands over his bare shoulders. "Being with you these days has made me jealous of younger women," she sighed.

He kissed her lips. This was their last night together and he'd developed a genuine affection for her, but he knew he wasn't in love with her.

"Will you call me when you're in New York?" she asked, opening her eyes and looking at him.

He rolled away from her and onto his back. He desperately didn't want to hurt her, but neither did he want to be dishonest with her. "Maybe not," he said gently. "If we continued the way we are, I'm afraid it would only complicate our lives later on."

For several moments, Ellen remained silent.

Jacob listened to the sound of her breathing, and at the same time he felt the pounding of his own heart.

"I love you," Ellen said quietly. "I know that wasn't the name of the game, but —" Her voice choked up and she paused before she could continue. "But you make me feel like a woman again!"

He took her hand and kissed the tips of her fingers. "You made me feel like a man!" Jacob said. "I haven't been with a woman for a long time. But there's more to a lasting love than what happens between two people in a bedroom. You've been married; you know what I mean, and even though I haven't been married, I know there's something more to it!"

"Jacob," Ellen said, "I would have been the first to smirk if I heard about a woman falling in love with a younger man. But now I no longer think it funny because it was so good…"

He let go of her hand and put his finger across her lips. "Don't," he told her. "Don't say something that you'll regret the moment after you say it."

"Oh Jacob, I love you!" Ellen said passionately. "I love you!"

He took her in his arms and held her very close.

Jacob arrived in New York in early October, between the high holy days of Rosh Hashanah and Yom Kippur. His thoughts were about his dead father. Traditionally, he was aware, his visit to his father's grave should have been made before Rosh Hashanah, but he had still been in Honolulu at the time. This was the best he could do.

It was early the day after his arrival that he, wearing his white service uniform, rented a car and drove alone to the cemetery in Elmont on Long Island, where his father was buried.

He stopped at the administration building to find out exactly where the grave was located. The man behind the counter gave him a questioning look and asked, "You sure you're in the right place?" he asked. "This is a Jewish cemetery."

Jacob suddenly understood. "Don't let the uniform confuse you," he said. "I'm also a Jew. I'm Mr. Miller's son."

"If you say so," the man answered, still doubtful. "The easiest way to get there is to drive straight up the road behind this building until you come to the crossway marked *Harrison*. It's about fifty feet on your left."

A short time later, Jacob parked the car and walked up the narrow path from the roadway to the grave. The leaves of the trees were already colored red, brown, and yellow in the cool nights of the early fall, and most of the grass was dying. He stopped at the gray marble headstone that had his family name carved into it. Around it there was space for six graves; his father had bought the plot some years before. If he remembered correctly, that was just after the war erupted in Europe and the diamond business had begun to recover after the Depression. "I have here," his father had said one night after dinner, "the deed for six graves. For me and your mother, for you, Miriam, and your husband, and for you, Jacob, and your wife." Jacob could still hear the pride in his father's voice as he spoke. Having a place for him and his family to be buried was very important, and being able to buy one large enough for his children and their spouses was an accomplishment, especially after the hard years of the thirties.

Jacob caressed the rough top of the stone. "There's so much I should have told you," he thought, "so much." There had been great disagreement between them when Jacob had chosen to apply for Navy flight training after he'd completed college. Yet, even with the differences between them — his father had desperately wanted him to become a rabbi — their love for each other never faltered. In the end, moreover, Jacob knew his father had become proud of him.

"You know, Papa," Jacob whispered, "you almost had a daughter-in-law. She wasn't a Jew, but you would have loved her just the same, because, Papa, I loved her!" He paused and with the back of his hand wiped the tears from his eyes. "She saved my life and gave up hers to do it. Papa, she died at sea. She doesn't have a grave. Share the *kaddish* I will say for you with her because I have nothing else to give to her. Nothing, Papa."

Jacob brushed the tears from his eyes again and was about to intone the *kaddish* when he heard a sound behind him. He turned to see a bent, wizened old man in a long black coat and a broad-brimmed black hat carrying an umbrella with an ornately carved wooden handle. It was an incongruous sight, since the sun was shining brightly with only a few small scattered clouds in the sky.

Jacob thought the man might be one of those rabbis who for some unexplainable reason did not have a congregation of their own, but eked out a meager livelihood by offering to pray for the dead. Jacob disliked them intensely. To him, there was something ghoulish in the way they followed people to gravesites, or worse, the way they often badgered the bereaved and sometimes became nasty when told their services weren't required.

The old man leaned on the umbrella, using it as if it were a support he needed badly. As Jacob stared at the Shamus, he suddenly realized that despite the initial impression of shabbiness, he was in fact expensively dressed. The sun glinted off a large square-cut diamond in a heavy gold setting on his left hand.

"It's right," the man said in perfect English, "that a son should come to his father's grave and say *kaddish*."

Jacob nodded uncertainly in reply.

"I know all about you, Jacob," the man continued. "I have been wondering when you were going to come."

"How do you know my name?" Jacob asked, feeling a trifle ill at ease. It was the most unlikely of places to encounter a stranger who knew his name. "Who are you?"

The old man smiled. "Name is Yitzhok Grunveldt, or, if you prefer, Isaac Grenville."

"How do you know me?"

Grenville lifted the umbrella and pointed at the gravestone. "Your father told me about his *kaddish*," he said, using the word this time as the traditional synonym for son.

Jacob looked at the Miller headstone. He didn't remember his father ever having mentioned anything about someone named Isaac Grenville. But then, his father had seldom spoken about any of the people with whom he had business dealings. "How did you know my father?" Jacob asked.

Grenville smiled. "We were in the trenches together in World War I," he said. "That's a whole lifetime ago. Later, your father brought me to this country."

"Brought you here?" Jacob exclaimed in astonishment.

"Paid for my passage."

Jacob stared at the old man.

But Grenville continued, "Paid for me and my wife, Ruth, may she rest in peace, to come here. Not with money, Jacob, but with diamonds. With diamonds, you could buy anything in Nazi Germany."

"But he never went back — I know he never went back there."

"He sent others. We came to this country and with your father's help, I started my bakery business. He let me have five hundred dollars to do it. I'll never forget."

Jacob was too surprised to speak.

"I made a lot of money. Now I don't have a *kaddish*, a son like you, and when my wife died, I was left alone. I don't have any family left. All the others died either in Hitler's camps or the gas chambers. I come here now," he said, looking around, "because Ruth is here and so is my friend Sam, your father. It's the place where I now feel most comfortable." Then, pointing with the umbrella to the cypress hedges around the graves, he added proudly, "I trim them myself. I don't like the way the caretakers here do it."

"Do you know my mother?" Jacob asked, finding it difficult to believe what he'd just heard.

"Yes," Grenville answered. "But if you ask her about me, she may say that I'm meshuga," he said. "But I'm not."

Jacob couldn't decide whether the man was crazy or not, but he said, for lack of anything better to say, "I certainly appreciate what you do to the hedges."

Grenville seemed pleased. "I'm glad I finally met you," he said. "Sam was very proud of you, and you should be very proud of him. He was a good man."

"I am proud of him," Jacob answered.

"Now I'll leave the two of you alone," Grenville said. Pointing with his umbrella back to the road where Jacob had parked his car, he said, "My chauffeur has probably fallen asleep!"

There was a black Cadillac directly behind Jacob's car. He had been so engrossed with Grenville that he hadn't noticed it before, or, for that matter, heard it when it had pulled up and stopped.

"May the Lord be with you," Grenville said.

"And with you too," Jacob answered politely as he watched Grenville turn and hobble away. He waited until the Cadillac had left and then, facing the headstone, he intoned the *kaddish*. When he was finished, Jacob picked up two smooth rocks and placed them on the headstone next to those that were already there. "Papa," he whispered, "one is for you and the other for Connie." Turning around, he walked slowly back to his car.

CHAPTER 12

By June 1946, Warren had completed Parachute Jump School at Quantico, Virginia, and was in the final days of a highly classified Office of Strategic Services course in cryptoanalysis. To be close to where the courses were conducted, Warren had rented a small bachelor apartment in a nineteenth-century brick building on the banks of the Potomac in Alexandria, Virginia. As part of his training, he found that he had been designated to act as a White House aide. This additional duty would give him the opportunity to accustom himself to the ways of diplomatic society as well as to meet important people. Though it was an honor to be on the list of White House aides, Warren did not relish the formality the social functions involved and would have preferred not to have been chosen. However, he guessed it was all part of Admiral Harly's plan for him.

One Sunday afternoon in late June, President and Mrs. Truman invited the world-renowned contralto Marian Anderson to perform at the White House. Warren, in beribboned white service uniform with a full-dress aiguillette draped over his right shoulder, found himself in the company of Mrs. Silvia Martins, a small, elegant, middle-aged woman, who in her white summer dress, seemed out of place in the crowded conservatory.

Warren sat next to Mrs. Martins throughout Miss Anderson's performance. He was especially moved by her rendition of several spirituals, including "Sometimes I Feel Like a Motherless Child" and "He's Got the Whole World in His Hands." Later, as he accompanied Mrs. Martins to the East Room for cocktails, she said, "Commander, I'm having a garden party and buffet supper a week from Saturday at four, and I would like you to come."

The sudden invitation surprised him. His conversation with the woman had been limited to social pleasantries and mutual admiration for Miss Anderson's stirring voice.

"Not a large party," she said, smiling at him. "A smattering of newspaper people and a few artist friends and writers. If you wish, bring a friend, a fellow officer."

"Thank you for the invitation," Warren responded, aware that she had subtly let him know that she didn't want him to arrive with a woman on his arm if he decided to accept.

"I can promise you good food and interesting conversation."

"I'll certainly try, Mrs. Martins, but I may find I'll be needed here."

"Of course, duty comes before pleasure. But if you can make it, I'd be pleased to have you. And I hope you will wear that beautiful uniform." Opening a white beaded purse, she took out an engraved card. "I live and work, as you can see, at the same address."

Warren looked at the card. "In New York?" he questioned.

She smiled. "In Greenwich Village. Isn't that where artists are supposed to live?" she asked with a mischievous twinkle in her brown eyes.

Warren hadn't thought of her as being anything more than a friend of someone connected to the White House. "I'm the first to admit," he answered, "I don't know where artists are supposed to live or, for that matter, about artists in general."

"That will really be refreshing," Mrs. Martins said, smiling. "And now, Commander, let us enjoy the rest of the afternoon. I must tell you beforehand, one very dry martini with an onion is my limit. But I do adore the hors d'oeuvre … and the company."

"Allow me to supply the martini," Warren responded gallantly, beginning to surmise his companion was someone of import. He headed to the bar, where a Navy steward's mate wearing a white mess jacket with the presidential seal on the right breast pocket was shaking up a fresh pitcher of martinis. As he waited in the queue, a man came up behind him and commented, "Wasn't that a marvelous performance?"

Facing him, Warren agreed. The man was avuncular-looking, with a round face, red cheeks, and glasses worn low on his nose.

"Admiral Harly sends his regards," the man whispered, bending close to Warren's ear.

Warren nodded. Over the past months, two other men had used the same opening gambit to identify themselves before taking up classified subjects. Apparently, this was more of the same.

"The name is Don Wolfe," the man said, extending his hand.

"Commander Warren Troost," Warren answered, sensing that Don Wolfe wasn't the man's real name.

Harly's cloak-and-dagger world was beginning to fascinate Warren.

"After the reception, Commander, I would appreciate a few moments of your time."

"Yes, sir," Warren said.

"I'll be seated out front in a black limousine with diplomatic plates," Wolfe said in a low voice as he turned abruptly away.

Warren stepped up to the bar. "Two martinis. One very dry with an onion and the other with an olive," he said.

A chauffeur dressed in a dark blue uniform opened the door of the limo. Warren entered and Wolfe patted the rear seat at his side.

"You'll be finishing your crypto course in another week," Wolfe said, "and then you'll report to the FBI's Special Training Section. Your identity for that period of time will be changed again." He removed a large white envelope from the inside pocket of his jacket. "Everything you need to know is there. After you have memorized every detail, burn it all," he said, handing the envelope to Warren. "In the meantime, you will continue your additional assignment as a White House aide under your own name."

"Who will I be this time?" Warren asked. In jump school, he had been a Marine first lieutenant, and in the cryptoanalysis course he was enrolled as an Army major.

"Warrant officer Allen J. Harris."

"That's a comedown from a major," Warren commented, for lack of anything better to say.

"We try to match you with someone who looks like you," Wolfe continued in a serious tone.

"Looks like me?" Warren questioned.

"All your identities at the different courses so far have been taken from men missing in action," Wolfe explained. "As you know, your own prints are always on file with the FBI. So are those, of course, of the MIAs. Since your orders have been written in their name, it hasn't been necessary for anyone to fingerprint you again, and that saves us the trouble of having to explain how come your prints don't match those of your assumed names … if anyone asks."

Warren pretended to understand. "For your info, sir, I've just been invited to a supper party by Mrs. Martins," he said. "I'm sure you know who she is. It's in New York, a week from next Saturday."

"Go, if you want to. She's a world-famous artist and sculptress, and is making a second reputation for herself as an art critic. She's often a guest at the White House."

"I certainly didn't figure her to be in the art world," Warren commented. "Isn't it strange that she should invite me to her party? I'm surely not the type she's used to. Besides, other than our very limited conversation after we met, we didn't seem to have a great deal in common."

"You're a personable young man, and if you showed up in your dress whites, you'd be an asset to her party, especially with all those ribbons."

They were motoring along Rock Creek Parkway. Even though the windows were cracked open, the inside of the car was hot and humid. Wolfe helped himself to a cigarette. "Oh, by the way, you — that is, Commander Warren Troost — will be transferred from the destroyer *Cooper* in Norfolk, to the AO-15, the *Ashoken*, but will continue to be on detached duty in this area as far as the record goes."

"Any particular reason?" Warren asked.

"The *Cooper* will be joining the Sixth Fleet in the Mediterranean, and about the same time the *Ashoken* is going into dry dock for an overhaul."

Warren puffed on his pipe. "I keep wondering what will happen if by chance I should meet an officer from the ship I'm supposed to be on. I can imagine the scene; he asks me my ship and I tell him and then he says, 'That's my ship. How come I've never seen you on board?' Then what do I do?"

Wolfe blew smoke out of the window, and with a straight face he said, "You've got two choices: either you tell him that you've never seen him aboard either, or have a fainting spell."

Warren laughed.

"You have a third choice."

"I sure as hell hope it's better than the first two."

"I'm not sure it is, but at least it will provide you with a quick switch. If you meet a man who you think is assigned to a ship, ask him what ship he's on first. Then you can just name a different ship."

"I wish I could just be Warren Troost all the time. It would simplify everything."

Wolfe waved the comment aside. "If none of the three saves your butt, find one that does." Then he said, "There is something else I want to discuss with you. You have a friend named Commander Jacob Miller?"

"Yes. Why? Is he coming aboard?" Warren asked. For the last year, Jacob had been assigned as executive officer of the Naval Air Station, New York, known as Floyd Bennett Field in Brooklyn.

"Aside from the fact that he's a hotshot pilot, what do you know about him?"

Warren thought for a few seconds before he asked, "Why the questions about him?"

"Answer mine, please."

"Not much. We're friends. We've known each other since Pearl Harbor. I know he's scheduled for duty in our embassy in Rome as assistant naval attaché."

"Know anything about his politics?"

Warren shook his head. "We don't talk about politics too often when we're together. Our favorite topic is women."

"Nothing wrong with that," Wolfe said.

"Now, will you tell me what this is all about?"

"I can only tell you that Commander Miller's loyalty has been questioned."

"You must be joking!"

"I'm not," Wolfe said, shaking his head. "Someone important in the Navy has raised the question, and as a result a temporary hold has been put on his assignment to Rome."

Warren took the pipe out of his mouth. "Christ, that's ridiculous. Whoever it is must be out of his head. Jacob is as loyal as I am. Christ, he was one of our best fighter pilots!"

"I was told to ask you about him."

"Does he know this is happening?" Warren asked.

"No."

"Are you absolutely sure?" Warren pressed.

"Yes. You know ... I know and only a few other select people who are doing his background check know."

Warren clamped his jaws together and frowned. "I sure as hell would like to know who's behind this idiocy," he muttered.

"I don't know, but whoever it is, he's someone with a lot of influence."

"If I decide to go to Mrs. Martins' garden party, I'm taking Jacob with me!" Warren exclaimed, feeling outraged that his friend's loyalty was being questioned.

"Good idea. Maybe you can come up with something that will lead us to the person who's responsible for creating this problem for Miller."

"It's not because he's a Jew, is it?" Warren asked.

"I'm a Jew," Wolfe answered. "I don't think that's it."

Warren remained silent.

"Well, it's about time we ended this session," Wolfe said, tapping on the sliding glass window above the driver's seat. "I'll take you back to Alexandria before we part."

The chauffeur slid the window open.

"Head across the river to Alexandria," Wolfe said.

"Yes, sir," the man answered.

Jacob and Warren, dressed in white service uniforms, were seated in a Checker cab en route to Greenwich Village. Warren had arrived in Brooklyn late in the afternoon the previous day and had spent the night at Jacob's apartment in an eight-storey building overlooking Prospect Park. After a leisurely dinner at Lundy's, a famous seafood restaurant on Sheepshead Bay, they had spent hours reminiscing about the war and the men they knew who had fought and died in it. Warren had called Jacob two days before to invite him to Mrs. Martins' party, and his friend had been overjoyed to hear from him. Jacob had assured him that with a cabbie's help, they'd have no trouble finding the Martins' house in the Village.

"If you were a drinking man," Jacob said teasingly as the cab entered Manhattan and headed down Canal Street, "we'd make a quick stop in the White Horse Tavern. It's only a couple of blocks from here."

"I really hope you know where the hell we're headed. The houses and the streets all look the same to me."

"If I was able to find the Japanese fleet off Midway, don't you think I'll be able to find the house where your friend lives?"

Warren stared at Jacob and said, "Hey, that's one thing we didn't talk about last night. Did you really find it all by your lonesome?" Warren asked half seriously.

"Well, yes. My squadron was out looking for it. I was the one who got lucky," he said. After a momentary pause, he added, "It almost seems as if that happened in another lifetime."

"I know what you mean," Warren answered, realizing that Jacob unwittingly had given him the opening he'd needed to ask the questions Wolfe wanted answered. "But sometimes that lifetime and this one kind of come together." Before Jacob could respond, he asked, "Jake, you ever have any trouble with your seniors? I sure as hell did. There was Hacker in the beginning and later on Captain Ross. I thought my career was over before it started."

"I guess I was just lucky. I had a few differences, but they never amounted to anything. The guy I had the most trouble with wasn't really Navy anyway," Jacob chuckled.

"What's funny?"

"This guy was from BuOrd, a scientist who was wearing a captain's uniform — a real horse's ass."

"He was with your team in Hiroshima?" Warren guessed.

"He was its leader," Jacob said. "We didn't hit it off from the start, and then it became worse over that woman doctor I introduced you to in Honolulu... But it really didn't mean a thing!"

"Are you talking about the woman, or the captain?"

"Both... 'It was just one of those things,'" Jacob sang flippantly, using Cole Porter's song to describe his brief relationship with Ellen Lane. "And as for the captain, well, I'm sure he's out of the Navy by now ... and back in BuOrd as a high-powered civilian." Warren thought to himself: *That could be the guy*. "You look like the cat that swallowed the canary," Jacob commented.

"I wouldn't know. I can't see myself," Warren said.

As the cab made its way toward Seventh Avenue, the signs of war seemed to have disappeared. People peered out from open windows and sat on slate door stoops. Good Humor ice-cream trucks cruised the streets, and at some corners men sold Italian ices off pushcarts. Soon the tenements gave way to stately brownstones and tree-lined streets.

"According to the address on the card," Jacob said, ending the silence between them, "the house should be about midway down the block." And he gave the cabdriver the number.

"You know," Warren told him, feeling inexplicably nervous, "I don't know why the hell I decided to do this."

"Because you want to see how an artist lives. It's educational!"

Warren made a face. "You wouldn't believe it, but for some reason, I have a premonition. Like something important is about to happen."

"I'm glad it's in your stomach and not in mine!"

"Don't you feel anything?"

"Hot," Jacob answered.

The cab stopped in front of the house, a turn-of-the-century, red sandstone three-storey building with a high stoop and a wrought-iron fence enclosing a small front garden. Along the curb, several very large cars were parked.

"This is the high-rent district," Jacob said irreverently.

"Are you superstitious?" Warren asked, persisting in his uneasiness. "Because I have a feeling about this afternoon. Maybe that's what really brought me here."

"I thought you wanted to see me," Jacob said, trying to lighten Warren's strange mood.

"Beside that."

"Well, all right! Just why *did* you come here?" Jacob asked.

"Just felt I had to."

Jacob adjusted his peaked hat. "Well, there's time to change your mind. We can go back right now to the White House Tavern I mentioned and..."

"Well, I've come this far. I might as well go the whole route," Warren said. Paying off the driver and motioning to

Jacob, he walked up the high steps to the large wooden door. "Standing by?" he asked.

"Standing by, Skipper," Jacob responded.

Warren pressed the bell button. Somewhere deep in the house, chimes played "Pop Goes the Weasel."

"At least your Mrs. Martins has a sense of humor," Jacob commented.

The door opened and Warren found himself looking at a wide-eyed, young black woman wearing a white apron over a black dress.

"Commanders Troost and Miller," Warren said, removing his cap and tucking it under his arm.

"Mrs. Martins, those sailors you've been expectin' are here," the woman called to the rear of the foyer. Flashing a big smile to Warren and Jacob, she said, "Yo' sho 'nuff do look nice in those pretty suits. Lord, I'm glad I don't have the job of keepin' 'em clean!"

"So good of you to come," Mrs. Martins exclaimed, sweeping down on them from the back of the hallway. She wore a loose-fitting, floor-length green gown.

"Please come in. Everyone is outside in the garden. Iris, take their hats."

"This is my friend, Commander Jacob Miller," Warren said.

"A pleasure to have you here," Mrs. Martins said, vigorously pumping Jacob's hand. "Please follow me. I'll introduce you to everyone by making one announcement; then, just circulate and meet people on your own."

Warren was quickly aware that in her own environment, Mrs. Martins was a different person. At the White House she had looked prim and elegant, almost as if she were an old-time girl-school mistress. But now she radiated an air of freedom and vibrancy.

They entered the garden by way of a door at the rear of an enormous drawing room at the back. The large yard was enclosed on three sides by a six-foot-high red brick wall into which arches had been deftly constructed. Chinese lanterns were suspended from tall poles, and in one corner a string quartet was producing soothing background music. Small groups of people sipping drinks were chatting with one another animatedly.

"Ladies and gentlemen," Mrs. Martins said loudly, "please give me your attention for a moment." She had to repeat her request two times before she was able to capture everyone's notice. "Please, your attention. These naval officers are my special guests. This is Commander Jacob Miller and this is Commander Warren Troost."

Immediately, the guests resumed their conversations. "The bar is the far right corner," Mrs. Martins said. "You'll find hors d'oeuvres on tables throughout the garden." Turning to Warren, she added, "Maybe as good as those in the White House! We'll dine a little later, but you're on your own for the moment. Have fun."

Warren thanked her.

"See you in a while," she said and, waving to one of her guests, she called out, "I'll be right there. Warren, when the crowd thins out a bit, I'll show you my studio, if you'd like."

"I'd like that very much," Warren responded as she left them standing on the top step.

"Something cool and spiked would taste real good now," Jacob said. They went down the steps and started to walk across the garden to the bar. "I think I'm going to have a good time here," Jacob commented. "I think — hey, are you listening to me?"

"Do you see that beautiful woman over there?" Warren said, stopping before they reached the bar.

"You're going to have to be more specific, friend. There are a lot of great-looking women here."

"To the right. That elegant strawberry blond with the bare midriff."

"All right, I see her."

"She's gorgeous," Warren exclaimed. His awed tone caused Jacob to glance quickly at his friend. From the expression on his face, Jacob knew that something magical was taking place.

"If you don't pull your eyes back in your head," Jacob told him, "she's going to feel them — oh, oh, she's turning around."

The woman's gaze settled on Warren, and suddenly her face lit up with a lovely smile.

"For God's sakes, Warren, stop staring at her. She's going to think all sailors are the same."

"I'm going to introduce myself right now," Warren said, starting to walk toward her.

Jacob grabbed hold of his friend's arm. "Warren, reverse course!" he exclaimed. "The men with her are looking daggers at you."

Warren pulled his arm away. "Listen, I can handle it." Going directly to her, he said, "Please excuse me, Miss —" He hoped she would give him her name, but the two men with her were glaring at him, and for an awkward moment she remained silent. "I just thought," he stumbled, "that I had met you —"

She came to his rescue with a soft, cultured voice, and said, "I don't think so, Commander. If we had, I would surely remember." She smiled again and turned back to her friends, who seemed about to become nasty over Warren's interruption.

"My mistake. I'm terribly sorry," Warren said, turning back toward Jacob.

"Let's get that drink, Skipper," Jacob said.

Warren allowed himself to be led to the bar. "I don't often react this way to a woman," he explained, drinking the bourbon on the rocks that Jacob ordered for him. "But by God, I know she's something special. I must get to know her."

"I know the feeling. But if I were you, I'd stay clear of her, especially when those big, ugly guys are with her."

"Remember, just before we entered the house, I told you about the weird feeling I was having?"

"I remember."

"Well, now I know why. My intuition was telling me I was about to meet someone who would affect my whole life."

"Your imagination is working overtime!" Jacob responded.

Warren turned to the bartender. "Give me another one of these." Seeing the worry on Jacob's face, he changed the subject. "So how come a guy from Brooklyn drinks bourbon?"

Jacob held his glass in front of him. "Yancy … John Yancy from the deep South started me on it."

"Did I ever meet him?"

Jacob shook his head. "No, you never met him. He died in my arms after he crash-landed on our carrier."

"At Midway?"

"Yes, at Midway."

Warren lifted his glass. "To John Yancy, and all of the other guys who never made it back to enjoy something like this."

"To all of them," Jacob responded, clinking his glass against Warren's.

"How about something to eat?" Warren suggested.

"All right," Jacob said. "Let's see about those hors d'oeuvres our hostess is so proud of."

On the way to the table, though, Mrs. Martins intercepted them and, taking both by the hand, said, "I want you to meet someone, my niece Hilary. Do you mind?"

"Not in the least," Warren answered.

She took them in tow and brought them to the far side of the garden, where two men were standing. "Commander Troost was my escort when I was last at the White House," she told the two men.

"Sidney Robbins," the taller of the two said, offering his hand to Warren.

"Walter Ray," the other man said, shaking Jacob's hand. "It's a pleasure to meet you."

Both men were reporters. Robbins for the *Daily News* and Ray for the *PM*.

Robbins was the more aggressive of the two and immediately wanted to know how each man had earned their Navy crosses. "I bet you're surprised that I can recognize the various medals represented by the *fruit salad* you men are wearing."

"Not in the least," Warren answered, resenting the man's patronizing tone.

"Readers always want to know about heroes," Ray said.

"I'm sorry," Warren answered, "but I can't help you. The war is long over!"

"Commander?" Robbins asked, looking at Jacob.

"Commander Troost is senior to me," he answered, suppressing a smile, "and if he can't help you, I certainly can't."

"Mrs. Martins," Warren asked turning to his hostess, who seemed to be enjoying the growing conflict between the men, "didn't you say there was someone you wanted us to meet?"

"Absolutely," she answered. "My niece Hilary... Sorry, guys," she said. Taking Warren and Jacob in tow, she started across the garden. "Now where is that girl? She was here just a few moments ago." Halfway across the patio, she paused and looked around. Smiling broadly, she exclaimed, "Ah, there she is."

They were headed directly toward the young woman whom Warren had approached a short time before. He looked questioningly at Jacob.

"Why not?" Jacob said.

"'Why not' what?" Mrs. Martins asked before Warren could answer.

"It's just our Navy way of talking to each other," Jacob answered lamely, hoping Warren would follow through with a more sensible reply.

"'Why not,'" Warren said, "means that we can't wait to meet your niece."

Mrs. Martins laughed as though she understood and then called out, "Hilary dear."

"Excuse me," Hilary said to the men she was with and approached them. "Yes, Auntie?"

As she came close, Warren's pulse began to pound. He was enthralled by her. All the women he had been with in the past, even Irene, suddenly paled in his memory and he wanted this girl. Without warning, he was in love. Hilary smiled as her gaze met his, and Warren felt a wave of joy throughout his frame as he recognized the warm response in her look.

"I would appreciate it if you introduce these young men to some of the other young people here," Mrs. Martins said.

"We really wouldn't want to impose —" Warren began, stumbling.

"I'll be delighted," Hilary cut in, not taking her admiring gaze off him. It was almost as though she and Warren were alone in the garden. Jacob sensed the attraction between the two and planned to move away as soon as politely possible.

"I'll leave you with Hilary," Mrs. Martins said.

For several seconds, there was an awkward silence until Warren said, "I had no idea you were Mrs. Martin's niece. I am glad that I met her and she invited me — us here."

"I'm happy about that, too," Hilary murmured without hesitation.

Warren's cheeks burned. He felt as if he were a schoolboy again.

"Come," Hilary said, "let's please my aunt and have you both meet some of these people and —"

"That will be great," Warren said and, turning to Jacob, added with mock seriousness, "What will you be doing, Jake, while we're doing that?"

"For Chrissakes," Jacob muttered, feigning anger, "who needs an enemy with a friend like you?" He left Hilary and Warren standing alone, gazing at each other.

By eight, the number of guests had thinned out, and Warren and Hilary sat in a corner of the garden on a wrought-iron loveseat. He had discovered that she was a high-fashion model and had often been on the covers of *Vogue* and *Harper's Bazaar* as well as several European magazines.

"Of course, there will come a time when new faces come on the scene, and I will give up being in front of the camera," Hilary said as she discussed the future. "Eventually, I'd like to become involved with the publishing end of the business. Become an editor."

"I don't know a thing about that life," Warren told her. "The only thing I know is the Navy."

"And I don't know a thing about the Navy," Hilary countered, "other than it has boats."

"Ships," he laughed.

"Ships," she repeated, smiling that intimate smile at him.

"Listen," he said, taking her hand in his, "I must see you again." His voice was edged with emotion.

Hilary frowned. "I want that, too. But I must tell you, I've been seeing a man on a steady basis," she said. "Usually he's with me, but tonight he couldn't be here... Now everything seems changed."

Warren, not understanding the meaning of her last words, let go of her hand. "It was stupid of me not to think there would be a man in your life." He managed a weak smile. "I really do want to thank you for making this evening something special for me." And he stood up.

"Where are you going?"

"To find Jacob, say our goodbyes to your aunt, and head for the nearest bar," he said. "I've probably made more of a fool of myself in the few hours I've been here than I have in years."

Hilary rose and sidled up to him. "And that's it?"

"There's nothing else, is there?"

She bit her lower lip.

"You tell me, is there?" Warren demanded.

"Will you take me home?" she asked in a whisper.

Startled, Warren looked toward the house. "I thought you lived here?"

"I have an apartment on Riverside Drive. Will you take me home?"

"Are you sure that's what you want?" Warren asked in disbelief. His heart skipped a beat and then raced.

She nodded.

Warren took a deep breath and, emboldened by her response, said, "I don't have to be back in Washington until Tuesday morning."

"You're not giving me any leeway."

"Only if you want some," Warren answered.

Again she bit her lower lip. "This isn't the way it's supposed to happen. I have never before met a man for the first time and hours later ended up in bed with him." Her eyes searched his face, seeking understanding.

"I don't know how it's supposed to happen," Warren said. "I only know that from the moment I saw you, I wanted you. And not for just one night … not for just days!"

"Yes, I believe that," she whispered again.

"Do you still want me to take you home?" he asked.

"Take me home!" Hilary said.

Warren expelled a long breath, smiled and said, "I'll tell Jacob he'll be going home alone!"

Hilary's eyes were closed, and her face was turned slightly to the right. In the soft light of the night table lamp, he could see a soft flush on her neck and her breasts. He nuzzled the underside of her jaw.

She smiled and her eager mouth sought his. He thrust gently into her.

Her lips parted and she moaned softly.

Warren put his lips to one nipple, then to the other.

She wrapped her legs around his. "Go faster," she begged in a breathy voice. "Yes. Oh, yes!"

Warren could feel Hilary's beautiful body tense as she turned her face up to his. He pressed his hungry mouth against hers and she slid her tongue in. Then she whispered urgently, "Do it to me. Oh do it! Do it!" The next instant she thrust herself up against him and, raking his back with her nails, she cried out for more.

Warren's senses fused into an explosion of pleasure that roared from his groin to the top of his head to the tips of his toes and with a cry of ecstasy, he buried his face between her warm, moist breasts. He was finally able to think about Irene without that old, overwhelming feeling of despair. She had become part of his past, and though he would never forget her, the memory of what might have been between them had been suddenly exorcised.

"You're very quiet," Hilary commented after a while.

"Resting," he answered evasively.

He rolled to her side and caressed her bare breasts. He heard himself saying, "Suppose I asked you to marry me, what would you say?"

"I'd say, 'Wow! what a fast worker!' In fact, I might think you're crazy," Hilary murmured.

"I see your point," Warren said. "But you know that old adage, don't you, that says, 'The arrival of one swallow doesn't make it spring.'"

"I'm not sure I know that one."

"Well, even if you don't, it could just as easily be said that one wonderful roll in the sack doesn't make a marriage!"

"I'm inclined to agree," Hilary said as she relaxed in his arms.

"But there're always exceptions to every rule," Warren offered. "I mean, it's as good a starting place as any... At least two people who have that going for them don't have to worry about that part, do they?"

"That seems reasonable."

He glided his hand from her breast to her cheek. "But just suppose I did ask you to marry me. What would you say?"

Drawing him to her, she whispered huskily, "I'd say, 'Keep talking. You're convincing me.'"

Warren sucked in his breath and, when he exhaled, said, "Darling Hilary, even if it's crazy, please marry me. I won't be able to live without you!"

"Bedded and wedded all in one night," Hilary laughed.

"What is that supposed to mean?"

"It means that I'm as crazy as you!" Hilary said. "Yes! I'll marry you, but only if you make love to me again, right now, so at least I'll know the first time wasn't all there is!"

"I can assure you, it wasn't all there is!" Warren sighed, wrapping her in his arms again.

CHAPTER 13

"Are you sure you have everything?" Tony asked. He had one arm around Miriam's shoulders and his other hand resting on his son Mike's head. Little Mike, named after Tony's uncle, clung to his father's winter overcoat. A December wind could be heard swirling around the house in the early-morning twilight.

"Jacob will be here about noon, and Warren and Hilary are coming in on the 4:15," Miriam said.

Tony smiled. "It'll be good to be together for Christmas. Dad, Mom, and Uncle Mike should be here by six, and we should be able to sit down to dinner by seven thirty at the very latest." He reached down, and, picking the little boy up, swung him high over his head. "Da, Da, Da!" Mike squealed in delight.

He brought his son level with his face. "Okay, Mikey, give Daddy a special Mikey kiss."

"Tiss, tiss," Mike said and, throwing his small arms around Tony's neck, he rubbed his nose against his father's.

"Wait until you see what I got you for Christmas," Tony said, putting the tot down on the floor. "God, I love that boy."

"I'd never know that unless you told me," Miriam responded archly.

Tony gathered her into his arms. "And I love you too," he said, kissing her and at the same time slipping his hand inside the top of her housecoat to caress her breast.

She held her hand over his.

"If I hold you any longer, I'll never get that boat to sea. I've got a full day of training for my guys ahead of me," he said, letting go of her. "I'll be back between five and six." He opened the door. "Hey, it's snowing. I can't remember the last time there was snow for Christmas."

"Be careful!" Miriam called after him.

Without looking back, Tony waved; then, pulling up his high collar, he bent into the blowing wind.

Tony and his XO, Lieutenant Wally Exman, were on the open bridge of the *Diablo*, a Trench-class submarine. A light, wind-driven snow limited visibility, but not enough to cancel the boat's schedule at sea.

"We'll commence our planned dives as soon as we get to deep water, off Montauk Point," Tony said, catching a glimpse of Race Point on Fishers Island, a thousand yards off the port bow. From time to time, spray enveloped the bridge as the *Diablo* plunged across Long Island Sound toward the open sea.

"Aye, aye, Skipper," Exman said, adding, "what a lousy day."

Tony checked the lookouts in the after part of the bridge. Two sailors in foul-weather gear were peering through binoculars, scanning ahead as best they could in the murky weather. "You men keep a sharp lookout," he cautioned them.

"Yes, sir," they answered in unison.

"They're part of the student crew," Exman explained.

Tony nodded. Today he had student submariners, both officer and enlisted, on board for instruction in diving operations. Out of a normal complement of a hundred enlisted men, fifteen were students — three officers and twelve enlisted — in their last phase of training before being assigned to fleet submarines.

An hour passed and the *Diablo* began to pitch heavily as she approached Montauk Point on her starboard bow and entered the Atlantic. The open bridge was becoming untenable.

"Skipper," a talker said, "radar reports a target bearing zero-five-zero. Range ten thousand yards. Speed ten knots."

"Get a course on her," Tony said.

The talker repeated the order.

"Probably a coaster," Exman commented, "or a tug."

"The contact's course is one-five-zero," the talker reported.

"That will put him well behind us," Tony said. "We'll keep course one-two-zero. I make Montauk Point abeam of us to starboard six thousand yards. We can start our dives anytime now. We'll snorkel to begin with."

Tony pressed the Klaxon control button for several seconds and as soon as its scream died, he said into his 1MC microphone, "Dive. Dive. Dive. Rig for snorkel."

The lookouts swung down from their perches.

"Clear the bridge," Tony ordered. "Clear the bridge."

The men dropped through the bridge hatch.

Tony was the last man off the bridge. He pulled the hatch down behind him, and the chief quartermaster dogged it down as both took their places in the conning tower.

The bow planes were rigged out, and the *Diablo's* bow began to pitch downward. The roar of boat's powerful diesels reverberated throughout the boat as the snorkel stack was extended.

"Periscope depth," Tony ordered, quickly removing his foul-weather gear. "We'll continue to snorkel for a while."

"Periscope depth," the dive control officer called back from the control room.

Tony listened to the opening and closing of valves throughout the ship as air was vented from ballast tanks and replaced by seawater. He watched the depth-gauge needle move clockwise. They were down twenty-five feet. Periscope depth was fifty-five.

"Coming to periscope depth," the diving officer in the control room called out.

The depth gauge registered forty feet.

The needle eased downward as Tony checked the boat's level. The inclinometer bubble was coming to center.

"Periscope depth," the DCO announced.

Tony smiled, nodded, and called out, "On the money." Then he turned to Exman. "Have the officer students report to the bridge. When they get here, take the conn while I give them a few pointers about the use of the periscope."

From his station, Exman switched on the 1MC. "Now hear this. Now hear this. Ensigns Baxter, Rice, and Sheer report to the bridge."

Within a minute, the three men were by Tony's side as he stood in front of the periscope. "Good morning, gentlemen," he said, smiling at them. "It's a pleasure to have you aboard today. This will be your last at-sea class until after the Christmas holidays. The next time we go out, it will be for a period of ten days during which will be included protracted attack situations. Right now, we are snorkeling at fifty-five feet — periscope depth. We are running on diesel power and charging our batteries at the same time. When we dive deeper, we will shut down the diesels and run on the boat's electric motors." During the past year and a half, Tony had said more or less the same thing to hundreds of students and had monitored dozens of practice dives. He enjoyed teaching his skills as much as he had enjoyed learning and using them himself. "As soon as we reach our assigned area, each of you will take the conn, bring the boat to the surface, and then back down to a cruising depth of two hundred feet. Each of you will surface and submerge the ship two times, and each of you will take turns later today conning her on the way back to our berth

227

in New London. Any questions…? None? All right then, let's see how this periscope works."

For the next half hour, the three young officers practiced raising and lowering the scope and scanning the horizon under Tony's supervision.

"Skipper, we've reached our designated area," Exman called.

Tony turned his attention back to his students. "Which of you wants to take the conn first?"

"I will —" Rice began.

Suddenly, a powerful explosion shook the *Diablo* from stem to stern. Tony and all hands in the conning tower were thrown to the deck as acrid smoke began to filter into the control room and conning tower.

"I have the conn," Tony shouted, scrambling to his feet and descending into the control room. He picked up the 1MC microphone and shouted, "General quarters, general quarters. All hands man your battle stations." Then, turning to the diving control officer, he ordered, "Surface! Surface! Shut down the diesels. Retract the snorkel."

"Fire in the forward battery room!" blared the control-room speaker box.

Another explosion rocked the *Diablo*, and the lights dimmed. Tony was slammed against the bulkhead. A burst of pain made him look at his right arm. The skin was torn open and the jagged edge of a broken bone protruded out of the wound. He was bleeding profusely.

"Skipper, damage control reports that we are taking on water and the bilge pumps are having trouble keeping up," Exman called.

This was Tony's worst nightmare realized. He staggered to his feet. Could he cope with this disaster?

"Damage control reports hydrogen-gas explosion in the forward battery compartment," a talker said. "Three dead and two missing."

Tony shook his head. He didn't want to hear anymore. He wanted to close his eyes and let whatever was going to happen, happen.

"Skipper, get a tourniquet around your arm before you pass out," Exman said.

Tony looked down at his bloody arm. He felt unreal, and the specter of Captain Yoshida in that prison camp long ago floated before his dazed eyes.

"Skipper, we're going down!" he heard Exman exclaim.

The depth gauge showed sixty feet, and the needle was moving clockwise.

Tony shook his head hard, and with a massive mental effort his mind began to clear. By God, he was going to survive this just as he had survived that bastard Yoshida! "Blow all ballast," he ordered. "Dive control, we have to get to the surface."

"Without the forward batteries, sir, our ballast pumps are laboring," Exman reported. "If we can put some way on the ship, the dive planes will help us up."

"All ahead full," Tony ordered. "Get those electric motors going."

"Skipper, engineering says we can't make more than two knots. Not enough juice," the engine-room signalman reported.

As Tony watched the depth-gauge needle move ever so slowly deeper, smoke and fumes were becoming heavy in the control room. "Oxygen breathers for all hands," Tony ordered. His arm throbbed.

"Skipper, we've got to lighten her," the diving officer called out. "We're at six-five feet. We need more electric power for our ballast pumps."

"Damage control, can you get us more juice on the ballast pumps?" Tony asked over the 1MC.

"They're trying," Exman said, answering the phone linked to the damage control center. "The fire is out in the forward battery compartment, but it's destroyed. Won't be any use for power. And we've lost contact with the forward torpedo room."

"Be sure that battery room is sealed off from the rest of the ship."

"There might be someone still alive in there," Exman reminded him.

"Seal off the forward battery compartment," Tony snapped. The source of the smoke had to be isolated and the risk of another explosion eliminated.

"Let me get something on that arm," a pharmacist mate said, approaching Tony.

"Have you taken care of the other men?" Tony asked, squinting at him.

"You need a bandage at least, sir."

"Skipper, let him do it," Exman said.

"Do it quickly," Tony responded, holding out his arm.

"Aye, aye, sir. Hold still. This will control the bleeding," the pharmacist mate said.

Exman handed Tony an oxygen breather. Tony waved it away with his good arm. He took several deep breaths and began to cough.

"Take it!" Exman exclaimed.

Tony nodded and, allowing Exman to put the breather mask over his nose, he breathed deeply. Then he said to the three students, "Lay aft and lend a hand wherever it's needed."

"Skipper," the talker said, "damage control reports ballast pumps are beginning to take effect."

Tony looked at the depth gauge. The needle remained stationary at sixty-five. Suddenly realizing how much he was sweating, Tony drew his right arm across his brow, and as he lowered it, he looked at the ship's clock. Less than ten minutes had passed since the initial explosion.

"Moving up, Skipper," Exman said.

Tony saw the jittery needle; it slipped counter clockwise to sixty feet, then fifty-five and hung there. At fifty-five feet, the tip of the radio antenna was out of the water. "Send a May Day," he said, "and keep sending until we get an acknowledgment."

Exman phoned the order to the radio officer.

"Skipper, engine-room says if we keep the ballast pumps going like they are, the best they can give is fourteen hundred rpm," the talker reported.

"That's enough to hold steerageway," Tony responded, pursing his lips. He had to use the electric motors to help drive the boat to the surface. "Go to fourteen hundred rpm," he finally said.

"May Day acknowledged," Exman reported.

"Fourteen hundred rpm," the engine-room talker said.

Tony took several deep breaths of oxygen. Smoke was beginning to clear in the control room.

The damage control officer came in. His face and hands were streaked with dirt. "Skipper, unless I get more power on those ballast pumps, they're going to burn out."

"We're down to fourteen hundred rpm," Tony answered.

"Those pumps need more juice."

Tony pursed his lips. "All stop," he ordered.

"All stop answered," the engine-room talker said.

"And just to be on the safe side," the DCO said, "we must cut the use of all unnecessary lighting."

"Shut all unnecessary lights," Tony ordered into the 1MC. He looked at Exman. "Keep the lighting here to a minimum."

"Aye, aye, Skipper."

The depth-gauge needle began to jiggle again, and this time Tony could feel the movement of the boat. She was moving through thirty feet…

"Stand by to surface," Tony ordered over the 1MC. "Start the diesels."

The depth-gauge needle swung into the green portion of the dial. The bridge hatch was thrown open, and a rush of cold, clean air filled the conning tower and control room. The diesels coughed, then began to roar.

"Open all deck hatches," Tony ordered as he clambered up to the open bridge. "And get somebody into that torpedo room to see what happened." Then he filled his lungs with the bracing air and slowly exhaled.

Moments later, the deck hatch over the forward torpedo room was thrown open, and one of the deck detail lowered himself into the space. With his teeth clenched, Tony waited impatiently for the man to reappear. After what seemed an interminable time, the top of the man's head appeared and before his face showed, he could be heard yelling, "They're alive, Skipper. They're all alive."

"XO, signal New London Port Control," Tony said with a sigh of relief, "that we're coming in under our own power."

"Aye, aye, Skipper," Exman answered with a smile.

Tony braced himself against the wind. He'd finally beaten Yoshida.

Under the bright white lights of the dock at the New London Submarine Base, a crowd of people waited silently for the *Diablo* to arrive. Besides the Navy officials there were several local politicians as well as a dozen reporters for New York and Boston papers.

Miriam clutched Jacob's right arm while Tony's parents and his Uncle Mike stood silently beside her. Warren was next to them. It was nine o'clock, and still no one had sighted the wounded sub.

"If they would only tell us something," Tony's father complained. "We've been waiting here for hours, and all we know is that the submarine is on its way in."

No one answered him.

"I hope little Mikey doesn't give Hilary a hard time," Miriam commented to Jacob. "You know she's over six months pregnant."

Overhearing her, Warren said grimly, "Don't worry, she'll be okay. She's glad to help out."

"You can't believe what this is like for me," Miriam said. "I must have dreamt just such a scene as this every time he went out for dive exercises. There is no such thing as a routine dive, is there?"

Jacob tightened his hold on his sister. For some reason, that plaintive question reminded him of Connie. He'd never told Miriam or his mother how Connie had been killed.

The screech of sirens came nearer. Then four ambulances approached and the Shore Patrol cleared a path through the throng for them to move onto the dock.

"That means there are casualties!" Mr. Trapasso said.

"Don't talk that way!" Mike told him. "Tony is all right!"

Suddenly a man came up to them. "I'm from the *Daily Mirror* in New York," he said, looking at Miriam. "I was told your husband is the *Diablo*'s captain."

"Yes," she answered.

"Is there anything you would like to say?"

"I hope everyone is safe," Miriam answered.

"Did your husband have any misgivings about —"

"That's it!" Jacob snapped. "She said what she had to say."

"Who are you?" the reporter asked.

Warren stepped forward. "I don't think you want to continue this interrogation under the circumstances," he said in a flat voice.

The reporter looked at him for a moment, nodded, and walked away.

"You'll have to face reporters," Jacob said to his sister, "whether you want to or not."

"You mean whether Tony is dead or alive, don't you?" she asked in a whimper.

Jacob uttered a deep sigh before he said, "Why don't you just wait and see —"

"Because I'm not you," Miriam answered. "Because I'm afraid of what will happen to me if he is dead. Because, I love him and —"

"Let me have her," Tony's mother said, leaving her husband's side and gathering Miriam in her arms. "Tony will be all right," she assured her. "You'll see, he'll be all right. There will be plenty of time to give him more sons."

Suddenly Miriam began to weep.

"You'll see," her mother-in-law cooed, switching to Italian. "You'll see I'm right."

"But I'm pregnant, Mama!" she cried.

"Does Tony know?" her mother-in-law asked in surprise.

"I was going to tell him tonight," Miriam wept. "We wanted another child."

"Everything will be fine," the older woman said, stroking Miriam's head. "You'll see, everything will turn out all right."

"I'm so frightened!" Miriam cried. "So frightened!"

In the distance, the throbbing sound of diesels became audible. "It's the *Diablo*," a woman yelled. "It's the *Diablo*!"

Through the darkness the red and green side lights of the boat appeared, and the crowd on the dock started to herd toward its edge.

"Please move back," a voice said over a bullhorn. "Please move back."

The crowd complied as corpsmen carrying stretchers left the ambulances and filed to the edge of the dock. Suddenly, the *Diablo*'s dark form emerged clearly in the darkness and motored slowly to the lighted pier.

"Can you see Tony?" Miriam asked, using a handkerchief to wipe her eyes.

"I'm not sure," Jacob answered. "There are men on the bridge."

The throb of the diesels stopped.

"Stand by to take fore and aft lines," someone called from the *Diablo*'s bridge.

"Was that Tony?" Jacob asked.

"I'm not sure," Miriam answered. "It didn't sound like him."

It took several more minutes to dock the *Diablo* and place a gangway over to her black hull. The corpsmen boarded her before she was completely tied up, followed by several submarine base officers.

"I see him!" Miriam shouted. "I see Tony! He's on the bridge!"

"Thank God! He's alive!" his mother cried in Italian. "Oh, thank you, Jesus, thank you for this miracle."

"He's been hurt," Miriam exclaimed. "There's a bandage on his left arm."

The corpsmen reappeared on deck with three stretchers, each with a black body bag lashed to it. They were followed by those injured men who were ambulatory.

"It's going to be a while before Tony will be able to leave the boat," Jacob commented.

"I'll wait," Mike said. "You can go back to the house if you want to, but I'm not moving till I see and talk to him."

Jacob didn't answer. From Miriam he'd learned about the close relationship between Tony and his Uncle Mike.

Members of the *Diablo*'s crew began to come ashore and were reunited with members of their tearful but thankful families. Reporters swarmed around them and after several minutes, the *Diablo*'s officers began to come ashore, led by Tony.

Miriam broke away from her mother-in-law and ran to him, followed by the rest of the family.

"Tony!" Miriam called. "Tony!"

He stopped and, using his right arm, brought her close and kissed her. "Everything is all right."

She looked down at his bandaged arm. "My God, what happened?"

"Just a bad fracture," he said soothingly. "I'll have it taken care of. But I'll be home for sure later tonight."

"Tony!" his mother cried and took him in her arms. "I knew you'd be safe," she said excitedly in Italian.

His father hugged him. "You had us worried there for a while," he said. "You really did."

"I was worried myself for a while, Papa."

Mike came up to him. "This is all the Christmas present I want," he said, hugging his nephew tightly.

"I beat Yoshida," Tony whispered in Mike's ear. "I beat him when the chips were down. Just like you said I could."

Mike grinned and gently slapped him on the back.

Jacob and Warren shook Tony's hand warmly and embraced him.

"Listen," Tony said, "Papa, you take Mama and everyone else home. I have to go to the hospital and have my arm fixed. I'll be home as soon as I can. But first I have to take care of some sad business."

"You should be with your family as soon as the doctors let you go," his mother scolded.

"Mama, I lost some men today," he said gently. "Some of them have family here. I must see those people tonight. It's my duty to do that."

"Oh Tony!" Miriam exclaimed.

"All right," Mr. Trapasso said, "we're all going home. Come on, let's go. My admiral has given the order."

Miriam looked up at Tony. "I love you," she said.

"I love you," he answered, kissing her again. "Now go home and tell Mikey I'll be home soon." He watched them until they were off the dock, then turned and walked to the ambulance.

CHAPTER 14

On his birthday, February 22, 1947, Jacob received orders appointing him naval attaché at the U.S. Embassy in Rome. This came as a real surprise, since he had expected to be ordered only as assistant attaché. He guessed the change resulted from his promotion to full commander a short time before.

Two days later, in a briefing on his new duties at the Office of Naval Intelligence, he was told that on occasion he'd be expected to travel in civilian clothes — in mufti — to other countries bordering the Mediterranean. During these excursions, he would gather military information on activities of "our friends" that might not otherwise be available.

The briefing lasted two hours; then he reported to the State Department, where a man in the Italian affairs section explained that part of his duties would be "ceremonial in nature on behalf of the Ambassador" but he also would be deeply involved in helping to finalize plans for rebuilding and modernizing the Italian navy.

On the morning of March 13, Jacob entered a huge room whose highly polished wooden floor reflected the sunlight streaming through the windows. The walls were hung with massive oil paintings in gilt frames. He presented his orders to the American ambassador, Byron Fairfax III, the former board chairman of Chemoil Products, of Wilmington, Delaware. Jacob had been told that Fairfax was one man who really looked ambassadorial, and played the role with such flair that few people realized he was not a career diplomat.

Fairfax was a lean, elegant man in a finely tailored dark silk suit. He rose from behind an ornately carved fruitwood desk with a gleaming top to shake Jacob's hand.

"You'll find, Commander," the ambassador said as Jacob seated himself in a chair in front of the desk, "that your duties here will not require any special effort on your part. Rome isn't the most politically sensitive spot in Europe right now, thank God, but it certainly is one of the most enjoyable." He smiled, showing even, sparkling white teeth. "You will be required to attend various official functions and, of course, there will be the usual routine reports to me and to your office of Naval Intelligence, which you should find not too demanding. The Italians are war-weary and they are mostly interested in getting on with the process of living and enjoying post-war life. You might even begin to think they are willing to leave the game of international intrigue to other players." He removed a gold cigarette case from the inside pocket of his jacket. "Care to try one?" he asked, extending the cigarette case toward Jacob. "They're Egyptian."

"Thank you, sir," Jacob answered. "I will."

"Take a few days to settle in," Fairfax told him, fitting his cigarette into a white ivory holder, "and then come see me if you need anything." He smiled again and asked, "Do you speak Italian?"

"No, sir," Jacob said, letting the smoke flow out of his nose. The cigarette was considerably stronger than any American brand.

"Any foreign language?"

"I had three years of college French and one of German."

Fairfax nodded. "With that background and some effort, you should be able to pick up enough Italian to take care of your everyday needs. You'll find the Italians much more tolerant of linguistic shortcomings than the French. And we have excellent courses right here in the embassy."

"I plan to learn the language as quickly as possible," Jacob assured the ambassador.

Fairfax nodded and said, "The only thing I have to add to what I have already told you is that you have one of the best assignments for a young naval officer in all Europe, but whether or not you will agree will depend, of course, on your perception of what 'best' is. I can tell you this: if you are looking for action as you have known it in the past, you may wish you were somewhere else. But if you can appreciate what is here — Italy is a living museum — you'll enjoy your assignment immensely. Welcome aboard!"

Fairfax concluded the meeting by shaking Jacob's hand again and telling him in a confidential, light tone, "When you shop, bargain for everything. Never pay the first price."

Using his diplomatic passport for identification, Jacob rented a three-room apartment on Via Pinciana, a small street opposite the Villa Borghese. The apartment was within walking distance of the embassy, located on the Via Veneto. He found that his new duties allowed him considerable free time, which he used to explore the city and the surrounding countryside. He spent an hour a day studying Italian in the embassy with several other embassy personnel taught by an Italian who spoke excellent English. He made occasional trips in mufti to Florence, Verona, Venice, and the region around Lake Garda to see if there was anything of military interest in those areas to report. He even labored through Gibbon's *The Rise and Fall of the Roman Empire*.

During his travels in Italy, Jacob soon learned that the ambassador had been right: the Italians wanted to forget about the war, even though signs of it were still in evidence almost everywhere but in Rome. For some reason, the German Army had not stood and fought in that city. There were places in the countryside in the north, near the Arno River and in the south around Anzio, however, where there were still burned-out German and American tanks in the fields.

Late one August afternoon, Jacob happened to be walking back to his apartment by way of the Spanish Steps. A lovely old fountain in the shape of a huge boat spewed streams of water high into the air. To the right, a flower vendor sold small bouquets of red and white roses; on the left stood the small house with whitewashed walls where the English poet John Keats had died. The sun-drenched steps were crowded with people enjoying the exquisite summer day as it dissolved into the long shadows of evening.

Climbing to the top, Jacob paused and looked back at the lovely scene below him. He was about to continue when a sudden gust of wind blew a wide-brimmed white straw hat off the head of a young woman halfway up the steps. The hat, caught in the breeze, sailed into the piazza in front of the church at the top, and came to rest a few feet from Jacob. Dashing after it, he picked it up.

The young woman breathlessly reached the top of the steps in pursuit of her hat. Jacob started toward her and, very much aware of her long russet hair, suddenly recognized the girl and came to an amazed stop.

She saw him and return recognition lighted in her eyes.

"I can't believe this! Aren't you Tara Hasse?" Jacob asked.

She smiled. "And you're Commander Miller, right?"

He nodded and extended the hat to her. The last time they had seen each other had been in Honolulu after he'd returned from Hiroshima. It was the night she'd been with Warren and he'd been with Ellen. If only he could remember the name of the restaurant where they had met so he could say something clever.

"Thanks a lot," she said. "I was afraid I'd lost it for good."

For a moment, neither of them spoke; then simultaneously each asked the other, "What are you doing here?"

"Please," Jacob said, "you tell me first."

"I'm here to study art," she said. "I've only been here two weeks. Now you tell me what you are doing here."

"I'm the naval attaché."

"I almost didn't know you in civilian clothes," she said with a shy smile.

"I wear my uniform only on official occasions," he explained somewhat lamely. He felt tongue-tied in the presence of this attractive young woman. "Other times, I dress like this."

"Just yesterday," Tara continued animatedly, "I received a letter from Warren telling me all about his son, Andrew, who will soon be four months old. You know Warren and I are real good friends."

"I remember. I was with Warren and Hilary last Christmas," Jacob said, thankful for a topic he knew something about. "We were at my brother-in-law's house in New London."

She nodded. "Yes, Warren wrote me about it and, of course, I read about your friend Tony's accident in the newspaper."

"Do you still make your home in Honolulu?" Jacob asked, wanting desperately to avoid any subject that might bring a quick end to this chance meeting.

Tara shook her head, and the movement caused her long hair to swirl from side to side. "I'll be in Italy for the next year, and then maybe I'll move to New York."

Out of the blue, Jacob remembered something that might prolong the conversation. "I read your mother's last book, *No Better World*. You must be very proud of her," he blurted.

"Yes, I am," Tara answered. "But it's sometimes hard to reconcile the mother with the writer in my own mind."

As he gazed at Tara, Jacob knew he didn't want to go back to his apartment and spend the evening alone, or, for that matter, with any of the other women he had been seeing. "Listen," he said, "if you don't have a dinner date tonight, how about having dinner with me? I know a few very good restaurants."

"I'd like that very much," Tara answered.

Jacob looked at his watch. It was only five thirty. Most of the restaurants would not open until seven. He glanced down at the fountain and saw a carriage horse drinking from it. "I have an idea," he said. "Suppose we take a carriage ride before dinner?"

She smiled in delight. "I've wanted to do that from the first day I arrived, but didn't have the guts to do it alone."

Jacob bowed from the waist and, speaking in Italian, he said, "Let's go, Miss Hasse. Your carriage awaits you."

She laughed. "That sounds very romantic … especially in Italian."

"I'm afraid the New York accent is still there," he commented, taking her hand and leading her down the steps. When they reached the bottom of the steps, he guided her to the flower vendor. "Which bouquet would you like?"

"You really don't have to —"

"I must," Jacob said. "With me it's a compulsion. Whenever I take a beautiful lady for a ride in a carriage, she must carry a bouquet."

"In that case," Tara answered, "I'll just have to choose one, won't I?"

"Yes."

"These look lovely," she said, pointing to a small cluster of red and white roses.

Jacob handed the bouquet to her and paid the vendor.

A few minutes later, they were seated in the rear of an open carriage that moved slowly away from the Spanish Steps.

For the next month, Jacob met Tara at every opportunity. They went to dinner and visited museums and the ruins of the Colosseum, where they were surprised to see thousands of cats. Together they explored the narrow streets of the Trastevere, where elements of Rome's underworld lived and thrived. They walked through almost empty streets of the old Jewish ghetto and stood for a long time in a deserted synagogue. When they were back on the street again, Jacob told Tara that his father had hoped he would become a rabbi, but he had wanted to fly. He spoke about his mother and sister and Tony. He even told her about his love for Connie.

Bit by bit, Tara revealed her innermost thoughts to him: her need to become an artist, to paint, how hurt she'd felt when she discovered that her mother and Warren's father had been lovers. Jacob found himself wanting to touch her whenever he was with her. When they were apart, she filled his thoughts.

One rainy Sunday afternoon Tara invited Jacob to her apartment, a three-room flat on the top floor of a four-story building behind the Piazza Navona. When he arrived, he found her dressed in blue slacks and a white short-sleeved blouse. There was wine, cheese, and freshly toasted bread on the table.

Jacob sat down at the table and sniffed the air: it was redolent with a spicy smell.

"I have a chicken in the oven," she explained. "But it's for dinner."

"Smells mighty good," he said, lighting a cigarette. "You never mentioned you could cook, or even liked to. I'm learning something new about you every day."

"I don't mind doing it when the spirit moves me," she said lightly.

"And, obviously, today the spirit moves you," Jacob joked. "Now, do you suppose that same spirit, or something like it, might move you to let me see some of your paintings?"

"Do you really want to see them?"

"I do," he said emphatically.

"All right," Tara said, taking his hand. "Come with me." And she led him into a small room with large windows along one end that she'd converted into a studio. "It has a northern exposure," she said, "which means that the light is at almost the same intensity throughout the day." She let go of his hand. "You stand over there against that wall, and I'll set the paintings up against this wall."

Jacob liked them. Some were still lifes, full of reds, yellows, oranges, and bright green. Others were pastoral scenes along with several portraits. "They're vibrant," he told her. "They're really good."

"You have the eye of an art critic," she teased with a smile.

"To show you that I'm willing to back my statement with hard cash, I'd like to buy this one," he said, and picked up an unframed self-portrait of her in which she was standing nude in front of a mirror.

"You don't have to buy it," she said, suddenly blushing. "I'll give it to you."

Jacob shook his head. "I want to pay —"

"No, I want you to have it," Tara exclaimed, her voice going up in pitch.

Jacob looked at her, and put the painting down. She was trembling. "Is anything wrong?" he asked, taking hold of her hands. His heart began to pound.

"I'm all right," Tara answered; then looking straight at him, she said, "You chose the one painting that I have been planning to give to you. Do you think I'm wicked?"

"I'll have it framed and put it up in my bedroom. That's where you ... er, it belongs."

Color came into her cheeks.

"Listen," Jacob said, "I've been thinking about us for days now."

"I have too," she admitted.

"I hoped you would," he said, suddenly having difficulty breathing. "Tara, I'm in love with you. I mean, I want to be with you ... all the time."

"I want to be with you," she whispered.

Jacob wrapped his arms around her and, drawing her to him, he kissed her passionately. "Marry me," he said. "Please!"

"Yes," Tara answered. "If you're sure —"

"I'm sure that I want to be with you whenever and wherever I can," he exclaimed.

She nestled against him and murmured, "That's the way I feel about you."

"You phone your mother and tell her; then I'll phone mine," Jacob told her.

"Are you absolutely sure it's what you want?" Tara asked.

"You're what I want," he said, sweeping her into his arms and, carrying her into the bedroom, he put her down on the bed. "I love you, Tara!" he whispered. "I always will!"

She took his face between her hands and brought it close to hers. "I love you too, Jacob," she whispered, "with all my heart!"

He began to unbutton her blouse.

It was Friday night of the Labor Day weekend. Tony had just finished putting Mikey to bed. Getting a bottle of beer, he was about to go out on the porch, where a cool evening breeze usually blew off the river, when the phone rang.

"I'll get it," Miriam called. A moment later, she said, "Tony, it's Papa."

Tony ambled out of the kitchen and into the hallway, where the phone was. He nodded to Miriam and said, "Go out on the porch. I'll be with you in a few minutes." She was due to give birth to their third child any day and seemed tired.

"I'm on, Papa," Tony said.

"Tony, you better come home."

"What?" Tony shouted.

"Tony —"

"What the hell is going on? Is Mama all right?"

Miriam edged closer to Tony, her abdomen awkwardly nudging him.

"It's Mike. He was shot," his father said with a sob.

"Mike?"

"Bad trouble, Tony."

"Is he alive?" Tony asked.

"Critical, Tony. The docs say he don't have much of a chance." His father's voice was filled with a mixture of agony and anger.

"Where is he?"

"The Sisters of Mercy Hospital."

247

"I'll be there," Tony told him. "You tell Mike I'll be there!" He put the phone down.

"What happened?" Miriam asked.

"Mike —" For several seconds he couldn't speak; then he told her what his father had said.

"Oh my God!" she exclaimed. Her right hand flew up to her mouth.

"I've got to go to him," Tony said. "I've got to be with him."

Tears streamed down Miriam's cheeks and she began to cry.

Tony put his arms around her. "I'll be back as soon as I can," he said. "I have to go right away."

"I know you do," she answered.

"If you go into labor —"

"I know what to do."

Tony let her go and, picking up the phone, called Commander Wayman, the submarine-base XO and arranged for an emergency five-day leave.

By the time Tony reached the hospital, it was three in the morning. His father and four of his soldiers were sitting in the lobby.

"Is he still alive?" Tony asked.

His father nodded. "When I told him you were coming, he smiled."

"Where is he?"

"Room 425. I'll go up with you. The elevator is at the end of the hall."

"Who hit him?" Tony asked as they waited for the elevator.

"One of Spilachi's torpedoes," his father answered with an outraged growl.

"Spilachi?" Tony exclaimed, spitting the name out.

The elevator arrived, the doors slid open, and they stepped into the car.

"There's been trouble between me and Spilachi," his father went on. "He's been trying to muscle me off the docks and take them over for himself."

"Since when?" Tony asked, wondering if what was happening now was the result of the way he'd treated Spilachi and his nephew that day a year before.

"The beginning of the summer," his father said as they stepped out of the elevator and into a long corridor. "Mike's room is the third one on the right."

Tony quickened his pace, but when he reached the open doorway he stopped abruptly. Mike was in an oxygen tent. There were tubes in both his arms and nostrils. A nun sat close to the bed.

"I'm his nephew," Tony said, answering her questioning look.

"Tony?" the sister asked.

"Yes," he answered, realizing that Mike must have been calling his name.

"He has been asking for you. But you must not tire him. He's very weak."

Tony crossed the threshold and, standing beside the bed, said in a strong voice, "Mike, it's Tony."

Mike smiled weakly and almost imperceptibly nodded.

Tony reached under the tent and, taking his hand, laced their fingers together. "You'll make it," he said, struggling to keep the pain and fear he felt out of his voice. "You'll play ball with Mikey again soon and wheel Sam around in the carriage."

Mike shook his head and began to speak.

"I can't hear him," Tony said, turning to the nun.

"You may lift the side of the oxygen tent."

"Mike," Tony said, "speak to me."

"Love you," Mike whispered, his eyelids fluttering open. "Love you."

Tony squeezed his uncle's hand and kissed him on the forehead.

"Woman's name," Mike said haltingly. "Della Hampton ... in Woodbridge ... in the phone book." He stopped and began to gasp.

The sister hurried to the bed. "You must go now."

"Stay," Mike whispered. "Find Della and tell her I loved her and the boys." The words were almost inaudible.

"I'll tell her, don't worry, Mike."

"Want her and my sons at my funeral... Promise me they'll be there."

"I promise," Tony said, feeling a sudden tightening of Mike's fingers around his own.

"I took care of her... She won't need anything." Mike took a deep breath and, slowly exhaling, said, "Hold me, Tony. Hold me."

Tony gathered Mike in his arms. "I love you," he said, his vision blurred by tears.

Mike smiled wanly, and the next instant his head lolled to one side. He was dead.

Tony gently laid Mike back down on the bed and, facing his father, said grimly, "You take care of everything here. I'll be at the house later."

"I never knew he had a woman and children," his father said in amazement.

"She's a black woman," Tony said when they were in the hallway. "But by God, she and her two sons will be at Mike's funeral. You heard him."

"If that's the way it's got to be, Tony, that's the way it will be. But what about your mother, what do you think it's going to do to her to see —"

"I'll explain it to Mama," Tony said as they entered the elevator.

They rode down to the main floor in silence.

Tony pulled up to a brick ranch house with a large lawn in front and a good-sized yard in the back. He'd phoned Della from the hospital and told her that he had something to tell her about Mike and that he was coming to see her.

As Tony got out of the car, the door to the house opened, framing a petite woman with graying hair tied in a bow behind her head and tortoiseshell glasses. He left the car and walked up the flagstone path to the door.

"Tell me what happened to Mike," Della said, looking up at him. Tony bit his lip.

"He's dead, isn't he?"

"Yes," Tony answered.

She swallowed hard and a look of anguish crossed her face. Moving out of the doorway, she said, "Come inside."

Tony followed her through the parlor into the kitchen.

"I just made a fresh pot of coffee," she said. "You look like you could use a cup. Sit down and I'll get it for you."

"Thank you, I could."

"What happened?" Della asked as she took two cups and saucers down from a cabinet and put them on the sink counter.

"He was shot," Tony said.

She trembled and seemed about to collapse.

Tony went to her and, putting his hands on her shoulders, he said, "Just before he died, Mike told me to tell you he loved you and he loved his sons."

Tears flowed down her cheeks and, lifting her left hand with a plain gold band on the ring finger, she said, "He was my husband. He married me and took me off the street. He was a good man."

Tony put his arms around her. He'd always suspected that Mike had married this woman he'd told him about that day long ago.

"He loved you too," she said, leaning against his chest, "and he knew you loved him. He always talked about you."

"Mike wanted you and his sons to go to the funeral," Tony continued. "He made me promise that all of you would be there."

Della shook her head. "That's no place for me and my boys."

"You're wrong, Della," he said, holding her at arm's length and looking straight at her. "What little happiness he had, you gave him. He told me he was so happy and proud that a beautiful woman like you could love a man like him."

"He was beautiful to me," she said in a choked voice. "I never looked at another man after I married him."

"He knew that, I'm sure," Tony responded.

"If I come —"

"No *if*," Tony said. "Mike wanted you there... I want you there. He was my uncle and you're my aunt."

"Negros —"

Tony shook his head. "You're Mike's wife. His children are my cousins."

"Now I know why he loved you so much: you're a lot like him," she sobbed.

"Will you come?" Tony pressed.

Della nodded. "I'll phone our sons; they'll be there too."

"Good!"

"Now sit down and have a cup of coffee," she said.

Tony went back to the table and sat down. This was the first time he'd ever been in a black person's home, and as he looked around, he realized it wasn't any different from his own.

Three days later, Tony, dressed in his white service uniform, stood in front of the family and friends in Romano's Funeral Chapel in Brooklyn and delivered the eulogy. Della and her sons, one a doctor and the other an attorney, sat between Tony's mother and father. Despite her almost full-term pregnancy, Miriam had come down with little Mikey from New London for the interment and sat quietly weeping in the pew.

Later, at the graveside in the Cemetery of the Sacred Heart, Tony, with his arm around Della's shoulders, waited until the grave was filled before leading the group back to the limousines.

After Della and her sons were dropped off at her home, Tony whispered in Sicilian to his father, "I want Spilachi for myself, understand? I don't want you or any of your men to go after him. That's the way it must be."

His father silently nodded. After a long pause, he asked, "When?"

"Today," Tony answered.

"He's got protection."

"It won't help him," Tony said. "Nothing will help him, or his nephew."

"What are you two whispering about?" Miriam asked.

"Nothing important," her father-in-law said. "Nothing to worry your pretty head about."

By the time they arrived at the house, the sky had clouded and the air became heavy with the threat of rain. Tony went upstairs to his old room and changed into street clothes. Then he went to the basement and took a "clean" snub-nosed .38 from his father's gun collection. Fitting a silencer to it, he loaded it and tucked it in his waistband under his polo shirt before he went up to the living room.

"I'm going out for a while," he told Miriam.

"It's raining and Mama says dinner is almost ready," she answered, frowning.

"I've got to go out," he said, going to the hall closet and taking out a light rain jacket. "I'll be back soon."

"When?"

"Soon," he said, opening the door.

Suddenly, Miriam was on her feet. "You're going after Spilachi, aren't you?" she cried in alarm. "You're going to kill him!"

At the sound of the raised voices, Tony's mother and father rushed into the room.

"Take care of her," he told them.

"Tony, don't go!"

He stepped through the open door.

"Tony, I won't be here when you come back!" Miriam shouted. "I mean it, Tony, I won't be here. You're throwing away our lives, Tony!"

He clenched his jaws together and slammed the door behind him.

A half hour later, Tony pulled up behind Spilachi's limo on the southeast corner of Cottonwood and Jefferson Avenues in north Newark. The limo driver got out of the car and came toward him.

"You want something here?" he snarled, bending close to the open window of Tony's car.

Tony grabbed the man's tie and, yanking his head through the rolled-down window, jammed the barrel of the .38 between the man's eyes. "Do exactly what I tell you or I'll blow your fucking head off."

The man's face went white.

"Take a step back. Keep your hands where I can see them," Tony said as he got out of the car. A moment later, he frisked the man and took a .357 Magnum from him. "How many more inside?" he asked.

"One and the boss's nephew."

"Good, I wanted Giorgio too," Tony said in Italian. "Listen, we're going in, but not through the front door. You're going to take me right to Spilachi, understand?"

The man nodded.

"Move!" Tony said.

They went around the side of the house and entered through a back door.

"So far so good," Tony said. "Now —" He stopped. He could hear someone else coming along the walkway toward the door. He pushed the driver against the wall inside the door and said, "Not a sound." A moment later it opened and as soon as the newcomer entered, Tony slammed the .38 down on his head. The man dropped to the floor.

"Christ, you broke his head open!" the limo driver exclaimed.

"Shut up and move!" Tony growled, prodding him with his gun.

"Mr. Spilachi is probably in that room there. It's his office," the man said, pointing to a closed door as they moved down a hallway.

"Open it," Tony whispered. "Don't try anything or you're dead!"

The man put his hand on the knob, slowly turned it and swung the door open.

Spilachi and Giorgio were seated at a large desk.

Tony pushed the man into the room. "Stay put!" he ordered. "Let me see your hands!" He kicked the door shut behind him. "You," he said to the driver, "get down on your belly."

"What?"

"Get down on your fucking belly or I'll break your fucking head open, too!" Tony said.

The man stretched out on the floor.

"Spilachi, you look like you just crapped in your pants. And Giorgio, you don't look much better. The two of you get out from behind that desk."

"I have a hundred Gs —" Spilachi started to say.

"Move away from the desk," Tony growled.

"What are you going to do?" Giorgio asked.

"Something neither of you will ever forget," Tony answered. He could feel the sweat run down his back.

He tightened his finger on the trigger. He wanted to kill the two of them on the spot, but he couldn't squeeze the trigger further. It would be in cold blood. He couldn't do it. Not even for Mike.

"Tony," Spilachi begged, "even if you're in the Navy, I'll cut you in."

"Giorgio, drop your pants."

Giorgio looked questioningly at his uncle.

"He's got a fucking gun on you," Spilachi told him.

Giorgio unbuckled his belt, unzipped his pants, and let them fall. "Now what?" he whimpered.

"The first part of a lesson," Tony said and, pointing the .38 at Giorgio's right knee, squeezed off a round.

Giorgio screamed and fell to the floor, clutching his shattered kneecap.

"Mother of God!" Spilachi cried, falling to his knees and extending his hands toward Tony. "Please, don't do anything to me. Please —"

Tony fired again.

Spilachi was thrown backward, his right shoulder smashed.

"You come anywhere near me or mine again," Tony said, breathing hard, "and I'll come back. Next time I'll cut your fucking balls off, understand, Spilachi?"

"Get me to a hospital!" Spilachi cried.

"You on the floor," Tony said. "Get up. We're going out the same way we came in."

In less than three minutes, Tony was in his car and on the way back to his father's house in Newark. As soon as he opened the door, he saw Miriam standing in the foyer. "I didn't kill them," he said. "But I should have. I just gave them a lesson."

"The baby is coming," she interrupted. "My water broke a half hour ago. Papa is taking me to the hospital."

"I'll take —"

"No, no, I don't want you to. I don't want you to!" she screamed.

Tony moved toward her.

Palms up, she thrust her hands out. "I don't want you anywhere near me. Not after what you did!" Miriam shouted.

His father came down the stairs, and at the same time his mother came from the kitchen. "Get her to the hospital," Tony said.

"Aren't you coming?" his mother asked in Italian.

Tony looked at Miriam. "Ask her."

"I don't want him," Miriam sobbed. "I don't want to be part of this. He's going to end up like Mike."

"Take her," Tony said to his father and, opening the door, he stepped aside to let them pass. He wasn't going to beg Miriam for anything, not even to be at the hospital for the birth of their third child... And, if it should come to that, though he loved her very much, he'd never beg her to stay married to him.

CHAPTER 15

"When the ambassador told me you were coming," Jacob said, vigorously shaking Warren's hand, "I couldn't believe it. I told Tara, and she said you must stay with us while you're in Rome." He led his old friend to a chair in front of his desk. "Sit down. My God, it's good to see you again. How's Hilary and the baby?"

"They're just fine. They're in New York," Warren answered. "How's Tara?"

"Fine, except for occasional morning sickness."

Warren grinned. "When is she due?"

"First week in November. Can you believe it? We'll be married over a year."

"It's hard enough for me to realize that I'm a father," Warren laughed, "but to come to terms with your being one will be impossible."

"I know exactly what you mean," Jacob responded.

Then Warren said, "I was sorry to hear that Tony and Miriam split up."

"I don't understand it," Jacob commented. "I know those two loved each other. And I heard they have another child, a daughter named Ruth."

"Do you know Tony resigned his commission?"

Jacob frowned. "No, I hadn't heard that. Now why the hell would he have done something like that?"

Warren shook his head. "There are some rumors around that he shot up a couple of Mafia guys to avenge his Uncle Mike. If that's true, maybe he figured his career would be finished if the Navy learned about it officially."

"He was a damn good officer."

Lowering his voice, Warren responded, "So are you, Jacob. That's why I'm here. I came to get you."

"Get me?" Jacob asked. "I don't understand." He leaned forward and planted his elbows on the desk. "Am I missing something? Aren't you on the *Ashoken*?"

Warren shook his head and smiled. "Only on paper."

"Okay, I'll accept that for now," Jacob said, sensing an atmosphere of intrigue. "But tell me why you need me?"

"Not here," Warren answered. "Let's walk and I'll answer your questions."

"All right," Jacob said, as he stood up. "We'll walk."

Within a few minutes they were on the Via Veneto, which was crowded with people walking to see and to be seen in the late afternoon.

"You know what's happening in Palestine," Warren said.

"The British are getting out," Jacob answered. "And the U.N. is going to vote on the formation of a Jewish state." He had been closely following the situation in Palestine for two reasons: first, to do so had become part of his official duties ever since the British had set up a naval blockade to prevent Jews from going to Palestine; and second, because he was a Jew, albeit a nonpracticing one. He understood the importance of Palestine finally becoming a Jewish homeland in the psyche of the Jews. And he knew, as the British had already found out, that the Jews were willing to fight for what they considered to be rightfully theirs.

"Yes, and that means the Jews and the Arabs will end up fighting each other just as the Jews and the British are now doing," Warren responded.

Jacob nodded. Over the past year, thousands of Jews who had survived Hitler's death camps had been using ports in Italy and Greece as staging points to run a British blockade and reach Palestine. The British Navy had intercepted dozens of their ships, and interned thousands of Jews on the island of Malta.

"Your ambassador and people in Washington have had you make several trips to the staging ports here and in Greece," Warren said.

"Less than half a dozen people were supposed to know that," Jacob responded in amazement.

"I make seven," Warren said sarcastically as they crossed a street. "The United States cannot become involved in the civil war that will erupt as soon as the British pull out, but we can't allow the Russians to become involved, either. This is a presidential-election year, and politicians are funny about what they say on one hand and do on the other. In this case, the president would like to help the Jews openly but can't. Therefore, clandestine assistance is the only option left."

Jacob didn't answer. The possibility that the Russians might intervene on the side of the Arabs had been included in his last report.

"They might not come in with men," Warren continued, "but even if they sent only guns and ammo, it might be enough to give the Arabs the edge." Jacob nodded, realizing his friend was operating in a cloak-and-dagger area outside the limits of Naval Intelligence. "There are certain things that can be done to stop the Russians," Warren continued. "Some, of course, are on a diplomatic level. Others take the form of undercover operations."

"That's a fancy way of saying espionage and sabotage, isn't it?"

Warren grinned, but didn't answer the question. He said instead, "Jake, your combat experience makes you particularly valuable to the operation that has been planned. Ambassador Fairfax concurs."

"What operation?"

"There's a ship that has the latest type of radar and sonar gear aboard. This ship is sailing into the eastern Med to monitor air, surface, and subsurface traffic in the area. If any vessel, plane, or submarine attempts to land military supplies anywhere along the Syrian, Palestinian, or Lebanese coast, the ship will vector in motor torpedo boats or combat aircraft, or both, to stop it."

"Will all supplies be stopped?" Jacob questioned, knowing, as he was sure Warren also knew, that the Palestinian Jews were getting their armament from ships that successfully ran the British blockade.

"Certain vessels will not be stopped. We'll be very selective."

Jacob nodded in understanding. "Now tell me where I come in and where you come in?"

"The master of that ship will take his orders from me. I'll be on board and you'll be with me."

Jacob stopped abruptly.

"Keep walking," Warren said.

"What would I do?"

"You'll be my right arm. It will be up to you to ensure that proper orders are given to the MTBs and combat planes if it comes to that."

"What if the opposition turns out to be Russian aircraft or naval vessels?"

"I never said there wasn't an element of risk," Warren answered wryly.

"The Russians have a battle force in the Black Sea!" Jacob said, lighting a cigarette. "Of course, they don't have aircraft carriers,but how about Turkey?Being a Moslem nation and—?"

Warren held up his hand. "Russia is the country we have to worry about." Then he said, "It's a voluntary assignment, Jake. But I thought you'd be interested in it."

"I am!" Jacob answered without hesitation.

"Good. You'll come aboard in Genoa sometime within the next ten days. I'll let you know exactly when. As far as anyone at the embassy will know, except Fairfax, of course, you'll be going on an extended assignment in France and England."

"How long will this extended assignment last?"

"It's now the end of April. By the middle or third week in May, the United Nations will vote on whether or not Palestine becomes the state of Israel. It is expected that the vote will be in favor of that happening, and it is also expected that the Arabs will immediately attack. So we will be involved until the smoke clears."

"Can you tell me something about the planes on our side? Who'll be flying them and where they're based?" Jacob asked.

"P-40s and P-47s and — I know you're going to like this — there's even a few ME-109s involved. They'll be flown by well-paid volunteers from the States and England, all former combat pilots. The planes are being positioned on landing strips in Cyprus as well as on a couple in Palestine in the desert. All will be close enough to make any strikes we call for."

"And the MTBs?" Jacob asked.

"Surplus PTs and a few Italian World War II boats we've acquired," Warren answered.

"Suppose we're questioned, or attacked by the Arabs, or say, the Russians?"

Warren took time to fill and light his pipe before he answered. "Officially, our government will not acknowledge our existence. I won't be an American and neither will you. We will have false British IDs and passports. You'll be listed as the ship's first officer and I as the captain."

"And the crew?"

"All experts in their assignments."

"Will the ship be armed?"

"Negative," Warren responded. "We don't want to give either the Russians or the Arabs any reason to think that we're anything but an old tramp steamer."

"So how will the radar antennae be concealed?"

"Most of it will look like regular ship's gear. The rest of it, Army SCR-584s, will be camouflaged as well as we can."

"Won't we look suspicious if we just steam back and forth for days on end?"

Warren chuckled. "I was wondering when you'd come to that. We're not going to do much steaming. We're going to be engaged in commercial fishing — a very legitimate business in that part of the Med — and we'll have engine trouble that will keep us in one location."

"And just how long do you think we'll be able to keep that up?"

Warren shrugged. "Long enough, I hope, to have been of some value."

"The odds look OK to me," Jacob commented. Smiling, he added, "And I want to play."

"Harry's Bar?" Warren questioned.

Jacob nodded. "Harry's bar," he said.

The two turned around and headed back along the Via Veneto.

Traveling in mufti, Jacob went from Rome to Milan by train and spent a day there before continuing on to Genoa. He boarded the *Pelican*, a rust-spotted freighter of Liberian registry, and was immediately escorted to the bridge, where Warren was discussing getting underway with the ship's master, an old seadog of uncertain national origin. Warren introduced him as Captain Josephs.

"We'll operate from back there," Warren said, pointing to a small chart house at the rear of the bridge. He smiled. "Don't let its size fool you. With a few things moved around and the right connections made, you'll have a first-class CIC set up. Captain Josephs is all set to go."

"I didn't see any additional radars on deck when I came aboard," Jacob commented.

"They're down in the hold. As soon as they're needed, they'll be hoisted topside."

Jacob nodded his head appreciatively. "This is even smaller than —"

Warren interrupted. "She's twelve thousand tons, has one screw, and in an emergency she'll make fifteen knots. In weather she lumbers along at nine, but she's a good old girl and has been in all of the oceans of the world at one time or another during her former life."

One of the bridge phones rang. Josephs answered it, and, addressing Warren, said, "Skipper, the engine-room says we're ready to move anytime you give the word."

Warren nodded. To Jacob he whispered, "We're waiting for our only passenger."

"Passenger?" Jacob asked, raising his eyebrows.

Ignoring the question, Warren suggested that Jacob make himself familiar with the ship. "I'll see you at dinner," he said. "Oh, Jake, there's something else I should remind you about."

"Yes, what is it?"

"This isn't one of our ships," Warren said. "The discipline isn't the same. Every man here, with the exception of you, myself, and three of my own men, is a civilian volunteer. Most had sea experience during the war, but they're not military. Mind you, I'm satisfied they'll do what they have to do to get the job done. They're getting paid well enough. But we can't expect them to react as we would expect the crew to do aboard one of our ships."

"I think I can handle it. Don't worry," Jacob answered, leaving the bridge. He found his cabin and unpacked his valise. Then he toured the ship. She was three hundred and fifty feet long and had a fifty-foot beam. Her hull was painted black; her superstructure amidships was a dirty white. She had one smokestack steadied in place with four braided steel guy wires.

The men Jacob saw acknowledged his presence with a nod, or by saying, "Hi!" Sometimes both.

About six, clouds began to roll in off the Ligurian Sea, and in a matter of minutes rain started to fall. Jacob was looking out the porthole in his cabin when he saw a black Cadillac drive up alongside the ship and stop. The chauffeur opened the rear door, and a tall man with a black patch over his left eye got out of the car. He took hold of a leather bag that was handed to him by someone else in the rear, said a few words, and quickly mounted the gangplank.

Within minutes after the passenger's arrival, the *Pelican* was underway. By seven, the ship's officers and the one-eyed passenger were gathered together in the small officers' mess for dinner. Using Jacob's assumed name, Steven Karole, Warren introduced him to each of the men. Then he said, "Gentlemen, Captain Josephs says that the engineer, Mr. Haines, assures us that we will be on station within ninety hours at the very most."

"Haines," one of the men said, looking at the engineer with a knowing look, "you can't even assure us who *you* are, so how the hell can you assure the skipper where *we'll* be ninety hours from now?"

The other men laughed and Haines, holding up his hands for silence, answered, "Then I'm in good company... As navigator, you'd have difficulty finding your way out of a closet... No, I'll change that... You wouldn't be able to find pussy, even if you fell into it!"

Other men joined in the crude banter, and soon the space was filled with a crazy quilt of ribald exchanges. Jacob and the one-eyed passenger did not contribute, but Warren gave as good as any of the others.

Jacob was keenly aware of the fact that Warren had not introduced him to the passenger, but he was even more aware of Warren's ability to seemingly become like the other men. If Jacob hadn't known that Warren was a U.S. Navy officer, he never would have guessed that he was.

By the next day, Jacob discovered that the engineering officer came from Levonia Avenue, not far from where he'd lived in Brooklyn, and had graduated from City College with a degree in mechanical engineering.

The second mate turned out to be a graduate student in English at Brooklyn College, while the radio officer, called Des McCabe, came from Dublin, Ireland. The electronics specialist, known as Harold Korman, had been born in Louisville, Kentucky, and taught electronic circuit design at Cooper Union in Manhattan. Most of the other crew had former sea experience. Several Jews who had been in German concentration camps and survived had numerical identification numbers tattooed on their left forearms. Though all hands seemed willing to speak about their past, Jacob realized that none of them were using their real names.

In the afternoon of the third day, Jacob joined Warren and Captain Josephs on the bridge. "The coast of Palestine is just over the horizon," Warren said, gesturing toward the ship's bow. "We're off the town of Ashkelon. Tonight, after we put our passenger ashore, we'll radio that we're experiencing difficulty with our boilers and will have to shut them down for repairs."

"Who do we radio?"

"A bogus office in Genoa," Warren answered. "But the message is intended to alert certain individuals in Palestine that we are in position."

"When do you think the balloon might go up?"

"The vote in the U.N. is going on now. I suspect the next ten to twelve hours should tell the story, at least as far as we're concerned."

"Just to satisfy my curiosity," Jacob said in a low voice, "who is our passenger?"

Warren smiled. "Someone you may have heard about."

"Try me?"

"Colonel Moshe Dyan."

"Ours?"

Warren shook his head. "Commander of the Jewish Brigade in the British Army during the war."

Recognition flashed through Jacob's mind when he heard the name. He didn't have to ask any more questions about the one-eyed passenger…

Although there were ferocious clashes between the Haganah, the army of the new state of Israel, and the Arabs on land, there was no action at sea. The *Pelican* remained off the Israeli coast for nine days without incident. At the end of the ninth day, Warren asked Captain Josephs to summon the entire company not on watch to the forward deck and announced,

"We have received word that Haganah is in control of every major city in Israel and that Arabs are in full retreat." The men began to cheer. "We have orders to leave our position at midnight tonight and return to Genoa." The men cheered again.

"Captain Josephs, do you think Haines can get all boilers on the line in time for our departure? And get all that fishing gear rigged in?"

"You can bet on it, Skipper," Josephs answered.

The Jewish men who had survived the camps began to sing the *Hatikvah*. Jacob knew the words in Hebrew and in English; he had learned them when he had attended Hebrew School a long time ago. Suddenly, Jacob remembered the passionate, off-key sounds whenever his father had sung it. "For you, Papa," he whispered and sang with the others.

At midnight Jacob accompanied Warren to the bridge, and Captain Josephs ordered, "All ahead full speed."

The engine-room telegraph operator repeated the command.

"Come to course two-seven-nine."

"Two-seven-nine," the helmsman answered.

Warren filled his pipe and, lighting it, said, "I'd have to admit that I was moved by what I saw on the foredeck, but I'm not sure I understand it. The men manning this ship have no real connection with Israel. I thought they were interested in the money."

"You're right, Warren," Jacob answered, lighting a cigarette. "But if you're a Jew, the birth of a Jewish state is a dream come true. And strangely enough, it has nothing to do with whether or not you want to live there. It is enough to know that it is there, that it exists."

Warren puffed on his pipe, sending smoke toward the bridge's low ceiling before he asked, "Do you feel that —? Is it enough for you to know that Israel exists?"

"I sang the *Hatikvah* too," Jacob answered. "It is enough!"

"You know this isn't the end to the fighting," Warren said. "The Arabs will try again and again!"

"My father, may he rest in peace, would have said, *If God had wanted the past, present and future to be all one, he would have created them that way. But He didn't. He created a past from which we can learn, a present for us to enjoy and a future for Himself.*"

Warren removed the pipe from his mouth. "Your father was a wise man," he said and was about to add, *and so is his son*, when suddenly the officer of the watch called out, "Skipper, two points off the starboard bow!"

"A submarine," Warren exclaimed after raising his binoculars.

A light began to flash on the submarine's bridge, and one of the bridge phones rang.

Jacob answered it. "Our signalman says we've been asked to identify ourselves."

"Tell him to give the ship's name and registry and to refuse anything after that," Warren said.

Jacob relayed the order.

"What's her range?" Warren asked the radar operator.

"One thousand yards and closing."

"Josephs, bring your ship right to course three-zero-zero."

Jacob immediately understood what Warren intended to do.

"Coming to three-zero-zero," the helmsman said, answering Captain Josephs' order.

Warren switched on the loudspeaker system. "All hands now hear this. All hands now hear this. Stand by for a ram. Stand by for a ram."

"If we had a couple more knots," he said tightly, "we'd have her for sure."

"A couple of more knots might just be enough to give your intention away," Jacob countered.

Ignoring Josephs, Warren said directly to the helmsman, "You take us straight into her. As close to her conning tower as possible. Aim for the red star if you can see it."

"Aye, aye, Skipper."

"Radar, what's our range?" Warren asked.

"Five hundred yards and closing."

Jacob could feel the sweat on his back and his legs, and drew his arm across his brow.

"They're on to us," Warren exclaimed. "He's coming around for a bow tube shot at us!"

The men on the sub's bridge disappeared.

"We need those extra knots," Warren said to Josephs.

Josephs phoned the engine-room. "Haines, give us everything you can. I don't give a fuck what we burn out, just do it."

"She's submerging," Warren said tensely.

Jacob watched the submarine's forward deck slip beneath the moonlit water.

"Range?" Warren asked.

"Two hundred fifty."

"God damn! I don't think he can get a shot off now," Warren cried.

The top of the conning tower was disappearing below the surface.

"How much water do we draw?" Jacob asked.

"Eighteen feet," Warren answered.

Jacob took a deep breath, exhaled, and shouted, "I think we've got him."

"Target gone," radar reported.

Moments later, the *Pelican*'s bow slammed into the submarine's conning tower. The *Pelican* shuddered, seemed to hesitate. Then, with the scream of metal grinding metal, she sliced through the submarine's structure like a knife through butter. Jacob and Warren were thrown against the forward bulkhead. Several of the other men lost their footing and wound up on the deck.

"Take her ahead, standard speed, Captain Josephs," Warren ordered, scrambling to his feet.

Josephs gave the order to the engine-room telegraph operator.

Jacob picked himself up and checked the fathometer. "Four hundred and thirty feet to bottom," he said.

Warren asked Josephs to have the helmsman bring the *Pelican* back to its former course. "We will report," he said in deliberate tones, "that we hit a very large unidentified object in the dead of night, very probably a whale. We're afraid we killed it. What do you think, Jake?"

"I'd have to agree with you, Skipper," Jacob said. "It was a very large object and, as you said, probably a whale."

CHAPTER 16

It had snowed two days before in New York, and the storm had slowed all traffic to a halt under a blanket of six inches of snow. But now, as the winter sun beat down and snow plows growled through the streets, grimy mounds of slush were piled high on the sidewalk curbs and gutters overflowed with dirty water.

"Coming up to it," Tony's driver said, easing the black limousine to the right. "Where do you want me to park?"

"In front," Tony answered. In the two years since he had resigned his commission and come to work for his father, Tony hadn't changed very much. His face was still boyish, but now there were tiny streaks of white in his black hair. He looked very much the successful businessman.

Today he'd been summoned to a morning meeting with capo Pasquale Sforza, the Mafia head of the Brooklyn and Manhattan waterfront. Things being the way they were, he couldn't refuse to come, but he would have liked to have told the son of a bitch to go screw himself.

The car pulled up in front of Brione's Italian Restaurant on Fourth Avenue in Bay Ridge. Tony waited until his driver opened the door for him. Though it was the first day of spring, 1950, a blustery wind tore at Tony's overcoat as he crossed the sidewalk. Brione's was a familiar gathering place for Mafiosos on special occasions, and he had been there many times in the past two years.

As Tony entered, the maître d' came up to him and said, "Please follow me, Mr. Trapasso."

"Haven't seen this place empty before," he commented as they passed through the main dining room with its subdued lighting and mirrored walls.

"It's only five o'clock," the man said. "By seven, there won't be a table available."

They moved through a narrow hallway and entered a room at the rear of the building. Two men wearing topcoats and broad-brimmed hats were seated behind a table. Behind him, Tony heard the sound of the door being closed. For a moment, neither he nor the men spoke. Instead, they gazed steadily at him. Tony recognized Pasquale Sforza, but he did not know the other, slightly built man with a pockmarked face and yellowish-brown eyes.

Suddenly the stranger's narrow lips stretched into a smile, and he began to quietly laugh in a strange, almost girlish way. As Sforza seemed to take a cue from the man and started to laugh obsequiously, Tony realized that the stranger must be Don Julio Nunzio. He, Luciano, and two other men controlled all mob activity from prostitution to trade unions in the United States. His nickname was Snake.

Tony felt a sudden surge of adrenaline. He had been called here because he and Sforza had been having trouble; Sforza wanted more of a cut. If he was going to be killed, it would not happen here.

They'd have him taken out sometime after he left. But now he had an opportunity to play his own hand with one of the big bosses. Tony pushed his hat back on his head. "Cut the shit and come to the point," he barked, "or I walk out of here."

The laughter instantly died.

"Who the fuck do you think you're speaking to, Admiral?" Nunzio challenged.

Tony pointed his finger at Sforza. "To him. He's your fucking puppet. He asked me to come here. So I'm here. Tell me what you want to say, and make it snappy."

Sforza started to stand.

Nunzio touched his arm and, when Sforza sat down again, he said in the Sicilian dialect, "I heard you had balls. They were right."

"And I heard you were smart."

Nunzio grinned.

Tony pointed to Sforza. "Get that ape out of here, and you and I will get things settled between us. If there is anything to settle."

Gun in hand, Sforza leaped to his feet.

"Put it away," Nunzio snapped.

Sforza glared at Tony. "I won't forget," he growled.

"I'm terrified," Tony chuckled.

"Leave us," Nunzio said, looking at Sforza.

"I —"

The expression on Nunzio's face changed. His eyes went to slits and, snakelike, it seemed his tongue was flicking the air.

Sforza returned the gun to his shoulder holster and walked stiffly to the door. When the door closed behind him, Nunzio said, "Sit down, Mr. Trapasso. Let's calm ourselves."

Tony took the chair and moved to the opposite side of the table across from Nunzio, whose expression had softened.

"I was sorry to hear that your father is ill," Nunzio said almost civilly. "He's a good man. Tell him I send my regards."

Tony thanked him, wondering what would come next.

"Now, what's this trouble between you and Sforza?" Nunzio asked. "I can understand your trouble with Spilachi, but Sforza is easier. All he wants is to make some money."

"He's stupid," Tony answered. "And stupid people are dangerous. They make the mistake of thinking they're smart. Pasquale can't see the trees for the leaves. He still believes that the way to make money is to come down on people. That's going out of style."

"And you don't?"

Tony looked straight at Nunzio. "If you think that's the way to do things, we're wasting my time and yours."

"Sforza said you got crazy ideas," Nunzio mused.

"We've got to change our way of doing business."

"Why?" Nunzio asked. "We all do very well with the way we've been operating."

"Because times are changing and we have to change with them," Tony replied heatedly.

"You've done well on the docks, with the numbers and —"

"Julio," Tony said, purposefully using the man's given name, "the New York and New Jersey waterfronts are going to change. Sooner or later, Washington is going to get interested in what goes on, and when it does, we'll be finished."

"Does your father —"

"My father knows only the old ways. But the old ways have to change."

Nunzio took a pigskin cigar case out of his breast pocket. "Cuban," he said, handing a cigar to Tony and taking one for himself.

Tony waited until they had lighted up before he steeled himself and announced, "Julio, I have some big ideas... I want ten million dollars from you to get them going."

"Jesus, is that all? Why not twenty?" Nunzio asked with a facetious grin.

"Fine, twenty million, if you can arrange it."

"And what would you do with twenty million dollars?"

"Buy successful, legit companies and run them," Tony answered. "I'd get out of the rackets. And you'd have a big interest in the legit businesses."

Nunzio tapped the ashes from his cigar onto the floor. "What kind of companies?"

"The kind that have control of their own markets. One of a kind across the board ... anything except banking and insurance."

"You're an ex-sailor," Nunzio said. "What do you know about business?"

"Plenty," Tony answered, "and for what I don't know, I'd hire people who do."

Nunzio blew a huge cloud of smoke toward the ceiling. "For twenty mil, what do I get in return?"

"Twenty percent of all profits."

"Forty."

"Goddamn it, Julio! I don't want to play a numbers game with you. Twenty percent is good and you know it."

"Not when you're playing with my twenty mil."

"Forget I ever suggested it. I'll go my own way."

"Where are you going to get that kind of money?"

Tony shook his head. "That's my problem, isn't it?" He stood up abruptly.

"Between you and Sforza, I have a regular pair of jumping jacks," Nunzio said. "Sit down, Tony, and let's get this settled between us now."

Tony dropped back onto the chair.

"I told Sforza to have you come here," Nunzio said, "because I started to hear rumors that you were doing things your way and not the way we wanted them done. Your father is an old friend of mine, and I don't want to do anything that would hurt him. You understand what I'm saying, don't you?

But if you don't want to do things our way on the docks, it might be worth twenty mil to get you out on your own."

"Twenty percent, Julio, and I get out. That's my offer. The deal has nothing to do with my father, and I don't give a shit what you heard, or didn't hear, about me. Do we have a deal or don't we?"

"You're not an easy man to do business with," Nunzio commented. "I don't like —"

"Twenty percent!"

Nunzio nodded. "All right. It will be worth the twenty mil just to see if you can make your ideas work."

"I've already made part of 'em work!" Tony said, shaking Nunzio's hand.

After completing a three-year tour in Rome, Jacob returned to the States at the end of March and was temporarily reassigned to the Eastern Sea Frontier Headquarters in Brooklyn as air operations officer.

He, Tara, and Sy, their one-year-old son, rented a three-bedroom apartment on Glenwood Road and Bedford Avenue in Brooklyn. From there it was an easy drive to the headquarters. Tara was able to continue studying art at the Brooklyn Museum, a twenty-minute subway ride from the nearby station, when her babysitter was available. They enjoyed Jacob's eight-to-five routine and were able to spend evenings and weekends together as a happy family.

As spring came on and the weather warmed, Jacob, like many other young fathers, often took Sy and his sister Miriam's children, Mike and Ruth, to either Prospect Park or to the small park on Bedford Avenue between Avenue X and Y for an hour's outing.

One Saturday afternoon while Jacob was sitting on a bench watching the children play, a voice said from behind him, "Hello, Commander."

Jacob turned.

His old friend and brother-in-law, Tony, was grinning down at him.

Jacob jumped to his feet and grabbed Tony's hand. "What a hell of a pleasant surprise, Tony. Sy is over there — with your kids."

"Before they see me, I want a few minutes with you," Tony said, going around to the front of the bench.

The two men sat down.

Tony was expensively dressed in gray slacks, a white shirt open at the neck, and a blue sports jacket draped over his shoulders. He was very tanned and when he put on the pair of sunglasses he'd been holding in his left hand, he looked theatrical.

"How are things going?" Tony asked, admiring his children on the park slides.

"Couldn't be better," Jacob answered. "I'm assigned to the Eastern Sea Frontier. It's like having a job in the real world: eight to five with most weekends and holidays off."

Tony nodded. "It was that way for me in New London," he commented. "You know, I've been trying to meet up with you, and only learned yesterday that you and Tara are back."

Jacob asked about Tony's mother and father.

"They're as well as most people their age," Tony said. "My father has been confined to a wheelchair and that's hard for him to take."

"I can imagine," Jacob responded.

"Do you ever get to see Warren Troost?" Tony asked, trying to get the amenities over.

"Now and then," Jacob answered. "Just now he happens to be in Washington. He tries to get to New York every weekend when he can. He and Hilary have an apartment in that new complex, Styvesant Town, on the east side. Hilary is a big wheel in the fashion world here in the city… That woman has all kinds of talent and ambitions!"

"Next time you see Warren, why don't you set something up for the three of us?" Tony suggested.

"I will. I'm sure Warren would like that."

Then Tony said, "Miriam probably told you why I had to get out."

"Something about a man named Spilachi —"

"Spilachi had friends in Washington. After I shot the bastard and his nephew, the word went out that I would be passed over. I wouldn't have gone any higher." He looked toward the black limousine parked at the curb on the Bedford Avenue side. "Now, instead of Spilachi having friends in Washington, and in the Navy Department… I have them." His voice hardened. "Believe me, Jake, I own the fuckers."

"Then you don't have any complaints, either," Jacob commented, aware that Tony was still wearing his wedding ring.

"Only one, and that's what I need your help with."

"Miriam?"

"I want her back. Now I can give her and the kids everything they want. She doesn't have to work. Did you know I send her a lot of money every week?"

"She told me," Jacob responded.

"And two days later, I get it back in the morning mail," Tony said tightly. "Jesus, she still doesn't understand that I couldn't let Spilachi get away with killing Uncle Mike. I'd have never been able to look at myself in a mirror again."

"She's a lot more headstrong than I ever thought she was," Jacob admitted.

"Pig-headed, I have to call it," Tony exclaimed, taking out a black alligator cigar case. "Try one, I have them specially made for me."

"That's good!" Jacob commented, after he let the smoke flow from his mouth.

"Do you know, she won't even see me?" Tony asked. "I mean, really see me."

For several moments, the two friends puffed on their cigars. Then Tony said again with deep feeling, "I want her back, Jacob. I've been with other women, but it was like — like using a piece of raw liver."

"Why don't you talk to her?" Jacob suggested.

Tony shook his head. "She won't listen … and I find it hard to beg," he said in a halting tone.

"If you don't tell her —"

"What I just told you," Tony said, "I've told no one else. I want you to talk to her."

"Even if I speak to her, I'm not sure she'll listen to me and, who knows, Tony, maybe she's right. She loves you, that much I know. But she can't stand the thought of you winding up like Mike."

"I'm sure she still loves me!" Tony commented positively. "If I was sure of anything in my life, I'm sure of that!"

"Tony, she doesn't want to be hurt —"

"Things are changing. My business is changing. I'm the president of several companies, and I'm going to buy another one soon."

"You're joking!" Jacob exclaimed. After a moment had passed, though, he said, "You're not joking."

"I'm a respectable businessman, and every time I buy a new company, I get farther away from the rackets."

"What about your connections on the docks?"

Tony shook his head. "I'll be out of that completely in a few weeks. Too much trouble … maybe later I'll get involved with the unions. But only on a legitimate basis."

"Mike and Ruth have spotted you," Jacob said, "and here they come."

"Daddy, Daddy!" Mike and his sister yelled almost in unison.

Tony stood up. "Will you speak to Miriam?" he asked, looking back at Jacob before he lifted his son in one arm and his daughter in the other and smothered them with kisses.

"Yes, I'll speak to her," Jacob answered.

"I owe you one."

Warren entered Admiral Harly's office in the new Pentagon building and was greeted warmly by the older man. "Did you know I'm putting in my retirement request at the end of July?"

Warren looked at him in surprise. He'd worked under Harly since '43, and despite the differences in rank and age, he had come to think of him as a friend who would be around forever.

"I will reach the mandatory retirement age then," Harly said, "and it's time to give someone else a chance at the job. My relief will be Vice-Admiral Wallace Kelly. I've already spoken to him about you and he's eager to meet you. Right now he's in Japan, but he'll be here in the middle of July. I suggested that he keep you around while he settles into the job."

"Thank you, sir," Warren responded, still trying to absorb the fact that Harly was retiring.

"That brings me to the next point. I read your report recommending that the Navy form its own commando-type force — sea, air, land teams you proposed calling them — and

I passed it up to the CNO with my recommendation that action be taken along the lines that you laid out. We both think Seals will be the logical extension of our underwater-demolition people."

Again Warren thanked Harly, but this time with enthusiasm in his voice.

"I can tell you're pleased about that," Harly said, looking owlishly wise.

"Yes, sir!" Warren said.

"And now to the final point," Harly said, "and this one is a personal one. It has been a pleasure to know you, Warren, to see you develop, and to have worked with you. I have every confidence that you'll make it to the top of the Navy, maybe even beyond. And if there's anything I can do in the future to help, I'm just a phone call away."

"The pleasure, sir, and honor has been mine. You have been an inspiration to me," Warren answered with respectful sincerity.

"Now, with that out of the way, suppose we leave the office and find a place where we can enjoy a couple of drinks and relax?"

"I'd like that, sir," Warren responded. "I'd like that very much!"

The rapid ascent of the elevator to the forty-fifth floor of Rockefeller Center reminded Jacob of fast fighter climbs, and he swallowed to equalize the pressure in his ears. He'd received a letter from the law firm of Slotnik, Caluchi, and O'Toole on the previous Monday, June 21, asking him to phone Mr. Slotnik on an extremely urgent matter. When he returned the call, he was told that his presence was required in the office to sign certain legal documents. When he tried to ask questions,

Slotnik put him off and said that all his questions would be answered if he could come to the office on Wednesday at ten.

The elevator came to an abrupt stop, its doors slid open, and Jacob stepped out in a gray-carpeted hallway. The names of the three law partners were neatly printed in black lettering on a free standing bronze placard.

Jacob approached the receptionist's desk and, when he identified himself, the young woman said, "Mr. Slotnik is expecting you, Commander Miller. Through the main door behind me, then straight down the hallway to the last office on the left."

Jacob nodded and thanked her. A few moments later he reached the open doorway of Slotnik's office and, to his surprise, the man was there to greet him.

"Commander," Slotnik said, "it's a pleasure to meet you. I'm sorry I sounded so mysterious on the phone, but the matter requires more than just some words over the phone, and as I already told you, your signature is required on several different documents."

Jacob was directed to a large leather club chair and Slotnik, a middle-aged man with a small gray goatee, twinkling blue eyes and graying blond hair, sat down opposite him in a high-backed chair, also covered in brown leather. In front of them on a low serving table was a tray with a Silex of freshly made coffee, cups, and saucers and a larger plate with an assortment of French pastries on it.

"Help yourself," Slotnik said, gesturing toward the tray. As he proceeded to pour himself a cup of coffee, he continued, "I'm sure you're wondering what this is all about. Let me explain. Sometime ago, you met a man named Isaac Grenville—"

"Yes, in the cemetery where my father is buried," Jacob answered, remembering the peculiar circumstances of that meeting some years ago.

"Isaac is dead, God rest his soul," Slotnik said.

"I'm sorry to hear that," Jacob said as he poured himself a cup of coffee. "He and my father, it seems, had been good friends."

"Isaac was a very wealthy man," Slotnik said, "very wealthy. And now, if you agree to the one single condition in his will, you will walk out of this office a very wealthy man, too."

Amazed, Jacob put the cup of coffee down. "I don't understand. I hardly knew Mr. Grenville. I met him only once —"

"Be that as it may, he has made you his sole heir," Slotnik said, "on the condition that you say *kaddish* for him and his wife on the anniversaries of their deaths and on Yom Kippur."

Jacob looked startled.

"Do you object to —"

"Mr. Slotnik, is this some kind of joke? If it is, I think it's in very poor taste."

"Commander, I never joke when money is involved, and in this case, when seven million dollars are about to change hands, I certainly would not joke."

"Seven million dollars!" Jacob exclaimed dazedly.

"Three million in cash. The rest in securities and real estate."

"I don't know what to say," Jacob gasped.

Slotnik smiled. "There's really nothing you can say except, of course, to agree to Isaac's condition."

"Certainly, I'll say *kaddish* for him and his wife," Jacob answered. "Had he asked me to do it the day I met him in the cemetery, I would have said yes!"

"I think he knew that, Commander," Slotnik commented. Offering his hand across the table, he said, "The documents are ready for your signature." With a twinkle in his eyes, he added, "Congratulations, Commander, I have a feeling that at this moment Isaac must be very pleased with himself."

When he returned home that evening, Jacob said nothing to Tara right away about his meeting with Slotnik. He was still trying to grasp the full meaning of the miraculous turn of events when he asked her to join him after dinner in their small living room.

Tara sat on the couch with her feet drawn up under her, while Jacob paced silently back and forth, not knowing how to begin with the momentous news. Now and then, he stopped and grinned at her.

"All right, I can tell you have something good to talk about. I bet I know: you were given a special promotion and —" she began.

"Wrong!" Jacob exclaimed with delight. "Guess again!" And he resumed his uncertain pacing.

"You've been transferred to Lower Slobbovia and you think I'll enjoy it... Oh, how am I to guess what's happened when you haven't given me a clue?" Tara teased. "Besides, I want to work on my painting tonight and you're keeping me here —"

"One more guess," Jacob said. "I'll give a clue. It has something to do with the letter I received from the lawyers."

"We're being sued by someone for a million dollars," Tara responded, slightly out of patience.

"Wrong," Jacob said, going to her. He knelt down in front of her and asked, "Have you ever wondered what it would be like to be wealthy?"

"Jake, I really do want to paint this evening," Tara said.

He put his arms around her waist. "Suppose you could have anything you wanted, what would you want?"

Without hesitating, she answered flippantly, "The time to finish my painting."

"Oh, come on. Name something you want," Jacob urged. "Something that you really want, but we can't afford."

"You're serious, aren't you?"

Jacob nodded. "Name it."

"A house, a place of our own," she sighed.

"Where?"

"Near the ocean. Maybe in the Hamptons! I've got really good taste."

"Anything else?" he persisted.

She hesitated.

"Tell me … anything else?"

"My own car," she said with a smile. "I'd like to have my own car."

Jacob drew her closer.

"What is this all about?" she asked.

"I love you, Tara," he said passionately. "From that first moment I saw you in Rome, I've loved you."

"You're not making any sense," she said, gently caressing the top of his head.

"Maybe not," he exclaimed excitedly. "But somehow, my loving you and the fact that you want a house and a car … and I want you to have them … somehow, everything is beautiful!"

"You're a nut," she exclaimed, "but a delightful one!" And she kissed the top of his head.

"Come the weekend," he said, "I'm going to buy you a house and car."

"What?"

"Tara, this morning in the lawyer's office I became a multimillionaire."

"Don't joke, Jacob!"

"Remember I told you about Isaac Grenville, my father's old friend?"

"Yes, the old man you met in the cemetery."

"He died without relatives and has left his entire estate to me. Three million in cash and the rest, four million dollars' worth, in securities and real estate."

"My God, are you sure?" she said, her voice rising in pitch. "I mean, what are we going to do with all that money?"

Jacob raised himself from his knees and sat down beside Tara. "One thing's for sure, we don't have to worry anymore about being able to afford anything we want!"

"What are you going to do about the Navy, Jake?"

"I haven't really thought about it," he answered; then taking her in his arms, he said, "First things first! The house and car for you on the weekend; then we'll think about other decisions we have to make."

"I don't think I want to work, now! Maybe I don't want you to work either!" Tara said joyously.

"I didn't think you would," Jacob answered, kissing her passionately.

Miriam finally agreed to meet Tony and he took her to dinner at Peter Lugers, a famous steakhouse with a turn-of-the-century ambience in the Williamsburg section of Brooklyn. Throughout dinner, their conversation was limited to disjointed starts and stops about their children, his parents, her mother, Jacob and Tara, and even about Warren and Hilary. Important-looking men often came to the table and shook Tony's hand. He introduced Miriam to them as his wife. Over coffee, Tony suggested they drive to Coney Island and walk on the Boardwalk.

"If you want," Miriam answered without enthusiasm.

"Maybe the park would be a better idea."

"I don't want to stay out too late," Miriam told him. "I have a lot of things to do tomorrow."

A few minutes later, he and Miriam were seated in the rear of the limousine. "Drive over to Prospect Park —"

"I'd rather go to the Boardwalk," Miriam said.

"Take us to Coney Island," Tony told the driver, and he pressed a button that raised the glass partition between the front and the rear sections of the car. Then he took Miriam's left hand in his. Earlier, he had noticed with delight that she still wore her wedding band. "I still wear mine too," he said, touching hers with the ball of his finger.

"I saw," Miriam responded softly.

"If we still are wearing these rings, why aren't we together?" he asked, trying to gaze deeply into her eyes.

"Tony, I don't want to talk about it!"

"But —"

"I agreed to see you because Jacob convinced me it was the right thing to do," Miriam interrupted.

Tony hesitated before he asked, "Are you sorry you came?"

Miriam shrugged her shoulders slightly, and turned her head to look out the window.

"Answer me!" he demanded, aware that they'd stopped for a red light.

"I'm not sure," she said. "I wanted to see you —"

Tony seized on that. "Why did you want to see me?"

Miriam turned her face toward him. "We shared a good life before you wrecked it."

Tony let go of her hand and in a low voice he said, "I loved Uncle Mike. There was nothing else I could do. I had to —"

Miriam stiffened. "I was about to give birth and you went off to kill someone."

"But I didn't kill anyone, did I?" he implored as the car started to move again.

"You sound almost sorry that you didn't," she said angrily.

"I couldn't," he admitted in a whisper. "I couldn't kill in cold blood."

Miriam remained silent.

"The children should have a full-time father, not someone they see once a week," Tony begged, gazing at her.

"You should have thought about that the night you walked out of your father's house," she said. Then she added, "When you were in the Navy, I lived with the possibility that you might be killed. That went with being a Navy wife, and I was proud of the things you had done and were doing. But the night you went after Spilachi, I realized that deep down inside you were a mobster at heart, one of the very kind you told me you hated. You were one of them!"

"It's not that way," Tony protested.

"All right, tell me the way it is," Miriam challenged.

"You know I couldn't stay in the Navy. You know —"

"You threw it all away just to prove yourself a man," she shot back at him. "You threw away your career, not to mention me and your children."

In the years that he and Miriam had lived together, she'd never spoken to him this way. Jacob was right. Miriam was a lot stronger than he'd ever thought.

"I think I want to go home now," Miriam said.

"We won't stay long."

She shook her head. "No, take me home."

"I love you, Miriam," he said. "And I know you love me."

"That doesn't matter," she responded haltingly. "That doesn't matter."

Tony put his hands on her shoulders and eased her around toward him. "Tell me what does matter?" he asked.

"I don't know."

"You matter to me," he said. "You matter very much."

"I don't want to live with the chance that you'll wind up like Uncle Mike," she responded. "I don't want to live with that hanging over my head."

"It won't happen," Tony said. "It won't happen because I won't let it happen. Things are changing."

"Jacob told me what you told him," she said more softly.

Tony nodded. "It's true, Miriam. I swear on the heads of our sons that it's true. I don't want to wind up the way Uncle Mike did, either!"

"No more shootings?"

"No more shootings," he answered, drawing her close to him.

She held him off.

"I'm a businessman now, a successful, legitimate businessman," Tony said. "And a successful businessman needs a wife, children, and a home." This time when he drew her close, she didn't resist. "I love you," he whispered, nuzzling her ear.

"I love you, too," Miriam responded.

Tony brought his lips down to hers and kissed her. "I've missed you," he told her. "I've missed you very much."

Jacob parked on Coney Island Avenue, a block south of Kings Highway. "We're within walking distance of five different automobile dealers," he said with excitement.

"I don't have the slightest idea of what kind of car I want!" Tara answered, as excited as he.

As they strolled along Jacob proclaimed dramatically, "Remember, Tara, today a car; tomorrow a house!"

Tara shifted Sy from one shoulder to the other.

"Give him to me," Jacob said, taking Sy in his arms. "Hey, boy, your mama is going to get a new car!"

They stopped for a red light on the corner of Kings Highway.

"Why don't you get one, too?" Tara said gaily. "You're driving a second hand heap now, and a rich fellow like you should have sporty wheels!"

"Not quite a heap, yet!" Jacob answered playfully. "I'll think about what you said!"

The light changed and they crossed the street.

"Maybe you should have worn your uniform," Tara said. "Maybe you'd be able to get a better price?"

"Tara, have you forgotten so soon?" Jacob reminded her. "We don't have to think about what something costs anymore, even if I'm not dressed for the part." He wore a pair of old chino pants, a tan polo shirt, and a long-beaked blue cap with the scrambled egg insignia of a Navy commander on the visor.

She threw her head back and laughed.

"You're beautiful!" Jacob exclaimed, suddenly aware of how the bright sunlight made her russet hair glisten.

Tara took his free hand and squeezed it.

"As soon as we're finished buying you a car, we're going to go to the Prospect Park Zoo; then we'll go into the city. We'll go to that Italian restaurant on MacDougal Street."

"I'd like that," Tara said.

"All right, you have your choice," Jacob told her. "Across the street is the Chrysler dealer. Here's the Buick. Up the street is the Chevy place and on the other side is the Cadillac dealer. On the next street, you'll find Lincolns and Fords."

"I don't know a thing about cars. What do you suggest?"

"I'm out to please you, Tara," Jacob answered. "Let's go over to the Studebaker place and see what they have."

"It'll be embarrassing if we don't buy," Tara pouted.

"The salesmen are used to browsers," he said, leading her into the showroom.

"They're certainly sporty-looking," Tara commented as they moved around from one car to another.

"The salesmen are watching us," Tara whispered.

"Do you like any of the cars?" Jacob asked.

"That blue convertible against the wall."

"Why don't you sit in it and see how it fits?" he said with a smile. He led her to the blue car. "Try it," he said, opening the door with his free hand. "Go on, sit behind the wheel."

Suddenly a salesman joined them and as he scanned Tony's attire, he said in a slightly condescending tone, "Folks, I hate to tell you this, but this is our most expensive model."

Jacob turned. The man was in his late forties and well dressed. Gold cufflinks studded the French cuffs of his white shirt, and a large diamond ring sparkled on the small finger of his left hand.

"You young people might do better to look at some of our other models," the salesman said.

"Just how expensive is this one?" Jacob asked.

"Ten five."

"Is that all? For another fifteen hundred I can buy the top-of-the-line Cadillac," Jacob observed pointedly, putting Sy down on the floor and holding his hand.

The man grinned as though he enjoyed the little joke. "By the way, my name is John Rice. Folks, I can see that you're a nice young couple and I wouldn't want to steer you wrong. This probably isn't the car for you."

"How does it feel?" Jacob asked, bending down to look at Tara.

"Good," she answered.

"Mister — I didn't get your name," Rice said.

"I didn't give it," Jacob answered. "But it's Jacob Miller." He didn't include his rank.

"Well, Mr. Miller, I can give you a real good price on our less expensive models. Ordinarily, we don't sell the cheaper cars for less than two hundred above our cost. But for you, I'll go back and check with the boss and see if I can convince him to cut that to one hundred on something I think you can afford."

"How about that same deal on this model?" Jacob asked as Tara eased out of the car and stood next to him.

"Listen to me," Rice said, "I'm offering you the best deal possible. Just look at that other car over there. Mrs. Miller, sit in it and see if you can see any difference."

"My wife wants this car," Jacob answered, putting his hand on the roof of the car.

"Mr. Miller, let me be frank with you," Rice said. "This car is—"

"Hey, John," one of the men called from the office, "there's fighting going on in Korea. Guys from your old division, the Twenty-fourth, are being sent in from Japan. Looks like North Korea has invaded South Korea."

"What does that mean?" Tara asked, clutching Jacob's arm. "Will you have to go?"

"I should have guessed you were in the Navy," Rice said, looking at Jacob's cap. "No, take my word for it, Mrs. Miller, it'll turn out to be just some Koreans killing other Koreans. I was with the Twenty-Fourth Infantry Division in the big one, and if they're in it, it'll be over in a few days!" He smiled at Jacob. "Come on, let me show you a car that makes sense for you."

"Jacob, maybe we should wait," Tara suggested in a quavering voice.

"I promised you a car and you're going to have a car," Jacob answered, putting his arm around her waist.

"Let me talk to my boss," Rice said.

"This car," Jacob responded.

"Hey John," the man in the office called, "the president has put all of our armed forces on alert. He said our guys in the Twenty-Fourth have already taken heavy casualties."

"Oh, Jacob!" Tara exclaimed.

"Write up the order," Jacob told Rice.

Rice shrugged and led them to his desk. "How will you finance —"

"I won't," Jacob answered. "I'll pay in cash."

"Cash, sir?"

"Cash," Jacob repeated. "Make the title out to Mrs. Jacob Miller. And have it ready tomorrow," Jacob said to the stunned salesman. Turning to Tara, he added, "OK, honey, let's get this little fellow to the zoo. It's a beautiful summer day and we're going to enjoy every minute of it."

Warren looked down at Hilary. Her eyes were closed, her lips slightly parted, and her neck and bare breasts still held the warm flush of their lovemaking. "I love you," he said in a low, husky voice.

Hilary smiled, opened her eyes and, wrapping her arms around his neck, she eased his lips down to hers.

Warren looked at the clock on the bedside table. "It's after noon and we talked about going into town to shop."

"It's Saturday and, thank God, I didn't have a modeling booking," Hilary said, "and, above all, you're here in bed with me and not in that silly old Washington!"

Warren eased himself upright and, propping his head up with one hand, he tenderly caressed her breasts with the other. "If our schedules let us," he said, "I'd like to take leave and go to Frisco. My mother could meet us there and spend some time together. She'd really enjoy Andy, now that he's walking around and beginning to talk."

"I don't know about going to Frisco," Hilary said. "Sometime in July I know I have to be in London and then in Athens for a few days."

"When did those two assignments come up?" he asked with annoyance, pulling himself into a sitting position and leaning against the headboard.

"Just recently," Hilary answered. "I've known about the possibility that I might have to go, and late Thursday it was finally firmed up. But listen to this: for the five days in London and three in Athens, I'll be paid thirty-five thousand dollars."

"We don't need the money. Between us we earn —"

"It's not only the money —" Hilary began.

"If it's not the money, tell me what it is," Warren interjected, trying not to become angry. They had had this kind of discussion on several occasions when Hilary's schedule had interfered with his plans.

"I'm going to be working with Henri Pascale."

"I don't know who the hell he is," Warren growled. "I only know that I'd like you to be with me."

"Maybe you'll be able to come with me?"

"Not on your life," he answered. "It wouldn't be fun. You're always exhausted after a day's shooting."

"Warren, don't sulk," Hilary said.

"OK then, Andy and I will go alone to visit my mother," he said.

Hilary reached out and touched his arm.

"It's hard enough when I have to be away, but that's —" Warren began.

"Someday soon," she said, "I'll either be editor of one of the high-fashion magazines, or start my own."

"Publish your own?" he asked, amazed at her ambition.

"It's possible… It's really possible with the right connections and financial help. I know all sides of the business."

Warren was silent. During the past years since the war had ended, he had learned a great deal about national and international political connections, but he knew nothing about the kinds of connections Hilary had just mentioned.

"You don't think I can do it, do you?"

"If it can be done, you'll do it," he said in exasperation.

"From the way you just said that, I can't help feeling that you'd prefer —"

"Hilary, I'm not against your doing important things," Warren cut in. "But I also want us to have a life together."

"We do and we will," Hilary answered, moving closer to Warren. "Come on and tell me you'll come to London and Athens if you can?"

"What about my mother? She was looking forward to being with us," he said, falling, as he always did, under her spell.

"She can come to London and Athens with us!" Hilary said. "Tell her we'll pay for everything. It will be our treat."

"You know what you are?" Warren asked.

"No. Tell me!" Hilary responded, reaching around the table on her side of the bed and turning on the radio.

"An operator," Warren answered. "A first class operator!"

"And that's bad?" she teased, wantonly fondling his genitals as she pressed her open mouth against his in a torrid kiss.

Suddenly, the song "Paper Moon" stopped and the announcer said, "We interrupt this program to bring you a late news bulletin from General MacArthur's headquarters in Tokyo. Sometime in the early hours of this morning, armed forces from communist North Korea invaded the Democratic Republic of South Korea. The North Korean army is moving toward the South Korean capital city of Seoul. Fighting is fierce and casualties are heavy. Elements of the United States Twenty-Fourth Infantry Division are in action against the invading forces. We will bring additional bulletins throughout our broadcast day. And now back to our regular program. Stay tuned!"

"What does that mean?" Hilary asked, sitting up.

Before Warren could answer, the phone rang.

Hilary answered it. "It's for you," she said, handing the phone to him.

"Commander Troost here," Warren said.

"Please state your serial number, Commander," the voice said.

Realizing the call was coming from someone in Admiral Harly's office, Warren gave his serial number.

"There's an aircraft waiting for you at the Floyd Bennett Naval Air Station. You are to return here without delay to meet with the admiral. Be prepared to proceed immediately to Japan."

"Wilco," Warren answered. He put the phone down.

"What is it?" Hilary asked.

"I've been ordered to —" He stopped. He knew that everything he'd do from now on would be under the strictest security.

"Where have you been ordered?" Hilary questioned.

Warren shook his head. "I must go to Washington right now. There's a plane waiting for me."

After he had thrown things into his bag, he came back to the bedside and looked down at her.

"Warren ... Warren, dear ... a half hour, or even an hour more, won't change things!" Hilary sobbed. "It might be a very long time before we can be together again!"

Warren got into the bed and took her in his arms.

"I love you," Hilary whispered.

He kissed her lips, her breasts, the hollow of flat stomach.

CHAPTER 17

In the predawn light of August 6, Jacob sat patiently in his F9F Panther jet at the head of the fighters on the attack carrier *Makin*. The drone of jet engines and, for Jacob, the more familiar throbbing of propeller-driven AD dive bombers engulfed the flight deck. The carrier was coming into the wind to launch its first support strike of the day.

The ship, with six escort destroyers, was steaming fifty miles east of the South Korean port city of Pusan, where the American Twenty-Fourth Division was surrounded on three sides by numerically superior forces of the North Korean People's Army.

The ten ADs, heavily laden with five-hundred-pound bombs, were already being flung into the air alternately from the port and starboard catapults. Jacob, strike coordinator of six other Panthers in the fighter escort, waited for the yellow-shirted taxi directors to lead them onto the cats. This would be Jacob's first combat mission since reporting aboard the *Makin* just three days before as the emergency replacement for its air group commander, who had been shot down the week prior.

As the last AD became airborne, the yellow shirt in front of Jacob signaled for the wheel chocks to be removed. With upraised arms and precise hand motions, he brought him forward to the port catapult. Jacob felt a slight jolt as the shuttle was attached to the nose wheel of his Panther and the bridle was tensed for firing.

The helmeted and goggled catapult officer raised his right arm and, circling the air with his index finger, called for one hundred percent power.

Jacob advanced his throttle to the stop and held it firmly there. He checked his instruments, positioned his head against the headrest, and, with his feet lightly on the rudder pedals, quickly saluted and lowered his hand to the stick.

The catapult officer dropped to his right knee and pointed with an extended arm to the bow.

The launch-control man in the catwalk pressed the 'fire' button, and with a whoosh of steam from the catapult track, Jacob hurtled toward the bow. The acceleration pushed him hard against the back of the seat, and in seconds his airspeed indicator showed 135 knots and increasing as the blue ocean fell away below him.

Jacob eased back on the throttle and began to climb to the pre-planned rendezvous point.

"Red Zero, this is Red Base. Do you read?" a voice from air operations aboard the *Makin* radioed.

"Loud and clear," Jacob said.

"At rendezvous, proceed to sectors W-12 and W-13 for targets of opportunity. The weather is clear."

"Wilco," Jacob answered, banking to the right. Glancing over his shoulder at the carrier, he saw two more Panthers climbing toward him and two just clearing the bow. The last two were on the cats. He checked the altimeter. He was at ten thousand feet and, needing oxygen soon, he secured his oxygen mask over his mouth and nose, and saw that the flow indicator on the ledge below his right arm was blinking properly each time he inhaled. He continued to climb.

"Red Zero, this is Red Base. All your birds are in the air. Good hunting."

"Roger," Jacob responded and then, addressing the AD leader, he radioed, "Red One, this is Red Zero. Circle at angels twelve below me."

The AD lead pilot said, "Wilco."

Jacob called the fighter leader. "Red Two, this is Red Zero. Join me at angels fifteen and be prepared to weave over Red One on our way in."

Jacob leveled off at fifteen thousand feet and began a large circle to complete the rendezvous. The ten slower ADs were already together, circling tightly below him. The Panthers were climbing toward him in three sections of two planes each. "This is Red Zero," he radioed. "We'll be looking for enemy vehicular traffic and troops. We'll descend to angels ten over the target area. Whenever a target is spotted, let me know where it is for attack instructions. Remember, we go in steep and fast. Don't take chances. We'll make our runs and get the hell out of there. Red One, Red Two, do you read?"

"Roger," both of the pilots radioed.

"Going down to angels ten," Jacob said, easing the stick forward. He had no idea how good the pilots of this air group were, or how they handled themselves in combat. Most had been on the line for only three weeks, and some had come to the air group directly from flight training at Pensacola. Only a few had fought in World War II. He himself had had only six-week transition training in jets before this sudden assignment as CAG Eight.

"Red Zero," Red Two called excitedly, "there are trucks at three o'clock."

Jacob checked the position. There was a convoy of ten vehicles moving east. "Red Two, we'll take 'em. Open out and follow me. I'm going in from the south," Jacob said. Leveling off and turning to the left, he made a 180° turn and armed his .50-caliber guns and rockets. "Let's go," he ordered, moving the stick forward and forcing his voice to be steady. His stomach balled into the knot he had known so well during his last combat mission in the battle for Okinawa in August 1945. As his Panther screamed toward the trucks, he said to himself, "Goddamn. Nothing changes."

"They've spotted us," Red Two radioed.

In front and below Jacob, the trucks were turning in panic off the road, and the troops were firing haphazardly at them with rifles. Jacob flipped the master armament switch on, and as the targets and men loomed larger and larger, he picked out a truck and squeezed the trigger on the stick with his forefinger. Instantly, he felt the plane shudder and saw the white tracers find their mark. The truck burst into flames. He released the trigger, pulled up, and pushed the throttle forward to climb rapidly. He looked over his shoulder. Six of the ten trucks were burning. "Let's go around and get what's left," he radioed. "Come in from the north this time."

The second run knocked out the remaining trucks, and Jacob radioed Red Two to reform above the ADs at ten thousand feet.

For the next half hour Jacob flew over the target area, but saw nothing moving. Then suddenly Red One radioed, "Red Zero, there's a large group of troops moving out of that mountain pass at eleven o'clock."

"Roger, I see them," Jacob answered. "We'll hold this position for a few minutes until they get more in the open. Red Two and I will make runs from the east — this time .50s and rockets. Then, Red One, you go in from the south and lay all your eggs on 'em."

"There sure is a piss pot full of them down there," Red One responded. "We can't wait, my guys are getting bored!"

To Jacob it looked as if it was a full battalion. "All right, remember, go in steep and fast." He kicked the plane over to the port side and began his run. This time there was heavy ground fire: machine guns and 40mm antiaircraft weapons.

At four thousand feet, Jacob commenced firing with his .50s. At three thousand, he fired all of the high-velocity rockets on the racks under his wings. The effect was devastating, and as he pulled out of his dive and looked back, he could see the enemy being pounded by the fighters behind him. As the last Panther pulled up, Red One and his ADs bored in viciously from the south. Bomb explosions rocked the area.

Jacob could see the terrain littered with casualties. "Red One, Red Two," he radioed, "good work. Now, ADs join up, and Red Two and I will take you home." He turned east and headed for the sea.

Jacob relaxed. The mission had turned out very well, especially for the first time out. The sun was well up and the sky was a beautiful light blue. His thoughts turned to more pleasant matters as he and the other Panthers crisscrossed above the ADs. He was hoping that he might have a letter waiting for him from Tara when he returned to the *Makin*. They had agreed before he left that she would fly to Japan to meet him when the ship put into port for R and R next month.

Jacob looked back as his flight headed east. On the horizon behind him were at least a dozen columns of dense black smoke. He radioed the ship. "Red Base, this is Red Zero. We're inbound."

"Roger, Red Zero, we have you. You should pick us up dead ahead of you in a few minutes."

Jacob acknowledged the information and once again allowed himself to think about Tara. He'd urged her to move to a bigger apartment, or buy a house, but she'd said, "I really wouldn't enjoy it without you, and —"

The radio crackled and a worried voice came on the air. "Red Zero, Red Two, this is Red Two Six. My engine is running rough."

"Where are you?" Jacob radioed, afraid the plane had been hit on the last run. He didn't know the men well enough yet to recognize voices.

"Tail end Charley, port side," the man answered.

"Red Two, continue on. I'll take a look at him," Jacob said. He slowed and dropped five hundred feet, allowing the other Panthers to pass over him. "I can't see anything," he radioed, moving under the distressed aircraft.

Without warning, black smoke erupted from the tailpipe.

"Eject!" Jacob shouted, kicking his Panther over to the port side, away from the crippled plane. "Eject!"

Suddenly the man began to scream, "I can't … I can't get to —!" The plane staggered and in the next instant exploded in a mass of flames, tumbling in a burning arc toward the sea.

Jacob swallowed hard in despair. He didn't even know the man's name.

Later that night, Jacob entered the wardroom and sat down at one of the tables. He had flown a second mission that day, and he was tired. He had just completed one of the most difficult letters he'd ever written to the parents of the pilot who had been lost that morning. The man's name was Dennis Holmes, a nugget fresh from Pensacola. He had been twenty-two years old.

"Mind if we join you, CAG?" a young man asked.

Jacob looked up and saw two fighter-squadron pilots. "Please," Jacob said, gesturing toward the empty chairs. Both were junior-grade lieutenants. The taller of the two introduced himself as Gary Jones; the other was Raoul Peterson. They had been commissioned in the Reserve before going to Pensacola.

"Our skipper said you were in the Battle of Midway," Jones said with awe in his voice. "Were you, sir?"

Jacob almost smiled. The way the question had been asked made him realize that to these young jet jockeys, Midway had taken place in ancient times and he was already an old man. "Yes, I was."

Both men grinned.

"Where are you men from?" Jacob asked.

"Santa Fe, New Mexico," Peterson answered.

"St. Louis," Jones said.

"Both places are far from the sea —" Jacob saw another, older man wearing captain's insignia coming toward the table.

"Holy Christ, I thought that was you, Miller," Captain Horace Dean exclaimed.

Jones and Peterson jumped to their feet.

"As you were," Dean said, shaking Jacob's hand. "My God, it's good to see you again. May I join you?"

"Certainly, sir," Jacob answered, wondering just how sincere that remark was in view of their previous run-ins years ago after Midway and, later, on board the *Shiloh*.

"The last time I saw you was after the *Shiloh* went down and we were picked up by the *Emerson*," Dean said. "I'll never forget that day!"

"When did you come aboard the *Makin*…? And what are you doing here, Captain?" Jacob asked, wishing fervently to change the subject from the tragedy of the *Shiloh*. He had succeeded in putting Connie in the past, and he didn't want her brought back into the present by Dean.

"Called by my country again. Same old business, press coordination," Dean answered, "and before I knew it, I was sent out to Japan. I was flown out here late this afternoon. What about you?"

"I'm the air group commander … CAG Eight!"

Dean shook his finger at him. "Congratulations. Truth is, I heard some interesting rumors about you not so long ago."

"I'm listening," Jacob said. He had never liked Dean and now felt a growing distaste for his inquisitive manner.

"You're probably the richest man in the Navy, maybe in all of the armed services." Jacob flushed but said nothing. "True?" Dean pressed. "It would make one hell of a release, you know. A guy who doesn't have to, out fighting in Korea."

Jacob remembered Dean well enough to know that once he was on to a story, he wouldn't let go until he had all the details. The reason for him being on board the *Makin* was becoming unpleasantly clear.

"You men have the best there is for your boss," Dean said patronizingly, looking at the two pilots.

"Come on, Captain Dean," Jacob said impatiently. "Give the guys a chance to find out for themselves!"

"Just letting them know how lucky they are," Dean laughed. "Now, about that rumor I heard?"

"Where there's smoke, they say there's fire," Jacob answered, deciding to see how far the bastard would go.

Dean grinned happily.

"Surely you don't expect to hear numbers," Jacob said with a straight face. "Just believe I'm not hurting."

"Enough to allow you to live a life of leisure once this war is over?"

"Let it go at that," Jacob answered. He was aware that Jones and Peterson were looking at him with another kind of respect from that for a Midway veteran.

"One more question," Dean said, "and then I'd like to know how it all came about. Do you intend to retire after the war?"

"No," Jacob answered firmly. "I will stay as long as the Navy will allow me to. I'm a career officer, and proud of it!"

Warren looked up from the papers on his desk. He was commanding officer of a Seal team of thirty-six highly trained enlisted men and two officers, lieutenant commanders Patrick Rogers and Christopher Knight. Both of them had had combat experience in the closing months of World War II as underwater demolition experts. The young lieutenant saluting him would be the unit's third officer. From the ribbons on his chest, he too had been blooded.

"Lieutenant Sean Branigan reporting for duty, sir," Branigan said.

Warren's eyes opened wide. The name hadn't registered when he'd first seen it on the orders transferring the man to the team, but now he remembered having been told years ago by Commander Hacker that his son, Sean, used his mother's maiden name, while his daughter kept his.

Sean resembled Hacker as Warren remembered the older man. He had the same red hair and freckles on his arms. But he also favored his sister, Irene, especially around the mouth.

"Sir?" Branigan said.

"I was aboard the *Dee* with your father during the last war," Warren answered quietly.

Sean stiffened. "Sir, I did not connect your name with that Troost. I seldom saw my father, and he only wrote to me on occasion."

Warren nodded. "And how about your sister?" he asked, struggling to keep the tightness he felt out of his voice. Almost any mention of Irene brought flashing into his mind the dreadful image of her lying dead — breasts hacked off by Japanese soldiers and mouth frozen open in a death scream.

"We exchanged letters now and then," Sean answered.

Warren rubbed his jaw. Obviously Irene had never written to her brother about him, or if she had, he did not wish to acknowledge it.

"We were not a close family," Sean volunteered.

"Some families are that way," Warren answered evenly, recognizing the same kind of rigidity in Sean that had been in him at the same age.

"Yes, sir," Sean responded.

"Why did you volunteer for this assignment?" Warren asked.

"When I heard about the Seal organization, I figured they'd go where the action would be and that's where I want to be. I was already UDT-qualified, as you probably know, sir."

"In a matter of days, we'll be going on our first mission," Warren said. "Between now and that time, you'll train with the team. In this outfit, there is little distinction between the officers and the men."

"Yes, sir," Sean answered.

"We live together and share the same recreational facilities. The officers in this unit function as leaders and administrators. The men are the heart of it. You will find that every man is an expert in many different areas, and every one of them can be totally relied upon to carry out his assignment. Have you any questions?"

"No, sir."

Warren nodded and said, "Welcome aboard, Lieutenant Branigan. That will be all for now."

"Thank you, sir," Sean responded as he saluted, did an about-face and left the office.

"I want to get back on active duty, sir," Tony said, standing in front of Admiral Harly's desk. "I know there's a shortage of trained officers."

"Commander Troost wrote to me about you," Harly said, leaning back in his chair. Though he had been scheduled to retire at the beginning of August, the chief of naval operations had obtained Congressional consent to allow Harly to remain on active duty for as long as the Korean emergency lasted. "I had your record checked and it is impressive," the admiral added.

"Thank you, sir," Tony responded, beginning to feel more at ease. "I asked Commander Troost to intercede for me because we were buddies in the last war."

Harly nodded, offered Tony a cigar, and took one himself before he began. "Let's look at the facts. You were involved in an incident some time ago that —"

"Excuse me, Admiral," Tony interrupted. "I resigned my commission voluntarily, and the authorities were never involved."

Harly blew smoke off to his right side. "Tony — may I call you Tony?"

"Certainly, sir."

"Tony, I'll be frank with you," Harly continued. "There is a complete file on you in the FBI. Some of your activities on the docks have been documented. Your current business dealings, though legitimate, have been monitored. Moreover, your continuing association with Mafia figures is well-known to the FBI and other government agencies. The fact is, your return to active duty at this time would be opposed by the Bureau and by those agencies."

Tony took a deep breath. Harly wasn't mincing words with him.

"That's the straight dope, Tony," Harly said, adding, "but there is another way for you to go."

"What would that be?" Tony asked, deeply disappointed by what Harly had just said.

Harly flicked the ashes from the end of his cigar into an ashtray, took a long look at Tony, and then said, "You can work with the CIA while you go about your regular business affairs."

Tony almost dropped his cigar. He was aware that the Office of Strategic Services, a hush-hush organization that dealt in international intrigue, had recently become known as the Central Intelligence Agency, but that was about all he knew of the subject.

"I can arrange it," Harly stated matter-of-factly. "You have a military background, which in certain situations will be useful, and your experience in other areas would be more useful."

"Do you mean in covert activities?"

Harly nodded. "If you agree, you can be sure you'll have opportunities to serve your country."

"What would I be? A spy?"

Harly laughed. "That's a hard word. Who knows? Actually, you'd be just what you are now — a businessman."

"Then when would I be working for, or with, the CIA?"

"From time to time, when asked to pursue special assignments," Harly answered.

"Are you connected —"

"Yes," Harly interrupted flatly. "Now, the question is, are you interested?"

"I'm interested," Tony said without hesitation.

"I'll set up a meeting for you right now," Harly replied and, picking up the phone, he began to dial.

CHAPTER 18

"Smoke if you have them and give me your attention. I have important information for you," Warren said, stepping onto a small platform in front of his men at one end of the Quonset hut. Earlier that day, he'd returned from a secret briefing at U.S. Naval Headquarters in Tokyo. "Men, the target for our first combat mission is the South Korean city of Inchon."

A low murmur came from the men. Inchon, the port for Seoul, was miles behind the present front. "Map, please."

The lights were switched off and a map of Inchon was projected on a screen behind him. "Our Marines will make an amphibious assault on Wolmido Island, which guards Inchon's harbor, and take it. Our task will be to neutralize the guns on Wolmido, and destroy the causeway between it and Inchon ahead of the Marine landings," he explained, identifying the island and the bridge with a pointer. "We will strike covertly one and a half hours ahead of a Marine battalion to reduce their opposition. When the island is secured, a main force of Marines will assault the mainland and be followed by Army troops. Any questions so far?"

"Sir, how will our team go in?" Commander Rogers asked.

"We'll use night cover and go ashore in rafts."

"Sir, do you have any detailed information about the island?" Knight asked.

"Yes, I do," Warren answered. "Next slide, please."

A composite consisting of an aerial photograph and cartographic map of the island came on the screen as Warren continued, "The island is a thousand yards wide at its widest point. Its terrain is rugged and we know it was extensively

312

tunneled by the South Koreans when they controlled it. The tunnels are being used by the present tenants, from the North. You can see their paths marked in red on the map. Also marked, with red stars, are the positions of the artillery we must take out. There are three positions. Each one has a crew of ten men on duty at any one time. Each position can fire independently, or have its fire controlled from a main control location at the top of this ridge, marked with a green square. The Marines will go for that after they hit the beach. Our job is to take out those shore batteries and blow the causeway." He paused and asked for questions.

"Skipper, do we know how many men are on the island?" a man asked.

"Not exactly. Could be five hundred, or twice that number," Warren said. "But we'll have the initial advantage of surprise. A half hour after we land, the Third Battalion, Fifth Marines will land. We will start our part on September 15 at 0430; the Marines will follow at dawn, 0600. The Marines and our team will remain on the island until the mainland assault takes place. That is scheduled for 1100, when there's enough water in the channel for the invasion force to steam into the harbor."

"What happens if the Koreans come off the mainland?" another man questioned. "They might try to bridge the causeway even though we've blown it, or they might come across the mud flats. If they laid down enough straw, they might make it across those flats."

"There will be gunfire support from our ships offshore, and the carrier *Makin* will be standing by to provide air strikes as needed."

"Skipper, do we link up with the Marines?" Sean Branigan asked.

"Yes," Warren responded, "but we maintain unit integrity." He paused for a few moments before he asked for additional questions. When he was satisfied that there were none, he said, "We will divide into four groups. Three groups of ten men will hit the three gun installations. Each man will carry in addition to his normal fighting gear ten pounds of RDX explosives. Group leaders will also carry the necessary detonating devices. The groups will be designated Able, Baker, and Charley, and will be led by Commanders Rogers, Knight, and Chief Hansen respectively. The fourth group, six men and Lieutenant Branigan, will be led by me. We will blow the causeway. Each group leader will be issued detailed operational plans. Our reassembly point will be on the island end of the causeway, where we will set up defensive positions to prevent enemy counterattack from the mainland. My radio call is Blue Frog. We board our transport at 1900 tonight. After this briefing, group leaders will report to my office. Gentlemen, I'll see you when we board ship. Lights, please."

The lights came on and the projector was switched off.

"Attention!" one of the men called when Warren stepped off the platform.

"As you were," Warren said. "Rogers, Knight, and Hansen, my office, please."

Jacob held Tara's hand as they rode the elevator to the top floor of the Imperial Palace Hotel in Tokyo, where she had registered on arrival from the States the day before. That morning at 0600, the *Makin* had tied up at the Yokosuka Naval Base. Jacob and the officers of his air group had been granted shore leave for seventy-two hours, and he had hurried immediately to the big city to be with her.

"When I registered," Tara said, "the desk clerk asked me if I was sure that I wanted just a room and not a suite."

"Damn! Because of Dean's article, we can't be ourselves anymore," Jacob lamented.

"You didn't expect it to be otherwise, did you?" she smiled.

Jacob shook his head. "Even the admiral called me to his cabin. I got the idea he wanted to be assured I didn't expect any special consideration. I simply told the old bugger I was just a run-of-the-mill professional naval officer."

"Did you think he believed you?"

"I'm sure I convinced him," Jacob answered as the elevator stopped and the door slid open. A Japanese man holding a leather attaché case was framed in the open door. "Going up?" he asked.

As the door started to close, Jacob held it open.

"You!" the man exclaimed as his face lighted in recognition. "Jacob, it's me, Yashi Kurokachi!"

"Yashi!" Jacob shouted, pulling Tara out of the elevator before the doors closed.

"Jacob!" Yashi said in a lilting English, and bowed deeply from the waist. "Jacob Miller! But now, I see, Commander Miller."

Jacob bowed amateurishly. "My wife, Tara, Yashi." Turning to Tara, he said, "This is my old friend, Yashi Kurokachi." The memory of that day in his raft at Midway came flooding back.

Kurokachi bowed again and, addressing Tara, said, "My great honor. Mrs. Miller, your husband is not only a hero in your country, but he is also a hero to my family."

Jacob flushed. "Tara doesn't know how we met, Yashi."

Kurokachi put his finger to his lips. "Please, allow me to tell her at dinner. You and your wife must be my guests. My wife would never forgive me if I did not insist that you join us for dinner."

Jacob looked questioningly at Tara.

"Of course, we will, Mr. Kurokachi," Tara accepted graciously.

"I will be in the lobby at five this evening," Kurokachi smiled.

"I'm happy to hear your wife and children survived the war," Jacob said, remembering they'd lived in Hiroshima.

Kurokachi shook his head. "They were all killed by the bomb," he said quietly. "Only a nephew survived, and he lives with me. You will meet him and my new family this evening."

"I am sorry," Jacob responded, "truly sorry." And he put his hand gently on the man's shoulder.

"I married again when I came home and now have another family, a boy named for you, Jacob. In my family, and in my son's family, and in the families of all my grandsons to come, the first-born son will always be named Jacob."

"I'm honored," Jacob responded in a low voice, again attempting a ceremonial bow.

"And I also have a daughter named Kumi," Kurokachi said proudly.

"I have a son, named Sy for my father Sam," Jacob offered, suddenly aware that Kurokachi looked prosperous.

"What are you doing now?" Jacob asked as they waited for the elevator to arrive again.

"I have a small electronics company," he said. "I have been meeting here today with some financial people from Hong Kong who might be willing to invest in my company," Kurokachi answered. "I am trying to expand."

The elevator stopped and the doors opened.

Jacob and Kurokachi bowed to each other and moments later, Jacob and Tara were again on their way up to the top floor and their room.

"Tara... Oh, Tara!" Jacob exclaimed, at the instant of his orgasmic ecstasy. "Tara, I love you, I've missed you, I love you!" as he felt her hands caress his bare back.

"I've missed you so much, too," Tara murmured. "This time it wasn't like any of the other times you were gone. This time, I constantly longed to be with you. I can't explain it!"

He kissed the tip of her nose. "I know the feeling," he said, settling down alongside of her in the large double bed.

"Sometimes I longed to have you inside me and feel your hands on my breasts! I would find myself weeping ... even my painting didn't help me stop wanting you."

He caressed her breasts tenderly. "I'm glad you came out here, even if it's for only three days... If only Sy could have come with you!"

"He asks about you all the time," she sighed. "He wants his daddy."

Jacob took a deep breath and slowly exhaled. "Damn! This is the life! It makes me realize how long it might be before I'll be back in the States!" Putting his hands behind his head, he gazed lasciviously at their naked reflections in the mirrored ceiling above the bed. "What do we look like making love?" he teased.

"Like we're enjoying it," Tara answered with a laugh.

"Next time I get to watch!" he suggested with a leer.

"That's only fair!" she giggled; then, hesitantly, she asked, "Have you — have you been flying combat missions?"

"Only against ground targets," Jacob answered. "The North Koreans don't have much of an air force, and what they had was shot out of the skies in the first few weeks of the war before I took over the group."

"Do you think it will last a long time?"

"I don't know," he said. "I don't want to think about it… Now, all I want to do is enjoy you…" And, drawing her closer to him, he felt the delightful warmth of her beautiful, naked body against him.

True to his word, Kurokachi met Jacob and Tara in the lobby of the hotel promptly at five and, after an exchange of greetings and bows, he led them to a waiting, chauffeur-driven Bentley.

They rode through a serene countryside punctuated by precisely laid-out rice paddies to Kurokachi's house, located about twenty miles outside of Tokyo. It was of typical Japanese architecture, rambling yet yielding an impression of pristine compactness and furnished in exquisite taste. At the door, they left their shoes and were offered soft woven slippers. After meeting Yashi's wife, Midori, a fragile, shy beauty about Tara's age, and the young children, who managed a few halting words of greeting in English, Jacob and Tara were led to the dining area. The table was low with cushions on four sides, and as the sliding screens were pulled back, they were delighted to see that the room fronted a graceful terrace, which in turn overlooked a small lake with a shrine rising from carefully placed rocks in its center.

The food was silently served by three smiling young women, and Jacob experienced for the first time the delicate taste of sushi among seven other courses of Japanese culinary triumphs.

Toward the end of the dinner, Kurokachi began the story of how he and Jacob had met. As he went on, tears gathered in Tara's eyes and she pressed her husband's hand.

"There we were," Kurokachi said, gazing intently at Jacob, "in the middle of the ocean — two small bits of humanity. I saw him before he saw me and I thought to myself, is he going to kill me? Of course, he could have very easily. He had a revolver, and I had been in the water a long time and was exhausted. To me it was a miracle that he told me to hold onto his small life raft and gave me a drink of his precious water. When the American destroyer came and picked him up, he insisted that I be taken on board. That was, is, and will always be the most revealing moment of my life. It was then that I learned what it means to be a real man."

Mrs. Kurokachi, who spoke surprisingly good English, said, "I am grateful, Commander, you did not shoot him."

Jacob smiled at her. Dressed in a traditional white silk, rose-embroidered kimono, she looked like an exquisite life-sized doll. "We are grateful to be here in your house," he responded with feeling.

Kurokachi filled his and Jacob's sake cups. "It was a strange way for two men to meet," he said. "But it happened that way, and now that our paths have once again crossed, my good friend, Jacob, I would like to think that there was some extraordinary reason for our lives to come together. Therefore, I propose that we continue to let them touch as often as possible."

"I will drink to that," Jacob answered, raising his cup.

"I offer you the hospitality of my home whenever you are in Tokyo," Kurokachi said. "Whatever is mine is also yours."

"I am honored," Jacob responded in a low voice.

Kurokachi nodded and the two of them drank.

Later, when Jacob and Tara had been driven back to the hotel and were in bed, Tara turned to him and asked, "Why didn't you ever tell me about Yashi?"

He shrugged, feeling slightly uncomfortable. He hadn't told her about John Yancy either or, for that matter, about many things that had happened to him in the past. "There didn't seem to be any point to it," he said lamely.

She sat up and leaned against the headboard. "That was a wonderful thing you did," she said. "Truly remarkable!"

Jacob joked, "I'm a remarkable man!"

"Yashi thinks so, and so do I! Seriously, I'm very proud of you."

Jacob put his hands behind his head. "It was my father who was the remarkable one, not me. Before I left for the war, he said to me, 'Never do anything that you'd be ashamed to tell your son.'"

"Do you think he would have approved of me?" Tara murmured quietly.

Jacob reached up and brought her down to his side. "Truthfully, I'm sure he would have been bothered by the fact that you're not Jewish, but he would have seen that you're a beautiful woman, a talented woman, and the woman I love. The combination of those three things would have made him accept with thanks what God had provided." He kissed the bare nipples of her breasts.

"If anything should happen to you," Tara whispered, "I wouldn't want to go on living."

"Nothing is going to happen to me."

"I mean it, Jacob," she said passionately. "I wouldn't want to go on living."

He put his arms around her and, gently rocking her, he whispered, "Nothing is going to happen to me, my love. Nothing."

"Oh Jacob, I'm so frightened... So very frightened that I might lose you."

He caressed her bare back. "How can I take your fear away?" he said gently.

"Aren't you ever afraid?" she asked.

"Yes," he answered. "I am. Every time I go on a mission, I have a gnawing fear ... but, then, something happens! I don't know what it is, but suddenly, I'm no longer afraid, at least not in the same way. I have a job to do and I must do it to the best of my ability! I'm more concerned for my men than I am for myself. Maybe that's what it is!"

She kissed him hungrily.

His hands moved over her supple body.

"This time," she reminded him coquettishly, "you want to be on the bottom!"

Jacob looked up at the mirrored ceiling. They did indeed look like they were enjoying it... Tara's head was tilted back, making a graceful curve of her neck. Her long, russet hair flowed over her bare shoulders, and his hands held the lovely roundness of her buttocks. He smiled and, closing his eyes, said in a low voice, "The mirror doesn't lie... I am enjoying this!"

Bending low over him, Tara answered in a breathless voice, "So am I, my love; so am I!" And she thrust herself down on him.

Jacob passionately kissed her lips.

Tony entered the Hotel Pierre cocktail lounge. It was his favorite spot in New York, and whenever he had to meet someone from the "Company," as he had learned to call it, this was often the place. He went to the bar, sat down on a soft-cushioned stool, and asked for a very dry martini on the rocks.

He reached over to a bowl of pretzels and helped himself. So far, since his association with the CIA had begun, he hadn't been called on to do more than meet a few people in Washington and in New York. He guessed he was being evaluated for future tasks.

As he sipped his drink, a man he had never before seen sat down on the stool next to him. "Name is McGrath," the man offered in a conversational tone. "But friends call me MG."

Tony understood at once. MG was the code word to identify the contact he had been told to expect.

"Hot as hell outside," McGrath commented. Though he was a tall, slender man, he was perspiring heavily.

He looked around. "Class," he commented. "Real class."

"What are you drinking?" Tony asked.

"Anything wet and cold."

"How about one of these?" Tony asked, pointing to his martini.

McGrath nodded.

"Make one for my friend," Tony told the barkeeper.

"Sure thing, Mr. Trapasso."

"Some beautiful women in here," McGrath observed.

"If you can't see them here," Tony answered, "you can't see them anywhere." Then he added, "You look warm, friend. Why don't we go over to that quiet table in the corner? Looks cooler over there."

McGrath nodded appreciatively and they moved to a secluded table. Without further ado, McGrath began, "We want you to set up a business in Hong Kong. Import-export would be fine, but if you can come up with something better, we'll go along with that too."

"How much capital will I have?" Tony asked.

"Two mil."

"When?"

"The sooner the better."

"Why —?" Tony began to ask just as a waiter came to the table and put McGrath's drink down. McGrath paused as the man left and took a sip of the martini. "The powers that be expect that sooner or later you'll be paid a visit by certain people who will offer you protection when they learn you are operating out of Hong Kong."

Tony smiled and said, "I know the scam."

"I thought you would," McGrath grinned. "At first, you are to refuse. But when they put the pressure on, you are to finally agree to accept their kind of protection."

"You still haven't told me just why I'll be doing this," Tony said.

"I don't know why exactly," McGrath answered. "But someone high up in the Company —"

"Tell me why you think it's being done," Tony cut in.

"I haven't thought a whole lot about it," McGrath answered impatiently. "I'm just a messenger. But I would guess that under the cover of conducting a business operation out there, you can help solve an international underworld problem that needs solving."

"I'll leave for Hong Kong next Monday," Tony said without further questions.

McGrath raised his glass. "To Hong Kong," he toasted.

"Hong Kong," Tony echoed, clinking his glass against McGrath's.

CHAPTER 19

Warren's seal team boarded the LST-44 in Yokosuka at 1900 on September 13 along with the men of the 3rd Battalion, 5th Marines under the command of Lieutenant Colonel John Raplet. The LST-44 got underway at 2030, taking position a thousand yards astern of the force-command ship, *Mt. McKinley*. The Seals occupied a space in the after part of the ship. Nine sections of bunks were stacked four deep along the bulkheads with a rectangular table in the middle of the compartment.

Within minutes of getting underway, Warren assembled his men around the table. "We'll be at sea for two days," he said. "Between then and now, I don't want any altercations between you men and the Marines. Is that clear?" His gaze moved quickly from man to man, and as he saw all of them nod in understanding, he continued, "You will be eating with them and that's where trouble could start. Don't, I repeat, don't quarrel over places in the chow lines. These Marines are tough and so are you. But I need every one of you for our mission. I don't want to have anyone in sick bay because he was hurt in a stupid fight. Branigan, you're in charge of that aspect of discipline."

"Yes, sir," Sean answered.

"My suggestion to all of you is to get plenty of rest."

After dismissing the men, Warren swung himself into the top bunk of the four assigned to the team's officers. As he listened to one of the men play a harmonica rendition of the popular song "Goodnight, Irene, Goodnight," he found himself thinking about Hilary. After completing her assignment in

London and Athens, she was back in New York. She wrote that she was taking two weeks off and spending them with little Andy and Warren's mother, Gloria, who had flown in from Honolulu. He was just drifting off to sleep when a voice came over the 1MC. "Commander Troost and Lieutenant Colonel Raplet, report to the bridge. Commander Troost and Lieutenant Colonel Raplet, please report to the bridge."

"No rest for the weary," Warren said, swinging himself down to the deck. A few minutes later, he and Raplet were on the bridge.

"In an hour or so," the captain said, "we're going to be running into heavy weather. There's a typhoon building off Kyushu, about fifty miles from where we will be. Make sure your men stay in their bunks as much as possible. I expect fifty knots or more of wind and heavy seas."

Raplet gave a low whistle. "If we're caught in that kind of weather for any length of time, I'm going to have a lot of sick Marines hitting that beach."

"If we're lucky, we should be out of it by late tomorrow morning," the captain said.

"And if we're not lucky?" Warren asked.

"Sometime in the evening," the captain answered.

"We're well to the west of the storm, but it's a big one and we're catching the outer edge."

Warren and Raplet left the bridge together. The wind had increased and the seas were getting heavy.

"I hope we get out of this by the time the captain says we will," Raplet said, "or my guys are going to have a lot harder time than Command thought they would."

Warren nodded. He understood Raplet's concern. He would have felt the same way if he were in the Marine's shoes. Hitting the beach in assault was hard enough on men, even in good weather. Fortunately, his own men had trained extensively in rough surf. Every one of them could handle himself and his equipment in what to others would be impossible conditions. *That's the reason for having Seals*, he thought somewhat smugly.

For a while, Warren and Raplet stood on the deck and gazed at the silhouettes of the blacked-out ships around them plunging silently through the angry, dark sea. Although it was the heart of summer, the tearing wind chilled them to the bone.

"After the last one, Warren, did you ever think we'd be doing this again?" Raplet asked pensively. "I know I didn't."

"Neither did I," Warren answered. During his planning meetings with Raplet over the past week, he had grown to like and admire this tough, seagoing soldier. His professionalism typified the strong link between the Navy and Marine Corps. Raplet had seen action in the assault on Guadalcanal and a half-dozen other combat landings years before.

"What's that old saying that goes, 'Now it's about time to earn our pay?'" Raplet mused. "Whoever said that first must have been thinking about men like us — and those guys sweating it out down below."

"No doubt about it, friend."

At 0400 on September 15 the gunfire-support ships of the invasion force, under the command of Admiral Thomas Strub, opened up on Inchon and on Wolmido Island. The darkness was punctuated with hundreds of muzzle flashes and searing arcs of light as projectiles flew toward the unsuspecting targets.

To the northeast, in the predawn twilight off Pusan, Jacob was catapulted off the *Makin*. Turning to the right, he climbed quickly to fifteen thousand feet, to his strike group's rendezvous. Their target was the rail yards at Pyongyang, the capital of North Korea. "We don't anticipate you will encounter any air opposition, but antiaircraft fire can be expected to be heavy," the air intelligence officer had said in his prelaunch briefing. "Your primary targets will be rail facilities and rolling stock in the western section of the city. Whatever other military vehicular traffic you see is fair game. The object of the exercise is to divert attention from the invasion force at Inchon."

Jacob looked to his right, where a flight of ten rocket-armed Panther fighters had formed into five sections of two each and were circling lazily. Below them, fifteen heavily loaded AD dive bombers were joining up in a classic V-of-V formation. Jacob pressed the radio button on his throttle, and called the bomber and fighter leaders. His voice sounded strangely muffled as he spoke into his oxygen-mask microphone: "Red One, Red Two, this is Red Zero. Fighters fly cover at angels twenty over the hawks on the way in. No unnecessary chatter on the air."

Red One and Red Two radioed, "Wilco."

Flying off to the side of the Panthers weaving over the ADs, Jacob radioed, "You all look good. Let's go," and took up a heading toward Pyongyang. Flying time to the target would be forty minutes.

"Now hear this," the address speakers of the LST-44 blared, "we are nearing the launch point. Seals, stand by to go over the side."

Warren and his men were already on deck and had inflated four large black rubber rafts. Every man wore a rubberized wetsuit and was lightly armed with a pistol and hunting knife. Other automatic weapons, explosives, and grenades in waterproof bags were already secured in the rafts.

A splashing rain was beating down. A half-hour bombardment had been lifted from Wolmido Island and now was being concentrated on the outskirts of Inchon.

The speakers came on again. "Three hundred yards to go. All engines stopped."

"One hundred yards," the voice announced. "We are two thousand yards off the beach."

"She's almost stopped, Skipper," Sean commented.

Warren nodded and looked over the men. Every man's face, covered with dark camouflage paint, looked evil. Only the whites of their eyes glistening in the dim, reflected light showed eager anticipation.

"Dead in the water," the voice on the 1MC said.

"Go!" Warren ordered.

The rafts were thrown over the side and men in groups of nine leapt into the water and clambered quickly into the rafts.

Warren and Sean were the last to leave the deck, and as soon as they were in their raft, all four paddled toward the dark land ahead of them.

Warren looked back over his shoulder. The ship was already underway again and turning seaward. She'd return when it was time to put the Marines ashore.

The rain seemed to be letting up. There was a light chop in the water, and the smell of acrid smoke from Inchon filled the air.

Two hundred yards off the beach, the water was shallow enough for the Seals to quietly slip in. Each man took his oilskin bag of explosives, slung his automatic carbine over his shoulder, and, half swimming, half wading, emerged from the water and quickly assembled. There was no opposition so far. Silently they split into pre-planned groups and headed for their assigned targets.

Warren guided his team toward the causeway. In a matter of minutes they were clambering over the slippery, seaweed-covered rocks at its base. As they had done so many times in practice, they quickly broke out the RDX explosives and positioned them for maximum effect on one side of the low bridge.

"Ready to set charges on the other side," Sean reported.

"Go!" Warren whispered. "Take three men with you."

Just as Sean's team was crossing the causeway, the sound of small-arms fire erupted from somewhere on the island. Two huge explosions belched fire and smoke into the air. The other Seals were doing their jobs.

"Koreans!" one of the men shouted. "The bastards are on the causeway coming this way."

Warren and the two men with him scrambled to the top. "Get those charges set," he shouted to Sean.

Enemy troops were running toward them from the mainland end of the causeway.

"Branigan!"

"Done, skipper," Sean yelled back. He and his men scrambled to the top of the causeway.

The enemy troops opened fire.

"Fall back," Warren ordered. In a low crouch, he and the rest of his team ran along the roadway toward the island.

"Company up ahead, too!" a man yelled.

A third explosion tore out of the island ahead of them.

Warren glanced over his shoulder. The North Korean soldiers were reaching the place where the charges had been set. "Hit the deck," he shouted, and immediately pressed a red button on a small radio transmitter strapped to his waist. The next instant an explosion tore away a huge section of the causeway, flinging debris and bodies high in the air. "Open fire!" he shouted, firing his carbine from the hip at the group of men running toward them from the island.

"We got some of them," one of the men shouted.

"They're falling back, Skipper," another man shouted.

Warren looked back toward the mainland. More than a fifty-foot section of the causeway had been blown out. No enemy was moving there.

"Skipper, the fuckers from the island are coming back for more!" a third man cried out.

"Branigan, get three men and take cover in those rocks on the other side."

"Aye, aye, Skipper," Sean answered and quickly chose the men to go with him.

"The rest of you, down on this side." Warren slid behind a huge boulder with a rounded top that gave him a clear field of fire as the enemy troops began to shoot savagely. Bullets ricocheted off the rocks, splintering them.

"Fire," Warren shouted. "Fire!" He sighted the carbine on one of the enemy and squeezed the trigger. The butt slammed against his shoulder. Again he fired. The man staggered and fell face forward.

Suddenly, another explosion tore out of the island behind the enemy, now grouped together two hundred yards away on the causeway.

"Keep firing!" Warren yelled.

Two more enemy soldiers went down.

"You," Warren ordered one of the men, "work your way along the base, close enough to drop a grenade on them."

"Aye, aye, Skipper."

As the man began to move down toward the water, Warren checked his watch. Fifty minutes had passed since they had left the transport. In another half hour, the Marines would storm ashore.

"Mortar round incoming," Sean yelled from his position on the other side.

The round exploded behind them on the roadway.

"Move forward," Warren shouted.

Another mortar round slammed into the rocks behind Sean, and a man screamed.

"Keep moving," Warren ordered, watching the man who was working his way along the base of the causeway.

Two more mortar rounds crashed into the rocks behind Warren.

The man at the base of the causeway climbed toward the top, paused, and lobbed a grenade with devastating effect into the enemy troops who had been confronting Warren's team. The gunfire stopped abruptly.

"Move!" Warren shouted, clambering up to the roadway and heading for the island. Moments later, Commander Rogers was running toward him with seven men. "The others?" Warren questioned as they joined up.

Rogers shook his head.

"More of our men, Skipper," Sean said.

Warren looked toward the island.

They were racing toward him. "Eight," he said.

"Two more coming," Sean said.

"Commander Knight was badly hit, sir," one of the men panted. "I saw him go down."

"Chief's coming with seven more," Sean called out.

Warren made a fast head count. Out of the thirty-six men he'd started with, he could account for only thirty. He didn't know if the others were dead or —?

"The LST is heading back in," one of the men yelled.

Warren looked at his watch. In a matter of minutes, the Marines would hit the beach. "Come on!" he said. "We're going to help those Marines finish the job we started on this island."

Jacob saw Pyongyang in front of him to the west. He switched on the radio. "Red Flight, this is Red Zero. You know what to do. I'll lead, and, Red Two, open out and follow me. Then your guys, Red One. Pick good targets. Steep and fast."

He flipped the master armament switch on, charged his .50-caliber guns, and armed his rockets for sequence firing. He eased the nose of his Panther down, adjusted his trim tabs for a steady dive as his speed increased, and began his run. The Panther streaked down. He watched the altimeter unwind counter clockwise. His eyes flicked to the air-speed indicator. He was at three hundred fifty knots, passing through eight thousand feet, and he retarded his throttle to keep that speed.

Second by second, details of the train yards were becoming clearer. To the right were the long, low, triangular rooftops of the repair shops. Scattered through the yard were switching engines and water towers. A coaling station was on the left.

Suddenly puffs of black smoke filled the air, and the white-hot trails of tracers from automatic weapons floated lazily toward him.

"Christ, what flack!" one of the Panther pilots exclaimed excitedly over the open radio circuit.

A burst to Jacob's port side jounced his plane. "Close," he muttered, "too fucking close." He realized he was sweating and his mouth was dry.

At four thousand feet he picked his target: a switching tower with a train approaching it. He began to ease back on the stick. He brushed his finger over the rocket-firing trigger. Instantly, two rockets trailing white smoke streaked toward the structure. Jacob pulled up and pushed the throttle forward. The Panther responded and as it clawed its way up, the switching tower burst into flames.

One of the planes behind Warren punched his rockets into the repair shops, leaving one in flames. Others raised havoc with several of the many trains that were in the yard. It all looked good to Jacob.

Jacob went to ten thousand feet before he leveled off. "Red One, Red Two, Zero here. I'm going back in for one more run. Follow me, Red Two. Then you, Red One," he radioed. Turning to the left, he began his dive. This time, he spotted an outbound train lumbering to the south. His point of aim was the locomotive.

The sky continued to be peppered with puffs of exploding, heavy-caliber antiaircraft fire.

"Red Two, this is Red Two Three. I'm hit," Jacob heard from a panicked voice over the radio.

"Tom, get out," a voice yelled.

Jacob glanced over his right shoulder. Behind him, a Panther was trailing black smoke. "Tom, eject!" Jacob heard Red Two order urgently. "Eject!" Meanwhile, the locomotive was looming larger and larger in his sight.

"Skipper, I'm losing control!" Tom cried in an agonized tone.

Jacob saw a wisp of smoke coming from the locomotive.

"He's going in!" a voice cut into his concentration. "Get out, Tom!"

Jacob bit his lower lip and forced his attention back on his target. He was down to three thousand feet at three hundred fifty knots. He sucked in his breath and counted to three before he pressed the rocket-firing button twice in rapid sequence. Two rockets raced toward the train, followed immediately by two more. He pulled back on the stick and pushed the throttle forward. He looked back over his right shoulder. The locomotive jumped the track, flashed into flames, and, tumbling into a ravine, took the first dozen cars with it. Out of the corner of his eye, he saw a Panther slam into the smoking repair shops. A ball of flame burst out of the already burning buildings.

Jacob shook his head and, clamping his jaws together tightly, he climbed back to ten thousand feet, leveled off, and waited for Red Two's remaining Panthers to join him. Red One was already in a steep dive, followed by his fourteen ADs. Their bombs blanketed the rail yard and smothered the antiaircraft defenses. They each climbed quickly to eight thousand feet and began to reform directly below the Panthers.

"Red Zero, bogies, three o'clock low, heading north," one of the AD pilots reported.

"I thought there wasn't supposed to be any air opposition," an AD pilot said half-jokingly.

Jacob radioed, "Cut the chatter!" The aircraft were to the west of the city and he recognized them as four Yaks, old propeller-driven planes. He estimated they were flying at about four thousand feet. "Red Two, take two sections and go get 'em," he ordered the Panther leader.

"Red Zero, they're dropping lower," a Red Two reported.

"I see that," Jacob answered. "If they get too close to the deck, you won't be able to follow them."

"They're going lower."

Even before the pilot spoke, Jacob sensed something was amiss. "Red Two, break off," he ordered. "Break off...! Come back to angels ten." As he scanned the sky, his eye suddenly picked up four more enemy aircraft well above him. They were black dots against a bright blue sky. "Bandits, twelve o'clock high," he radioed his flight. "Red One, take off for home. Red Two and I will see what it's all about."

"Okay, jet jockeys, they've got the altitude," Jacob said, "but we're going to take it back. Let's do some fancy flying." He banked sharply to the right and began a steep climb.

The enemy planes were closer now and holding formation.

"Holy Christ, Red Zero, they're jets!" a pilot shouted over the radio.

"Those damn Yaks were just flying decoy," another pilot said.

"Cut the talk and let's go for them," Jacob snapped. When he had been in Tokyo, he'd met some Air Force pilots who told him that some of their guys had tangled with North Korean MiG-15s, a Russian-made jet fighter, and had found it a "tough kill to make."

The MiGs were almost directly above them.

"Why the hell don't they break formation?" one of the pilots wondered.

"I said, cut the chatter!" Jacob snapped, checking the positions of his pilots. Two sections of two each were on either side of him and one, a pilot nicknamed Cue Ball, who had been Tom's wingman, was alone at nine o'clock. "Cue Ball, this is Red Zero," Jacob said. "Join up, you're my wingman. Everybody, guns hot."

"Roger," Cue Ball answered and immediately maneuvered his plane into position.

Still in formation, the MiGs flashed by high above the Panthers.

Jacob sucked in his breath, expecting them to dive and engage. He could clearly see the red star on the underside of their wings. Slowly, he exhaled.

"Red Zero," Red Two radioed, "looks like they don't want to play."

Jacob checked his fuel gauge. There was more than enough to get back to the *Makin*, but not enough for more combat. "They're going bye-bye and so are we. Going to angels twenty. Let's go home." Then he radioed, "Red Base, this is Red Zero. Returning with Red Two, Red One should be approaching you."

"Red Base awaits you at Zulu 5," the ship answered. "Zulu 5."

"Roger, Zulu 5," Jacob said. "ETA 20 minutes."

The successful invasion at Inchon unhinged the NKPA's left flank and, coupled with the massive American breakout at Pusan at the same time, the Allied forces began a drive northward.

Three weeks after the U.S. landings at Inchon, an Armed Forces' radio broadcast reported that American troops crossed the Thirty-Eighth Parallel, which had been the dividing line between North and South Korea.

On the evening of October 7, Tony, on his way back from Hong Kong, arranged to meet Jacob and Warren in Tokyo. Jacob's ship, the *Makin*, had returned to Yokosuka for another R and R period, and Warren was back in Japan to rebuild and continue training his Seal team.

"To victory," Tony said, raising his cup of warm sake, "that's what we should drink to first. In a matter of a few weeks it will be all over, and you guys won't have to risk your sweet butts anymore."

"To not having to risk our butts," Jacob responded, lifting his cup.

"To victory," Warren added.

The three of them were seated on straw mats around a small red-lacquered table in a private room in a traditional Japanese restaurant. A delicately painted shoji screen was opened, allowing them to look at a Zen garden illuminated by a number of brightly colored paper lanterns.

"How did you know about this place, Jacob?" Tony asked. "It's certainly off the beaten track." Even in the wavering play of light coming from the lanterns, he could see that both of his friends carried the tragedy of war with them in their eyes. He knew the look all too well. He wistfully admitted to himself that among those who had it was a indefinable bond that he no longer could share.

"A friend of mine told me about it," Jacob answered.

"A Jap?" Tony asked sharply.

Aware of Tony's hatred for the Japanese, Jacob answered quietly, "A friend is a friend, Tony, even if his country was once an enemy. I never knew Yashi Kurokachi personally as my enemy; I've only known him as a friend."

Tony lowered his eyes.

"Come on," Warren suddenly said, "all three of us are friends, good friends … no, the best of friends!"

Tony looked up. "Okay, so there was one good Jap and Jacob happened to save him from becoming shark bait." Then he smiled and exclaimed, "Damn it, I know you're right. Excuse my stupidity."

"What the hell were you doing this time in Hong Kong?" Jacob asked, hoping to change the subject.

"Business again," Tony answered, wondering if Warren knew about his connection with the Company, "my second trip. But forget about me. I have some things to tell the two of you. First, Jacob, before I left New York the last time, I saw your mother. She's fine and, as I think you know, I gave Tara a hand when she — you — bought the house she wanted in the Hamptons. Since the real estate agents out there are sharks, I called a few friends who know about the area, then went out with one of them and Tara to see the place before she spoke to the real estate agent and people who owned it. Jacob, you're going to love it. It has a beautiful view. From one side you look out over the ocean, and from the other you see acres of farmland."

"Thanks for helping her, Tony. I really appreciate it."

"With our influence, she got it, as you know, for 50 thousand," Tony said without further elaboration. "In ten years' time, the house and the land you have around it will be worth ten, maybe fifteen times that."

"Land? What land? I thought it was a house," Jacob responded. He hadn't yet heard all the details of the deal from Tara. In fact, he'd been greatly surprised when Tara wrote after her trip to Tokyo that she was ready to move.

"Six acres … and I bought an additional six, three on either side of you," Tony said. "It's a damn good investment for the two of us."

"As long as Tara likes it —"

"Likes it," Tony exclaimed, "she loves it! She even named it Seascape."

Jacob repeated the name and said, "I like the sound of it."

Tony looked at Warren, chuckled, and said, "How nice it is when your brother-in-law is also your friend. But now it's your turn. First, Hilary and Andy are fine. Second, I saw your mother in Honolulu. She's thinking of moving to New York so she can be close to her grandchildren."

"Hilary mentioned that," Warren commented. "I think it would be a good idea."

"Now," Tony said, "are you ready for this, Warren? The word is out that your wife is going to be appointed fashion editor of that magazine she works for."

"When?" Warren asked, completely surprised by the news. Hilary hadn't written a word about the possibility, and when he spoke to her on the phone the previous Sunday, she hadn't mentioned it then either.

"Soon," Tony answered.

"That's something she really wants."

Tony nodded. Because it was a good investment, his holding company had recently bought the magazine, and when he returned, he intended to arrange for Hilary to have the job she wanted. After all, her husband was his friend, but he needn't know strings were about to be pulled.

"She'll be able to spend more time with Andy," Warren added.

"Absolutely," Tony agreed.

"To Tony, the bearer of good tidings," Warren said, raising his sake cup.

"To all of us," Jacob said.

"To all of us," Tony and Warren echoed in unison.

"All right, amigos," Tony asked, "who'll do the ordering here? I'm starved."

"I've managed to pick up something of the language from Yashi. Enough to get what I want in a place like this," Jacob offered.

"Please, no fish," Tony said. "Even after all this time, I can't eat it. Any other seafood is fine. But —"

"No fish!" Jacob assured him.

"It's great to be with you guys again," Tony said. "Really great to be with you again!"

CHAPTER 20

Warren trudged wearily in the darkness to his tent in a secluded area of the Marine Corps air station at Iwakuni, Japan. He had spent the last four hours in his Quonset hut office preparing a progress report for Naval Forces, Japan, Headquarters in Atsugi and now he was looking forward to a hot shower and a few hours' sleep.

Warren entered the dimly lighted tent and glanced at the twenty-four-hour clock hung on the center ridge pole: it was 22:30. Suddenly, he spotted a pale blue envelope on his small desk. It was a letter from Hilary with a November 21, 1950 date. It had only taken five days for the letter to come from New York. Warren reached over to a small table for a letter opener and slit the top of the blue envelope. He was hoping to be home by Christmas. General MacArthur had publicly stated that most of the men fighting in Korea would be back in the States in time for the holidays. He already had heard some talk about him and his men being reassigned to either San Diego or Norfolk within the next ten days. The fighting in Korea was just about over. American troops and their allies fighting under the flag of the United Nations had, in some areas, reached the Yalu River, the dividing line between North Korea and China.

Three blue tissue paper sheets were filled with Hilary's small, neat, densely packed script. Warren thoroughly enjoyed her letters. She wrote almost the way she spoke. He began to read.

My Darling,

I can't begin to tell you how much I miss you. I wish we could spend Thanksgiving together. Your mother, me, and Andy have been invited to

have dinner with Tony, Miriam, and Tara at Tony's new house in Long
Beach, New Jersey. I really feel as if Tony, Miriam, and Tara are family.
And —

A sudden knock on the door stopped Warren's reading. "Yes," he called out, moving his eyes from the letter to the door.

"Skipper, it's Frasse," one of the men called. "We're picking up some strange stuff on the radio… Commander Rogers thinks you'd better hear it."

Warren swung himself out of the bunk. Rogers was the team duty officer and wouldn't call him unless the matter was urgent. "I'll be there in a few minutes." The short-wave radio was in the outer room of his office in the Quonset hut.

Rogers was waiting for him at the door. "Either it's someone's idea of a joke," he said, "or some of the Marine units up near the Yalu are coming under attack by the Koreans."

"Come on, those guys are just sitting there, waiting for the order to pack up and go home," Warren said as he closed the door and walked over to the radio.

"It comes over sporadically," Rogers said.

Warren stood in front of the radio. "At the frequency —"

The radio began to emit static. Then a voice said, "This is Charley company, we're under attack. This is Charley company, we're under attack. The Koreans are all around us…"

"That's what I heard before," Rogers explained.

"How the hell could we pick that up?" Warren asked.

"The skip effect," Rogers answered. "On a cloudy night, you can pick up all sorts of transmissions."

Warren nodded. "Any other reports like that one?"

Rogers shook his head. "No, sir."

Suddenly the phone began to ring. Picking it up, Warren identified himself.

"This is Captain Baily, Operations Officer, COMNAVFORJAP," the voice on the other end announced. "As of now and until further notice, Commander, the admiral wants your team standing by in Condition One."

"Yes, sir," Warren answered, suddenly stiffening. "We're to go to Condition One," Warren said, putting the phone down. "Something must be happening in Korea."

"Do you think the Chinese have come into it?" Rogers asked.

"Christ, if they have," Warren exclaimed, "it's a whole new war."

"Now hear this. Now hear this." The voice on the 1MC broke through Jacob's sleep. "Now hear this... Flight quarters. All pilots report to the ready room. All pilots report to the ready room. Air group commander and squadron CO to air intelligence."

Jacob switched on the light in his cabin and looked at his watch. It was four o'clock in the morning. He rubbed his eyes and quickly dressed.

Minutes later, he entered the ready room. Captain Paul Wiggims, the strike briefing officer, was already on the small platform. Behind him was an enlarged map of North Korea, which Wiggims used to define the day's strikes.

"Gentlemen," Wiggims said when everyone was finally seated, "I apologize for having gotten you out of bed." He spoke with a Southern accent. "But we've received an urgent call for air strikes in these areas." And he tapped the map with the rubber-tipped pointer. "Ch'onghch'on, Kumu-ri and Sinanju. There units of the First Marine Division, the Ninth

Infantry Regiment and First Cavalry Division are under heavy attack from ChiCom troops."

A buzz of disbelief came from the pilots.

"Gentlemen, it appears that the Chinese have crossed the Yalu River in division strength," Wiggims said, silencing the men with his words. "If that is true, then several thousand of our men are at risk of being completely surrounded. During this strike and the others that will no doubt follow in the days to come, you can expect to encounter MiG fighter opposition. You are not permitted to follow them across the Yalu River. There will be Air Force planes operating in the same or adjacent areas. Any questions?"

"Just how bad is the situation on the ground?" Jacob asked.

"It's not bad, it's damn near being grave, according to the reports on the radio. Any other questions? None?" He looked at his watch and said, "All right then, we'll be ready to launch in ten minutes."

Jacob pickled off his two napalm tanks on a target area just north of Sinanju, where, in the gathering daylight, the ChiComs were massing for another attack. The searing red flames of the jellied gasoline spread for hundreds of yards over the area. As he climbed steeply away from the target, he looked back over his shoulder. The Panthers following him dropped their napalm tanks.

"On target, Red Leader," the first cavalry forward observer on the ground radioed. "That'll cook the bastards!"

Jacob and his men were flying this mission without being guided to their targets by a tactical air controller. One had been in the air minutes before the squadron had arrived and had been shot down by small-arms fire.

"OK, Red Two, now rockets!" Jacob radioed. He'd climbed up to ten thousand feet and was circling until the rest of the Panthers joined up.

"I read you," the FO cut in. "Go for Alpha-four."

Jacob repeated the coordinates and quickly located them on the chart board. Alpha-four was in the Kumu-ri area, between the target they'd just bombed and the outer perimeter of the American position. "Red One, you have Alpha-4," Jacob radioed the AD leader, who was circling at nine thousand feet. "Red Two, follow me!" He pushed the stick forward and, steepening his dive, he pointed the nose of his Panther at the still smoldering target area. He was passing through three thousand feet when suddenly an unfamiliar voice came over the radio. "Bogies four o'clock high. Bogies four o'clock high."

"See 'em," another voice answered.

"Christ, there's ten of them!" the first voice exclaimed.

"MiGs!" a third voice yelled.

Jacob glanced at as much of the sky as he could see. It was empty.

"You hear that, Skipper?" Raoul asked.

"Yes. Those are Air Force guys," Jacob answered, looking at his altimeter. He was down to one thousand feet. "We're coming in," he told his men. "Remember, as soon as you fire, get the hell out of there as fast as you can." He was down to eight hundred feet. The ground was racing up toward him. He could see the ChiComs run for cover. Directly in front of him was a large stack of boxes. He pressed the rocket-release button on his stick once, twice, and a third time. The six rockets streaked away from his plane. He pulled up on the stick and pushed the throttle forward. Behind him, the earth erupted into flames.

"Good work," the FO commented. "Looks like you hit an ammo dump."

Jacob's plane was in a steep climb. "Red Two, rejoin at angels ten," he radioed.

"Wilco," came the answer.

Suddenly, Jacob caught sight of the air battle between the Air Force F-80s and the MiGs. The sharp blue sky to the northeast of Sinanju was crisscrossed with contrails. This was the first time he or his men had ever seen more than one or two MiGs at a time, and those had always been at a distance.

"Bogies nine o'clock high," Raoul reported.

Jacob looked. "I count eight," he said after a moment.

"Ten," Peters responded. "Two are low."

"FO, this is Red Zero," Jacob radioed. "We've got bandits coming in at nine o'clock."

"Have them in sight," the FO answered. "Thanks for the help. Good luck."

"All right, men," Jacob told his men, "let's head those bandits off at the pass." He put on his oxygen face mask, set the control valve to Normal, then kicking his Panther into a sharp left turn, he eased back on the stick and pushed the throttle full forward. He and the other Panthers clawed skyward to eighteen thousand feet. He radioed the AD leader, "Red One, collect your birds and get the hell out of here. Enemy fighters."

"They've spotted us," Red Two answered, trying to keep the excitement out of his voice.

The formation of a dozen MiGs turned toward Jacob's squadron. They were at the same altitude.

"Okay, men, go for them!" Jacob exclaimed. He was sweating now, and his voice had a tightness to it. This was going to be the same kind of air-to-air combat he had fought against the Japanese fighter pilots in World War II. Only now the planes and the enemy were different.

Jacob chose one of the MiGs on the far left and aimed his plane at it. His guns blazed; his tracers mixed erratically with those coming from the MiG.

The MiG rolled off to the right and streaked under him.

Out of the corner of his eye, Jacob saw a plane burst into flames. He couldn't tell whether it was one of his or MiG.

"On your tail, Skipper!" Raoul yelled.

Jacob pulled back on the stick. The plane screamed.

"Got him in my sights!" Raoul shouted. "I got him. I got the fucker, Skipper!"

Jacob breathed deeply and as his vision cleared, he eased the stick forward. A MiG suddenly came into his sights. He squeezed the trigger twice, giving the enemy two short bursts.

Black smoke streamed out of the MiG's jet engine.

Jacob delivered another short burst.

The MiG exploded into a ball of flames.

Jacob streaked over him, executed a roll, and climbed. "Check your fuel," he radioed. He had enough for another two, maybe three minutes of dog fighting. After that, he'd have to break off and head back to the *Makin*.

"Red Two, one of our guys is going down," a pilot named Bond called.

Jacob saw him. He was off to the right and a few thousand feet below. There wasn't any smoke coming from the plane. The plane began to spin. "Eject," Jacob yelled. "Eject!"

"Can't, Skipper," a faint voice answered. "Shot up ... no hands!"

Jacob clenched his jaw.

"That's Smitty. Get out, for God's sake, Smitty!" Bond shouted. As the plane staggered in the air, its nose came up, and suddenly it snapped to the right and began to spin.

Jacob saw Smitty's plane slam into the ground and explode into flames.

"Skipper, they're breaking off," Peters radioed.

The ten MiGs reformed into a formation and flew west toward China.

"Let's go home," Jacob radioed. "Join up at angels fifteen." He felt drained. The air battle had lasted only five minutes. But to him it seemed as if it had been going on for hours. No, more than hours. For more time than he wanted to remember!

On the afternoon of December 5, Warren and two dozen other officers, from lieutenant commanders to captains, were seated in a room at the Yokosuka Naval Base. Warren knew most of them personally, or by sight. Three had been in his graduating class at Annapolis, but because he'd been promoted to a full lieutenancy during the war, he was now a rank ahead of them.

None of the assembled officers had any idea why they'd been ordered to report to that particular room, though all of them knew it had something to do with what was happening in Korea, where the quick American victory against the NKPA had quickly disintegrated under the onslaught of the Chinese communists. The Marines had fought their way out of encirclement at the frozen Chosin and with various army units were fighting their way toward Korea's east coast.

Finally the door on the right side of the front of the room opened, and Admiral J. W. Picker entered. He was a tall, dignified-looking man with gray hair and dark blue eyes. Picker was the overall commander of the American naval forces in the Japan-Korea area.

The assembled officers instantly rose to attention.

"Gentlemen, please be seated," Picker said. He waited a moment before continuing. "As all of you know, our forces in Korea are under ferocious attack by Chinese troops, whose numbers are estimated to be ten times ours.

"General MacArthur has ordered a strategic withdrawal of the First Marine Division, the Seventh Infantry Division, and the Tenth Corps to the port of Hungnam, on the east coast of Korea." Even as he spoke, a huge map of North Korea was projected on the wall behind him. "Hungnam is here," he said, touching the map with a pointer.

"Our task will be to extricate the ground troops from this port as expeditiously and as safely as possible." He paused. Except for the sound of the men breathing, there was absolute silence in the room.

"Despite the constant enemy fire and the extremely harsh weather conditions — even now, as I brief you, a second blizzard is battering our forces and the temperature is thirty below zero — the withdrawal to Hungnam is taking place in good order, though casualties are heavy. The first troops are expected to reach Hungnam some time on the ninth of December. We'll be there ready to take them off the beach. Any questions?"

"Sir, will we still control the port, or will we have to secure it first?" one of the officers asked.

"We now hold the port," Picker answered. "But the Chinese troops will probably attempt to prevent our troops from entering them. We will counter that effort with strikes by aircraft from carriers steaming offshore and land-based aircraft operating from the south. In addition we will employ, wherever needed and wherever possible, naval bombardment to suppress enemy fire and limit his ability to hamper the withdrawal of our forces."

After a slight pause, COMNAVFORJAP continued, "The approaches to the harbor have been heavily mined by the enemy, and a path through these minefields will be cleared before our ships enter them. But the presence of mines will constitute an ever-present danger. We do not have sufficient time to sweep the entrances completely clear of the mines. This means that there will only be one narrow channel in and out. To safely navigate through it will require excellent seamanship, and this brings me to the reason why you have been summoned here.

"Each of you, by your past performance under enemy fire and difficult conditions, have exhibited an unusual degree of ship handling and command excellence. Each of you will be assigned to command a vessel that will be part of the evacuation fleet. These vessels are not Navy ships. They have been pressed into service in order to accommodate the thousands of our men and tens of thousands of civilians who want to flee from the communist-dominated north.

"The crews which you will command are not Navy and more than likely will be polyglot and of uncertain response should your particular ship come under enemy fire. Any questions?"

"Sir, how many civilians are expected to leave?" an officer asked.

"Between fifty and a hundred thousand," Picker answered. "Your ships, gentlemen, will be crammed with them."

"Sir, will our vessels take troops and civilians, or only civilians?" another officer asked.

"Only after all of our troops are safely on board will civilians be taken aboard any of our vessels," Picker said. "On the way out of this room, each of you will be handed your assignment and charts of the particular harbor to which you will go. All of you are permitted to choose one of your subordinates as your XO. This choice must be governed entirely by your estimation of the man's ability to function in a difficult situation and, should the need arise, take your place as captain. Gentlemen, I wish you good luck," Picker said.

The map of Korea vanished from the rear wall.

As Picker stepped off the podium, a silence fell over the room; all hands rose to attention.

"As you were," Picker instantly responded and as he reached the door, he stopped. "Commander Troost, will you please accompany me to my office."

Totally surprised, Warren answered, "Yes, sir." A few minutes later, he was seated in front of Picker's desk.

"Smoke if you wish," the admiral said.

"Thank you, sir," Warren answered, taking his pipe out of his jacket pocket.

"I knew your father and mother," Picker said. "Your father and I served on the same destroyer during World War I, and then later on our paths crossed at several different duty stations. How are your mother and sister?"

"Well," Warren said, puffing on his pipe. "My mother is in New York with my wife and son. And Lillian is doing some acting in Hollywood."

Picker nodded. "Your mother was a beautiful woman," he commented wistfully.

"She still is," Warren answered, wondering if Picker had once been his mother's lover.

"Warren — I hope you don't mind me addressing you by your given name?"

Warren shook his head. "Not at all, sir."

"The success of your mission at Wolmido has had a profound effect upon the upper echelons of command, including myself. Additional UDT units will be formed and trained along the lines that you have trained your men. And now there's another, even more dangerous assignment for you and your men at Hungnam," Picker said. "The city must be totally destroyed. Nothing must be left for the communists. Your team will be responsible for the demolition of the electric powerhouse and the gantry cranes on the main pier. Any other targets you consider of value to the ChiComs are fair game. Do you understand?"

"Yes, sir," Warren answered calmly, despite the whirling in his stomach. "How much time will we have to complete the assignment?"

"My best guess is that it will take a week, possibly ten days to completely load our troops and civilians. Maybe longer. During that time, the Chinese are expected to mount ferocious attacks against those units fighting rear-guard actions. You are bound to come under intense enemy fire, especially at the power station, which is located in the northwest section of the city. The destroyer Holmes will be standing in the harbor to pick you up."

For a few moments, neither man spoke. Then Picker said, "Your father would have been very proud of you, Warren."

"Thank you, sir," Warren answered. "It's kind of you to say that."

"Please send my regards to your mother the next time you write to her," Picker said.

"I certainly will."

"My aide, Commander Hopewell, will give you the necessary charts and maps for your mission," Picker said, standing and extending his hand across the desk.

Warren stood up and shook the admiral's hand.

"Good luck, Warren," Picker said.

"Thank you, sir," Warren answered; then letting go of Picker's hand, he saluted.

Picker returned the courtesy.

"Shaggy Dog, this is Red Zero," Jacob radioed from the cockpit of his Panther. This was his fifth sortie for the day. Below and in front of him was the port of Hungnam and the fleet of ships waiting to evacuate the retreating Marines and Army units. "I'm approaching the coast. I have twelve blue chickens and six red hawks inbound for you, angels eighteen. ETA five minutes. Over."

"Welcome to the zoo," the Marine tactical air controller answered. "We're waiting for you with bated breath."

"What's the local weather like?" Jacob asked.

"Scattered clouds at five thousand. Visibility limited."

"Roger," Jacob answered, looking over his right shoulder. His six Panthers, arranged in three sections of two aircraft each, were weaving protectively above the twelve ADs, each loaded with two tanks of napalm and four five-hundred-pound anti-personnel bombs.

"Red Zero, let me know when your feet are dry," Shaggy Dog radioed.

"I'm over Alpha-Zero," Jacob answered. "Advise."

"I have you in sight. You'll see me over Alpha-Four. Eleven o'clock low from your position. Over."

Jacob scanned the horizon and in moments picked up the tactical air controller's light plane. "Gotcha, Shaggy Dog," Jacob radioed. "Chickens ready to lay their eggs and deliver heat and light wherever needed."

"Stand by, Red Zero," Shaggy Dog answered. "I'll get the addresses from Papa."

"Standing by," Jacob answered. He waited for the Tracon pilot to coordinate a strike against the ChiComs mortar and machine-gun positions on either side of the valley. Cover was also required for the Marines of the First Division and the Army's retreating Seventh Division.

"Red Zero," the tactical air controller said. "Papa's boys are getting hurt at Bravo-one. Over."

"Red One," Jacob called to the AD flight leader, "send four of your flock to Bravo-One and take care of the problem."

"Wilco, Red Zero. Red One Nine, take three with you and do it."

"Red Zero," the TAC radioed, "we need help at Bravo-Four and Six."

Jacob directed Red One to answer Papa's call for help. He watched Red One Nine's flight of ADs swoop down over the targets at Bravo-One. As they pulled up from their dives, the ridge top exploded into fire.

"That should help a lot, Red Zero," Shaggy Dog said.

The other three targets were a mass of flames.

The ADs climbed back up under Red One's directions to their orbiting altitude.

"Real good work," Shaggy Dog radioed. "But Papa says he has problems at Bravo-Two. Heavy small-arms fire coming from there."

"All Red Ones on Bravo-Two," Jacob ordered.

"Roger," Red One answered.

"Red Zero, keep a sharp lookout for Weasels," Shaggy Dog cautioned. "There's bound to be a few in the barnyard."

"Wilco," Jacob responded; then to his fighter pilots, he said, "Keep alert."

The twelve ADs were strung out in a long line. Jacob watched the first one bank steeply to the right and go into a dive. The others followed at regular intervals. In moments, huge dark clouds of debris filled the air.

"Red Zero, we're taking ground fire," Red One reported.

Suddenly, as one of the ADs started to pull up, it seemed to falter, and the next instant smoke began to pour from its engine.

"Skipper, I can't control her," the pilot radioed.

"Jerry, get the hell out of there," Red One shouted.

"I'm trying," Jerry yelled. "The canopy —"

The plane's nose dropped suddenly and the next instant it slammed into the ground, exploding into flames.

"Red Zero, you can send your chickens back to home plate. Sorry as I can be, about that one. Papa says they really helped," Shaggy Dog radioed.

"Thanks," Jacob answered and ordered the ADs back to the carrier.

"Red Zero, can you expend your Roman candles on Papa's targets?" Shaggy Dog asked.

"That's why we're here!" Jacob responded.

"Bravo-Six," Shaggy Dog radioed, "the enemy are thick as flies up there. I'll mark it with smoke."

"Red Two," Jacob said, speaking to the Panther leader, "take interval. We'll go in fast. Make it count. Follow me!" He rolled to the right and dived toward the target.

Jacob checked his altimeter. In seconds, his screaming jet had dropped from twenty thousand to ten thousand. He looked back over his right shoulder. The five Panthers were following him. "Remember, steep and fast." The white target-marking smoke was directly in front of him. He pickled off his six rockets, pulled back on the stick, and climbed to twenty thousand.

"Neat, real neat," Shaggy Dog commented as the rockets tore into the top of the ridge.

Jacob looked down at the long columns of Marines moving toward the port of Hungnam. The columns seemed to extend deep into Korea. Tens of thousands of men were desperately trying to escape.

"Red Zero, thanks," Shaggy Dog radioed. "Again, sorry you lost a chicken."

"Thanks for the consideration," Jacob answered.

"Red Zero, Red Zero, this is Red Rover," the air operations officer aboard the *Makin* radioed. "We're at Victor George. Can you give me an ETA?"

Jacob made a quick check of his instruments. "Red Rover, ETA two zero minutes."

"Roger, Red Zero," the AOO answered.

"Holy Christ," one of the pilots shouted, "I'm taking fire! Where'd that bastard come from?"

Jacob glanced around. He couldn't see directly behind him. "Who's taking fire?"

"It's me, Tom. I'm tail end Charlie," the pilot answered.

"Red Zero, tallyho, four bogies six o'clock high," another excited voice called out.

Jacob kicked his plane into a tight right turn. "Tom," he radioed, "are you all right?"

"She's still flying," Tom answered.

Jacob saw a MiG fighter closing on him. He tightened his turn. The force of six Gs caused his vision to momentarily blur. But in a matter of moments, he could see the contrails of the other planes as they swirled through the sky in a classic dogfight.

The MiG tried to follow Jacob, but overshot and zoomed past.

Jacob reversed into a left turn, climbed, and as he eased the stick back, caught the MiG in his gun sight. He pressed the trigger. The six .50s in his wings chattered. A series of white arcs leaped from his plane to the MiG. The next instant, a puff of black smoke erupted from the MiG and it became a ball of fire.

"Red Zero, one's coming up on your tail," one of the pilots called, "but I'm on his tail."

Jacob kicked the aircraft into a right turn.

"I got the son of a bitch," Red Two yelled. "I smoked him!"

Jacob caught a glimpse of the falling plane just before it disappeared into the clouds below.

"Red Zero," a pilot radioed, "they're breaking off."

"Man, I'd just like to be able to go after those fuckers once," another pilot responded.

"Join up," Jacob ordered and turned toward the sea ... and home plate at Victor George.

Warren and his UDT team went ashore under a leaden sky at Hungnam at 1300 on December 24, and, passing long columns of exhausted Marines and soldiers, immediately deployed toward the powerhouse.

From the north and west of the city came the intermittent, flat-sounding boom of ChiCom mortar rounds.

"Remember," Warren cautioned, "there's more than a good chance that infiltrators are either in, or around the powerhouse. Don't take chances. Shoot first!" He had repeated the same thing, in almost the same words, a couple of dozen times since they had left Yokosuka aboard the destroyer,

Holmes. But now, as they made their way through the city's deserted side streets, it assumed a super-reality.

The team moved in an infantry wedge-shaped formation. The point man, Gruber, was ten yards in front of the main body. Behind him were two bazooka men with weapons held at the ready. Each of the rest of the men were armed with automatic carbines. The officers carried .45s and all of the men had some kind of side arm holstered around his waist. All had a standard Marine issue K-bar knife strapped to his lower leg and carried four grenades in bandoliers across their chests. Six men at the rear carried canvas bags packed with powerful RDX demolition charges.

Sean Branigan was with Warren behind the BARs. Chief Hanson was in the middle of the wedge and Lieutenant Rogers brought up the rear.

"Kind of spooky," Sean whispered.

Warren nodded. "Pass the word to Rogers to keep a sharp lookout, especially at windows and roofs."

"Wilco," Sean answered and dropped back to tell the man behind him what Warren had said. "Done, Skipper," he said, falling back into step alongside Warren.

Suddenly, the point man's right hand went up.

Warren signaled the team to halt. "Stay here," he said to Sean and trotted up to Gruber.

"Powerhouse is off to the right, Skipper," Gruber said. Warren saw it before he was told. "Not much of a powerhouse."

Warren examined the low brick building through his field glasses. The glass in many of its windows was missing. The top of the smokestack had been blown away. There was a small mound of coal to the building's right with two upturned wheelbarrows nearby. About a hundred yards to the left of the powerhouse, the crumbled walls of a roofless farmhouse gave mute testimony of heavy fighting in the area.

"Don't look as if it's worth the powder to blow it up, sir," Gruber said, gazing at the silent plant.

"Probably isn't," Warren answered, "but our orders are to demolish it and that we will." He put his field glasses back in the case and signaled Sean to bring the men forward. "That's our objective," he said, gesturing toward the powerhouse when the men joined him. "All of you know your jobs. When we're a hundred yards from it, Hanson, Gruber and four demolition men will proceed inside and set the charges. The rest of us will cover them until they rejoin. Remember, the charges have three-minute fuses, so they have to get out fast." He looked at Hanson. "It's up to you, Chief, to make sure nobody is left inside. Use the front door to get in and out."

"Aye, aye, Skipper," Hanson answered.

Warren looked at his watch. "It's 0630," he said. "We should be in position by 0700. Let's move out. Gruber, take the point."

Gruber trotted forward.

Warren began to walk. There were six hundred and fifty yards between them and the power plant as they approached it from the left side.

Glancing up, Warren spotted a formation of twelve ADs, with Panther jets weaving above them, cross the shoreline from the east and head inland. Moments after the planes flew over them, explosion after explosion echoed across the city, and mushrooms of fire and smoke rose in the air west of the city.

"That was the first time the fly-boys hit the enemy today," Sean said. "It's going to be a long day for everybody."

"This clear weather can't last. It's beginning to cloud over," Warren observed. "Christ! All we need is more snow!"

At Warren's signal, the demolition men broke off and went ahead with Hanson in the lead. The men entered the powerhouse. Warren stationed the rest of the team in covering teams.

Sean and ten men took position in front of the mound of coal. Rogers and ten men deployed to the farm building and Warren, with the rest, faced the plant's door.

Hanson's team began to set charges of RDX on the turbines and the electric generators, working quickly. Quiet engulfed the building.

Outside, Warren checked his watch. "Three minutes," he said. Even though it was bitterly cold, he was beginning to sweat.

Gruber came out of the furnace room and thrust his thumb up as he joined Hanson.

"Go!" Hanson shouted, pointing to the door.

"All charges are set —" Gruber began.

At that instant, Warren heard two short bursts of automatic fire erupt from somewhere inside the plant.

Goddamn! The bastards must have been lying in wait inside! "Branigan, come with me!" He raced toward the door. As he entered he saw Hanson, Gruber, and three other men face-down on the floor. Another man was trying to crawl toward the door.

"I'll get this man out, Skipper. Cover me!" Sean yelled, dragging the wounded Seal toward the door.

At the same instant Rogers, from his position, saw a portion of the coal mound begin to slide downward and the dull, metallic muzzle of a machine gun protrude from the pile. "Hit the deck!" he yelled. "Machine gun in the coal pile." He sprayed the pile with a burst from his carbine.

Suddenly the high whistle of an incoming mortar round pierced the air, followed by the sharp crack as it exploded in front of the power station.

"Rogers, take that machine gun out! Now!" Warren yelled from the doorway. He glanced at his watch. "One minute before the powerhouse blows!"

Rogers raced toward the coal pile, pulled the pin from a grenade, leaped up, threw it, and dropped down again in a single fluid motion. The explosion sent coal soaring into the air and bared the remains of a camouflaged machine-gun nest.

"Now," Warren yelled, dashing out of the door. He ran to Sean and helped him carry the wounded man away from the building.

In the next instant, a tremendous explosion tore the powerhouse apart. What was left of the smokestack teetered slowly back and forth and plunged to the ground with a roar.

Warren and Sean continued to run, dragging the wounded man between them toward the farmhouse.

They reached the safety of a low stone wall surrounding it and, with the help of the other Seals gathered there, pulled the man over it. Another mortar round exploded in front of the wrecked powerhouse.

"This is about all the cover we're going to have," Warren said, feeling as if his lungs were going to burst.

Sean nodded.

"We've got to knock out that mortar," Warren gasped. "They're over there," pointing to the area behind the leveled coal mound.

"I can try to circle it and get behind them," Sean suggested.

Warren yelled to one of the BAR men and two others. "Go with Branigan," he ordered. Then to Sean he said, "I'll come in from the front and draw their fire!"

Sean nodded, lifted himself up, and, motioning to the men to follow him, loped away in a crouch.

Warren looked at the wounded man. The man had been hit in the right side of his upper chest, just below the shoulder. But it was so cold the blood had already coagulated and bleeding had stopped. "We'll get you to an aide station as soon as we can," he soothed.

The man nodded. "I'm holding on, Skipper," he said.

"Rogers," Warren called, "get the men back to the ship if Branigan and I don't make it. Don't go looking for wounded. Just get your ass back to the ship."

"Aye, aye, Skipper," Rogers answered reluctantly.

Warren called for the other BAR man and three others. "We'll spread out and keep them busy. Okay, let's go." He was up and over the wall. The next instant, he was running a zigzag course toward the remains of the coal pile.

Rifle fire snapped from inside the farmhouse.

A man screamed, threw up his hands, and fell face forward.

"Keep going," Warren shouted, suddenly aware that it was snowing.

The BAR man fired from his hip.

"Close enough!" Warren yelled and, dropping to the ground, immediately began to fire his carbine.

"Jesus, Skipper, my legs are hit!" the BAR man shouted.

Warren did a double roll to his left and wound up alongside the man. "Can you crawl back to the wall?"

"I can try," the man answered.

Warren took the BAR and the ammo for it. "Go," he ordered, leaping to a crouch and firing the cumbersome weapon in the direction of the mortar position. "Okay, you guys," he called to the men behind him, "let's make it even hotter for them!" Firing, he leaped up and resumed his zigzag run toward the coal pile, firing his carbine blindly from his hip. A searing pain slashed across his right side and he stumbled, dropping his weapon. The next moment his legs crumpled under him. His vision blurred. The sharp crack of a grenade filled his head. Before he sank into the onrushing blackness, he heard Rogers yell, "I'm coming, Skipper!"

Warren's eyes were half closed. On his right a young Marine lieutenant lay heavily sedated, after having had both legs amputated at the knee. The doctors had tried to save them, but they had been too badly smashed by shrapnel a day before the lieutenant's unit had reached Hungnam. The bed to Warren's left had been occupied until early that morning by a crusty Army major, who had the left side of his face shot away. Somehow, the major had managed to cut his wrists and had almost bled to death before a passing nurse saw the blood-soaked sheets under the desperate man.

After surgery, the doctor had assured Warren, "You'll be up and in business again within a couple of months. In the meantime, just thank God you were hit where there aren't too many vital parts!"

The fact that his wound wasn't terribly serious didn't lessen the pain or discomfort. But, aware of the terrible condition of most of the men in the ward, he realized just how lucky he was. If he believed in anything, he certainly believed in luck. Without it, a man was totally lost.

Suddenly, Warren realized there were people at the foot of the bed. He opened his eyes.

"We thought you were asleep, Skipper," Rogers said.

Sean, standing next to Rogers, smiled encouragingly.

"How are you feeling?" Rogers asked.

"Stiff, but otherwise all right," Warren answered. Gazing at them, he said, "Thanks for getting me out."

"We got all except Hansen, Gruber, and four others out," Sean replied softly.

"I know," Warren answered. The day after his surgery, Admiral Picker had called and said, "I have recommended that you, Rogers, and Branigan be awarded the Navy Cross. Your team was splendid!"

"Skipper, no matter what, we wouldn't have left you there," Rogers said. "Hell, we even finished off those gantries!"

Warren smiled. "I know that, too. I can't tell you how proud I am of all of you!"

"We managed to get back to the *Holmes* by 'requisitioning' a few rowboats! We were the last to leave, and as soon as we climbed on board, our ships began to shell the waterfront. Those big guns opened up and the shoreline disappeared into rubble. On the way back to Japan, we were told that the enemy hadn't expected that to happen. They fought right down to the water's edge, which was a big mistake for most of them!"

"How long will you be in the hospital, sir?" Sean asked.

"Two, maybe three weeks," Warren replied. "After that, I get to go home for a while. And be with Hilary and Andy for a while."

"Lieutenant Rogers is our acting skipper," Sean said.

Rogers flushed. "Only until —"

"You'll make a good one," Warren said.

"We'd better be going now, Sean," Rogers said, seeing that Warren seemed tired.

"Thanks for stopping by," Warren responded. "Give the men my best wishes."

"You go ahead," Sean said to Rogers. "I'll join you in a minute."

"Sure thing, Lieutenant," Rogers answered and, nodding to Warren, he left.

Sean waited for several moments before he said, "I just wanted you to know that I started the paperwork to change my surname to Hacker."

Warren nodded. That was as much of a thank you as he was going to get. But it was enough. "Hacker is a good name," Warren replied, offering his hand. "A damn good name."

"You gave it back to me," Sean said.

CHAPTER 21

At 10 p.m. on June 22, 1953, the phone on Tony's night table rang. Miriam looked up from *The Adventures of Augie March*, a novel by Saul Bellow, that she'd received from the Book-of-the-Month Club in the morning mail. "Aren't you going to answer it?" she asked after the phone had rung a second time.

"If it rings a third time, I know whoever is on the other end really wants to speak to me," Tony said. He'd been reading an article in the latest issue of *Time* magazine about the fierce fighting that was going on ridges along the Thirty-Eighth Parallel in Korea while the armistice talks at Panmunjom were still bogged down in ridiculous details. The war was almost three years old, and these armistice talks had been going on for more than a year and a half. During that time there had not been any let-up in the fighting. The war had cost tens of thousands of lives.

"You're becoming weird."

The phone rang a third time and Tony picked it up. "Mr. Trapasso, this is Chief Stern of the East Hampton Police —"

"What's wrong?"

"Your sister-in-law, Mrs. Miller, has — I think you had better come out here," Stern said. "Mrs. Miller is in the hospital."

"The boy?" Tony questioned, feeling his stomach tighten.

"What is it?" Miriam asked.

Tony shook his head. "Is the boy all right?" he questioned again.

"He's all right," Stern replied. "Confused and frightened. But he's all right."

"I'll be there as soon as I can," Tony said and put the phone down. "Tara has been in some kind of an accident."

"Oh my God, no!" Miriam exclaimed. "I spoke to her this afternoon. She'd gotten a letter from Jacob yesterday telling her he's the operations officer on carrier division's staff. She said he didn't have to fly any more strike missions, and she was so happy about that. Is Sy all right?"

"The chief says he is," Tony responded as he got out of bed. "Mario will drive me out there."

"I'm going with you," Miriam said.

Tony was about to say no, then he changed his mind. "Just leave a note for the maid that she can see when she wakes up. Tell her we'll be back sometime tomorrow afternoon."

"You promised Mike you'd take him to the Dodgers game," she said, pulling the nightgown over her head.

"I know. He'll just have to take a rain check on it," Tony answered, going into the bathroom to splash his face with water. Whatever happened to Tara had to be serious, or Stern wouldn't have phoned. "We'll go to the hospital first," he called, drying his face with a towel.

It was almost three o'clock in the morning and raining when Tony and Miriam arrived at the hospital. Stern was waiting for them in the small lobby. "She's in Room 103," he said, leading them past the security guard.

"What happened to her?" Tony asked as they approached the room.

Stern hesitated. "Why don't you visit with her first and then we'll talk? I took the liberty of hiring a special nurse for her."

"No problem. I'd have done the same thing," Tony responded as they entered Tara's room.

The nurse stood up. "They're family," the chief told the nurse.

Tara was in the center of the bed. An IV was in each arm.

"Oh no!" Miriam exclaimed, looking at Tara. "Oh no!" She turned away and buried her face in Tony's shoulder.

Tony put his arms around her. Tara's face had been smashed. Her nose was broken. Both lips were badly cut. "What happened?" he finally managed to ask.

"From what little information we have, it appears that she interrupted a burglary, and was beaten and raped."

Tony sucked in his breath and slowly exhaled. "Any leads?" he asked tightly.

Stern shook his head. "Whatever footprints there might have been had been washed away by the rain."

"Did the boy see any of it?" Tony asked.

"I don't know," Stern said. "He's pretty frightened. I have him over at my place. I thought being around my kids — well, I just didn't want to keep him over at the station house."

"I appreciate that."

"The doctor says she's going to need a lot of plastic surgery," Stern said.

Miriam lifted her head from Tony's chest. "Do we tell Jacob?" she asked. Then to Stern, she said, "Her husband is on his second tour of duty on a carrier off Korea."

"Yes, I know. He and I had a long conversation on Decoration Day weekend. He said he'd just finished a tour of duty training all-weather jet-fighter pilots at Atlantic City, and would soon be going back to the war."

"His knowing isn't going to help her," Tony said, "and it might hurt him. Let's see how things go in the next few days before we make any decisions."

"She's in bad shape mentally," Stern commented. "But maybe in a few days she'll come out of it. Right now she needs as much rest as she can get."

"In the morning, we'll make arrangements to move her to a New York hospital," Tony said.

Stern nodded.

"There's nothing we can do here," Tony said, putting his arm around Miriam's shoulders. "Let's find a motel and get some sleep."

She nodded. "Who would do something like that?"

"An animal," Tony answered fiercely.

"Your husband is right," Stern said. "A human animal."

Jacob was in the wardroom drinking a cup of coffee and wondering why Tara hadn't been writing as frequently as before. Even more to the point, her letters were typed and oddly impersonal, almost as if she wasn't writing them. Suddenly the room phone rang. One of the other officers answered. "Commander Miller," he said, "report to the admiral's sea cabin."

"On my way," Jacob answered, quickly swallowing the last of the coffee.

Sawyer was a thin, wiry man, with a reputation for demanding excellence in himself as well as in his staff. At their initial meeting, Sawyer had made it clear that Jacob's past record didn't mean anything to him. He'd said, "You're here because I need an operations officer for the carrier division. Now you're going to have to prove to me that you're the best damn operations officer in the Navy, or by God, I'll get me one who is."

"Sit down," Sawyer said. "I've received word to stop strikes on targets north of the Thirty-Eighth Parallel. It seems that the armistice negotiations at Panmunjom are finally going to be successful."

"I hope so, sir," Jacob answered. "Those talks have been going on for eighteen months. So far they've agreed to disagree about everything, even whether the table at which they meet should be round, square, or rectangular."

Sawyer puffed on a cigarette. "A pessimist," he chuckled. "A man after my own heart."

"With all due respect, not a pessimist, sir," Jacob answered. "But a realist. I've come back to a war that in eighteen months hasn't changed. At least when I was flying strike missions, we'd run into a few MiGs now and then, but now the men fly for weeks without seeing one. We deliver our ordnance wherever it's needed. But —"

Sawyer held up his hands. "I know what the story is, Commander, but we are doing a good job —" He smiled. "You're doing a good job. I'm glad to have you aboard the *Sharpsburg*."

"Thank you, sir," Jacob answered.

"Headquarters says we could see a sharp increase in fighting as the talks near their conclusion. I guess the ChiComs will try to grab as much real estate as they can before the fighting stops."

"Probably," Jacob agreed.

"Should these negotiations actually come to something, I have been invited to attend the official signing ceremony, and I will be allowed to bring one member of my staff with me. I'd like you to be that member."

Surprised, Jacob answered, "Thank you, sir. It would be an honor."

Sawyer nodded. "It would be an honor to all of us to bring the fighting to an end."

"Yes, sir," Jacob answered. "That certainly would be an honor."

Warren was on the bridge of the destroyer *Holmes*. He'd taken command of her on May 1, 1953, after having spent the previous eighteen months in Washington D.C., where he was assigned to Planning and Operations.

This was the beginning of Warren's second tour. After he'd been wounded, he'd spent a month in New York on sick leave and then had returned to Japan, where he had been liaison officer between the American and British staffs. But now he was back in the war, and his ship was about to commence a routine fire-support mission for an Army unit that occupied a position on the east coast of Korea, on the Thirty-Eighth Parallel.

"Radar, check the distance to the shore," Warren said.

"Three thousand yards," the radar officer answered.

"Ahead one third," he said.

"Ahead one third answered," the engine-room signalman responded.

Warren peered through the murky blackness. Only the vaguest hint of a land mass was visible through continually shifting predawn mist.

"Signal light, Skipper," his XO said. "Two points off starboard bow. Signaling Fox 1."

"Got it," he said. "Answer the ship's name."

"Aye, aye, Skipper," the XO responded and passed the command to the signalman at the signal light.

"Engine-room, stand by to stop all engines," Warren said.

"Engine-room standing by," the engine-room signalman replied.

"Fox 1 is ready and waiting," the XO reported.

Warren was just about to order full stop on all engines when his Radio Officer said, "Skipper, a high-priority message is coming out of Headquarters. All fire-support missions canceled. Repeat, all fire-support missions canceled. All fire-support ships return to base. All fire-support ships return to base."

"Fox 1 is signaling, mission canceled," the XO said.

"Acknowledge," Warren responded, then to the helmsman, he said, "Come to one-six-zero."

"Coming to one-six-zero," the helmsman answered.

"Engine-room, two thirds ahead," Warren said.

"Two thirds ahead answered," the engine-room signalman responded.

"Do you think the Chinese are really going to sign at Panmunjom?" his XO asked in a low voice.

"I sure as hell hope so," Warren answered.

The sky over Panmunjom early in the morning of July 27 was spotted with sunlight through heavy gray clouds. The night before it had rained, and the ground in front of the building where Jacob and Admiral Sawyer stood was still wet. They had arrived by copter at 0930.

Jacob, though conscious of the historic event he would soon witness, was deeply troubled by the letter he'd received the previous day from Tony. Tara had suffered some kind of "mental breakdown and had to be institutionalized and will require long-term care. Her doctor suggests that it might be beneficial for her to see you. Under the circumstances, I am sure you would be given an emergency leave. If you run into any obstacles on your end, let me know and I'll see whether I can move things on this end. Sy is with us, and though he misses his mother and father, he appears to be weathering the situation pretty well." Jacob knew Tara well enough to know that something terrible must have happened to break her.

"It's beginning," Sawyer whispered.

Jacob nodded and, deciding that he'd request an emergency leave as soon as he and Sawyer were back on the *Sharpsburg*, he focused his attention on Lieutenant General William K. Harrison, the commander of the United Nations delegation. The general and several of his aides started toward the wooden building that the Chinese had put up during the 1952 recessed armistice talks. As Jacob and Sawyer joined the other Navy, Marine, and Army officers, he realized that while the Americans were entering the building from one side, the Chinese were coming in from the other side.

There were three tables in the room, two with chairs and between them a smaller one without a chair. On one of the larger tables was the U.N. flag and on the other the flag of North Korea.

General Harrison sat ramrod straight at one table, and General Nam II of North Korea took his place at the other table. Neither man acknowledged the presence of the other.

At precisely 1001, they began to sign the eighteen documents presented to them. The signing took ten minutes. When it was over, both men left without speaking to the other. The fighting was officially over. But peace, real peace had not been gained by either side.

Jacob was somehow reminded of the lines, "How does the world end? Not with a bang, but with a whimper." Perhaps, he thought, it will end not with a whimper, but with deadly silence.

A NOTE TO THE READER

Dear Reader,

If you have enjoyed the novel enough to leave a review on **Amazon** and **Goodreads**, then we would be truly grateful.

Sapere Books is an exciting new publisher of brilliant fiction and popular history.

To find out more about our latest releases and our monthly bargain books visit our website:
saperebooks.com